William Davies

The Pilgrimage of the Tiber

from its Mouth to its Source - with some account of its tributaries. Second Edition

William Davies

The Pilgrimage of the Tiber

from its Mouth to its Source - with some account of its tributaries. Second Edition

ISBN/EAN: 9783337287771

Printed in Europe, USA, Canada, Australia, Japan

Cover: Foto ©Andreas Hilbeck / pixelio.de

More available books at **www.hansebooks.com**

THE PILGRIMAGE OF THE TIBER.

ST. PETER'S AND THE VATICAN, FROM THE BANKS OF THE TIBER.

THE

PILGRIMAGE OF THE TIBER,

From its Mouth to its Source:

WITH SOME ACCOUNT OF ITS TRIBUTARIES.

By WILLIAM DAVIES.

"Et terram Hesperiam venies : ubi Lydius, arva
Inter opima virum, leni fluit agmine Tybris."—
VIRGIL, Æn. ii. 781.

["And you shall come to the Hesperian land,
Where Lydian Tiber flows with gentle stream,
By fruitful fields of men."]

SECOND EDITION REVISED.

LONDON:
SAMPSON LOW, MARSTON, LOW & SEARLE.
1875.

LONDON :

PRINTED BY WILLIAM CLOWES AND SONS,
STAMFORD STREET AND CHARING CROSS.

PREFACE TO FIRST EDITION.

IT is somewhat singular, in these days of much travelling, that the course of the Tiber, the most classic of all streams, should either never have been completely explored or else no account should have been given of it in its entirety, either in the Italian or English language, as far as I am aware. This is all the more remarkable as it is not only crowded with interesting associations at every turn, but its course also embraces an unsurpassed continuity of the most beautiful and varied scenery that is to be found even in Italy, the favoured land of beauty, poetry, and song.

It is several years since the project was formed which is here carried out. It was first intended that it should have been a joint work between Mr. C. I. Hemans and myself; Mr. Hemans having been a long resident in Italy and a close student of its historical antiquities. This, however, Mr. Hemans' uncertain health and numerous engagements prevented him from undertaking. The plan was altered. I took upon myself the task of writing the whole book, looking to his large local knowledge for indications and confirmations where my own was deficient or uncertain. He has also been of very ample use in directing me to authorities. Although the substance of this work is otherwise my own, it would be impossible to overrate the value of the assistance he has rendered to me in these respects.

Although we were both familiar with a good part of the river previously to the journey here described, yet on this occasion we conscientiously made the whole tour of it, from its mouth to its source, in order that nothing should be omitted in the account of its course. The journey took about five weeks, leaving out the excursions made from Rome. We were accompanied by two artist friends, one the length of the whole journey, and the other from Perugia ; both of whom lent the aid of their pencils to illustrate our progress.

Though not very easy to define, my plan of selection in writing this book has been a very special and precise one to myself. It may be indicated by the term picturesque. I have not attempted to write a guide book or a history. I have thought it enough to have chosen those events and circumstances which group themselves about my subject wherever their importance and interest may have made their introduction desirable from a picturesque or illustrative point of view. I have only given as much personal adventure as might serve to string my narrative upon. A few old stories will be found here, associated or connected with the ancient river, which I hope it will not be thought are repeated once too often. I did not think, however, when treating of the Tiber as a subject that this was the place to omit them. The pictures given from local historians of the mediæval condition of some of the Tiberine towns, and country, will, I believe, be new to most English readers. The chapter upon the popular songs of central Italy will also probably afford an insight into a quite fresh field of literature, as I do not know that any of them have been brought forward before in the English language.

As regards the illustrations, it was intended that my artist friends should have prepared their own drawings for the engraver, had not their absence from England prevented them from doing so. They have no cause, however, to complain of the way in which their sketches or drawings have been copied. For myself, I must record my special obligations to the engraver of my little drawings, which, for the most part, have been reproduced with perhaps as much fidelity as the nature of the material will allow.

In conclusion, I can only say that I have left no known source of information unexamined, nor any spot within my limits unexplored, likely to furnish matter of interest. If it were not too presumptuous I should express the hope that my reader may find some analogous pleasure in reading my book to that which I had in making the journey of which it gives the account.

It may be mentioned that the terms "right" and "left," occurring in these pages, refer to the upward journey.

ADVERTISEMENT TO SECOND EDITION.

I HAVE to thank several friends and friendly reviewers for the suggestion of a few new episodes which have been here added to my account of the Tiber; some inadvertences of the former edition have been also corrected, so that it is hoped the volume may now present a tolerably complete account of the classic stream of my pilgrimage from the point of view selected for illustration.

CONTENTS.

ILLUSTRATIONS.

⁕ The whole of the Illustrations are engraved by J. D. COOPER.

Map of
CENTRAL ITALY
Showing the Course of the Tiber.

English Miles.

PILGRIMAGE OF THE TIBER.

CHAPTER I.

INTRODUCTORY.

BEFORE entering on the more special description of the Tiber and its course I will here give my readers a few general facts concerning it.

We are told that the Tiber was first called Albula on account of the light colour of its waters ; but that afterwards it took the name of Tiberinus from a certain Alban king, who, being slain on its banks, was carried down by the flood. It probably was only called "white" by a figure of speech—just as Virgil called it " Cœruleus Tibris " from the hue reflected on its waters. The tawny-yellow or chestnut colour that really belongs to it, and serves to distinguish it so specially in the lowlands, is communicated by vast quantities of earthy deposit, of which it contains about seventeen per cent. at times of flood, gathered during its course from the regions of Umbria. It takes its rise in the central Apennines, where they trend towards the Adriatic, in the direction of Urbino, on Monte Fumajolo, almost within sight of Rimini. It is joined in its course by many tributaries, which have been variously numbered according to what has been thought worthy of the name. The principal ones are the Anio, the Nar, the Chiana, and the Topino, into which the Clitumnus discharges itself.

B

It flows in a south-westerly direction. Its whole length is about two hundred and sixty miles, its breadth below Rome about two hundred yards. Its current flows at the rate of about three miles an hour. Its elevation at Rome is eighteen to twenty feet above the sea-level. It quickly narrows in the upward direction ; and at Ponte Felice, near Borghetto, not quite sixty miles from its mouth, is now unnavigable for large vessels. It has always been subject to disastrous overflowings ; records of which abound in every historical account of it from the earliest times. Frequent mention is made in earlier epochs of vast numbers of serpents left by these floods wherever they spread, which sometimes added the calamity of pestilence to that of deluge. It would appear from this that the fauna of the contiguous districts must be changed, since they are now seen no longer : perhaps owing to its denudation of wood. The aspect of its neighbourhood must have altered greatly from the time when the wide Campagna stretched its breadth of undulating country in the pride of culture from its shores, and its sides were lined with groves, villas, and mansions from Ostia to Otricoli, a distance of almost seventy miles from its mouth. Some have supposed that its bed has been raised since the historic period ; this, however, can scarcely have been the case to any appreciable extent, as the position of the earliest bridges marks pretty much the same water-level as that which must have prevailed nearly two thousand years back.

During the Middle Ages the water of the Tiber formed the principal drink of the Romans. It was borne for sale through the city on the backs of asses. The mother of Cola di Rienzo was one of these water-vendors. So much was it valued above other waters that the Popes Clement the Seventh and Paul the Third never travelled far without taking a supply of it with them. One can scarcely imagine this muddy fluid to be preferred ; unless, indeed, there were some remnant of the ancient reverence for the stream still lingering to a later period.

Its current is a dangerous one. It goes seething through the Campagna like a boiling caldron. He must be a clever swimmer who would breast its treacherous eddies and spreading whirlpools in safety.

How many memories rise up in the mind as we look at it, and think of the splendid triumphs it has witnessed and of the dark deeds performed on its banks! It was to its shores that legend sent the heroic Hercules to wash the Iberian heifers after having slain the monster Geryon. It saw Æneas pass to deeds of valour and glory when the saffron-coloured morning rose in the sky and the well-wooded banks were vocal with the songs of many birds. Hither the frenzied Bacchanalians used to rush at dead of night with frantic cries and wild contortions—raving women with floating hair—plunging inextinguishable torches into the stream, symbols of the unquenchable passions that tore and consumed them. Here the sick slaves and abandoned children were left to perish unpityingly, the miserable victims of cruelty and superstition. Borne upon its tawny bosom the consul Æmilius entered Rome in a royal galley of sixteen tiers of oars, proud in the gorgeous spoils of the conquered Macedonia, when the whole city flowed out to meet him. Its bed received the body of the flagrant and scandalous emperor Heliogabalus drunk with crime and loathsome through every vice, after he had been massacred by a maddened populace and dragged about the streets of Rome with shouts of ferocious joy. It was into its waters that the ashes of the noble champion of freedom and truth, Arnold of Brescia, were cast, one more victim to the cause of unappreciated philanthropy and liberty. By the Tiber Pope Gregory the Eleventh returned to Rome, together with the functionaries of the papal court, in all the splendour of ecclesiastical pomp, after the seventy-two years' exile of the papacy at Avignon in Provence, landing at St. Paul's amidst the acclamations of vast crowds, whence he was escorted triumphantly into the city. These and a thousand other memories seem to be written on its turbid

wrinkles as they flow down to the sea, bearing everything
into oblivion, and veiling the dark secrets of which it has
been the unwearied witness through the long course of
unnumbered centuries.

But it is time to commence our journey.

HEAD OF THE TRAJAN CANAL, NEAR OSTIA.

CHAPTER II.

FROM OSTIA TO ROME.

WHEN I went to Italy, in the spring of eighteen hundred and seventy-one, for the special purpose of exploring the Tiber, it was but supplementary to a long previous residence in that country, which had already made me acquainted with a good part of its course. In the first instance, I took up my quarters in Rome, revisiting the various places in the neighbourhood ; some of them more than once. Whilst there I was able to go down the stream to Ostia, in a steamer that leaves Rome weekly for the mouth of the river, for a short time during the spring. On this occasion, and subsequently, I was much indebted to Mr. Welby, the proprietor of the navigation of the river, for much kindness, courtesy, and information. If the Cæsars were to come back, what would they say to an Englishman being in virtual possession of the stream they reverenced so sacredly and guarded so jealously ! Yet such at present is the case.

Early one morning, just when the sun was throwing his first rays over the top of the Aventine, H. and I hastened to the Ripa Grande, and soon after found ourselves steaming down the river at a pretty good speed, owing to the rapidity of the current. Our party was a very animated one, consisting altogether of Italians, who were going for a day's run to the sea-side, or to spend a week there with their families. A plethoric band did its best to keep up the spirits of the company by blowing its loudest. Mirth and hilarity prevailed on every hand. Meals were improvised and every one seemed gay and happy.

Agreeably to the plan of this volume, I shall not detain the reader during this part of the journey, but take the stream in its upward course from Ostia.

In two hours we found ourselves at Fiumicino, a strong wind blowing from the sea, and rolling the white breakers far on the strand.

Immediately on our arrival we left the crowd of holiday makers, taking our way across the Sacred Island to Ostia.

The Tiber enters the Mediterranean by two mouths, the one below Ostia, which is its natural one, the other at Fiumicino (which we had just navigated), an artificial canal formed by the Roman Emperor Trajan in order to avoid the shoals and sand-banks which obstructed its natural passage. These two outlets are distant from each other about three miles. There was a still earlier cutting made by Claudius from a point higher up the river, which flowed into the sea more to the north, the silting up of which made the present one necessary; it led into a port long since left inland by the retiring sea, now only showing a few ruins near the hamlet of Porto. The irregular angle formed by the two streams is called the Isola Sacra, or Sacred Island, once famous for the worship of Venus, its fertile summer pastures and abundant winter roses. Now its aspect must be vastly changed. It is a dreary desert of marshy ground, over-grown with the ash-pale asphodel, rampant reeds and lean, bristling rushes ; roamed by herds of half-wild oxen with enormous horns, which eyed us menacingly as we passed, as if resenting our intrusion on their territory. Here and there a lonely tower or wall rises, forlorn witness of the desola-tion around. To the right of the river is the ancient town of Ostia, once on the sea, but now withdrawn far from it, buried in ruin, choked with thistles, hidden under green corn-fields, which the wind waves over the graves of a thousand households. Everything seems to mourn ; whilst the sadness is made still more touching by the numerous streets, temples and houses which modern excavations have made bare, showing them pretty much as they were left hundreds of years ago. A few of the most important and interesting may be examined.

Turning a little from the river, we first observe the naked but substantial walls of what has been supposed a temple of Jupiter of about the second century. A very noble building it must once have been, for on the surface of its brickwork are yet to be seen the holes by means of which it was covered with marbles. A tessellated road extending for a long distance leads us to a wide and imposing flight of steps which were once flanked by Corinthian columns—they are now despoiled of their covering, doubtless a costly one—to the threshold, across the whole breadth of which a solid monolith of African marble is laid, about eighteen feet long and four wide, probably being at least as thick. The interior consists of a vast hall or chamber, almost square, with niches at the sides for statues. At the extreme end facing the entrance, the altar still remains in a despoiled condition, above which is a raised tribune with cells on each side. Over this altar must have stood the image or statue of the presiding deity of the place. There are no means of lighting from without excepting through the doorway—a characteristic common to the temples of both Greece and Rome, in which, perhaps, a solemn and mysterious gloom may have been desired. Beneath this hall is a subterranean chamber supposed to have been used as a place of preparation for the priests before the celebration of the rites of worship. At one side of the temple, and exposed to the open air, is a *peribolos* or columned enclosure of the sacred precincts of the temple. In it are to be seen some magnificent fragments of marble architectural mouldings.

As the temples of Ostia represent several distinctive forms of religious worship, a slight sketch of their nature in connection with them may not be unacceptable to the reader.

The worship of Jupiter constituted one of the loftiest religious functions of ancient times. He was represented as a majestic figure with a long flowing beard, seated upon a throne, holding a thunderbolt in his right hand and a victory in the other, having at his feet an eagle bearing away Ganymede. The upper part of his body was naked, the lower clothed. All these characters were supposed to have a mystic meaning; the throne denoting stability and security of empire; the nakedness of the upper part of his body, that he was only visible to the higher intelligences and in the celestial parts of the universe; the clothing of the lower part, that he was hidden from the inferior world. The sceptre in his right hand signified his omnipotence; the victory in his left, that he was invincible; and the eagle, that he was the lord of heaven.

His worship commanded the highest honours. The first day of every period was dedicated to him by festivals, sacrifices, or libations. He was the Lord of Light; the white colour was sacred to him. The victims most commonly offered to him were a goat, a sheep, or a white bull with gilded horns : the lesser offerings made to him were salt, flour, or incense. His chariot was supposed to be drawn by twenty-four white horses; his priests wore white caps; the consuls were robed in white when they offered their first sacrifices to him. The oak and the olive were consecrated to him. His worship was largely followed by the Roman ladies.

Probably the lofty ceremonial of the homage done to him here would be but the shadow of the more splendid rites of the Capitol of Rome, which was considered specially his seat; but enough is left to us in the proportions and grandeur of this fine temple to certify that his worship even here was no mean thing, and that it bore the significance of the highest form of religious pomp and display.

Not very distant from this is another temple, with a long colonnaded approach, dedicated to another kind of worship, that of Cybele and Atys. This mysterious form of religion, or rather superstition, looms out to us through the lurid ages, a dark symbolism and outgrowth of some of the most confusing and incomprehensible elements that lie at the bottom of human nature. It is the communion of those wild and mysterious passions that seem always lying in wait for the unwary to hurl them in their stormy arms on the waves of ever-unsatisfied desire, which bear in their train the furies of anguish, remorse, madness, and self-despair.

Cybele appears primarily to have represented the Earth : the great fruitful mother of organic being. The worship of the earth under one form or other is the most ancient and extensive of all worships. It ruled the religious mind of races long passed away. But what is the most remarkable of all, it would appear as if traces of its symbolism still exist in some modern forms of Christianity. In the Capitoline gallery of sculptures at Rome is a bas-relief of a priest of Cybele, bearing in one hand an *aspergillum* for the scattering of consecrated water, and in the other a long scourge and a shell, in which are fruits and a pine cone. From his head depend two strings of beads of recurrent sizes, long enough to have served the devotional purpose of the modern rosary without being taken off. At the sides, besides some musical instrument, are sculptured a censer, a *pedum*, or crooked staff, which may have answered to the ecclesiastical pastoral crook. Lastly, there is the Phrygian cap, of such a form that it might appear to shadow forth the tiara of modern times.

Diodorus Siculus says that Cybele was the daughter of Meon, king of Lydia, and Dindyme, his wife. The king not desiring that she should be brought up, caused her to be exposed on Mount Cybele (from which she took her name). She was, however, suckled by the leopards and other savage animals. Being here discovered by some shepherdesses, she was carried to their home and brought up amongst them. As she grew up she surpassed her companions as much in wisdom and beauty as in the qualities of genius and invention. She made the stops to the flute, and introduced the use of timbrels and drums. Her love for children, of whom she had saved many from various diseases, gave her the name of Mother in the Mountain.

Cybele then fell in love with Atys, afterwards called Papas. She was subsequently led by accident to the court of her father, who, discovering her amour, caused Atys to be slain, together with the shepherdess who had first found and rescued her. Upon this she became delirious, and ran through the country shrieking and beating drums. The Phrygians about this time, suffering cruel distempers and severe famine, consulted an oracle, and were thereupon desired to bury Atys and honour Cybele as a goddess. Annual sacrifices were instituted in her honour, and afterwards a stately temple was built to her in the city of Pessinus, in Phrygia. Here her worship was celebrated with great uproar : her priests beating tabrets and striking bucklers with spears, dancing furiously with wild contortions and frantic gesticulations, dark and evil doings being mixed with these violent devotions.

She was generally represented as a matron holding keys to symbolize the undeveloped treasures of the earth. She wore a wreath of oak : her temples were round, and crowned with turrets to signify the cities built upon the earth. Her chariot was drawn with tame lions, in allusion to the power of culture : the various instruments she bore represented implements of culture.

Catullus, in one of his odes, describes in a few wonderful lines with the vigour of a master hand the initiation of Atys. After having taken the initiatory rite, by mutilating himself, he seizes the musical instruments and calls upon his fellows to join him in the new worship. "The whole band," says the poet, "forthwith yelled with quivering tongues, the light timbrel booms, the hollow cymbals clash, and up to Ida goes the impetuous rout with hurried steps : with them goes Atys with his timbrel, raving, panting, like one lost and demented, and leads the way through the murky forests,

like an unbroken heifer shunning the burthen of the yoke.
Swiftly the Gallæ follow their hasty-footed leader. So when
they reach the home of Cybele, wearied with excessive
exertion they fall asleep fasting.   Heavy sleep covers their
drooping eyes with languor, and their raving phrensy subsides in soft repose."* Still more finely touched in, perhaps,
is the bitter repentance of Atys at his awaking—a repentance
that only adds to his fury. Then Cybele lets loose her lions.
"'Up, fierce beast, up,'" she says ; "'go, hence with him, in
madness, make him return hence, smitten with madness,
into the forest, who audaciously desires to fly from my
sway. Up! beat thy flanks with thy tail: lash thyself:
make the whole region resound with thy roaring: toss
fiercely thy tawny mane on thy tawny neck.' So said
terrific Cybele, and unfastened the yokes with her hand.
The beast, inciting himself, pricks up his impetuous spirit,
runs, roars, and breaks down the bushes in his headlong
course.   But when he reached the verge of the foam-
whitened shore, and saw soft Atys near the breakers, he
made a rush. The bewildered wretch fled into the wild
forest, and there he remained all his life long the bond-slave
of Cybele."†

       * "Simul hæc comitibus Atys cecinit notha mulier,
           Thiasus repente linguis trepidantibus ululat,
           Leve tympanum remugit, cava cymbala recrepant.
           Viridem citus adit Idam properante pede chorus.
           Furibunda simul, anhelans, vaga vadit, animi egens,
           Comitata tympano Atys, per opaca nemora dux,
           Veluti juvenca vitans onus indomita jugi,
           Rapidæ ducem sequuntur Gallæ pede propero.
           Itaque, ut domum Cybelles tetigere, lassulæ
           Nimio e labore somnum capiunt sine Cerere.
           Piger his labantes languore oculos sopor operit,
           Abit in quiete molli rabidus furor animi."
   † Translation in Bohn's series.
        "Agedum, inquit, age ferox, i: face ut hinc furoribus,
           Face ut hinc furoris ictu reditum in nemora ferat,
           Mea libere nimis qui fugere imperia cupit.
           Age, cæde terga cauda: tua verbera patere:
           Face cuncta mugienti fremitu loca retonent:

The story of the arrival of the image or symbol of Cybele at Ostia and the carrying of it to Rome, is one of those wonderful legends which are made more of by the poet than the historian. It is told by Livy, and finds a lengthy narration by Ovid in one of his finest descriptive poems. It is thus related.

In the year of Rome five hundred and forty-seven, or about two hundred years before the birth of Christ, in consequence of the fall of numerous showers of stones the Sibylline books were consulted, when a prediction unknown before was found therein, which said that whenever Italy should be invaded by a foreign enemy, the foe should be conquered if the image of the Idæan mother should be brought from Pessinus in Phrygia to Rome. This discovery produced a profound consternation. At the same time notice was received of an approaching contest from the Pythian Apollo at Delphi, in which the Romans should be victorious : also at this time a speedy termination was expected to the war in Africa. It was finally concluded that the oracle at Delphi must be consulted on the best means of obtaining the object pointed out by the Sibylline books. They there learned that it was to be obtained by means of king Attalus, and that they must appoint the best man in Rome to receive it. They then went to the king of Pergamus, who conducted them to Pessinus, where a sacred stone was put into their hands, which they were told was the mother of the gods, to be conveyed to Rome. The honourable distinction of receiving it fell upon Publius Scipio Nasica, whose father had been recently killed in Spain ; upon what grounds

---

Rutilam ferox torosa cervice quate jubam.—
Ait hæc minax Cybelle, religatque juga manu.
Ferus ipse sese adhortans rapidum incitat animum:
Vadit, fremit, refringit virgulta pede vago.
At ubi ultima albicantis loca littoris adiit,
Tenerumque vidit Atyn prope marmora pelagi:
Facit impetum. Ille demens fugit in nemora fera.
Ibi semper omne vitæ spatium famula fuit."   O. LXIII.

history is silent. He was accordingly sent to Ostia for the
purpose. When the ship in which it was carried arrived
within sight, Scipio sailed out to meet it, and receiving the
stone reverently, placed it in the hands of the matrons, who
passing it from one to another, conveyed it to Rome. Ere
it reached the city all the people poured out to meet it.
Frankincense was burned at every door and propitiatory
prayers offered. It was then borne into the temple of
victory on the palatine, crowds of persons bringing presents
and celebrating the auspicious occasion. The stone was set
in silver and worshipped under the name of Cybele. Some
have conjectured it to have been an aerolite. The frequent
mention of showers of stones by ancient writers leads to
the conjecture that falls of meteorolites may have more frequently taken place than they do now ; or possibly they
may have been volcanic stones thrown from a long distance ;
if, indeed, the accounts are not fabulous altogether.

Adjoining some baths whose mosaics and marbles still
attest their former splendour, is a third temple, dedicated to
Mithras, the sun-god. The principal court still retains its
original plan together with traces of the colonnade by which
it was surrounded, doubtless open to the sky, but communi-
cating with a wide chamber of brickwork masonry, which
leads through an atrium into an interior one. On the
floor of the court, which is of marble, a mosaic inscription
signifies that L. Agrius Calendio gave and dedicated the
temple (or perhaps only the mosaic) to the invincible sun-
god Mithras. In a raised apse near the altar once covered
with costly marbles were found three statues of Mithras and
priests, with traces of gilding on the vestments, each bearing
a torch ; one lowered, another lifted, the third, upon which
a priest leans, being extinguished. Fragments of other
sculptures were also found there.

This singular form of worship, probably of extreme
antiquity in the East, appears to have been first made
known in Italy by the companions of Pompey the Great
on their return from the Oriental campaigns under that

general in the century before the Christian era; but it does not seem to have prevailed much in the western world until two or three centuries later.

Mithras was regarded as belonging to the realms of both Light and Darkness: as the genius between the Sun and the Moon: as the Reconciler between the Persian deities Ormuzd and Ahriman, who were the authors of Good and Evil: as the Demiurge or Creator of the Universe: as the conductor of souls through the signs of the zodiac, first, to mortal life in the world, and then to the supreme source of all things through death. According to some, he not only fashioned the world, but contains in himself the seeds of all life—just as the Nicene creed defines the Holy Ghost, the Lord and Giver of life. He also partakes of the passions and sorrows of men, here offering another analogy with Christianity; and finally triumphs over Darkness and Evil.

The symbolism by which he is represented may be thus explained. Mithras slays a bull, which represents the fructifying earth, whose flank being open causes the vivifying blood to flow forth. Spring stands beside him as a youth with an uplifted torch; also symbolized as a growing tree. Autumn as an old man with a reverted torch, is the bearer of ripened fruits, represented as a tree also. A serpent, a scorpion, and a dog (standing for the constellations through which the sun passes during the summer months) prey upon the bull, or assist the god in causing its blood to flow. The eagle and the hawk, symbols of the Oriental deity Ormuzd, sometimes soar near. Progressive mystic initiations formed a prominent part of Mithraic rites, as in those of Cybele. The two trainings, however, differed considerably; the votaries of Cybele being educated through noise and uproar, those of Mithras in stillness and seclusion. The initiation of the latter was performed in caves where, secluded from light and all company, the probationers underwent eighty different kinds of tortures or expiations. Many were not able to endure these severe preparations, and died in the noviciate: often enough those who survived were so crazed and shaken in mind, as never to recover their former condition. A relief found in the Tyrol represents the Mithraic worshippers seated at a feast, which would remind one of the *Agape,* or " Love-Feast," of the early Christians. There is a raised platform round the Mithreum of the newly-discovered temple at the church of San Clemente at Rome, which, it is thought, may have served such a purpose. An interesting discovery of a tablet consisting of the figure of Mithras, surrounded by an egg-shaped zone, on which are represented the signs of the zodiac, was made at Borcovicus (now Housesteads), on the Roman Wall in Northumberland.* In the same cave was found an altar with a dedicatory inscription.

Leaving these temples, it is saddening to walk through the deserted streets and houses of this bygone town. Floors covered with rich mosaics are now left open to the sky : mutilated statues keep forlorn state amongst unshorn grass and rank weeds : large jars for corn and wine, sunk into the ground, witness of buying and selling before Death had struck the last bargain : the worn pavements mark the passage of vehicles : everywhere are seen the signs of life and activity, long since ended, of an energetic and pros- perous people, whose former home is usurped by the humming bee, the burly beetle, and the music-loving lizard.

Vastly different from the spreading solitude now before us must this inhospitable coast have appeared when Æneas, after his long voyage, found its welcome shelter, so finely described by Virgil in the opening of the seventh book of the Æneid, if, indeed, it be anything more than a poetic fiction. He says : "And now the sea began to blush with the morning rays, and in the lofty firmament saffron aurora

* There is an engraving given of this in the Rev. J. Collingwood Bruce's work on the Roman Wall, p. 398. I am not able to read its symbolism clearly from the engraving. It would be curious to see if it numbered thirteen signs of the zodiac, as used by the Anglo-Saxons, an example of which may be seen round the doorway of the Church of St. Margaret at York.

shone in her car of rosy hue, when the winds at once dropped, and every breath of air suddenly subsided, and the oars labour in the lazy water. And here Æneas from the sea beholds a great grove. The Tiber divides it with his pleasant stream, a river with whirling eddies, and yellow with thick sand ; here it bursts forth into the sea ; around and above were birds of various plumage, which, haunting the banks and channel of the stream, charmed the air with their song, and flew in the grove. The prince bids his comrades turn their course, and put their prows towards the land, and gladly takes shelter in the shady river."*

The mouth of the Tiber, according to Dionysius, was first adapted for a sea-port, and the city of Ostia (which means a port, or entrance) built by Ancus Martius, the fourth king of Rome, somewhat more than six hundred years before the Christian era. The harbour was reconstructed and additions made to it by the emperor Claudius, six or seven centuries later. He carried out pillars on each side, and formed a mole to protect the entrance, sinking the huge vessel in which the obelisk now standing in front of St. Peter's at Rome had been brought from Heliopolis, and raising a lofty lighthouse upon piles laid upon it.

The silting up of this harbour caused another to be subsequently undertaken by the emperor Trajan, and a new canal cut, which is the branch of the river still navigated, known as the Fiumicino, or little river.

---

* Globe translation.

"Jamque rubescebat radiis mare, et æthere ab alto
Aurora in roseis fulgebat lutea bigis :
Cum venti posuere, omnisque repente resedit
Flatus, et in lento luctantur marmore tonsæ.
Atque hic Æneas ingentem ex æquore lucum
Prospicit. Hunc inter fluvio Tiberinus amœno,
Vorticibus rapidis, et multa flavus arena,
In mare prorumpit. Variæ circumque supraque
Assuetæ ripis volucres et fluminis alveo
Æthera mulcebant cantu, lucoque volabant.
Flectere iter sociis terræque advertere proras
Imperat, et lætus fluvio succedit opaco."

Strabo says that in his time (about the beginning of the Christian era) Ostia had no port, owing to alluvial deposit, and that numerous vessels plied in the open sea as lighters to freight and unload the larger ships, which could not even be anchored near the shore without danger. It was desirable to relieve those vessels of a part of their burden which were going to Rome, in order that they might make a speedy voyage up the river. In the fourth century the place began to fall into decay, and was shortly afterwards all but abandoned. Its destruction was completed by the Saracens in the ninth century, at which period we hear of it again as the Gregoriopolis of Pope Gregory the Fourth, who built the present hamlet, sur-rounding it with walls. In the same century it received a notable defeat in an engagement with the Saracens, which is represented by Raphael on the walls of the Stanze at the Vatican. It maintained a military position of importance for long afterwards during the Middle Ages. Early in the seventeenth century it again fell into neglect and disuse, the melancholy and deserted place we now see it.

Those of my readers who are acquainted with the remark-able dialogue called 'Octavius' by Marcus Minucius Felix, upon the relative claims of Paganism and Christianity, will recollect that it is described as having taken place at Ostia. Minucius, supposed to have been an African by birth, was a lawyer at Rome, living, probably, in the third century. The dialogue is carried on by two friends, Cæcilius, a heathen, and Octavius, a Christian, Minucius being placed between the two in the character of umpire or listener. After describing their walk from Rome to Ostia, whither they went for the benefit of the sea at the Autumn vacation, he pictures their arrival at the shore. He says, "There the gentle surges had smoothed the outermost sands like a pleasure walk ; and as the sea, although the winds blew not, is ever unquiet, it came forward to the shore, not hoary and foaming, but with waves gently swelling and curled.

C

On this occasion we were agreeably amused by the varieties of its appearance ; for as we stood on the margin and dipped the soles of our feet into the water, the wave alternately struck at us, and then receding and sliding away, seemed to swallow up itself." He proceeds to describe their saunterings on the beach in the same graphic and picturesque manner.—" We walked slowly and composedly, and coasted along the easy bend of the shore, beguiling the way all the while with accounts of navigation given by Octavius. Having walked far enough for pleasure without fatigue, we returned by the same way, and we came to that place where small vessels are laid upon a frame of oak to prevent their being rotted by contact with the ground. There we saw some boys eagerly engaged in the game of throwing shells into the sea. The nature of the game is this: from the beach they choose a shell, thin and polished by the waves ; they hold it in a horizontal position, and then whirl it along as near the surface of the sea as possible, so as to make it skim the surge in its even motion, or spring up and bound from time to time out of the water. That boy is conqueror whose shell both runs out farthest and bounds oftenest."

Presently they sat down, when the dialogue was opened by Cæcilius urging the claims of heathenism against those of Christianity. He was replied to by Octavius with so much force and cogency that he became converted on the spot. Nothing can be more calm and impartial than the manner in which the claims of each are viewed and commented upon. Although the dialogue may have lost some of its point as a repertory of argument, it is still valuable for its large mode of treatment as well as for the account which it embodies of the two systems of religion, as they stood at that time, both in themselves and in regard to each other.

A very touching incident is brought home to us here in the death of Monica, the mother of St. Augustine, in the year three hundred and eighty-seven. After his

conversion they were returning to Africa in company with
a newly baptized court-officer Euodius, when his mother
was taken ill, and after nine days' sickness she died.
St. Augustine gives an affecting description of her last days
and their rapturous communion of spirit in the 'Confes-
sions.'   He says, " The day now approaching whereon she
was to depart this life, (which day, Thou well knewest, we
knew not,) it came to pass, Thyself, as I believe, by Thy
secret ways so ordering it, that she and I stood alone,
leaning in a certain window, which looked into the garden of
the house where we now lay, at Ostia ; where, removed from
the din of men, we were recruiting from the fatigues of
a long journey for the voyage.   We were discoursing then
together, alone, very sweetly ; and 'forgetting those things
which are behind, and reaching forth unto those things
which are before,' we were enquiring between ourselves
in the presence of the Truth, which Thou art, of what sort
the eternal life of the saints was to be, 'which eye hath not
seen, nor ear heard, nor hath it entered into the heart
of man.'   But yet we gasped with the mouth of our heart
after those heavenly streams of thy fountain, 'the fountain of
life,' which is 'with thee ;' that being bedewed thence according
to our capacity, we might in some sort meditate upon so
high a mystery.   And when our discourse was brought to
that point that the very highest delight of the earthly senses,
in the very purest material light, was, in respect of the
sweetness of that life, not only not worthy of comparison, but
not even of mention ; we, raising up ourselves with a more
glowing affection towards the ' Self-same,' did by degrees
pass through all things bodily, even the very heaven, whence
sun and moon and stars shine upon the earth ; yea, we were
soaring yet, by inward musing and discourse and admiring of
Thy works ; and we came to our own minds and went beyond
them, that we might arrive at that region of never-failing
plenty, where ' Thou feedest Israel ' for ever with the food
of truth, and where life is the ' Wisdom by whom all ' these
'things are made,' and what have been, and what shall be."

C 2

Five days after this she fell sick and fainted, and on her recovery she said, " Here shall you bury your mother." It had been her wish to have lain beside her husband, but perhaps in the nearness of that sublime vision the veil of the flesh had been melted away in the light of the Eternal, and the immortal and spiritual life already entered upon before leaving this. "On the ninth day of her sickness," says Augustine, "and the fifty-sixth year of her age and the three and thirtieth of mine, was that religious and holy soul freed from the body." After Augustine had closed her eyes, an attendant boy broke out into a loud lament, but being checked, an awe-struck silence prevailed, when Euodius began to sing a psalm, wherein many religious persons presently joined them. With faithful self-command Augustine refrained his "flood of grief ;" but he adds pathetically, " I knew what I was keeping down in my heart." She was buried without tears but not without sorrow. Thus passed away one of the world's types of women, loving and lovely to the utmost perfection of loveliness.

A little to the north of Ostia and the Island is situated the ancient Portus or port of Claudius. It will be remembered by the student of ecclesiastical history as having been the seat of a bishopric occupied in the early part of the third century by Hippolytus, one of the noblest ornaments and most heroic martyrs of the primitive Church, affording a fine example of that singleness and simplicity with which it was first governed. He lived in the early part of the third century, and wrote the Refutation of all Heresies (first attributed to Origen). Its chief value now is that of a history or account of the various religious faiths of his time. Bunsen, in his ' Hippolytus and his Age,' thus sums up the character of this remarkable man. " This noble character and warm heart, combined with a rare knowledge and able use of speculative as well as moral Grecian philosophy, an enlightened and effectual zeal for infusing the hellenic element of thought and intellectual liberty into the Western Church, and that conscientious struggle for truth, against falsehood and violence, which was crowned by martyrdom ; these are the eminent qualities which made Hippolytus dear to his congregation and to the Churches of the East and West, and which ensure to the author of the Refutation an honourable place among the good men and the leading minds of ancient Christendom."

By far the most conspicuous object presented to us on the whole undulating deltaic country which carries the eye to the gloomy belt of pines which lines the coast here, is an old castle, consisting of an enormous round tower and four square walls, companioned by a solitary stone-pine that spreads out its huge head of foliage high in the air, a little bent with the sea-winds against which it has so long battled. This castle was built by Sangallo for the warlike cardinal Della Rovere, who afterwards made his way to the papal throne rather by force of arms than the higher and more peaceable virtues of Christian life. He was called Julius the Second. " The elevation of Alexander the Sixth," says Roscoe, in narrating the circumstance, " was the signal of flight to such of the cardinals as had opposed his election. Giuliano della Rovere, who to a martial spirit united a personal hatred to Alexander, insomuch that in one of their quarrels the dispute had terminated with blows, thought it prudent to consult his safety by retiring to Ostia, of which place he was bishop. Here he fortified himself as for a siege, alleging that he could not trust 'the traitor,' by which appellation he had been accustomed to distinguish his ancient adversary."

Near Ostia are some salt pits, or marshes, in which the water of the sea is received and then evaporated. The salt thus produced is of a yellow hue, owing to an admixture of the waters of the Tiber. These were formed by Ancus Martius, and must not be confused with those exacted from the Veientes as hostages of peace by Romulus when he overcame them at Fidenæ, since those must have been on the other side of the river ; on the Etrurian, and not the Latian side, as Canina justly remarks.

Dante makes Ostia, "*Dove l' acqua di Tevere s' insala*"
(where the water of the Tiber becomes salt), the entrance into
Purgatory, as symbolical of the seat of the church at Rome.

If the reader is not already tired of this dreary region,
let him prolong his walk southward about two miles to

CASTLE AT OSTIA.

Castel Fusano, a modern castellated mansion, ghostlike in
its lonely gloom, belonging to the Chigi family. It is
situated in the skirts of a forest of pines, stretching for
miles along the coast. Being not very distant from the
sea, it was fortified to withstand the attacks of the Barbary
corsairs in the seventeenth century. It is a large, solid-
looking residence ; its roof being on a level with the lofty
trees, whose umbrageous tops look like a garden suspended
in the air. But by what sombre shades is it surrounded !
Funereal plumes of dark pines hang over glassy pools of
stagnant water, grown with reeds and rushes and rank
grass, as if they mourned the lonely desolation of the spot ;
and if any cheerful breeze comes by, laden with pleasant

murmurs of the sea, it sinks to a whisper there, and dies amongst the branches with a feeble wail. Even the sunshine puts on a sobered look within these dismal precincts, whilst Melancholy sits brooding in the solitude, with Miasma and Malaria by her side, fed with the consuming fires of slow fever and shivering ague. It has an eery sound, too, the wind at night in these dusky pines, when the December clouds have crushed the day down to a narrow streak at the horizon, and the dry reeds shriek with subdued voices, and the withered weeds, gaunt and grey, wave and whisper ominously. Then let the sad heart keep away from them, for they will tell it over and over again in wearisome tones all the sorrow that ever it knew.

This forest is the ancient Silva Laurentina. It is the site of one of the most touching episodes in the Æneid of Virgil—the deaths of the fast friends Nisus and Euryalus, in the war waged by Æneas against the Rutulian king Turnus, in dispute for the hand of the fair Lavinia.

One night as they were both on guard together, Nisus, in the desire to distinguish himself, inquired of Euryalus, "Do the gods inspire men's souls with this ardour, or does each man make a god of his own strong passions?" and then went on to say that the Rutulian watch-fires were slowly dying down, and that, overcome with wine and sleep, their enemies no longer maintained their guard, and proposed to go to Æneas, that he might summon a council, and allow them to enter the enemy's camp. Having obtained permission, they went thither. After slaying a number of their sleeping foes, and lading themselves with booty, they prepared to return, when they were met by a troop of horsemen sent from the town of Latinus, who, espying the helmet of Euryalus, challenged them. They fled into the forest, relying on the darkness to conceal them ; but Euryalus was surrounded and taken. Although Nisus had reached a place of safety, yet, missing his friend, he turned back in search of him. Presently he discerned the horsemen, and unperceived, threw several darts with fatal effect. After searching in vain for the source of these missiles, their leader, Volscens, ran upon Euryalus, exclaiming that his life should pay for both. Nisus immediately hastened from his hiding-place and confessed himself the author of the mischief; but too late to save his friend, in whose body the sword of Volscens was already buried. Rushing furiously with whirling sword upon Volscens, Nisus plunged it into his throat, and then throwing himself on the corpse of his friend, died, pierced with many a wound, their blood mingling on the turf.*

After a long day's ramble we found ourselves once more in the vicinity of Fiumicino, but knowing that the little place would be filled to the utmost, we went into a small road-side *osteria*, not offering, it is true, a very luxurious interior—in fact it very much bore the appearance of an English stable on the first entry; but experience had taught us that we should here very likely find tolerable cookery in a rough way, decent wine and a clean white napkin, however coarse; in no particular of which were we disappointed.

The salt placed upon the table was noticeable as being of a similar kind, and made in the same place as that which had been in use thousands of years before, produced by evaporating the salt water on the flats at the mouth of the river, as already mentioned.

When we reached Fiumicino the afternoon sun was sloping downwards, and the steamer at the head of the canal was panting and blowing as if to inform the passengers that the hour of departure was approaching. We strolled down to the coast. Immense breakers were rolling up the sand, and the little wooden jetty was deluged with the waves.

No sooner however had we begun to ascend the canal of Trajan, and the roar of the ocean to die on the ear, and the old ruins to grow less in the distance behind us, than the wind sank, and a calm pervaded the atmosphere. The canal is not quite straight, but follows a somewhat sinuous

* Virg. Æn. ix. 176.

direction. Along its banks the remains of brickwork are still visible. Two or three tall poplars with crowning masses of foliage, looking like pines, stand at the head of it. Soon we entered the ancient stream. As the labouring vessel panted and pushed its difficult way up the swift current, a soft evening sun spread a rich mantle over the surrounding prospect. The blue sky, the glittering river laden with infinite memories, the sweeping Campagna, the distant mountains, so faint and thin that the white villages and towns upon them appeared to hang suspended in the air—all seemed to take the magic of the time, clothing themselves rather in the hues of a beautiful dream than the substantial colours of waking reality. On the steep sides of the river tiled tombs are seen, some gaping to the light, others still sealed, in which repose the ashes of the dead, sometime to be exposed rudely by the swelling current or the curious inquiry of the antiquary. All along, too, traces of masonry may be observed just above the water's edge ; probably the remains of houses and other buildings which occupied its banks. As we passed along the shores the wide difference between their present and former condition was thrust upon my mind. I imagined them covered with fair gardens sloping down to the water's edge, with long alleys of trees and trimly cut shrubs and bushes. I imagined the weary citizen retired for his *villeggiatura*, from the toil and bustle of Rome, standing with wife and child by his balustraded terrace as the slow ship was towed up the river by labouring oxen, or the slave-rowed galley dipped its tiers of oars into the whirling current, fighting its way to the far-off city between sombre masses of pendulous foliage. Now, indeed, all is changed. The white heron watches for his prey on bare banks, or flaps across the stream with the slow beat of his broad wings ; skimming sand-martins flutter over its eddying surface ; various kinds of piper haunt the water's edge ; the wheeling hawk lingers and sails in the air ; the many-coloured bee-eater burrows in the crumbling banks, or flies over, uttering his low, soft whistle, whilst great herds of

shaggy cattle stand where the river has left a dry bed
of sand or mud, whisking their tails and enjoying the
coolness.

To all this the people on board the vessel appeared to be
for the most part supremely indifferent. Nor should it be
matter of surprise. Italians are so accustomed to the beauty
and antiquities that everywhere surround them, that it is
no wonder that a great proportion of them should pass un-
remarked. If they had always to bear with them the great
burden of the past, records of which meet them at every turn,
there would be no room for the thoughts and feelings of to-
day. So they, not unwisely, perhaps, gave themselves to the
enjoyment of the hour, laughing, joking, chatting, eating and
drinking with the utmost gaiety and good-humour. The band
grew louder and louder, probably on the strength of the
wine of Fiumicino, blowing till it was red in the face, and
hardly ever pausing to take breath. I stood on the captain's
deck, alternately gazing at the prospect and watching the
animated scene beneath. Presently a band of sailors (if
such they might be called who had come to assist the working of the vessel) came and sat below me. There were men
old and young, together with a number of boys, whose
duties seemed to be chiefly that of hopping about like frogs,
of which every Italian vessel that ever I sailed in was
always full. I counted fourteen of these able assistants
once on a Neapolitan ferry-boat. One of this particular
group took some salt, and laying it upon the deck without
so much as blowing the dust away, set his heel upon it to
reduce it to powder, which was the signal to begin. I
cannot tell what they ate, nor what they drank, but if it
were not of the best, its deficiencies were amply compensated by the mirth and contentment that prevailed amongst
them.

Perhaps the most picturesque point of the river between
Rome and its mouth is Dragoncello, a lonely *tenuta*, or
farm-house, situated on an elevation clothed with trees and
verdure, which Nibby identifies as the probable site of

Ficana, conquered by the Romans under Ancus Martius.[*]
Not far from here is Magliana, now turned into a farm-
house and buildings, though formerly the favourite residence
of several of the popes.   It consists of a long extent of low
grey buildings lying on the left bank, situated in a plain
surrounded by sweeping hillocks.   On the south rise the
Alban hills, and more to the east the more elevated Sabine
range, with its tender and beautiful lines.   A lofty stone
gateway gives entrance to the court, which is flanked on
two sides by the principal buildings turreted and castellated,
having a fine fountain in the middle.

Some frescoes attributed to Raphael ornament the walls.
It is now a dreary and desolate range of building, but
was once the favourite retreat of Leo the Tenth during the
hunting season.   It was here that he took his last illness,
the circumstances of which are thus narrated by Ranke in
his 'History of the Popes.'

"At the diet of Worms, in the year fifteen hundred and
twenty-one, where the religious and political affairs of
Europe were discussed, Leo concluded a treaty with
Charles the Fifth for the reconquest of Milan," then under
the dominion of Francis the First of France.

"Leo was at his villa at Magliana when the news of the
entry of his troops into Milan was brought to him.   He
gave himself up to the feeling which is wont to accompany
the successful termination of an enterprise, and contemplated
with pleasure the festivities with which his people were preparing to celebrate his triumph.   Up to a late hour in the
night he went backwards and forwards from the window
to the blazing hearth; it was in November.   Somewhat
exhausted, but full of joy and exultation, he returned
to Rome.   The rejoicings for the victory were just ended,
when he was attacked by a mortal disease.   'Pray for
me,' said he to his attendants, 'that I may still make you
all happy.'   He loved life, but his hour was come.   He
had not time to receive the viaticum, nor extreme unction,

[*] See Livy, i. 33.

So suddenly, so early, so full of high hopes, he died as the poppy fadeth."

"The Roman people," adds Ranke, "could not forgive him for dying without the sacraments, for spending so much money, and for leaving debts. They accompanied his body to the grave with words of reproach and indignation. 'You glided in like a fox,' said they; 'you ruled like a lion, you died like a dog.' Posterity, however, has stamped a century, and a great epoch in the advancement of the human race, with his name."

Passing by Tor di Valle, where the emissary of the Alban Lake, made before the fall of Veii, discharges itself into the river, the church of San Paolo alle Tre Fontane comes into view, a little removed from the banks on the right, about two miles distant from Rome.

On the spot where this church stands St. Paul is said to have been beheaded. There is a fragment of a column shown on which he is supposed to have suffered. Near the altar are three several springs of water, said to mark the places where the head fell and rebounded. On the floor some curious and rude mosaics from Ostia symbolize the four seasons. There are also two other churches near. One of them contains some fine mosaics of the modern school. But the most interesting of the three is an old basilica built by Honorius the First in the year six hundred and twenty-six, affording an excellent sample of the earliest form of Christian architecture in its transition from the ancient pagan temple. It has eight arches on either side, supported by pilasters. The roof is open woodwork, the wide nave being without chapels. In the front of the church is a portico supported by granite columns.

The neighbouring monastery is inhabited by Trappist monks. It would be difficult to imagine a more dreary spot than that of this little settlement. Buried in a hollow of the Campagna, surrounded by desolate hills laid bare in many places for the pozzolana earth which they contain,

removed from other habitations, in an unhealthy locality,
it must surely be trying **to the** resident religious community. Perhaps, however, the wholesome rule of living
by the labour of their own hands, the quiet retirement and
peaceful thoughts nourished **thereby, may** enable these
recluses **to support so uncircumstantial an** existence with
satisfaction.

A mile nearer to Rome, and close to the river, the Basilica
of St. Paul stands, which early tradition marks as his burial-
place. This splendid temple occupies the position of what
was formerly one of the noblest monuments of Christian
architectural art—the ancient Basilica of St. Paul, **once**
under the protection of the kings of England, begun **in the**
year three hundred and eighty-eight on the site of one still
more ancient over the remains of a Roman Christian lady.
This was destroyed by fire in eighteen hundred and twenty-
three, and **of** all its costly marbles **and mosaics only** a few
fragments **were** saved. Large **sums** were immediately
collected and set aside for its restoration. Whatever **the**
former building may have been, it **is not easy** to imagine
anything grander in **its** manner than that which has now
taken **its place.**

It has a spacious nave surmounted by large mosaic
portraits of the popes from the earliest times ; four ranges
of enormous polished granite columns on either side supporting **a** ceiling of carved and gilded woodwork : the **floor**
is of polished marble, in which these columns are reflected
as in a mirror. The **fine** altar and baldacchino borne on
pillars **of alabaster,** the noble mosaics saved from **the**
ancient church in the apse, the precious stones **of costliest**
inlay with which **the** church is lined, the open, **airy look**
communicated **by** the abundant light falling everywhere on
objects of splendour, fill the **mind** with amazement and
defy description. **It must be confessed,** however, that the
tender and reflective nature **of the** Christian religion would
seem to demand a more **pensive** atmosphere, more subdued
lights and quieter surroundings whereon to rest the eye in

its most devotional moods.   This gorgeous fabric would more remind one of the ordered grace and elegance of some magnificent pagan temple of old than of the toned and softened accessories with which Christian worship loves to surround itself.

Perhaps the more thoughful visitor will be better satisfied with the tranquil images presented to the mind in the tasteful fancies of the adjoining cloister.   Gracefully carved columns supporting the roof inclose a square patch of picturesque garden-ground.   Once these columns were inlaid with mosaics, but time and sacrilegious hands have now carried them almost all away.   Here the sunshine rests, seen from pleasant shade, where the good brothers of former days have walked and mused in the still hours of recreation. There yet seems to linger an ancestral devotion about its quaint flower-beds and crumbling walls which time cannot destroy.

Nothing can be conceived more unattractive than the external appearance of this wonderful temple.   Bare, blank walls of light blink with straight, ugly-looking slits for windows, whilst the campanile is a monumental epitome of architecture gone mad.   Pile upon pile of incongruous masonry climb to a height of ugliness it would be hard to match in the whole history of architectural follies.   Perhaps, however, in neglecting the outside of the building the architect may have had the artistic intention of surprising the spectator with the contrast between the exterior and interior. If he had any such aim he certainly could not have carried it out more effectually.

Just after passing St. Paul's the inconsiderable stream of the Almo empties itself.   It was famous in ancient days as the spot where the image of Cybele and the utensils belonging to her worship were annually washed with great state and pomp.   Ovid, speaking of the ceremony, says, " There is a spot where the rapid Almo flows into the Tiber, and the lesser stream loses its name in the greater.   There does the hoary priest in his purple vestments lave the lady

goddess and her sacred utensils in the waters of the Almo." *
The custom is also alluded to by other writers. This
stream flows from the so-called Grotto of Egeria by the
reputed temple of Bacchus on the Campagna, and is afterwards crossed by the Appian Way ; but its source really
lies in the Alban Hills near Marino, from which place it
is conveyed to the Grotto by a subterranean channel.

As we followed the windings of the river the dome of
St. Peter suddenly met the sight and as suddenly vanished.
The sun had long since set. The stars came out above
our heads, shyly at first, and then more brightly. The
mirth and merriment died away to a more reflective silence,
and when we slid up to the quay the outline of the lofty
Aventine, with its convents and churches and crowning
cypresses, was softened in the silvery light of the moon and
one fair planet that burned brightly beside it. Pale lights
glimmered in the street. Friends bade each other farewell,
and the faint murmurs of the city came to us muffled
through the stillness of night.

* "Est locus, in Tiberin qua lubricus influit Almo,
    Et nomen magno perdit ab amne minor.
  Illic purpurea canus cum veste sacerdos
    Almonis dominam sacraque lavit aquis."

Fasti, iv. 337.

THE BASILICA OF SAN PAOLO, FROM THE TIBER.

CHAPTER III.

ROME. FROM THE PROTESTANT CEMETERY TO THE TOWER OF ANGUILLARA.

WHAT a strange sensation is that which overpowers the traveller on his first arrival in Rome! With what varied and innumerable associations is his mind filled! The very name of it is laden with memories which breathe a vitality through the vanished centuries, ensouling the present with the mighty energies and active life of the past. At first everything seems to bear a consecration to him; but presently his reverence gives place to a tender and loving" interest, which familiarity seems rather to increase than diminish: so that nobody who has once visited Rome wishes it may be for the last time.

The first object that meets the eye on entering the city by the upward course of the river is the Protestant burial-ground. It is situated on a gentle slope falling from the ivied walls—a beautiful spot, planted with tall cypresses that rise above its graves, dispensing a solemn gloom about their muffled precincts. There is, perhaps, no place in Rome so soothing as this tranquil corner in the evening hours, when the throstle sings his latest song and the cawing jackdaw retires to rest. Then everything seems to be surrounded with an atmosphere of repose. The far-off sounds of the city lulled to a faint murmur, the increasing dimness, the drooping immortelles, and the quiet graves— all breathe a pensive peacefulness through the mind, making death appear no more a mystery and a sorrow—

the painful dislocation of time—but the natural consummation of life waiting until the individual shall be merged into the great Being of the universe.

On the highest part of the ground, underneath the ancient wall, lie interred the ashes of the poet Shelley. It will be remembered that he was drowned in a boat off Spezia, with his friend Williams. Many days afterwards his body was found by Captain Trelawny, so disfigured and mangled as to have been scarcely recognisable, had not a volume of Sophocles in one pocket and the poems of Keats in another left no doubt of his identity. In consequence of the stringent regulations then in force in that part of Italy, the corpse was not allowed to be taken inland; so it remained for a while buried in the sand. Permission was subsequently obtained to burn it; and for this purpose an apparatus was prepared by Captain Trelawny and a pyre raised upon which it was placed. As the flames began to surround it salt and frankincense were thrown upon it, and oil and wine poured over it. When the rest of the body was consumed the heart remained entire. It was snatched from the subsiding flames by Captain Trelawny, and this, together with his remains, was deposited in a box and finally interred where they now lie.

It must have been a picturesque as well as a mournful spectacle. Lord Byron and Leigh Hunt were present, together with a number of soldiers and the Health officer. The background to this tragical ceremony is clearly sketched by the graphic pen of Captain Trelawny. He says: "The lonely and grand scenery that surrounded us so exactly harmonised with Shelley's genius, that I could imagine his spirit soaring over us. The sea, with the islands of Gorgona, Capraji, and Elba, was before us; old battlemented watch-towers stretched along the coast, backed by the marble-crested Apennines glistening in the sun, picturesque from their diversified outlines, and not a human dwelling was in sight." One can well imagine the heavy column of smoke rising, the grouping of the soldiers and the saddened faces of the friends of the poet, to whom the bright sunshine and fair prospect would appear like a mockery during the fulfilment of their melancholy task.

His tomb, a flat slab of marble at a corner of the cemetery, bears this inscription : " Percy Bysshe Shelley. Cor Cordium.   Natus IV. Aug. MDCCXCII. obiit VIII. Jul. MDCCCXXII.

> " Nothing of him that doth fade,
> But doth suffer a sea change
> Into something rich and strange."

The words Cor Cordium, "heart of hearts," refer to the above-mentioned circumstance of his heart having remained entire from the funereal flames.   The cool seclusion of this dim nook, surrounded by green leaves and peeping flowers, might be such as the ethereal poet himself would have selected during his life-time for a last resting-place.

Not far from here, but in a more neglected place now disused, lies the body of the unfortunate John Keats : unfortunate in that the laurels planted whilst he lived had scarcely time to grow ere he died, and that misprision should have preyed on a sensitive mind, embittering its last days, and calling around it clouds of sorrow where only sunshine should have reigned.   On his marble head-stone is sculptured the fitting emblem of a lyre with broken strings, with the motto dictated by himself :

> " Here lies one whose name was writ in water."

It is strange that the hearing and appreciation which is frequently refused to a man during his life should be often given cordially enough at his death.   Like the Roman king to whom were brought the Sibylline books, we reject the full offer of the present in scorn, too glad to seize the moiety afterwards on any terms.

Rising up behind this tomb, far above the sheltering firs, is the pyramid of Caius Cestius, a huge monument and mausoleum, which was the last resting-place of a Roman prætor and tribune of the time of Augustus : one who was once wont to prepare the feasts of the gods, **but who has** himself long since been made the spoil of decay. In the Capitoline Museum are two **curious** *cippi* **or** inscribed tablets, once belonging to **this tomb, erected** by his executors, setting forth **that Caius had** desired **in** his will that he might be buried in **Attalic vestments.** These were rich robes, **very costly, woven** of gold and other expensive **materials, which took** their name from Attalus, king of **Phrygia,** and were introduced after the overthrow of that **kingdom in** the century before the Christian era. **The** inscription goes on to say, that as it had been forbidden by law [probably enacted about the time of his death] that these robes should any longer **be** used in burial, **the** executors had spent the value of them in raising this tomb to his memory. Near the pyramid was found an enormous bronze foot, supposed to have belonged to **a colossal statue** of the silent indweller in this durable house. The **house** remains, but the tenant has departed for whose conservation it was built. For not even in our **bones and** ashes may we **be** immortal, or cheat corroding Time **of his proper** prey.

On the same side of the river, **and** just beyond the limits **of the** cemetery, a wide and lofty hill rises, called Monte **Testaccio,** which at first looks **as if** it were **a** natural **elevation** of the ground, but on examination proves to **be** nothing but the sherds of broken *amphoræ,* or wine jars. **It is** almost inconceivable that so large an accumulation could be the result of fragments so small. It was doubtless once the site of the manufacture of these articles, **the** broken ones being thrown aside as useless ; **having its** position here in order to be near the warehouses **and the** wharf where the wine was first landed and stored. Climbing this hill to the summit, marked by a black cross, the **eye sweeps** the whole country round. **Beyond** the graveyard **and** the pyramid and **the low-lying** city, the varied undulations of the Campagna **spread** to the distant mountains, crossed by dim **aqueducts** and straight roads. One of these is the Via Appia, with its border of tombs and the vast mausoleum of Cecilia Metella, the wife of Crassus, almost two thousand years old, still standing though stripped of its ancient pride.   To the right the Tiber winds by the church of St. Paul, beneath the range of the Janiculum, into the city : over a shoulder of the hill the dome of St. Peter lifts itself, together with the more distant Monte Mario crowned with spiring cypresses and its single stone-pine.

On the same side of the river, and a little further along, are a series of docks and quays lately opened up ; parts of which remain as entire as when they were in use.   Sloping pavements for the convenience of landing goods are laid bare, the maker's name stamped upon the tiles being as fresh and legible as ever.   The doors of the warehouses still remain ; and many parts of the walls, consisting of small blocks of tufa, built lozenge-wise (called *opus reticulatum*), are still intact.   A small symbol sculptured in stone assigns each division of the quay to its proper use ; immense perforated blocks projecting from the brickwork serving to attach the vessels.   The upper section constituted the marble wharf, large masses of which in various stages of working lie scattered about ; columns roughed out, blocks half sawn and pediments prepared for the chisel of the finer workmen.   One of these is curious as showing the manner in which they proceeded to mark out columns in the solid block before working.   It is singular that the modern marble wharf should have been fixed at almost the same spot, the position of the ancient one only having been discovered within the last few years.

Opposite to this wharf or dock-yard (*navalia*), on the ground lying between the Janiculum and the river, was "the little farm of four acres," once held by the magnanimous Lucius Quintus, called Cincinnatus.   Its position was formerly assigned to the *prati*, or meadows, higher up the river ; but the recent discovery of this wharf has indubitably fixed its site, since Livy describes it as across the river from Rome, just opposite to the docks.   It was known in old

Roman days by the name of the Quintian meadows from
its occupation by Cincinnatus ; the circumstances of which
it is worth while to put together in passing ; particularly as
modern historians generally give it no more than a bare
mention.

It happened at a certain time in the early republic of
Rome that there arose a great deal of difference and jealousy
of power between the tribunes who were the representatives
of the people, and the patricians or nobles. One of the
latter, and amongst the most distinguished by birth and
fortune, was Lucius Quintus, who had a son named Caeso,
a young man of good parts and education, brave and well
favoured, having a certain measure of patrician pride, who
espoused very warmly the cause of his party, measuring his
language—for he was very eloquent—by no temperate rule.
He was for this reason as much hated by the people as he
was approved by the class to which he belonged. The
tribunes, desiring at once to curb his haughtiness and show
their power, preferred a charge against him, suborning dis-
honest witnesses ; for which, indeed, there was some slight
colour in his conduct, but no substantial foundation in fact.
It was in vain that his father disproved the capital allega-
tions made against him, pleading the inexperience of youth
for the rest, and pointing to the acts of bravery which he
had already performed, and the honours they had won him.
On the false testimony of one Volscius, a slanderous, ill-con-
ditioned man, he was cited to appear before the senate, but
allowed his personal liberty on the bail of his father together
with nine others, for his appearance when called upon by the
senate ; but preferring a voluntary banishment, he went and
settled in Tyrrhenia. Not content with paying his own part
of the surety, Cincinnatus paid all the others also the sums
in which they had been bound with him, the exaction of no
part of which was abated.   For this purpose it was necessary to sell almost all his property, only reserving to himself a small farm of four acres, lying across the Tiber, as
before described.   To this place he went with his wife and

E

family and a few slaves ; occupying himself in rural pursuits
and tilling the ground laboriously.   But when the office of
consul with Claudius became vacant a year afterwards, he
was unanimously chosen to occupy the post, to the consternation of the people, who expected that he would repay
upon them the wrong done to his son.   They had little,
however, to fear from one to whom justice was law and
probity a possession.   When the messengers arrived to
accompany him to Rome he was found ploughing in rustic
garments.   As he paused in his labour, wondering what
could be the object of a visit from so many persons, he was
requested to go into his cottage and dress himself in a more
becoming manner.   The delegates then saluted him as consul, and covering him with the official robe bordered with
purple, and bearing before him the axes and other ensigns
of magistracy, he was led into the city.   Before departing,
however, he tenderly embraced his wife, commending the
family concerns to her best care and attention, tears of
regret starting to his eyes at leaving untended his little
possession.

Dionysius, who tells this story circumstantially, says,
" What induces me to relate so many particulars is to let
the world see what kind of men the Roman magistrates were
at that time ; that they worked with their hands, and were
temperate ; that they were not uneasy under innocent
poverty ; and were so far from aiming at regal power, that
they refused it even when offered."

Right nobly did Cincinnatus discharge the duties of his
office, never once showing the least prejudice or interest
in the distribution of justice.   It is true, he used much
firmness in subduing the disorders of the people, which had
then risen very high ; but, at the same time, he fulfilled the
magisterial function with so much mildness and equality,
and was so humane and considerate in the discharge of it,
that he raised the reputation, not only of the magistracy itself, but also of the whole aristocracy ; and when the senate
would have had him continue in the consulship after the

prescribed term had expired, he both refused it and blamed those who pressed it upon him, resigning the power and importance of his position, and returning to his former place of abode and mode of life.

He was not however permitted to remain long in retirement. Shortly afterwards Rome was engaged in a war with the Æqui; and the state finding itself involved in much difficulty, it was agreed on all hands that a dictator must be appointed, and that dictator must be no other than Cincinnatus.

So they sent for him once more, bringing before him horses magnificently appointed, together with the four-and-twenty axes, the purple robe, and other insignia, formerly the privilege of royalty alone; at which he sighed, saying that this year's crop would also be lost for his pressing business. He did not refuse to go, however; and appointing some change of command in the Roman army, marched against the enemy, whom he overthrew with great slaughter, bearing thence abundant spoil and very large honours. But perhaps the part of his conduct which most of all merits praise is, that after six months from his appointment to the dictatorship, during which he received all the distinction which could be paid to the most honourable position, he laid down his office and went to his former simplicity of life; neither could the senate persuade him to accept the least part of the lands he had conquered nor any money, slaves, or other reward; and though friends and relations came forward with considerable presents, he refused them all; preferring his country cares to courtly ease, and his poverty to all the wealth and splendour that could be offered to him.

This was not the last service that Cincinnatus rendered to his country, but it is enough to justify what Dionysius says of him, that "he was not only the greatest statesman but the ablest general of his time:" and that he was one of those—

Who did give
Themselves for Rome, and would not live
As men good only for a year.*

---

* Ben Jonson.

Just above the modern marble wharf rise the abrupt heights of the Aventine hill. It is the highest of the ancient seven hills of Rome, and perhaps presents the most picturesque appearance. Legend says that Romulus and Remus desiring to build a city on the spot where they had been exposed and brought up, quarrelled as to whose name it should take, and that they determined to settle the matter by augury of birds. Upon this Romulus stationed himself on the Palatine and Remus on the Aventine. First Remus saw six vultures and then Romulus twelve, upon which Remus contended for priority of time, Romulus for superiority of number, whereupon the quarrel was renewed and Remus slain. Some say Remus was slain for jumping over Romulus' wall. To the circumstance of the augury has been attributed the name of this hill (from *avis*, a bird); others again derive it from Aventinus, one of the early kings. It used to be covered over with thick laurels, and had many mysterious old stories connected with it. One of these is told by Virgil in the eighth book of the Æneid, which is as follows :—On this hill was a cave, supposed to have been on the steep side facing the river, inhabited by a monster, half human in shape but wholly savage and imbruted in his nature. He was the son of Vulcan ; belching forth hot flames from his den, slaying men, and producing much mischief. He was called Cacus. Hither Hercules brought his herds to pasture, when Cacus, seizing upon four of his finest bulls and as many of his best heifers, dragged them up the hill by the tail, in order that they might not be tracked by their foot-prints, and so stowed them away in his cave. When Hercules was about to depart he missed the bulls and heifers which had been stolen, and searching for them he was not able to find them. Just as he was going away, however, his cattle beginning to low, one of them in the cave answered in the same manner. Hercules boiling with fury sought over the hill, at last discovering the mouth of the cave, which was closed by a huge stone. By pushing a larger mass of rock upon it from above the impediment was dislodged and the cave exposed to view. Cacus immediately began to vomit forth flames : but Hercules casting himself into the cave grappled with him and at last succeeded in strangling him. A periodical feast used to be kept in commemoration of the event. This legend has been supposed to refer to the early volcanic condition of the hill.[*]

Another legend not less curious relating to this place, is told by Ovid in his 'Fasti.' The substance of it is as follows :—

In the days of Numa the people were much dismayed by the heavy rains and the lightning which fell thickly and frequently. So that the priest-king consulted the goddess Egeria on the occasion. She bade him calm his fears, and told him that the lightning was to be averted by atonement, referring him for further instructions to Picus and Faunus, Roman divinities, at the same time telling him that they would afford him no information except by compulsion, and that he must secure them with chains when he caught them. At the foot of the Aventine hill there was a grove of oak, in the centre of which was a grassy plot and a constant stream of water trickling from the rock, which was covered with green moss. At this stream Faunus and Picus were accustomed to drink. Here Numa sacrificed a sheep, and then placed cups of wine about the fountain, concealing himself in a neighbouring grotto. Presently the forest gods came to refresh themselves, but instead of water, drank the wine that had been laid for them ; afterwards going to sleep. Then Numa issued from his hiding-place and fixed their hands in manacles. When the gods awoke they struggled in vain to free themselves. Then Numa stepped forwards and, asking forgiveness for what he had done, begged them to tell him how the lightnings might be averted. Faunus replied that he asked them a question which they could not answer, but promised to summon

[*] Virg. Æn. viii. 184.

Jove himself to his assistance if he would only free them
from their bonds.   Upon this Numa set them at liberty ;
whereupon the tops of the Aventine forest trembled and
the earth yielded to the feet of Jove.   Numa at first was
overcome by the vision, but presently recovering himself,
stated his desire.   Jove then told him that he must "cut
off a head."   "Of an onion in my garden," said Numa.
"Nay, but of a man," said Jupiter.   "Yes, the topmost
hairs," said the other.   "You must take a life," said Jove.
"The life of a fish," replied Numa.   Jove, diverted with the
ingenious answers of Numa, laughed, and said, "See to it,
then, that with these thou dost propitiate my missiles, thou
man not to be daunted in a conference with the gods.
Moreover, when to-morrow's sun shall have risen I will give
thee the sure pledge of empire." *

This promise was fulfilled the next day in the fall of the
celestial shield, which was supposed to contain in its safety
the welfare of the empire : so that in order that it might
not be carried away, Numa caused a number of counterparts
to be made, preserving the secret of the true one.   The
shields were periodically carried through the streets of Rome
with dancing, festivities, and great rejoicings.

Although fortified by Romulus, the Aventine was first
included in the city by Ancus Martius.   After Virginia had
been slain by her father to protect her from the cruel
violence of Appius Claudius, he and the soldiers he commanded stationed themselves on the Aventine in rebellious
opposition to the overgrown patrician power in the decem-
virate, which was at that time abolished.   Subsequently
Lucius Icilius, to whom Virginia had been betrothed, who
had been made a tribune, caused the Aventine to be built
upon for the special use and advantage of the people.

There were many temples upon the hill.   Amongst the
most celebrated were those of Juno Regina, whose image
Camillus brought from Veii at its fall, Jupiter Libertas built

* Fasti, iii.

by Caius Gracchus, Diana Aventina, and Bona Dea, the good goddess.

Bona Dea, or Fauna, was sister, wife, or daughter of Faunus. She was the embodiment of chastity, her worship being wholly restricted to women. She only revealed her oracles to females. Her temple was built on the rocks of Aventine, "hating the eyes of men" (oculos exosa viriles). It was consecrated by Claudia, a maiden of reputed virtue. On the first of May, her festival was held in the house of some consul or prætor, probably in order that it might be more private, sacrifices being made for the whole Roman people. The Vestals conducted the worship, which was chiefly attended by women of the higher order. The statue of the goddess was decorated with vine leaves and had a serpent placed about its feet. The women also wore garlands, the house being adorned in the same manner ; the myrtle alone being excluded, because it was with a staff of myrtle that Faunus killed Fauna **before** she became a goddess.

Once when these rites were being celebrated by Pompeia, the wife of Julius Cæsar, Clodius, a libertine of illustrious family, introduced himself into the house in women's clothing, with the desire of meeting Pompeia, whom it would appear was privy to his coming. Whilst her maid was in search of her Clodius was discovered by his voice, which caused a great uproar. The lights were extinguished and the proceedings broken up. When this came to the ears of Cæsar he at once divorced Pompeia, and when it was urged that there could be no real accusation against her, made use of the memorable saying, that the wife of Cæsar **must be** even above suspicion.

Although **the** rites in honour of this goddess **doubtless** began in all earnestness and sincerity and from an elevated enthusiasm, **yet** if we are to believe **the** Latin satirical writer Juvenal, who flourished in the first century, they must have degenerated at that time **to the** worst and lowest forms of demoralization.

Valerius Maximus relates that in the days of Servius

Tullius, there was born an unusually large cow belonging to a patrician family in the Campo Sabina, whence the augurs and priests said that whoever sacrificed it at the temple of Diana on the Aventine, his country would have the empery of the world. Its owner on hearing this went with great joy to sacrifice the cow in order that the Sabine people might become rulers of the human race. The priest of the temple told him that before it was killed the sacrificer must wash his hands in the Tiber. Then whilst the Sabine went for that purpose, the priest sacrificed the cow himself, thus obtaining for the Roman people the advantage of the offering.

The Aventine is associated with the fate of the fine-spirited reformer and friend of the people, Caius Gracchus. After the death of his brother Tiberius, who had laboured so hard in the same cause, Caius gave himself with no less vigour to withstand the oppressions of the nobles and promote the freedom of the people. But at last, the opposite party being too strong for him, he was treacherously deserted by his own. Objecting that force should be used in the cause he advocated, he retired to the temple of Diana at the foot of this hill without drawing his sword, and would have put an end to his life if he had not been restrained. It is said that he kneeled down here, and in the bitterness of his disappointment prayed that the Romans for their baseness and cowardice might never know the name of freedom. This happened near the temple dedicated to liberty which his grandfather had built. He thence fled over the Pons Sublicius to the grove of the goddess Furina, which was on the site of the modern hospital and prisons of San Michele; where he was miserably slain, himself dealing the mortal blow. A reward of its weight in gold being offered for his head, it was filled with lead by one Septimuleius and borne to Opimius the consul, on the point of a spear. This was in the year one hundred and twenty before Christ, about thirteen years after the death of his brother.

In considering the character of the ancient Roman people no trait is presented to us in a stronger light than that of their intense superstition; overbearing and blinding, in some directions, all judgment and reason. No expedition was organized without the omens being consulted. The disposition of the entrails of a bird could influence or change the most reasonable and matured conclusions. A chance word, a false step, the sight of a bird or animal, any trivial occurrence upon which faith in the supernatural could fix itself was seized upon to determine the most momentous occasions, to govern the most stupendous enterprises, to supersede all the judgments of counsel and consideration. Of course their indomitable steadfastness in what they did undertake generally served them in the place of divinity, and no doubt to their half-reasoning minds, seemed to confirm and justify their creed. Reported showers of stones, streams of blood, the spontaneous movement of statues, and other exorbitant phenomena were placed in the same category with the slightest deviation from ordinary law ; as for example, the birth of a malformed child or animal, or even the simple fall of the electric fluid. All these had to be expiated by solemn sacrifices to the gods on sacred days set especially apart for that purpose. The fundamental cause of this doubtless arose from that inward respect for law which formed the nature and essence of the Roman character, the slighest deviation from their conceptions of which was ranked with the supernatural and the monstrous. A curious and picturesque circumstance taking place on the spot under consideration affords an illustration of this. It is told by the historian Livy.*

A shower of stones being reported to have fallen at Veii ; a stream of blood having appeared, and a temple been struck by lightning at Minturna, as also a gate and a wall at Atella ; a wolf having torn a man at Capua, and a monstrous child been born at Frusino (which was cruelly placed into a chest and thrown into the sea), it was supposed

* xxvii. 37.

the Divine Powers were angry and needed propitiation. Accordingly, thrice nine virgins were deputed to go through the city singing a hymn. Whilst they were learning this hymn in the temple of Jupiter Stator, the temple of Juno Regina on the Aventine was struck by lightning. This was construed into a prodigy appertaining to the matrons, who were required to bring a present to the goddess of the Aventine, both those of Rome and those within ten miles from it. This was accordingly done ; a contribution being made from their dowries, of which a gold basin was made and carried to the Aventine, a day being set apart for another sacrifice and procession ; which consisted of two white heifers led from the temple of Apollo through the Carmental Gate, after which were borne two images in cypress of Juno Regina ; then came twenty-seven virgins all clothed in white, singing the praises of the same goddess : these were followed by the decemvirs crowned with laurel, and wearing purple-broidered robes. Arrived at the Forum the procession stopped, and the virgins, who were connected by a cord passing from hand to hand, moved, beating time with their feet to the music of their voices ; finally ascending the Aventine, where the decemviri made a double sacrifice, depositing the cypress images in the temple.

It is a striking picture. Often and often, standing at the foot of the hill in the bright sunshine, have I imagined the whole circumstance of this impressive ceremony, as if no decades of centuries intervened. I have seen in my mind's eye the procession pass along the streets of the city, the people looking on with hushed voices and serious faces : and then, the dance of the damsels in the forum, their lithe bodies moving to and fro, not springing in the blithe merriment of a festival, but scarcely lifting their feet from the ground, as their treble voices swell the solemn hymn and a feeling of awe creeps over the minds of the spectators ; and, last of all, the train of sacrifice, followed by the matrons of the city and adjoining country, with a vast concourse of people in their wake, slowly winding the heights of the Aventine to its summit, until they stand in front of the altar smoking in the dim and magnificent temple before the colossal figure of Juno erect in dignified majesty, the object of reverence to all eyes.

But now no longer is the "seat of Juno eternal on the Aventine." It became gradually less populous from the sixth century, though not actually abandoned till the tenth. In the thirteenth century there was an attempt to revive its condition under Pope Honorius, but this was ineffectual. It is now for the most part disused as a place of residence on account of its unhealthiness, and partly, perhaps, on account of its elevation. It is principally covered by walled vineyards and waste corners that bear no trace of its former population, its convents and churches forming almost its sole structures. Of the latter of these (two of them with convents attached) there are three on the steepest part, facing the river.

The first is generally called that of the Priorato from the priory attached to it, belonging to the renowned Knights of Malta. This order was a union of the military and religious functions. It originated in the year one thousand and forty-eight in a hospital built in the East by some people of Amalfi to succour pilgrims visiting the holy sepulchre. It afterwards extended widely, numbering the rich and great amongst its members. Its principal establishment in England was the priory at Clerkenwell, the chief of which had a seat in the upper House of Parliament, and was styled First Baron of England. In the height of its prosperity the brotherhood was bound by religious vows, giving itself specially to the succour of the sick and befriending of pilgrims. It flourished greatly during the middle ages, and though for some time not much more than a name, only appears to have practically died out at the beginning of the present century. This church adjoining their priory contains several very fine Renaissance monuments in which the effigies of some of these old world heroes, noisy enough in their day, no doubt, sleep quietly and unnoticed now in dusty marble.

In this monastery Hildebrand, afterwards Pope Gregory the Seventh, passed his early years under the care of his uncle, who was the abbot. This remarkable man was born of poor parents at Soana in Tuscany, as is generally supposed, though this has been disputed, in the year one thousand and twenty. His education was completed in the monastery of Cluny in France, after which he returned to Rome, and taking orders, was afterwards entrusted with the full management of affairs under Alexander the Second, ultimately obtaining the position of cardinal. When Alexander died and the funeral was going forward at the church of St. John Lateran, the cry arose on all hands, " It is Hildebrand whom St. Peter elects as his successor !" At first he resisted, but finally accepted the pontificate, at the same time writing to King Henry the Fourth of Germany, requesting him not to sanction the election ; assuring him that if he did so, he should visit his conduct for several abuses and scandals with great severity. The prerogative of sanctioning the appointment of a new pontiff was at that time the privilege of the German crown ; this being the last occasion upon which it was used. Henry, however, without more ado, ratified the election, sending a prelate to attend the consecration who was not even in priest's orders.

No sooner had Gregory attained the throne than he at once began his attack upon the prevalent abuses of the time, the incontinence of the clergy and secular investiture, or the control of the laity over the benefices of the church. Against this latter reform Henry rebelled, which brought matters to such a condition, that the pope excommunicated him, absolving all his subjects from the oath of their allegiance. This produced a rebellion in the empire, so that Henry, in order to keep his imperial seat, was compelled to go and ask pardon and absolution of the pope. He went. It was winter and the most inclement of seasons when he passed over Mont Cenis with his wife, undergoing much difficulty and incredible hardships. He found the pope at Canossa in North Italy on a visit to the Countess

Matilda, who was there entrenched in a strong fortress.
Three days elapsed before the pope would receive him,
three days he stood between the inner and outer cincture of
the fortress, his retainers and attendants being outside,
bare-footed, bare-headed, fasting till the evening, expecting
the pope's message.   At last it came.   He was ushered
into the presence, and there obtained the benefits of absolution and benediction.   They were seeming friends, and
sat down together at table in amicable converse ; but it was
for the last time.

As soon as Henry had subdued the rebellion, by crushing
its head, the Duke of Suabia, he once more set the pope at
defiance.   Gregory then recognised the vanquished Rodolph
of Suabia as emperor of Germany, whilst Henry on the
other hand proceeded at once to raise up an antipope in the
person of the Archbishop of Ravenna as Clement the Third.
Pressing his advantage still further, Henry found himself in
Rome in possession of the city (his army occupying the
position of this very hill), the unfortunate Gregory being
compelled to shut himself up in the castle-fortress of St.
Angelo.   Here it might have gone hard with him had not
the Norman adventurer Robert Guiscard, whom the pope
had made duke of Apulia, come forward with a large force
and set him at liberty.   Upon this Henry withdrew his troops,
fearing to meet the larger force of the Norman.   The pope
was then escorted to Salerno by Robert, where he died in
the year one thousand and eighty-five ; his last words, " I have
loved justice and hated iniquity, therefore I die in exile."

The view from the terrace-garden of this convent is very
beautiful.   Through a vista of ilex trees the dome of
St. Peter overtops the town.   The river leads the eye
through the city with its quaint bridges and ancient bell-
towers, as it flows between this hill and the Janiculum on
the other side.   It is a true conventual residence.   The
noises of the world only reach it in muffled and subdued
tones.   Heaven is above it and the world beneath it.
What more can the aspiring soul require ?

Adjoining this is the church of St. Alessio, or Alexius. It is said to be situated upon the place called Armilustrum, where the ancient feast for the purification of arms used to be held in early Roman days. It is here also that we are told the Sabine king Tatius, one of the founders of the city with Romulus, was buried. The first church occupying this position was built where stood the house of Euphemianus the father of Alexius, in the ninth century. It was originally dedicated to St. Boniface. The legend of Alexius is amongst the most interesting and romantic in the whole calendar. It is thus told by Mrs. Jameson in her 'Sacred and Legendary Art.'

" In the days when Innocent the First was pope, and Arcadius and Honorius reigned over the East and West, there lived a man in Rome whose name was Euphemian, rich and of senatorial rank. He had a house and great possessions on the Aventine hill, but he had no son to inherit his wealth. He and his wife, whose name was Aglae, besought the Lord earnestly to grant them offspring. And their prayer was heard ; for after many years they had a son, and called him Alexis. And Alexis from his childhood had devoted himself to the service of God, and became remarked by all for his humility, his piety, and his charity. Although outwardly he went clothed in silk and gold, as became his rank, yet he wore a hair shirt next his body ; and though he had a smiling and pleasant countenance towards all, yet in his chamber he wept incessantly, bewailing his own sinful state and that of the world, and made a secret vow to devote himself wholly to the service of God.

" And when he was of a proper age his father wished him to marry, and chose out for his wife a maiden of noble birth, beautiful and graceful and virtuous, one whom it was impossible to look on without being irresistibly attracted. Alexis, who had never disobeyed his parents from his infancy upwards, trembled within himself for the vow he had spoken, and seeing his bride, how fair she was and how virtuous, he trembled yet the more ; but he did not dare to gainsay the words of his father. On the appointed day, the nuptials were celebrated with great pomp and festivity ; but when evening came, the bridegroom had disappeared, and they sought him everywhere in vain ; and when they questioned the bride, she answered, 'Behold, he came into my chamber, and gave me this ring of gold, and this girdle of precious stones, and this veil of purple, and then he bade me farewell, and I know not whither he is gone !' And they were all astonished, and, seeing he returned not, they gave themselves up to grief ; his mother spread sackcloth on the earth, and sprinkled it with ashes, and sat down upon it ; and his wife took off her jewels and bridal robes, and darkened her windows, and put on widow's attire, weeping continually : and Euphemian sent servants and messengers to all parts of the world to seek his son, but he was nowhere to be found.

"In the meantime, Alexis, after taking leave of his bride, disguised himself in the habit of a pilgrim, fled from his father's house, and throwing himself into a little boat, he reached the mouth of the Tiber. At Ostia he embarked in a vessel bound for Laodicea, and thence he repaired to Edessa, a city of Mesopotamia, and dwelt there in great poverty and humility, spending his days in ministering to the sick and poor, and in devotion to the Madonna, until the people, who beheld his great piety, cried out, 'A saint !' Then, fearing for his virtue, he left that place, and embarked in a ship bound for Tarsus, in order to pay his devotions to St. Paul. But a great tempest arose, and after many days the ship, instead of reaching the desired port, was driven to the mouth of the Tiber, and entered the port of Ostia.

"When Alexis found himself again near his native home, he thought, 'It is better for me to live by the charity of my parents than to be a burthen to strangers ;' and, hoping that he was so much changed that no one would recognize him, he entered Rome. As he approached his father's house, he saw him come forth with a great retinue of servants, and, accosting him humbly, besought a corner of refuge beneath his roof, and to eat of the crumbs which fell from his table : and Euphemian, looking on him, knew not that it was his son ; nevertheless, he felt his heart moved with unusual pity, and granted his petition, thinking within himself, 'Alas for my son Alexis ! perhaps he is now a wanderer and poor, even as this man.'   So he gave Alexis in charge to his servants, commanding that he should have all things needful.

"But, as it often happens with rich men who have many servitors and slaves, Euphemian was ill obeyed ; for, believing Alexis to be what he appeared, a poor, ragged way-worn beggar, they gave him no other lodging than a hole under the marble steps which led to his father's door, and all who passed and repassed looked on his misery ; and the servants, seeing that he bore all uncomplainingly, mocked at him, thinking him an idiot, and pulled his matted beard, and threw dirt on his head ; but he endured in silence.   A far greater trial was to witness every day the grief of his mother and his wife ; for his wife, like another Ruth, refused to go back to the house of her fathers ; and, often, as he lay in his dark hole under the steps, he heard her weeping in her chamber, and crying, 'O my Alexis ! whither art thou gone ?   Why hast thou espoused me only to forsake me ?'   And, hearing her thus tenderly lamenting and upbraiding his absence, he was sorely tempted ; nevertheless he remained steadfast.

"Thus many years passed away, until his emaciated frame sank under his sufferings, and it was revealed to him that he should die.   Then he procured from a servant of the house pen and ink, and wrote a full account of all these things, and all that had happened to him in his life, and put the letter in his bosom, expecting death.

"It happened about this time, on a certain feast day, that Pope Innocent was celebrating high mass before the Emperor Honorius and all his court, and suddenly a voice was heard which said, 'Seek the servant of God who is about to depart from this life, and who shall pray for the city of Rome!' So the people fell on their faces, and another voice said, 'Where shall we seek him?' And the first voice answered, 'In the house of Euphemian the patrician.' And Euphemian was standing next to the emperor, who said to him, 'What! hast thou such a treasure in thy house, and hast not divulged it? Let us now repair thither immediately.' So Euphemian went before to prepare the way; and as he approached his house, a servant met him, saying, 'The poor beggar whom thou hast sheltered has died within this hour, and we have laid him on the steps before the door.' And Euphemian ran up the steps and uncovered the face of the beggar, and it seemed to him the face of an angel, such a glory of light proceeded from it, and his heart melted within him, and he fell on his knees. And as the emperor and his court came near, he said, 'This is the servant of God of whom the voice spake just now.' And when the pope saw the letter which was in the dead hand of Alexis, he humbly asked him to deliver it; and the hand relinquished it forthwith, and the chancellor read it aloud before all the assembly.

"But now what words shall describe the emotions of his father when he knew that it was his son who lay before him? and how the mother and the wife, rushing forth distracted, flung themselves on the senseless body, and could with difficulty be separated from it? and how for seven days they watched and wept beside him? and how the people crowded to touch his sacred remains, and many sick and infirm were healed thereby? But all this I pass over; let it suffice that on the spot where stood the house of Euphemian, the church of St. Alexis now stands. The marble steps beneath which he died are preserved in the church, in a chapel to the left of the entrance, and beneath them is seen the statue of the saint lying extended on a mat, in the mean dress of a poor pilgrim, his staff beside him and the letter in his hand."

F

The third and adjoining church is that of Santa Sabina. It is in the basilica form. It was first built in the year four hundred and twenty-five, on the site of the house of the saint from whom it takes its name. It has been frequently restored. It consists of a nave and two side aisles, separated by twenty-four antique Corinthian columns of fluted white marble, of uniform height and thickness. It is supposed that these columns formerly belonged to the temple of Juno Regina, which probably stood here. In the convent attached to this church, St. Dominic once dwelled. An old orange tree, planted by his hand, still stands an object of reverence in the garden. It was here that Thomas Aquinas secluded himself, in order to be out of the reach of the importunities of his relations, who wished to dissuade him from the religious life.

More removed from the river, is the church of Santa Prisca, which, tradition says, occupies the site of the house where St. Peter lived whilst in Rome, adding many souls to the church.

Leaving the Aventine, the range of white buildings on the left includes the hospital, schools, and prison of San Michele. Stretching in front of it is the Ripa Grande, or port of the river, beneath whose tall beacon-tower numerous vessels lie with sails furled. A little beyond this we come upon the foundations of the old Pons Sublicius, only to be seen when the river is low. This, the oldest and most celebrated of the Roman bridges, was built by Ancus Martius. After frequent repairs it was totally destroyed by a flood in the eighth century. This is the bridge that Horatius Cocles is said to have defended so bravely, single-handed, against the van of an army. The banished Tarquins in their wish to reinstate themselves, had fled for assistance to Lars Porsena of Clusium, the renowned king of a powerful people, who accordingly marched against Rome with an allied army of vast numbers. After making himself master of the Janiculum, a long range of rising ground here flanking the course of the river, he thought also, without much more trouble, to do the same by the city. But on approaching it, he found its **near banks** lined with Roman troops. A very severe engagement then immediately commenced, in which the Romans, finding themselves worsted, strove to regain the city; but the **ingress** being limited to this one bridge, it **threatened** to fall into the **hands** of the enemy, **had not the** bravery of Publius Horatius,—or Horatius Cocles, as he was called, from having lost one of **his** eyes **in** battle—and two others, Spurius Lartius and Titus Herminius, prevented it. They stood their ground, fighting bravely until the whole of the army had passed the bridge, when the two latter retired. But Horatius, calling out that they should break the bridge behind him, still maintained the fight, until the shouts of the **Romans** had told him that it **was** accomplished, when, **weary and** wounded, he jumped into the river, with difficulty regaining the other side.

One may imagine the joy with which **he** was welcomed, with no more serious wound than was curable; and with what an honourable halt he limped through life ever after-**wards.** On the moment, he was crowned, and conducted into the city with songs, everybody rushing out to look at **him with** wild and delirious joy. From bare stores each individual contributed to his provision; and not only had he as much land allotted to him as he could plough **round** in one day with a yoke of oxen, but also, whilst **he was** still living, his bronze statue stood in the most conspicuous part of the Forum, a continual witness of his bravery and the value his nation set upon it.

It was during this war that Mucius Scævola, **having** crossed the river for the purpose of assassinating **Porsena,** when found out, thrust his hand into **the fire to show** his indifference to bodily suffering; **and** the Roman maiden, Clœlia, swam over it with a **band of her companions** who had been given in hostage to the Etrurian king.

Dionysius mentions a very peculiar ceremony which used to take place on this bridge. He says that in the earliest days of ancient Rome, human victims were sacrificed to the god Saturn as the deity of universal Nature; but that Hercules, wishing to abolish these, instituted other sacrifices to be immolated on an altar of fire, allowing the people to retain so much of their custom as to bind figures in the likeness of men, hand and foot, and cast them into the Tiber, in order to satisfy any lingering superstition they might have. This ceremony was retained long afterwards. In the middle of May each year the priests assembled, after having made sacrifices, together with the Vestal virgins, the prætors, and citizens, on the sacred bridge [Pons Sublicius], and thence cast into the river thirty pageants resembling men, which they called Argivi. Ovid, in speaking of the same ceremony, says these dummies were made of rushes, and thrown into the river by the Vestal virgins. To learn the origin of this custom he invokes the spirit of the Tiber—the old river-god—who informs him that it arose from the ancient Argive settlers desiring that their bodies might be thrown into the river at their death, so that, perchance, they might be washed on to the shores of their native land. But that afterwards, the custom being displeasing to the survivors, these effigies were substituted.

On the right of the river, between the remains of the Sublician Bridge and the Island, the inconsiderable stream of the Marana (ancient Aqua Crabra) flows into the Tiber, near to which, on the same side, is the Piazza della Bocca della Verità, which takes its name from a large-mouthed antique mask, which probably formed the outlet to some fountain or the opening of a drain in the impluvium or central court of a house. There was a mediæval tradition that if a person making a deposition on oath were to place his hand within the mouth of the mask, perjury would be punished by his not being able to withdraw it. Here between the Tiber on the one hand and the Palatine and the Aventine on the other, were the Velabrum and Forum Boarium, used as markets in the more developed condition of the ancient city: in its early days, before the Cloaca

Maxima had been constructed, their whole extent was nothing but an undrained marsh covered with stagnant pools of water. Several temples were situated here : one to Hercules, one to Fortuna, and another to Mater Matuta ; yet, although two of them still remain in tolerable preservation, archæologists differ as to the name to be attached to each, as well as in respect to the position of the third. The elegant little circular structure commonly called the temple of Vesta, has no sort of authority for its name. The temple of Vesta, in which the ancile or sacred shield was kept, alluded to by Horace as having been thrown down by an inundation of the river, must have been nearer the Forum. Bunsen believes this structure to have been a temple of Cybele, Canina that of Mater Matuta. Standing immediately above the river, it forms a beautiful and picturesque object. It once consisted of a fine peristyle of twenty fluted columns of marble, one of them being now destroyed. The entablature also is lost. It is now turned into a little chapel, though not used ; the roof being covered with red tiles.

The other temple, called that of Fortuna Virilis, the name of which has also been disputed, is said to have been first raised in the time of the kings, but has been subsequently rebuilt and restored. It is constructed of travertine and tufa. There are four columns at the front and seven at the side remaining visible. The interspaces are walled up, as it is also used now as a modern church. The columns are Ionic and support a fine entablature and frieze with the heads of oxen and garlands sculptured upon it. Not far from this temple is a rich and elaborately carved archway of white marble raised by the bankers and cattle merchants of the place in honour of the fratricidal emperor Caracalla. The representation of his brother has evidently occupied a position near to that of his own, but has been erased, the inscription also having been altered. What is left of the sculptured form of the emperor is noticeable as being in strong and favourable contrast with his bust in the Capitol, in which every evil thought and malicious intention appear to meet.

To complete the list of antique monuments in this place must be mentioned a four-pierced arch, that of Janus in the Velabrum, such as it is supposed stood sometimes at cross-roads. It is a very solid structure of white marble, but is held to be of the declining period, probably that of Septimius Severus, that is, the second or third century of our era.

Just at the foot of the bridge are the remains of an ancient mansion of brick with some ornate mouldings, some antique fragments being built into the wall. There is a long Latin inscription upon it from which it has been conjectured to have belonged to the tribune Cola di Rienzo. The architecture has been supposed to be of the eleventh century.

Livy tells us that shortly after the battle of Cannæ (two hundred and sixteen years before Christ) several prodigies having occurred, amongst the rest, two Vestal virgins having broken their vows whilst a messenger was being sent to Delphi to inquire of the oracle, extraordinary sacrifices were made; a Gallic man and woman and a Greek man and woman being let down alive into a pit fenced round with stone, in the Cattle Market (Forum Boarium)—not the first victims it had received, he says; a proceeding which he condemns as not being generically a Roman rite.

This place is also notable as having been the spot upon which the first gladiatorial combat took place in Rome— given on occasion of the funeral of the father of Marcus and Decius Brutus, two hundred and sixty-four years before Christ.

On the side of the piazza farthest from the river is the church of Santa Maria in Cosmedin, attached to which rises a mediæval campanile, the tallest, as it is one of the finest in Rome. The church, too, is very interesting, though it has been much spoilt by restorations and alterations. It was founded by Adrian the First late in the eighth century, and rebuilt early in the thirteenth by Alfanus, a Roman chancellor, whose epitaph attributes to him the large distinction of having been 'an honest man' (vir probus).

Just below the little round temple the Cloaca Maxima empties itself into the river. This is considered one of the most stupendous engineering works of antiquity. Livy attributes it to Tarquinius Priscus, the fifth king of Rome. It is an immense stone archway constructed of large blocks of peperino, some of them nearly five feet in length and more than three in thickness, put together without cement, for the purpose of a drain or sewer. The inner vaulting reaches to the height of twelve feet. It passes from the region of the Velabrum to the Tiber, a distance of eight hundred feet. It formed the outlet of the principal part of the sewerage of ancient Rome, and even now remains apparently as solid and firm as when it was first built.

Near the Cloaca Maxima may be traced very substantial remains of a travertine structure—in good solid blocks—which is supposed to be the "pulchrum littus" or quay formed in the very earliest days of ancient Rome. Nearly opposite to this are some huge heads of lions, also in stone, projecting from the bank, discovered by Mr. Parker a few years ago. They were used for the purpose of attaching vessels. Here the river is spanned by the Ponte Rotto or Broken Bridge : it is the ancient Pons Æmilius completed in the second century before Christ. It has undergone subsequent restorations. In the year fifteen hundred and ninety-eight a severe flood carried away two arches. The deficiency is now supplied by a suspension bridge, which joins the remaining portion to the other shore. At its piers are fixed revolving nets made in the shape of a shallow purse or bag, fixed upon cross bars, which thus turn by the force of the stream, depositing their spoils, when there are any, into a piece of canvas stretched at the side to receive them. From this bridge the body of the monster Heliogabalus was thrown into the river. It might have been a favourite place for suicides, since Juvenal, in one of his satires, facetiously asks his friend Postumus, why he should think of getting married as long as there are halters and lofty windows and the Æmilian Bridge is so ready at hand. The views from it, both up and down, are very commanding, and embrace some of the most notable sites and objects of the ancient and mediæval city.

Another conspicuous object on the left is the Tower of Anguillara. It was once one of the most formidable of those numerous castles of the Middle Ages, the occupiers of which kept Rome in continual embroilment. Dreadful places they were; rightly styled by Petrarch "proud towers, enemies of heaven." Rome once bristled with them. Even now the gloomy walls and narrow loophole windows of those which remain bear a sinister aspect, frowning in the sunshine as though they belonged to the kingdom of darkness rather than the free and unsuspicious realm of day. The very manner of their fabrication spoke of faction and the bitterness of party. The flat turret indicated adherence to the Ghibelline cause; a triangular indentation cut on the summit, attachment to the opposite Guelph interest; as did also cross frame-work in the windows. On their ground floors were frequently constructed horrible instruments of feudal revenge and tyranny called *trabocchetti:* trap-doors being made to allow the miserable victims who passed over them to fall into dark prison-like wells, closed alike from rescue and discovery. These were sometimes shaped to a point at the bottom, so that the unfortunate wretches who became immured within them could not even stand upon their feet or retain any posture of repose for a single moment.

Of the fortification of the Anguillara stronghold there is not much left beyond the tower, a façade wall, and a brick archway. The top of the tower is now put to a very different purpose. Between the roof and the walls there is an open space forming a kind of *loggia* which commands a fine view of the surrounding country. At the season of Christmas a mimic representation of the Nativity is constructed called the *Presepio,* and artfully placed to receive the Campagna and Alban hills as a background, by means of which a very pretty artistic effect is obtained.

CHAPTER IV.

*ROME. FROM THE ISLAND TO THE
PONS TRIUMPHALIS.*

WHEN we stand upon some of Rome's most classic
spots it is impressive to recall the words of the
elegiac poet Propertius, in which he addresses the stranger,
calling upon him to look round on all that lies before him
of the mighty city in the pride of its pomp, and bidding
him remember that before the coming of Æneas it was nothing but a grassy mound upon which the herds of Evander
strayed and fed, that the temples glittering before him in all
their splendour at first only rose in honour of earthenware
gods, when a rude shrine was no shame, and Jupiter thun-
dered from a bare rock ; when the sole living creatures the
Tiber met on its way were the oxen that grazed upon its
banks, and the rocky shelves of the Aventine were the only
hearth of the little brotherhood of Remus, and were rule
and kingdom enough for them. It is impressive to recall
this and look round with the expansive gaze of to-day. Of
all the gold and marble that dignified the verse of the poet
nothing left but heaps of crumbling dust and a denuded
name ! Once more rank weeds choke the place of palaces,
and the costly shrine is usurped by mean habitations and
noisome heaps of rubbish. The very gods have vanished
before the potency of inductive science, leaving no trace
behind them but the broken fragments of their marble
effigies.

There is perhaps no place in Rome which offers so strong

a contrast between the past and the present as the one we
have now reached, that is, the Sacred Island "which the
river surrounds with its divided wave," and the adjacent
banks ; for it was chiefly here that the ancient city stood ;
and not at the northern extremity, which constitutes the
more fashionable quarter of modern times.

The story given of the origin of this island is a curious
one. Higher up the river, and on the right or more
northerly side of it, occupying, perhaps, the greater part of

ISLAND OF THE TIBER.

the ground upon which the modern city is built, was a large
field or open space which in early days had been consecrated by public decrees to the god Mars, and was used by
the youth of Rome whereon to practise martial and gym-
nastic exercises. It was called the Campus Martius, a
name which is still given to a part of the same district,
though it is now covered with houses. This ground had
been taken by the last of the tyrant kings Tarquinius, for
his own property, and sown with corn. On his banishment

through the instrumentality of Brutus, the royal effects were given over to the people, all except the produce of this **field,** which then stood ripe to harvest, **or,** perhaps, already reaped ; but as the ground had been dedicated to a sacred purpose, it was not thought lawful to make use of it : it was therefore thrown into the river, with whatever shrubs and **trees had grown there ;** thence floating down to where the **island now** stands.   Being here arrested, the silt of the river accumulated upon and around it, resulting in the for-**mation** of this island, though probably it has been artificially modified at various times.

The story of its consecration is told **by Livy and Ovid.** It is an old fable, but full of significancies.

In the fifth century of the city, a little less than three hundred years before **the birth of** Christ, a **dire contagion** spread itself, not only over **Rome,** but the whole country **of** Latium, insomuch **that** the people, distracted with so many deaths, sent messengers to Delphi to **consult** the oracle **as** to what means should be taken **to** cause its termination. The Delphic reply told them **that they must** seek their remedy nearer home ; **for** that **it was not** Apollo but **Apollo's son** whom they wanted.   **On** further inquiry they were directed to Epidaurus in Argolis, where they were assured they should find him whom they sought.   Thither **they** accordingly went, and summoning the elders, informed **them of** the words of the oracle and besought them that **they** might carry away the divinity which they **had come in** search of.   Upon this there was a great consultation, some contending that the image should be permitted to be **taken** away, others again as strongly advocating that **it should be** retained.   Thus they deliberated until nightfall, **when the** consideration **was deferred ; the Roman leader** being left in the temple.   As he slept in the night he had a dream, and **in** his dream the **statue of the god** became animated, bidding him mark the serpent that entwined his staff, and telling him **that he should be transformed** into a similar serpent, but of vastly larger dimensions, as became a god. When the assembly met again in the morning they besought the god to let them know his will and pleasure by an indication as to what course of conduct they ought to pursue. As they thus accosted the statue, the god himself suddenly emerged from the foot of the altar in the form of a snake of enormous proportions covered with glistening plates of gold, shaking the whole structure from marble pavement to gilded roof. As he erected himself, rolling his eyes of fire, the priest who stood by with his hair bound in a white fillet, raised the cry, "Behold the god!" assuring the people and praying that the nation might be assisted in their rites. The serpent hissing loudly three times, turned round as if to bid farewell to the temple, and then glided over the polished pavement strewed with flowers, taking his way to the ship which lay in the harbour. When he reached the vessel he placed himself within it, resting his head upon the stern. They sailed many days until they arrived at Antium, where they were obliged to put in shore on account of stress of weather. Here the god, abandoning the ship, went to pay a visit to the shrine of his parent Apollo, and then returning, placed himself within it as before. Thus entering the Tiber, notice having already been received of their coming, they were welcomed by a vast assemblage of persons. On each side of the river, altars were erected, from which dense fumes of incense rose into the air. When they came to Rome, the serpent raised himself as if looking for a place of habitation, and here, where the river extends its arms on either side, leaving this island in the middle, he forsook the ship, and resuming his celestial form, brought health and happiness to the afflicted city.

It was in commemoration of this event that the island was fashioned into the form of a ship. Huge blocks of travertine and peperino still remain about the prow (pointing down the stream), imitating on a grand scale the

form of planks upon which are chiselled the figure of a
serpent twined about a rod, and, farther down, the head of
an ox. A temple was raised to Æsculapius, in which his
statue was placed, which probably stood in the fore part of
the simulated vessel, hospitals for the sick occupying the
sides, a tall column or obelisk rising in the midst to represent a mast ; temples were also dedicated to Jupiter and
to Faunus. To these was added a prison, in the days of
Tiberius, in which persons of distinction upon whom a sentence of death had been passed, were confined for ten days
previously to execution ; their respite afterwards being
extended to thirty.

The sick persons who visited the temple of Æsculapius
hoping for a cure, generally remained within it one or two
nights. It was then supposed that the god appeared to
them in a dream revealing the means of their recovery.
Sometimes, under conditions prescribed by the priests,
parents were permitted to expose their children on this
island. Sick slaves also, whose recovery was either doubtful
or tedious, were brought hither and abandoned. Claudius
enacted that should a slave so renounced survive, he should
have his liberty.

The island is now called San Bartolomeo from a church
probably built on the site of the old temple of Æsculapius,
dedicated to that saint. This church was founded by Otho
the Third, in the year one thousand. It is in the old basilica
form. Twenty-four antique columns of red granite, supposed to have belonged to the ancient temple, divide the
nave from the aisles. It is said to contain the body of St.
Bartholomew. This, however, is contested by the inhabitants of Benevento, who profess to have the real body in
their keeping.

As if to maintain its ancient character, there is a modern
hospital on the island belonging to the order of St. John
Calabita (a Spanish saint by whom it was founded), into
which all comers are received, of whatever nationality. Such

an institution in such a place perhaps marks more strongly than anything else the march of centuries, the difference between then and now, the wide contrast between Christian compassion and pagan superstition and cruelty.

The island is joined to the mainland by two bridges, one on either side : the one to the left called Ponte di San Bartolomeo (the ancient Pons Cestius), the other Ponte Quattro Capi (ancient Pons Fabricius). This bridge obtains its modern name from some four-headed Januses which surmount the parapet. The first, which is to the left looking up the stream, joins the island to that part of Rome known as the Trastevere, or transtiberine quarter, which is supposed to contain a more distinctively ancient Roman type of race than that on the east side of the river. This bridge was built about fifty years before the commencement of the Christian era by the prætor Lucius Cestius, who may have been the father of that Caius whose monumental pyramid has already passed under notice. It was restored in the year three hundred and seventy of our reckoning, by the Emperors Valentinian, Valens, and Gratian, as may still be read on the inner parapet wall. The other bridge, Pons Fabricius, connecting the island with the opposite shore, was built some twenty or thirty years later. This bridge is mentioned by Horace in one of his satires, in which he makes the dilettante Damasippus say, that being desperate, he stood upon it, with his head covered, ready to cast himself into the waters, when his friend Stertinius coming by persuaded him to become a stoic instead.*

The views from these bridges are very picturesque. Quaint abutments and arched jetties stretch themselves into the river, the trasteverine channel of which is filled with old black floating water-mills with slow-revolving wheels, each surmounted by the pious symbol of a cross. These mills are interesting as having been first used by

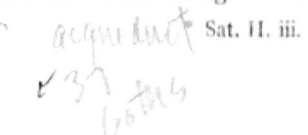

* Sat. II. iii.

Belisarius when Rome was besieged by the Goths in the year five hundred and thirty seven: the aqueducts having been broken and the streams arrested that turned the mills of the Janiculum. As the use of horses or mules would have caused an increased consumption of the diminishing stores of the city, Belisarius placed these mills where the current of the river was the strongest. The Goths becoming aware of this, turned large logs and tree-trunks down the stream, which at first were productive of some damage, until a strong chain placed across not only averted the mischief, but caused a barrier to be formed which kept out the boats of the enemy.

Close to the Ponte Quattro Capi on the island there is a tower which has been evidently cut down from its original altitude. It has a noticeable name in history from its having been occupied by the Countess Matilda, and formed the asylum of the popes Victor the Third and Urban the Second. This remarkable champion of the church was the daughter of Boniface, Count of Modena and Marquis of Tuscany. She was born in the year one thousand and forty-six. Partly from her father and partly from her deceased husband she inherited the rule of the most extensive states in Italy. A widow at thirty, and without any children, she gave herself wholly to the protection and aggrandizement of the papacy. Endowed with a strength of mind and character beyond her sex, her attainments and energies placed her amongst the foremost personages of her time. She spoke the languages of the various soldiers who served under her banner, and corresponded in several tongues. She not only collected a comprehensive library, but caused a new code of civil law to be drawn up by capable persons. She headed her own troops in battle. She was cheerful, cool, courageous, and of good bodily presence: probably, however, not of very warm or tender affections, or else these qualities were overborne by the more vigorous and masculine ones, since she separated from both her husbands; her marriage with the second

having been only dictated by prudential political considerations. Her latter years were spent in the practice of an
austere piety. When she died she bequeathed all her
possessions to the church ; but endless disputes and contests for many years rendered the bequest little more than
nominal.

In the immediate vicinity of the same bridge, on the
mainland, are the ruins of the Theatre of Marcellus. It
was begun by Julius Cæsar and completed by Augustus,
who dedicated it to his nephew Marcellus, the son of his
sister Octavia, the beloved youth who was to have been
his successor to the empire, had not a premature death
carried him away at the unripe age of eighteen, to the
deep sorrow of all Rome. It was on the occasion of its
dedication that Pliny tells us a tame tiger was exhibited
on the stage ; the first ever seen at Rome. Seven hundred
wild beasts were at that time slaughtered within it for the
gratification of the people. It was used as a fortress in
the Middle Ages. The palace of the Orsini now occupies
a part of the ground upon which it stood. Out of the
forty-one arches on each of the three stories in which it
was built, only twelve remain over the two larger ones,
worn and broken, and partly buried in the ground. The
bottom story is formed into shops, whose dingy accessories
are quite in keeping with the blackened ruin. It is in one
of Rome's most characteristic quarters, and the artist or
stranger who would see a little genuine Roman life of the
lower order, cannot do better than go there in the evening,
when the noisy groups give themselves to chaffering or
gossiping. It may be worth his while also to enter one of the
dirty little wine-shops in the neighbourhood, where perhaps
he will see the ancient—it might be called the classic—
game of *morra* played across the benches; which is done
by the two who are. engaged in it suddenly throwing out
the fingers of one hand, both calling out a number loudly
at the same instant, the one who guesses the aggregate
number of fingers thrown out winning the turn. Some-

times these games end in disastrous quarrels, when knives are drawn and bloodshed ensues. In the shops, whose dim recesses seem made on purpose for the pencil of a Rembrandt, a little lamp may be seen burning before a picture or image of the Virgin whose lineaments are scarcely discernible through the surrounding gloom.

Just past the island, on the right bank of the river, is the Ghetto, or Jews' quarter. The forefathers of this colony were first brought to Rome as slaves by Pompey, fifty years before the birth of Christ. At first their fate was a hard one : they suffered nothing but persecution and indignities, until Julius Cæsar somewhat relieved their position, purchasing thereby their tears and prayers at his death. Augustus gave them still more liberty, assigning them a quarter in Trastevere. All their sorrows were renewed during the reign of Tiberius, and they continued to suffer the worst persecution from Nero to Vespasian. Domitian drove them out of the city altogether, so that they were compelled to roam the country, miserably poor, many of them resorting to disreputable modes of gaining a livelihood. In the twelfth century they would appear to have regained a little more freedom : but in the year fifteen hundred and fifty-six they not only lost all their privileges but were confined within the limits of the present Ghetto by the harsh and intolerant Caraffa of Naples, Paul the Fourth, who established the censorship and inquisition in Rome. He compelled every Jew to wear a badge ; the men yellow hats, and the women yellow veils. The Jews remained in the more or less severe confinement of these limits for two centuries, subjected to all sorts of arbitrary restrictions and oppressions. Their permitted occupations were narrowly defined ; thus driving them to many dishonourable shifts and practices merely to support themselves. They were compelled to listen to a sermon preached against their religion every Sunday. Under Gregory the Sixth they were bound to decorate the Triumphal Arch of

G

Titus, that commemorated their own defeat and fall, also the road leading to the Coliseum. Under Paul the Second, in the latter half of the fifteenth century, they had to run races at the time of carnival, almost naked, and with ropes about their necks, amidst the jeers and howls of the populace. They were obliged to be within their quarter at a certain time of night, or they were locked out. It was only at the accession of Pius the Ninth, in eighteen hundred and forty-six, that the walls of the Ghetto were levelled with the ground and a larger degree of liberty allowed to them.

The place is still full of character ; the tall houses are all crowded together ; the principal street is so narrow as almost to exclude the light of day ; women sit sewing at the doors of the dark recesses which serve for shops ; the men offer their wares for sale, chiefly consisting of cloths, stuffs, and cast-off clothing, children run about or group themselves at the thresholds ; the whole place is of the dirtiest and most unsavoury possible, and yet, strange to say, not unhealthy : fevers, cholera, and other endemic diseases, it is said, are less prolific there than in other places. Behind all this dinginess there is wealth too : costly stuffs lie treasured within those grimy walls, embroideries and tapestries of high value are buried there, and, doubtless, many a long purse of gold. The colony numbers about four thousand persons.

The Ponte Sisto is a comparatively modern bridge. It was built in the latter part of the fifteenth century on the ruins of the ancient Pons Janiculensis constructed by Caracalla in order to pass to his garden on the transtiberine side of the river. The views from this bridge are very quaint and characteristic. Tall houses rise straight from the water, soiled with mud as if they had grown out of it, with jutting loggias and irregular balconies, still further varied with an informality of window and a picturesqueness of accessory delightful to the eye of the artist. In garden terraces built on broken archways of brick crumbling namelessly under the corroding effects of the river, bushy orange trees reveal their golden fruit glowing amongst dark green leaves, and trellised vines with long tendrils distribute their grateful shade. Farther still, and high above the houses, the vast dome of St. Peter rises, with its expansive curves all softened and harmonised, thrusting its tall cross into the very skies, and farthest of all, the dim blue ridge of the Janiculan range fringed with a few cypresses and the graceful ornament of the full-foliaged stone-pine.

A little higher up from this bridge is the Palazzo Farnese on the one hand, and the Villa and Palace of the Farnesina on the other. The first of these, begun by Vignola and finished by Michael Angelo, is considered one of the finest pieces of architecture in its style extant. The Farnesina is chiefly noticeable for its frescoes by Raphael. They were painted for a rich merchant of Siena, named Agostino Chigi, a great promoter of the arts, who built the palace and resided there. It is said that whilst working upon these frescoes Raphael fell in love with the daughter of a neighbouring baker, which caused him so to neglect his work that his patron requested that she might be brought to the palace, that the painter might talk to his _innamorata_ and proceed with his occupation at the same time. If the portrait called the Fornarina which he has left to us be a faithful likeness of that lady, her beauty was certainly not striking ; perhaps the want of it was compensated by vivacity of manner and exuberance of wit. This same Chigi was a man of some note also. The first books in the Greek language, printed in Rome—Pindar in the year fifteen hundred and fifteen, and Theocritus in the following one —were printed for him and in his own house : the edition of the latter, I believe, still keeps a name for its accurate reading. In this palace he once entertained Leo the Tenth and his whole court with great sumptuousness and magnificence at one of the most costly feasts given in modern times ; after which, the dishes and plates, all of silver, upon which it was served were thrown into the Tiber ; Agostino,

G 2

however, like a prudent man as he was, taking care that they should be fished up again afterwards.

The low-spired church here seen, on the Janiculan heights, is that of San Pietro in Montorio, and not very distant from it the convent of St. Onofrio, interesting for its association with the last days of the poet Tasso. He had come to Rome for the honour of a public coronation at the Capitol, such as Petrarch had received. The excitement was too much for his delicate frame enfeebled by so many vicissitudes. He was taken to the convent to die. "I have been brought," he says in his last letter to Antonio Costantini, "to this monastery of Saint Onofrio, not only because the air is recommended by the doctors above that of every other part of Rome, but to commence my conversation in heaven, so to speak, from this elevated spot, and with the intercourse of these devout fathers." He died, after a brief illness, on the twenty-fifth of April in fifteen hundred and ninety-five.

Advancing still upwards, the conspicuous church with its elevated dome on the right is that of San Giovanni in Fiorentini, a modern structure not otherwise noticeable ; opposite to which is the Lunatic Asylum. A little farther the river makes a sudden bend in an easterly direction.

Here an extensive building stretches itself along the left bank, the Hospital of Santo Spirito. This was the first foundling hospital established in Europe. It was founded by the excellent and Christian-minded Pope Innocent the Third about the beginning of the thirteenth century, who was so shocked at hearing of the numbers of small children drawn up by the fishing nets from the river, that he devised this as a remedy. It has been rebuilt and enlarged at successive periods. The system of the clandestine deposit of children has since grown European ; though, I believe, it has never prevailed in England. In a by-street on the other side of the building, there is a grated projection sufficiently large to receive a young child, in the inside of which is a cushioned cradle, in which the infant is placed, when a turn is given to the apparatus, and the child is immediately separated from the ties of every earthly relationship. Denied the maternal care, it is no wonder that more than one-half of these unfortunate creatures should perish in infancy. How many a mother has stood trembling beside that dark grating with a heart full of tears and bitterness, straining to behold to the last moment the face of her helpless offspring, to resign which appears like resigning her very self, her own soul ; and once the fatal separation made, has turned from it with a pang more painful than that of death itself! Not always, however, are these innocent victims of circumstance quite lost to their parents. Some token or other is sometimes preserved, recognition afterwards taking place ; but such re-meetings must be rare and difficult. Generally, the grave can be no more silent than the walls of this ill-starred abode. Not infrequently married persons—even of those having families of their own—adopt one or more children from this institution. The building is not, however, entirely occupied by foundlings ; its large extent embraces accommodation for numerous sick patients ; and doubtless, many have reason to be grateful for the friendly shelter of the Tiber-washed walls of the Hospital of Santo Spirito.

Precisely at this curve of the river, and where it is the nearest to St. Peter's, at low water may be seen the remains of the ancient Pons Triumphalis. It was across this bridge that the barbarous but splendid spectacle of the Roman Triumph used to pass. This, as every one knows, was the public festival held after a great victory, only accorded on high and stringent conditions, when the whole conquering army together with the spoils of the vanquished and their principal personages, accompanied with all the pomp of military and civic circumstance, were passed in review before the people.

Let us rebuild the bridge in imagination and stand upon it, spectators of one of these wonderful pageants, to realise which nothing is wanting in the records of history.

Long before the break of day the whole city is up.
Everywhere scaffolds and galleries are erected from which
to behold the coming spectacle, to bear the least service in
which has been a source of canvassing and rivalship for
many a day. All the people are dressed in white: nobody
so poor that he cannot find a garment for this occasion.
Gorgeous temples reveal their dim interiors smoking with
incense and garlanded with flowers. Bustling officers clear
the centre of the streets, pushing back the eager crowds.
All night, and long before, the army encamped outside of
the city has been making preparation for its triumphal
entry into it. It is that of the consul Paulus Æmilius,
returned from the conquest of Macedonia : a man of noble
and fine traits, though not altogether free from the barbarities
incident to his time. Now every avenue is crowded : white
garments flutter everywhere. Friends look for friends
wherewith to congratulate. Eagerness and expectation
show themselves in every face. Hark ! they come. The
restlessness of the multitude subsides. Nearer and nearer
the music sounds. Now they pass the bridge upon which
we stand, in order to enter the city. The procession is
headed by the magistrates and the whole body of the
senate arrayed in their robes of office. Then appear the
statues, pictures and colossal images taken from the vanquished, piled up on two hundred and fifty chariots, accompanied by persons bearing boards on which are written
in large letters the names of the conquered cities, together
with plans and drawings of them, also models in wood
and ivory. Then innumerable waggons laden with the
finest and richest armour of the Macedonians, both brass
and steel, all cleaned and polished for the occasion, disposed in the most artistic manner as if tumbled in heaps
by chance, yet loosely bound together so as to clash in
the movement, thus producing a kind of reminiscence of
their deadly purpose in warfare. From amongst shields,
greaves, habergeons, quivers and helmets, sword-points
bristle, flashing in the sun. Then follow three thousand

men, bearing four hundred and fifty vessels filled with silver coins, four to each vessel ; others carry cups, bowls and goblets of gorgeous workmanship, set out to the best advantage. After these come the trumpeters, not with notes of peace, but blaring out a fierce war-peal—the charge for onset—till every soldier's blood bounds and tingles in his veins, as he clutches his sword the tighter, and sets his feet more firmly to the ground. Then come troops of young men robed in ornamentally-bordered garments, leading to the sacrifice a hundred and twenty oxen with gilded horns and heads adorned with ribbons and garlands, no suspicion in their mild eyes of the fate that awaits them. Along with these are boys carrying basins of silver and gold for libation. Then follows the gold coin borne in seventy-seven vessels, each of three talents. Then the consecrated bowl of ten talents, made of gold and set with precious stones, which Æmilius had vowed to the god of the Capitol ; followed by the whole service of gold plate from the royal table of Perseus, the Macedonian king. Then the chariot of Perseus, in which his armour is placed together with his diadem—symbol of kingly rule now no more. Presently come the children of the fallen monarch, together with their servants, teachers and other attendants weeping and stretching forth their hands, imploring mercy and pity for their charge. And now a very saddening episode occurs. Amongst these children are two little boys and a girl, brought up in all the wealth and luxury of royalty, henceforward to be the slaves of a ruthless conqueror. So young are they that they do not even perceive their unfortunate position, but with childish prattle look about them in wonder at the magnificent pageant by which they are surrounded. Their very insensibility makes their situation the more touching, compelling even the sturdy Romans to confess their humanity in compassionate floods of tears as they pass. Perseus himself follows, dressed in black, looking like one absolutely stunned and deprived of reason in the severity

of his misfortune, surrounded by his servants and dependents, who appear to regard his grief, forgetful of their
own. No wonder he should look sad. To be conquered
by a foreign enemy meant the loss of everything then ; not
only rule and state, not only liberty and, perhaps, life—for
the loss of these things to a brave man might have been
borne—but there was also the knowledge that the wife,
family and friends of the conquered were all involved with
him in common ruin, and perhaps reserved to fates worse
than his own—this it was that stabbed bravery to the
heart and made courage itself tremble. Not even could he
say, my children will call me father when I die, and keep
my name alive amongst men. His whole household shared
his condition. Pity for others knew no drop of mercy for
him. The inexorable cancelled his name from the book of
the living, not even allowing him a recording tombstone
when he died. To be conquered was to be annihilated,
converting the page of existence into an empty and dreary
blank. No wonder that Perseus should look distracted
and disconsolate. In these Triumphs nothing of humilia-
tion was spared to the conquered. By the current brutality
of the time, not only did they submit to the indignity
belonging to the position of a vanquished people, but
hired wretches walked beside them, ridiculing them and
taunting them with their downfall, heaping shameful reproaches and scornful jests on their already too hard
fortunes. But the procession does not wait. Soon all
traces of sadness are lost in the moving pageant. Four
hundred crowns are borne by, the tribute of the several
vanquished cities, given in token of fealty to their conquerors. Last of all Æmilius himself appears : a man
well worthy to be looked upon, as the historians confess,
even without these insignia of state about him. He rides
in a chariot magnificently decorated, dressed in a purple
robe shot with gold, bearing a laurel branch in his right
hand, followed by his two sons, Quintus Maximus and
Publius Scipio—sons by birth, though now calling another

by the name of father, for these are given away in adoption. They are accompanied by other illustrious personages. Then comes the whole army; first the cavalry, troop by troop, then the cohorts, each in its order, the soldiers carrying boughs of laurel and singing verses in praise of their commander and his deeds, or in ridicule of their fallen foes.

It is a proud position, that which Æmilius occupies at this moment; honoured by the whole city, and that city the greatest on the earth's surface. Right royally he bears himself amidst the radiance and splendour around; the object of attraction to the eyes of gazing thousands: so that it might naturally be supposed, that if ever a man had reached the top of human ambition, and found the full happiness of glory, honour, praise, popularity and reverence, it was Paulus Æmilius that day. Let us see if it was really so —if all was satisfied desire, calmness and contentment beneath the purple robe and laurel crown.

Æmilius was a tender-hearted man, as tenderness went in those days: he loved his own, no doubt, very dearly. He had two sons still left to him, sole heirs of his name and fortune—two others, the fruits of a first marriage, he had given in adoption, as has been said. The youngest was twelve years of age—that period of promise when the character first begins to dawn on the soul—the true infancy of manhood, the spring of the human year. Many a time had he been brought outside the gates of the city to witness the bustling preparations for the coming triumph, till his young heart beat high with joy. Long days before, the proud father had anticipated the pleasure of making the boy a sharer of his honours. He would sit by his side in the chariot; how his eyes would sparkle with delight in the splendour of the occasion—an occasion which he would remember to the last day of his existence, proud to be able to say, Æmilius was my father! But fate had decreed it otherwise. Five days before the crowning consummation of the general's glory, his darling boy sickened and died.

Think if it were all happiness beneath that silk and gold ; if no pang of sorrow shot through the father's heart, be-dimming the brilliancy of the pompous spectacle and turning its gorgeous panoplies into the wearisome tediousness of a miserable and empty piece of vanity. Three days after-wards his remaining son will likewise be snatched from him by inexorable death, and the bereaved father be left child-less.

Three long days has it taken for this procession to pass under review. Now it is over. It will find a sickening termination. It will go to the Forum, to the foot of the Capitol, where many will be cruelly put to death— where a black prison yawns, dark and loathsome, filled with horror and the shudderings of despair, whose tomb-like vaults to this day seem to renew echoes of the anguish they have known, in which will be plunged the kingly Perseus, shorn of every beam of royalty, to suffer and pine till unusual clemency shall afford him from all the world a little less repulsive corner, where, overcome by his misfortunes, he may sicken and starve, perishing miserably. Of his children let us not inquire further. Enough to have lingered for a moment on the black spot that gave a deadlier hue to the crimson stains which render infamous the barbaric splendours of a Roman Triumph.

Many such proud processions has the ancient river here witnessed, as those old arches on the Via Sacra testify with their broken sculptures and half-obliterated inscriptions, so lordly in their glory, so extravagant in their ostentation, that in order that the head of an emperor even might not be turned by them, it was found necessary to place behind him a slave to whisper in his ear, amidst the wild shouts of *Io triumphe !* which tore the skies, Cæsar, remember that thou art but a man !

CHAPTER V.

ROME. FROM THE BRIDGE OF ST. ANGELO TO THE PORTA DEL POPOLO.

THE traveller following the upward course of the Tiber finds no more characteristic and impressive prospect than that which meets his gaze when he has left the bridge and castle of St. Angelo behind him, and, looking backwards, he sees the dome of St. Peter's and the tomb of Hadrian stand within the limits of the same vision, the grandest of ancient and modern monuments, side by side; the one a memento of the hope of immortality in the conservation of the bodily frame, the other of the faith in it through the culture and development of the spiritual and insubstantial part of our being. Neither from the picturesque point of view could anything be finer; particularly if seen under the glow of the downward-sloping sun of a rich and mellow afternoon. Then the animated stone figures which stand upon the bridge seem to wave their garments and flutter their wings in the bickering light, and high up on the summit of the lofty tower, the bronze angel, touched with the ethereal gleam, seems to tremble too, as if longing to take his flight into the liquid glory by which he is surrounded, and bid farewell to the earth for ever. Then, beyond the bridge and the impassioned figures that guard its parapets, the dome of St. Peter's rises, majestic, vast, dim and broad in its proportions; more like some huge growth of earth and sky than a fabric raised stone by stone through the laborious efforts of human skill and industry.

The bridge was built by the emperor Hadrian about the year one hundred and thirty-six, for the purpose of passing to his tomb which lay just on the other side of it. It was called Ælius from one of the names borne by that emperor. In the Middle Ages it shared the history of the mausoleum and was the scene of many a fearful struggle and terrible tragedy. In the lawless time of the eleventh century Cencio, the son of the prefect, erected a high tower near it, from which he exacted toll or black-mail on the passers,

CASTLE OF ST. ANGELO.

and once imprisoned the pope himself (Hildebrand) within it, who was, however, rescued by a popular rising. In the jubilee year fourteen hundred and fifty some portion of the bridge gave way under the pressure of a crowd of persons returning from the papal benediction, when almost two hundred were killed. Two chapels were afterwards built on the right bank for the benefit of the souls of those who had perished ; but these being made use of by the army led by Bourbon at the time of the siege of the castle,

they were demolished and the statues of St. Peter and St. Paul
placed there instead.   Afterwards, the parapet was built and
statues of angels bearing the instruments of the passion
placed upon it.   The angel of the cross is by Bernini, the
others by his pupils.   Much as it is the fashion to speak
slightingly of these, one must allow that whatever be their
demerits as works of art their position and general
picturesqueness would make their removal a matter of
regret to every one who has once seen their agitated forms
against the sturdy and immovable walls of the old mausoleum, or giving value to the quiet and exquisite curves of
the dome of St. Peter's.

On the left bank, and close to the river, the mausoleum of
Hadrian or Castle of St. Angelo stands, apostrophised by
Lord Byron :

> Turn to the mole which Hadrian reared on high,
> Imperial mimic of old Egypt's piles,
> Colossal copyist of deformity,
> Whose travell'd phantasy from the far Nile's
> Enormous model, doom'd the artist's toils
> To build for giants, and for his vain earth,
> His shrunken ashes, raise this dome: How smiles
> The gazer's eye with philosophic mirth,
> To view the huge design which sprung from such a birth !

To give the whole history of this majestic monument of
Rome's bygone splendour, would be to give the history of
Rome itself since it was built.   A sketch of the vicissitudes
it has passed through, together with a more detailed
narrative of some of its most important and picturesque
phases, must serve our purpose here.

The mausoleum of Augustus in the Campus Martius
being fully occupied when the ashes of Nerva had been
deposited therein, Hadrian laid the foundations of a still
vaster and grander place of imperial sepulture on the opposite side of the river and lower down, intended, perhaps, to
outvie the former in magnificence and grandeur.   And what
foundations !   Whoever will go carefully over the explora-
tions figured in Piranesi's 'Antichità Romane,' will gain a

new idea of the marvellous workmanship accomplished by
those wonderful Romans of old.   Down below the sunless
bed of the Tiber these stupendous substructures lie, stone
biting into stone, arch reversed upon arch, wall set upon
wall ; not as men build, but as Nature builds when she
raises her fastnesses for the eagle.   No wonder that it
should stand : it would be a wonder, rather, if it should
ever fall whilst Time itself lasts.   Though Hadrian began
it, he did not complete it.   It was finished by Antoninus
Pius, in the Christian year one hundred and forty.   In the
elaborately drawn restoration of Canina, based upon all
known authorities as to its former condition, it may be
recalled more or less clearly to the mind's eye.   The
entrance was without a portico, on the ground floor, above
which was raised a tier of tablets going round the whole
building, probably having upon them inscriptions to the
dead.   At the four angles of the square basement were
placed equestrian statues.   Above this rose another story
with fluted Ionic columns supporting a handsome frieze or
pediment, with statues placed between each column, and
upon this another in the same manner, excepting that the
columns were of the Corinthian order.   The several stories
diminished gradually in area as they went higher ;   the
whole being surmounted with a conical roof crowned with
the large pine-cone of bronze, now in the gardens of the
Vatican.   It was entirely covered with Parian marble, its
sculptures being of the same material.   From its enormous
size it must have been one of the most striking and imposing monuments ever raised by human hands.   It is nine
hundred feet in circumference, and the external wall is
about fifty feet in thickness.   Immediately within this
wall was an inclined plane (a part of which still remains),
along which a carriage might have driven to the summit.
A square chamber occupied the centre of the building, in
which the sarcophagi stood, the cinerary urns being placed
at the sides.

This tomb was not the only monument that the indefatigable emperor, whose name it bears, left behind him. He made a tour through a great part of the Roman empire, embracing Europe, Asia, and Africa. He reached Great Britain, where he caused the wall to be built, dividing the northern from the southern portion, fragments of which still remain. At the foot of the hills near Tivoli he raised a palace of vast extent, which was supposed to be the epitome of all he had seen in his travels. Its extensive ruins still speak its former grandeur. Many fine works of art were found there. He himself was the second to be placed within the tomb he had reared ; an adopted son who died before him being the first. Hadrian died at Baiæ, whither he had gone for his health, his remains being brought to the mausoleum by his successor, Antoninus Pius.

The next laid in it was Antoninus Pius himself, who left a good name behind him. He was the adopted son of Hadrian. His reign of twenty years constituted one of those bright epochs which have the happiness to be almost silent in history. His whole study was for the welfare of his country. War, violence, and crime had nothing to record during his wise and judicious rule. He framed laws, made sanitary regulations, assigned funds for relieving the children of indigent parents, repaired to the best of his power the losses and miseries suffered from earthquakes and other natural causes. Yet with all this he loved the country and country pleasures, as the most elevated and energetic minds almost always do. He had a full voice, a commanding presence, and an impressive personality ; like a sterling coin with a good image stamped upon it, not to give it value, but to confirm it valuable.

The next who found a dwelling in this lordly sepulchre was a hero indeed. It was Marcus Aurelius Antoninus, nephew and foster-son of Antoninus Pius, whose name must be a star of light to every student of practical morals. He was born in Rome in the year one hundred and twenty-one, and adopted by his uncle, before he was made emperor, on the death of his father, which happened when

he was quite a young boy. Even then he was a very
earnest student, and practised himself in the austerities of
the stoic sect of philosophers. Early elected to the most
weighty offices of state, he justified the public trust, fulfilling in the most unimpeachable manner every function
deputed to him. When Antoninus Pius died, he divided
the empire with his foster-brother, Lucius Verus, although
he had reached the ripe age of forty, and might very well
have retained the power in his own hands. He maintained
an unbroken friendship with Lucius, overlooking that the
latter was opposed to him in almost all the finer elements
of character, giving himself up to the unworthy pleasures
of degraded sensuous enjoyment. In the meantime, Aurelius ruled as a good man ought to rule, acting as one who
lived in the service of the state, and not upon it. Dion
Cassius tells us that he applied himself to the most minute
offices, never saying, doing, or writing anything negligently ;
giving even slight affairs the fullest attention, from an
opinion that an emperor ought to do nothing hastily. He
avoided the precedent of failing in little things, lest it should
extend to greater. He would frequently remain the whole
day through in the senate. Not the least of the blessings
of a good man's rule is that the preference of councillors
and officers must. be given to good men also. Aurelius
selected old and tried hands to second his high intentions,
and found them ready to assist him in ruling well. But this
great man's life was not altogether spent under the royal
purple and surrounded by imperial splendour at home. For
five arduous years he campaigned in central Europe through
all the vicissitudes of a severe climate, leaving kingly
halls for inclement skies, and every amenity of life for the
hard course of military discipline ; and this with a suscep-
tible constitution, and much bodily weakness. His fearless-
ness and forbearance were exemplified in the fact of a
conspiracy against him being discovered, which was crushed
by his generosity and coolness without a single punishment ;
and when the letters and papers were brought to him

discovering the plot, he had them burnt without looking at them. He died towards **the end of** the second century at Sirmium, the capital of **Pannonia, his ashes** being **borne** to repose in his native city. **They have perished ;** but **the** memory of a **great good man does not perish** so easily. Marcus **Aurelius read a great lesson to** mankind which will live **whilst men live.** Life **for him was a field of** duty, **in which the only** ills were vice, ignorance, and error of judgment and opinion—the ignoring, in fact, of the highest **laws of** our nature and being : the sole good being virtue, **purity** of life, temperance and justice in energy and **in** action. He never forgot these. His whole life **was a** sermon preached from that most potent **and** influential **of** all pulpits, act and practice. He was no self-apologist ; **his** life needed no explanation. Fortunately, however, **for us,** we are' not left altogether to infer the principles by **which** he was governed. From **time to** time he noted down the rules and laws by **which he was, or desired to** be, actuated. Translated into all languages, they **have been a** handbook ever since to every one to whom the **main object in** life is practically to live up to its highest principles ; and, in this **respect, form an** admirable appendix to Christian doctrine, with **which,** indeed, they **in a** great measure identify themselves. **It is** true the Christians suffered persecution during **his** reign ; **but** it is almost certain from what is known of the man, that it could not have been by his command. **It** has been very reasonably urged that Christianity **at that** period may have been misrepresented as a political **faction.** At least, it was a more or less secret society, **and all secret** societies at that **time** were forbidden. **Again, even at so early an epoch,** it is possible that there **may not have been** wanting individuals, enthusiasts **who wished to** establish it on a temporal basis and dominion, which would naturally cause it to fall under the punishment of the Roman laws and jurisdiction. Internal evidence at least acquits Marcus Aurelius of having been a willing **party to** anything like **cruelty or** oppression.

H

A bronze statue of him seated in majestic action on horseback, to this day stands on the top of Rome's proudest eminence, the Capitoline Hill, and worthily occupies the exalted position. An epitome of all that is noble in Roman character, he shows us how much may be done in one lifetime, and what a grand thing a lifetime may be made. Lord of a large proportion of the material world, he found his vastest empire within, holding a mightier rule than that of kingdoms, and crowned with a loftier monarchy. No wonder he should have been loved by the people he left behind him. So great, indeed, was their affection for his memory, that there was scarcely a house of note in which his marble bust or figure was not found. Thus it is that even now in Rome there is hardly a gallery, public or private, wherein his dignified and gracious form does not stand before us, and his mild but earnest countenance look on us in marble clearly yet through the vicissitudes of almost two thousand years.

As if this tomb must be a microcosm and contain samples of all the good and bad in the world, its next occupant was in the utmost contrast to those already laid in it. It was Commodus, the wicked son of an excellent father. How such a monster, indeed, could have proceeded from so noble a parent is one of those problems of time and humanity which it is impossible to solve. It seemed as if he justified the proverb of the old song : "Full young doth it prick that will be a thorn," for he appeared to take to vice as naturally as his father Aurelius was born to virtue. He was full of meanness, cruelty, and vanity. He danced and sang in public, and acted as a buffoon. He assumed the character of Hercules, and went about clothed in a lion's skin, and bearing a club. He fought at gladiatorial games, but took care to be encased in stout armour, and to carry a heavy sword, whilst his adversaries were naked, armed with weapons of tin or lead. One knows not whether most to abhor the enormities of which he was guilty, or to despise the pusillanimity of the Roman senate and people who submitted to him, and even flattered his excesses. He killed many thousands of wild animals, but always from behind a screen. He never went out without his sword, nor without using it. One day he had determined to put to death some persons about to be made consuls. A little child finding the fatal tablet on which their names were written, carried it to Marcia, his wife. Poison was administered to the tyrant, but being slow in its effects, he was despatched by an athlete, sent in for that purpose, who strangled him. The senate, whilst congratulating Pertinax his successor, poured curses on the corpse of Commodus, and wanted to drag him through the streets, and throw him into the river; but this Pertinax would not permit. He too was borne to the place of emperors, and laid, an unworthy occupant, within their tomb.

After him came Septimius Severus, who died at York, in the year two hundred and eleven, whose ashes were also brought hither; and, last of all, Caracalla, his son, sometimes called Tarantus, after a certain gladiator, who, as Dion Cassius tells us, "was very little, very ill-made, and very much a villain." He repeated the worst follies and cruelties of Commodus. At an early age he slew Geta, his brother, who had flown to his mother's arms, with whom he should have divided the empire, and many thousands of persons afterwards supposed to be favourable to him. He then gave himself up to bestiality and pleasure, quite neglecting the affairs of the empire. No wonder he should have been haunted by spectres through the gorgeous halls of the Palatine—his father and his brother Geta, with swords pointed to his bosom at night. No wonder that he should have turned to incantations and strange rites to find a little rest, and been disappointed. The spirits he summoned were avenging ones—his own; no gods answered his unregarded prayers. Torn by remorse, he passed from one distraction to another, until his miserable life was terminated at the age of thirty by the hand of the assassin after a reign of seven years.

He was the last emperor laid in the Mausoleum. From

the death of Severus, in the year two hundred and eleven, it remained closed for two hundred years, until the beginning of the fifth century, when it was used as a fortress against the Goths under Alaric. He, however, burst into the tomb, desecrating its places of sepulture and carrying off all the treasured urns and sarcophagi that he found within it. In the year five hundred and thirty-seven it was again attacked by the Goths under Vitiges, and vigorously defended by the brave Roman general Belisarius, who, when the castle—for henceforth, no longer a tomb,—it became a fortress—was on the point of being taken, saved it by casting down upon the enemy the marble statues with which it was decorated. A little later an event occurred from which it obtained a new name and significance.

About the middle of the sixth century there was born in Rome one of the great lights of the church and noblest ornaments to Christianity, Gregory, the first pope of that name, justly designated the Great. He was of an illustrious family: his father being a senator and his mother coming of an historic race. He applied himself vigorously to study in his youth. At the age of thirty he was made prætor, or chief magistrate and governor of Rome. On the death of his father he founded a monastery in his own house on the Cœlian Hill, and afterwards six others in Sicily. When his year of prætorship had terminated he took the monastic habit, spending his time in study, fasting, and religious observances. One day in passing through the market he saw some British youths exposed for sale, and on inquiring who they were, was told they were called Angli or Angles. "Call them not Angles but angels," he said, "for surely their faces fit them for such a dignity and companionship," adding that it was lamentable that, having exteriors so fair, there should not be God's grace within. Having petitioned the pope to send missions to their country, and finding no one willing to undertake the task, he started himself privately. No sooner was this known to the people than the whole city was in an uproar; and, running to the pope one day as he entered St. Peter's, they earnestly besought him to order his return, saying that by his going St. Peter was offended and Rome ruined. He was overtaken, and with much reluctance induced to abandon his intended journey. He subsequently, however, sent St. Augustine and others to fulfil an office which it was denied to him to perform. It was during a residence of three years in Constantinople, whither he had gone upon a diplomatic errand, that he wrote his voluminous and important work upon the Book of Job. When he was made the secretary of Pope Pelagius the Second, he still remained in his monastery, but on the death of that pontiff, in the year five hundred and ninety, he was unanimously elected to the papacy. He did all he could to avoid a dignity courted by so many, and actually wrote to the emperor of the East, entreating him to annul the election. At last, escaping through the well-watched gates of the city in a basket, he went and hid himself in a cave in the middle of a wood ; but being discovered, he was promoted to the see and consecrated. It was no affectation of modesty that caused him to act thus. In writing to Theoctista, the emperor's sister, he says, "I have lost the comfort of my calm, and appearing to be outwardly exalted, I am inwardly and really fallen ;" in a letter to the patrician Narses, "All that the world thinks agreeable brings to me trouble and affliction ;" also to St. Leander, whose acquaintance he had made in Constantinople, "I remember with tears that I have lost the calm harbour of my repose, and with many a sigh I look upon the firm land I cannot reach. If you love me assist me with your prayers."

The time at which Gregory ascended the throne was one of sore trial and distress at Rome. A tremendous inundation of the Tiber had occurred. The air was poisoned by vast numbers of serpents left by the receded waters. A terrible plague had broken out ; of which, indeed, his predecessor had died. Dismay and terror reigned on every hand. Of course, at that time, when the laws of nature were so little understood, the affliction was at once attributed to the retributive visitation of God, pretty much as it would have been a few centuries previously. The Deity was angry and must be propitiated. Accordingly, Gregory organised a vast procession with great fasting and humility. A picture of the Virgin Mary, said to be by St. Luke, now in the church of the Aracœli near the Capitol, was borne through the city. The story goes that when they reached the Ælian bridge—from this event taking the name of St. Angelo—heavenly voices were heard singing in the air,

> Regina cœli lætare,
> Quia quem meruisti portare
> Resurrexit sicut dixit.
>   Alleluia !

[Rejoice, O Queen of Heaven, for that he whom thou hast been worthy to bear, has risen as he had promised. Hallelujah !]

To which Gregory answered,

> Ora pro nobis Deum.
>   Alleluia !

[Pray to God for us. Hallelujah.]

And all the people replied,

> Ora pro nobis Deum.
>   Alleluia !

Upon this there appeared in the air an angel, hovering over the ancient mausoleum, sheathing a bloody sword, and the plague was staid : not, however, before eighty persons in the procession had been struck down mortally as it passed through the streets ; a result more serious than surprising, perhaps, under the circumstances.

The words of the anthem above quoted are still to be seen inscribed over a tabernacle in the church of the Aracœli, near the Capitol, and a record of the event written upon parchment is in the archives of the adjoining convent. On St. Mark's day it is still celebrated ; when a procession of ecclesiastics, together with several religious communities, after passing through various parts of the city pause at the bridge, singing the same antiphon, Regina cœli lætare. It was not, however, till long afterwards that the mausoleum took the name which it now bears. The bronze figure of an angel in the act of sheathing a sword which stands upon the summit is only the work of the last century.

To pursue the story of Gregory a little farther.

He seems to have concentrated in himself some of the highest and finest qualities of manhood, anticipating his age in some respects by many a century. Coming to the throne at one of the saddest periods of civilized history, when the church was distracted with schisms and heresies, and over-run with abuses; when the heart of society was rotten to its centre, and vice, selfishness, and injustice were rife everywhere, he stretched forth the hand of love and not of terror, and never utterly in vain. When the bishop of Terracina had caused the Jews to be robbed of their synagogue, he commanded that it should be restored to them; saying, that they were not to be compelled, but converted by meekness and charity; and when a rich Jew of Cagliari, converted to Christianity, placed Christian symbols in a synagogue, to the offence of others, he reproved him, and commanded that they should be withdrawn. Tender-hearted as a child, he knew no fear: he was a lion in the cause of right; and yet his boldness was united with so much tact and fine judgment that he almost never came into collision with absolutely opposing forces. When Romanus, the exarch or governor of Italy for the emperor, in the year five hundred and ninety-two, broke a solemn league entered into with the Lombards, taking Perugia and several other towns, so that the Lombards in revenge besieged the very walls of Rome, Gregory acted with the utmost promptitude, raising an army for the defence, yet he so far prevailed upon the enemy by well-timed diplomacy as to cause them to retire without further damage: after which he severely reproved the exarch for his perfidy. He attended personally to the wants of the poor, amongst whom there was then much necessity, some

of them being received and entertained at his own table;
proper officers being appointed to relieve others. Once
when a man was found dead at a street-corner, it was
presumed through starvation, he denied himself the sacrament for several days. He did not scruple even to sell
the too luxurious appointments of the church in order to
redeem captives taken by the Lombards—his own income
being wholly spent on others, and not on himself. When
the Archbishop of Ravenna used the pallium not only at
mass, but at other functions, Gregory wrote to him telling
him that no ornament shone so fairly on the shoulders of a
bishop as humility. In his letters to his vicars and stewards
abroad, he enjoins mildness and liberality towards vassals
and farmers; disapproving anything like oppression, and
requiring that time should be allowed for the payment of
debts, and instalments taken. His care and consideration
extended to the utmost limits of his reach. He counted
the whole human race to have claims on him. His touch
vibrated through the hemisphere, and beyond it. He never
forgot the least in the greatest: he had that rare faculty.
The cares of kingdoms allowed him to listen to the complaint of a beggar. The affairs of state not only permitted
him to remodel the economy of the church to its simplest
particular, but to write many books, still famous in ecclesiastical and religious literature, and pen a vast number of
letters, still authorities in matters of church ordinance and
religious morals. He studied and practised music diligently,
first naming the notes by letters. One form of ecclesiastical
music still keeps his name—the Gregorian. When John,
the Archbishop of Ravenna, reproved him for cowardice in
seeking to evade the distinction of the papacy, he wrote a
book on the Pastoral Care, setting forth the danger and
difficulties together with the duties and obligations of that
sacred function—more arduous than the acquirement of
any art or science; first treating of the disposition requisite
for so high a calling, then of the duties belonging to it,
then what kind of service and care the flock demanded of

the pastor, and last of all, the obligations of self-watchful-
ness and self-examination which must constantly attend
the pastor himself if he would not be one of those

> Blind mouths, that scarce themselves know how to hold
> A sheephook, or have learned ought else the least
> That to the faithful herdsman's art belongs.*

Another of his famous books he called Dialogues:
perhaps the least valuable of all his writings. It is full of
wild stories of supernatural interference, miracles of saints,
and other extravagancies, which may very fairly be referred
to the age in which he lived, rather than to the man.
Besides these, he wrote numerous Latin hymns, still used
in the services of the Roman church, of which the well-
known Veni Creator is one. All this was done amidst
failing health and a thousand distractions.

After a course so good and noble, this pattern to the
human race expired in the year six hundred and four,
about the sixty-fourth of his age. He reigned thirteen
years six months and ten days—his biographers cannot
spare one from the enumeration.

The name of Gregory was subsequently numbered
amongst the most honoured of the church to which he
belonged. With the other three saints revered as " Doctors "
of the Latin church his memory was celebrated by rites
ordered to be universally observed by Boniface the Eighth
in twelve hundred and ninety-five. If ever a man deserved the name of saint it was he. He finds his last
resting-place in St. Peter's, and it is the most fitting one ;
that many may pass his tomb, and none without a memory
of the great man whom it covers.

From about the year nine hundred and twenty-three the
castle was occupied by a Roman lady named Marozia,
infamous daughter of an infamous mother. She was
patrician by birth, of great beauty, obtaining much power
and wide possessions by the worst means. She first

* Lycidas.

married Alberic, Count of Tusculum and Marquis of Camerino, who was traitor enough to induce the Hungarians to invade Italy, which so enraged his countrymen that he was driven from his stronghold and died at Orte. His widow returned, and again obtained possession of the castle, marrying Guido, Marquis of Tuscany, who attempted to make himself master of the temporal power of Rome. The pope's brother was assassinated in the Lateran Palace, at that time the papal residence, and the pope himself, John the Tenth, taken to the castle of St. Angelo, where he was strangled ; her own son, who was then only twenty-five years of age, being elevated to the papacy under the title of John the Eleventh, and made a mere instrument in the hands of his mother under the control of his brother Alberic. He was afterwards deposed and imprisoned within the fortress. Shortly after the murder of John the Eleventh Guido died, and Marozia took for her third husband Hugo, Marquis of Provence, just elected King of Italy at Pavia, who was so well received at Rome, that he left his army without the gates. A few months afterwards, when they were one day dining within the castle, Marozia asked her son Alberic to bring the king water to wash his hands. He performed the task so awkwardly that the water was spilt ; upon which the king struck him. Full of indignation, Alberic left the castle, and appealing to the people, inveighed against the tyranny of the king. His words took effect. An insurrection ensued, and the king, without attempting a stroke in his defence, was let down from the walls of the castle and escaped. Alberic made himself master of the fortress and of Rome, maintaining his position during four powerless pontificates, for a space of twenty-two years. On his accession he condemned his mother to a perpetual imprisonment within the fortress of her power, where she died. Her progeny occupied the papacy to three successive generations.

Towards the end of the tenth century a patrician of

Rome, by name Crescentius, placed himself **at the head** of the citizens in order to shake off the temporal **rule of the** papacy, which at that time was largely subservient **to** German influences, the pope himself, Gregory the Fifth, having been placed upon the throne by his cousin, young Otho the **Third of** Germany, who was then but sixteen years of age, **whilst Gregory** only numbered twenty-five years. **Crescentius raised up** an antipope and drove away Gregory, **who went to** Pavia, and recalling Otho, returned to Rome **in his company.** The antipope was taken and suffered the **most** cruel mutilation at the hands **of** his ruthless adversaries, who compelled him to ride seated backwards on **an** ass, in the torn vestments he had usurped, through **the** streets **of** the city. Crescentius entrenched himself **in the** fortress **of** St. Angelo ; but after **some resistance capi-**tulated, on condition that his life and liberty **should be** spared. No sooner, however, had **Otho entered** the **castle** than Crescentius, together **with** twelve **of his followers, were** beheaded, and their bodies suspended **from the battlements ;** Stefania, the beloved and beautiful wife **of** Crescentius, being subjected to the most brutal **violence.** Disquieted **by** remorse **for these** misdeeds, **and perhaps** moved by **the superstitious fear that the end** of the world was ap-**proaching, as was the** general belief and prophecy at **that** time, Otho undertook a pilgrimage to the sanctuary of St. Michel on Monte Gargano, in the kingdom of Naples. On his return he fell sick by the way, when Stefania caused it to reach his ears that she had great power and skill in the art of healing. She was summoned **to his couch, and,** lulling **all** suspicion **by her** blandishments, ad-ministered to him a dose of **poison, thus revenging at the** same time her husband's wrongs **and** her **own.** Otho died at Paterno, on the **borders of the Abruzzi, on the nine-**teenth of January, in the year **one thousand and two, the** last representative **of the imperial house of** Saxony.

The building began **to assume its present appearance** towards the end of the fourteenth century. Its walls were raised. It was surrounded by strong fortifications. The walled corridor connecting it with the Vatican was built in the year fourteen hundred and eleven. It would be impossible here to follow all its later vicissitudes. One historic picture, however, must be presented of the important position it occupied during the siege and sack of Rome by the conjoined forces of Spain and Germany in the year fifteen hundred and twenty-seven.

Charles the Fifth, emperor of Germany and Spain, after driving out the French from the greater part of Italy, (Francis the First having been taken prisoner at the battle of Pavia, in the year fifteen hundred and twenty-five), became an object of jealousy to Pope Clement the Seventh, who, to curb his growing power, allied himself with the French and some of the Italian States. Charles' army was led by the Duke of Bourbon, who was kinsman to the king, but had renounced the interests of France and joined the service of its enemy in consequence of some of his estates having been confiscated, and his stipend as constable withdrawn through the disappointed passion of Maria Louisa, the king's mother, who had fallen in love with him.

Under these circumstances the army approached the walls of Rome, both the military and civil inhabitants of which felt so secure in their fancied power and the supposed weakness of the enemy, that they took few or no precautions to avert the misfortune that awaited them. Not until the enemy was at the gate was it thought necessary even to store and victual the castle of St. Angelo, the main fortress of the city.

Yet with all this confidence the records of the time give a list of omens and prognostics of the horrors about to ensue, some of them reminding one of the old superstitions of Greece and Rome. Long before the enemy approached the gates of the city a man from Siena, in the character of a prophet, described as of "mature age, dark skin, naked, emaciated, and apparently very religious and devout," went

about predicting the certain ruin of the priests and of all
the Roman court, and the resuscitation of the church ; fore-
warning the people in a loud and fearful voice that the
hour of repentance had come, for the scourge was at hand :
and though put in prison he still stoutly maintained his
prophecy, gaining many to believe him.   Another warning
was, that an image of the Madonna at the church of Santa
Maria, in Traspontina, had been struck by lightning, her
crown being shivered, and the Infant broken to pieces in
her arms.   Another accident also was interpreted to be
of sinister import : the host placed in the tabernacle on
Holy Thursday had fallen from its receptacle to the ground.
"Assured signs," says the chronicler, "quite sufficient to
reasonably intimidate every devout Christian."

After maintaining a vigorous contest outside of the city,
the enemy found a weak place near Santo Spirito, where
a house had been built into the walls, and here they at
last effected an entrance.   As soon as the news had spread
through the city the greatest consternation prevailed.   The
pope was hurried immediately to the castle, crying out
that he had been betrayed, and lamenting the slaughter
and lawless outrages which he saw from the windows as he
passed along the narrow corridor.   Everybody rushed to
the castle ; so that, amongst cardinals, prelates and others
who had forced their way into it, there were no fewer
than three thousand persons.   It was defended by Cellini,
amongst others, who acted as a gunner on the occasion.
If his own account is to be believed, he performed almost
superhuman feats of courage and skill, killing the Duke of
Bourbon (Guicciardini, however, says he was shot on a
scaling ladder outside of the walls) on his first approaching
the fortress.   The defence was maintained for almost a
month, but being at last obliged to capitulate, the pope
was confined a prisoner within it, until he made his escape
to Orvieto, carrying with him the tiara-jewels sewn into
his garments by Benvenuto Cellini, who little thought that by
so friendly a service he was laying the ostensible founda-

tion for the subsequent miseries which he suffered within the very walls he had so gallantly defended.

There are several accounts extant of this terrible occurrence, from one of which, bearing the name of Jacopo Buonaparte, a few extracts may be made. In pursuing his narrative he says, "No less horrible a spectacle was it to see the men of a grey old age, whose grade and aspect were full of gravity and reverence, who had been honoured and respected of all for the high authority vested in them in Rome; for their virtues, good sense, and position, now scorned and outraged ; neither learning, arts, nor religion serving to exempt people from such disgraceful treatment. It appeared truly as if that city which was accustomed to be the conqueror of all nations, the seat of honourable triumphs, the abode of glory, and the true and assured domicile of religion, had been reserved for these evil-doers in order that they might raise a shameful trophy to infamy and dishonour of the most esteemed men within it."

In another place the historian proceeds: "How many rare and valuable relics covered with gold and silver were despoiled by bloody and homicidal hands, and in derision of religion cast down to the ground! The heads of St. Peter, of St. Paul, of St. Andrew, and of many other saints, the wood of the Cross, the Thorns, the holy Oil, even the consecrated Host were shamefully trampled under foot. Nothing else was to be seen in the streets but plunderers and vile scoundrels carrying great bundles of rich stuffs, ecclesiastical ornaments, and large sacks filled with various sorts of vessels in gold and silver, savouring more of the proud riches and vain pomps of the Roman court than of the humble poverty and true devotion of the Christian religion. Vast numbers of prisoners of every quality were to be seen crying and shrieking, hurried rapidly along by bands of ultramontanes to the wealthy chambers where their treasures were stored. Numerous dead bodies lay about the streets, some cut to pieces, covered with mud and their own blood ; whilst others, only half alive, lay miserably on the ground. Often enough, amidst the frenzy, girls, men, and boys were seen to jump from the windows, either voluntarily or by compulsion, in order that they might not fall a living prey into the hands of this embruted and ferocious people."

The details of the miserable sufferings of the Romans at this unhappy time are too harrowing to follow closely. The most horrible cruelties alternated with the most abominable blasphemies ; as if the incarnate spirit of evil had itself broken loose and was determined to do its worst. Amongst other sickening outrages a priest was put to death with the greatest ignominy and cruelty for refusing to give the sacrament ("ah, hard earth, why dost thou not open!" exclaims the historian in narrating the circumstance) to a dressed-up ass. Some arrayed themselves in sacerdotal vestments and mocked the service of God at the altars of the churches with horrid oaths and blasphemies. We are told that during this Brocken-feast of horrors the Spaniards were at first much worse than the Germans ; but that afterwards the latter, seeing that the cruelties practised by their comrades were followed by success in producing a larger quantity of booty, set themselves to supersede all others in brutal ways and inventions. " For which reason," pursues the historian, " it is impossible to imagine a torment, however intolerable, to which, on account of their insatiable avarice, their wretched and miserable prisoners were not repeatedly subjected. With how much patience these were endured by dainty and delicate prelates and effeminated courtiers it is easy to comprehend, knowing how difficult it was for them in their prosperous fortune to support, I will not say severe ailments of the body and heavy troubles of the mind, but even so much as the bite of a fly."

Ranke, in his ' History of the Popes,' describing this event says, " The imperial army entered Rome two hours before sunset. Without a leader to check their ferocity the bloodthirsty soldiers, hardened by long privation, poured

like a torrent over the city.   Never did a richer booty fall
into the hands of a more terrible army ; never was there
a more protracted and more ruinous pillage.   The splendour
of Rome fills the beginning of the sixteenth century ; it
marks an astonishing period of the development of the
human mind ; with this day it was extinguished for ever."

The interior horrors of the castle of St. Angelo as a
prison have been graphically described by Platina, the
biographer of the popes, who was confined here under Paul
the Second in fourteen hundred and sixty-eight, accused
of conspiracy ; but, it would appear, without any proofs
of guilt.   He says that after he and some others had been
taken to the castle, the pope sent his vice-chamberlain
Vianesio of Bologna, who, to follow Platina's own words,
"caused us to suffer every sort of torture to make us
confess what we did not know.   On the first and second
day many were tortured, a great proportion of whom
fainted in their agony.   You would have thought at that
time that the tomb of Hadrian had been converted into
the bull of Phalaris, so terribly did its hollow concave
resound with the cries of the miserable young men."   He
then describes his own tortures by the rope, condemning
the conduct of the vice-chamberlain, whose office should
have forbidden his presence on such an occasion, who, he
says, sat making unseemly jokes "on outspread carpets as
if at a wedding, or rather at the supper of Atreus and
Tantalus."

Eleven years after the sack of Rome above described,
Benvenuto Cellini, the celebrated artist in precious metals,
was a long time confined prisoner in the castle by Pope Paul
the Third, under the accusation of having stolen some of the
pontifical jewels at the time of his predecessor's flight to
Orvieto.   Cellini himself, however, says that he was entirely
innocent, and that his imprisonment was an act of jealousy
on the part of the pope's favourites.   No narrative can do
justice to his sorrows but his own in that most inimitable of
all autobiographies, a few particulars from which may be

given here. It was in vain that he pleaded for evidence of
his crime or the means to clear himself. In no respectful
manner he urged the injustice of his accusation, which in
that arbitrary state of legislature served but to aggravate
his punishment. He was placed in a dungeon feebly
lighted : but fortunately met with a friendly countryman,
a Florentine, in the constable of the castle. From him he
received many indulgences, and finally was permitted considerable liberty on his parole not to misuse it, until he fell
under suspicion of abetting a monk in the fabrication of a
duplicate key. From this charge he exculpated himself,
explaining that the wax in which the model was formed
had been stolen from some which he had used for modelling
small figures. The severity, however, with which he was
treated on this occasion caused him to think of attempting
his escape from the castle. For this end he managed to
retain some of the sheets of his bed instead of sending
them to be washed, which he cut into strips and carefully
secreted. He was aided in his project by an extraordinary
circumstance which will be best told in his own words.

"The constable of the castle had annually a certain
disorder, which totally deprived him of his senses, and
when the fit came upon him he was talkative to excess.
Every year he had some different whim ; one time he
fancied himself metamorphosed into a pitcher of oil ;
another time he fancied himself a frog, and began to hop
as such ; another time, again, he imagined he was dead,
and it was found necessary to humour his conceit by
making a show of burying him : thus had he every year
some new frenzy.. This year he fancied himself a bat, and
when he went to take a walk, he sometimes made just such
a noise as bats do ; he likewise used gestures with his
hands and his body, as if he were going to fly. His
physicians and his old servants, who knew his disorder,
procured him all the pleasures and amusements they could
think of ; and as they found he delighted greatly in my
conversation, they frequently came to me to conduct me to

I

his apartment, where the poor man often detained me
three or four hours chatting with him. He sometimes
kept me at his table to dine or sup, and always made me
sit opposite to him, on which occasion he never ceased to
talk himself, or to encourage me to join in conversation.
At these interviews I generally took care to eat heartily,
but the poor constable neither ate nor slept, insomuch that
I was tired and jaded with constant attendance. Upon
examining his countenance, I could perceive that his eyes
looked quite shockingly, and that he began to squint. He
asked me whether I had ever a fancy to fly. I answered,
that I had always been very ready to attempt such things
as men found most difficult; and that with regard to
flying, as God had given me a body admirably well calculated for running, I had even resolution enough to
attempt to fly. He then proposed to me to explain how I
could contrive it. I answered, that when I attentively
considered the several creatures that fly, and thought of
effecting by art what they do by the force of nature, I did
not find one so fit to imitate as the bat. As soon as the
poor man heard mention made of a bat, his frenzy for the
year turning upon that animal, he cried out aloud, ' It is
very true, a bat is the thing.' He then addressed himself to
me, and said, ' Benvenuto, if you had the opportunity, would
you have the heart to make an attempt to fly ?' I answered,
that if he would give me leave, I had courage enough to
attempt to fly as far as the meadows by means of a pair
of wings waxed over. He said, thereupon, ' I should like
to see you fly ; but as the pope has enjoined me to watch
over you with the utmost care, and I know that you have
the cunning of the devil, and would avail yourself of the
opportunity to make your escape, I am resolved to keep
you locked up with a hundred keys, that you may not slip
out of my hand.' I then began to solicit him with new
entreaties, putting him in mind that I had had it in my
power to make my escape, but through regard to the
promise I had made him, would never avail myself of the

opportunity. I therefore besought him for the love of God, and as he had conferred so many obligations on me, that he would not make my condition worse than it was. Whilst I uttered these words, he gave instant orders that I should be secured and confined a closer prisoner than ever. When I saw that it was to no purpose to entreat him any farther, I said before all present, 'Confine me as close as you please, I will contrive to make my escape notwithstanding.' So they carried me off, and locked me up with the utmost care."*

From this moment Cellini's mind was fully made up. First of all he formed his sheets into bands, which he sewed together, and having managed to obtain a pair of pincers, he commenced to draw out the nails from the iron plates of his door, which he did with a great deal of difficulty, particularly as he was occasionally visited during the night to satisfy the fears of the constable. As fast as he drew out one of these nails, the form of the head was imitated in wax mixed with rusty filings, so as to deceive the eye ; the various articles being hidden in the ticking of his bed, from which he managed to divert inspection. At last his preparations being completed, he put his project in practice in the following manner.

"One holiday evening, the constable being very much disordered, and his madness being at the highest pitch, he scarce said anything else but that he was become a bat, and desired his people, that if Benvenuto happened to make his escape, they should take no notice of it, for he must soon catch me, as he should, doubtless, be much better able to fly by night than I ; adding, 'Benvenuto is only a counterfeit bat, but I am a bat in good earnest. Let me alone to manage him ; I shall be able to catch him, I warrant you.' His frenzy continuing thus in its utmost violence for several nights, he tired the patience of all his servants ; and I by various means came to the knowledge of all that passed, though I was indebted for

* This and succeeding quotations are taken from Roscoe's translation.

my chief information to the Savoyard, who was very much attached to me.

"As I had formed a resolution to attempt my escape that night, let what would happen, I began with praying fervently to Almighty God, that it would please his divine majesty to befriend and assist me in that hazardous enterprise. I then went to work, and was employed the whole night in preparing whatever I had occasion for. Two hours before daybreak I took the iron plates from the door with great trouble and difficulty, for the bolt and the wood that received it made a great resistance, so that I could not open them, but was obliged to cut the wood. I, however, at last forced the door, and having taken with me the above-mentioned slips of linen, which I had rolled up in bundles with the utmost care, I went out and got upon the right side of the tower, and having observed, from within, two tiles of the roof, I leaped upon them with the utmost ease. I was in a white doublet, and had on a pair of white half hose, over which I wore a pair of little light boots, that reached half way up my legs, and in one of these I put my dagger. I then took the end of one of my bundles of long slips, which I had made out of the sheets of my bed, and fastened it to one of the tiles of the roof that happened to jut out four inches, and the long string of slips was fastened to the tiles in the manner of a stirrup. When I had fixed it firmly, I addressed myself to the Deity in these terms. 'Almighty God, favour my cause, for thou knowest it is a just one, and I am not on my part wanting in my utmost efforts to make it succeed.' Then letting myself down gently, and the whole weight of my body being sustained by my arm, I at last reached the ground.

"It was not a moonlight night, but the stars shone with resplendent lustre. When I had touched the ground, I first contemplated the great height which I had descended with so much courage ; and then walked away in high joy, thinking I had recovered my liberty. But I soon found myself mistaken ; for the constable had caused two pretty high walls to be erected on that side, which made an inclosure for a stable and poultry-yard. This place was fastened with great bolts on the outside. When I saw myself immured in this inclosure, I felt the greatest anxiety imaginable. Whilst I was walking backwards and forwards, I stumbled on a long pole covered with straw; this I with much difficulty fixed against the wall, and by the strength of my arms climbed to the top of it ; but as the wall was sharp I could not get a sufficient hold to enable me to descend by the pole to the other side. I therefore resolved to have recourse to my other string of slips, for I had left one tied to the great tower. So I took the string, and having fastened it properly, I descended down the steep wall. This put me to a great deal of pain and trouble, and likewise tore the skin off the palms of my hands, insomuch that they were all over bloody, for which reason I rested myself a little. When I thought I had sufficiently recruited my strength, I came to the last wall, which looked towards the meadows ; and having prepared my string of long slips, which I wanted to get about one of the niched battlements, in order to descend this as I had done the higher wall, a sentinel perceived what I was about. Finding my design obstructed, and myself in danger of my life, I resolved to cope with the soldier, who seeing me advance towards him resolutely with my drawn dagger in my hand, thought it most advisable to keep out of my way. After I had gone a little way from my string I quickly returned to it ; and though I was seen by another of the soldiers upon guard, the man did not care to take any notice of me. I then fastened my string to the niched battlement, and began to let myself down. Whether it was owing to my being near the ground and preparing to give a leap, or whether my hands were quite tired, I do not know, but being unable to hold any longer, I fell, and in falling struck my head, and became quite insensible.

"I continued in that state about an hour and a half, as nearly as I can guess. The day beginning to break, the cool breeze that precedes the rising of the sun brought me to myself; but I had not yet thoroughly recovered my senses, for I had conceived a strange notion that I had been beheaded and was then in purgatory. I, however, by degrees recovered my strength and powers; and perceiving that I had got out of the castle, I soon recollected all that had befallen me. As I perceived that my senses had been affected, before I took notice that my leg was broken, I clapped my hands to my head, and found them all bloody. I afterwards searched my body all over, and thought I had received no hurt of any consequence; but upon attempting to rise from the ground, I found that my right leg was broken three inches above the heel, which threw me into a terrible consternation. I thereupon pulled my dagger with its scabbard out of my boot. This scabbard was cased with a large piece of metal at the bottom, which occasioned the hurt of my leg; as the bone could not bend any way, it broke in that place. I therefore threw away the scabbard, and cutting the part of my string of slips that I still had left, I bandaged my leg as well as I could. I then crept on my hands and knees towards the gate, with my dagger in my hand, and upon coming up to it, found it shut; but observing a stone under the gate, and thinking that it did not stick very fast, I prepared to push it away. Clapping my hands to it, I found that I could move it with ease; so I soon pulled it out, and effected my egress. It was about five hundred paces from the place where I had had my fall to the gate at which I entered the city.

"As soon as I got in, some mastiff dogs came up, and bit me severely; finding that they persisted to worry me, I took my dagger and gave one of them so severe a stab, that he set up a loud howling; whereupon all the dogs in the neighbourhood, as it is the nature of those animals, ran up to him; and I made all the haste I could to crawl towards the church of Sta. Maria Transpontina. When I arrived at the entrance of the street that leads **towards the** castle of St. Angelo, I took my way thence **towards St.** Peter's gate ; but as it was then broad daylight, I reflected that I was in great danger, and happening **to** meet with **a** water-carrier, who had loaded his ass, and filled his vessels with water, I called to **him and** begged he would put me **upon the beast's back, and** carry me to the landing-place of the steps of **St.** Peter's church. **I** told him that I was an unfortunate youth, who had been concerned in a love-intrigue, and had made an attempt to get out at a window, from which I had fallen, and broken my leg ; but as the house I came out of belonged to a person of the first rank, I should be in danger of being cut to pieces if **discovered.** I therefore earnestly entreated him to take me up, **and** offered to give him a gold crown ; so saying, I clapped my hand to my purse, which was very well lined. The honest waterman instantly took me upon his back, **and** carried me to the steps before St. Peter's **church, where** I desired him to leave me and to run back to his **ass.**

"I immediately set out, crawling in the same manner I **had** done before, in order to reach the house of the duchess, **consort to** Duke Ottavio, natural daughter to the emperor, **and who had** been formerly married to Alessandro, the late Duke of Florence. I knew that there were several of my friends with that princess, who had attended her from Florence ; as likewise I had the happiness of being in her excellency's good graces. This last circumstance had been partly owing to the constable of the castle, who, having a desire to befriend me, told the pope that when the duchess made her entry into Rome, I prevented a damage **of above** a thousand crowns, that they were likely **to suffer by a** heavy rain ; upon which occasion, when **he was almost** in despair, I had revived **his** drooping courage, by pointing several pieces of artillery towards that tract of the heavens where the thickest clouds had gathered ; so that when the shower began to **fall, I** fired my pieces, whereupon the clouds dispersed, and the sun again shone out in all **its** brightness. Therefore it was entirely owing to me that the above day of rejoicing had been happily concluded. This coming to the ears of the duchess, her excellency said that Benvenuto was one of those men of genius who loved the memory of her husband, the Duke Alessandro, and she should always remember such, whenever an opportunity offered of doing them services. She had likewise spoken of me to Duke Ottavio, her husband. I was, therefore, going directly to the place where her excellency resided, which was in Borgo Vecchio, at a magnificent palace. There I should have been perfectly secure of any danger of falling into the pope's hands; but as the exploit I had already performed was too extraordinary for a human creature, and lest I should be puffed up with vain glory, God was pleased to put me to a still severer trial than that which I had already gone through.

"What gave occasion to this was, that whilst I was crawling along upon all four, one of the servants of Cardinal Cornaro knew me, and, running immediately to his master's apartment, awaked him out of his sleep, saying to him, 'My most reverend lord, here is your jeweller, Benvenuto, who has made his escape out of the castle, and is crawling along upon all four, quite besmeared with blood; by what I can judge from appearances, he seems to have broken one of his legs, and we cannot guess whither he is bending his course.' The cardinal, the moment he heard this, said to his servants, 'Run and bring him hither to my apartment upon your backs.' When I came into his presence, the good cardinal bade me fear nothing, and immediately sent for some of the most eminent surgeons of Rome to take care of me; amongst these was Signor Giacopo of Perugia, an excellent practitioner. This last set the bone, then bandaged my leg and bled me. As my veins were swelled more than usual, and he wanted to make a pretty wide incision, the blood gushed from me with such violence, and in so great a quantity, that it spurted into his face, and covered him in such a manner, that he found it a very difficult matter to continue his operation. He looked upon this as very ominous, and was with difficulty prevailed upon to attend me afterwards ; nay, he was several times for leaving me, recollecting that he had run a great hazard by having anything to do with me. The cardinal then caused me to be put into a private apartment, and went directly to the Vatican, in order to intercede in my behalf with the pope."

This, however, was not the last time that the unfortunate Cellini saw the inside of the castle. Undermined by his enemies in the favour of the pope, he was finally immured in a worse dungeon, on the horrors of which he dwells very graphically in his biography. It was then that his religious feelings were fully awakened, and the fiery and mettlesome bravado stained with so many homicides, wasted with long confinement and the lack of light, want of proper food and all the wholesome necessaries of life, was reduced to the devotional visionary for whom life had no longer any attraction. When they came one day to place him in a still more horrible dungeon, he says, " I never once turned about, nor took any notice of them ; on the contrary, I worshipped God the Father, surrounded with a host of angels, and Christ rising victorious over death, which I had drawn upon the wall with a piece of charcoal that I picked off the ground." Blackened with torches, dim with antiquity, the figures still remain, barely discernible, the monument of his bitter sufferings.

It was long before he was set at liberty. Finally, in an impressible moment the pope consented to his enlargement, and soon the self-assertive and audacious braggart, the impetuous brawler and wonderful artist was as spirited, active and energetic as ever.

Amongst other dark episodes in the history of this castle-tomb may be mentioned the imprisonment of Benedetto da Foiano, a popular preacher in Florence in the times of the Medici. He was a follower of Savonarola, and in the struggle against the Medicean power in the year fifteen

hundred and twenty-eight Benedetto did all he could to
excite the people in defence of the republic. He is described
as a man of fine personal appearance, of much learning and
singular eloquence, drawing together vast audiences. He
was betrayed to Malatesta Baglioni by a traitorous soldier
who had undertaken to favour his escape, and sent to Pope
Clement the Seventh (himself a Medici), by whom he was
immured in a dark and noisome dungeon in the castle of
St. Angelo, where, in spite of the friendly desires of the
governor of the castle to mitigate the resentment of the
pope against him, after many months, wanting every
decency and comfort, the little bread and water allowed to
him were gradually diminished until he died miserably ;
the too hard fate of an energetic and earnest reformer.
" Truly," says the historian Varchi in relating this pitiable
story, " he was worthy of a greater and better fortune, or
should have been gifted with less learning and eloquence."

From this period the castle remained in undisturbed
possession of the papal power, until the year seventeen
hundred and ninety-eight, when it was taken by a republican
French garrison, nine thousand strong, who did some
damage to the outer works by setting fire to a powder
magazine. It was afterwards retaken by the Neapolitans
for the papal government. In the year eighteen hundred
and eight it was again taken by the French, and only escaped another occupation six years afterwards by a speedy
capitulation.

It would, indeed, appear as if this wonderful pile were
indestructible. When taken from the French occupation
for the antipope in one thousand three hundred and seventy-
nine, the irate Romans set themselves to destroy it altogether ; but after labouring with all their might upon it for
several days, they made so little impression that they gave
it up in despair. Grim and stern it still keeps watch over
the river, unchanged through all changes, defying decay and
the ruthless hand of Time.

Immediately past the bridge on the right bank of the

river stands the Apollo theatre, the opera house of Rome. It is built on the site of the old Torre di Nona, a prison in which criminals were placed previous to execution. It was from this place that the unfortunate Beatrice Cenci and her step-mother were led to execution. Here another bridge crossed the river, the Pons Vaticanus. Piranesi and some other archæologists claim it for the Pons Triumphalis. There is now little to indicate its site excepting a few remains, on which the modern theatre is built.

Advancing along the river, spreading meadows sweep from the left bank to the very foot of the Vatican. The region of the old Campus Martius lies on the right, now entirely covered with streets and houses. Presently we arrive at the Ripetta, or wharf, consisting of a picturesque flight of steps, the material for which was taken from the Coliseum. Here a ferry-boat attached to a rope carried across the stream, passes to and fro by the force of the current. On the same side as the wharf, separated from the immediate banks of the river by a street, is the round mausoleum, or tomb of the family of Augustus, the first emperor of Rome, by whom it was built. It is now surrounded with buildings ; and it is only here and there that fragments of the ancient masonry (*opus reticulatum*) are visible. With the help of Strabo's description, it is not difficult to form an idea of its primitive magnificence. It was covered with white marble and surmounted by a tumulus of earth planted with cypresses, and crowned by a colossal bronze statue of the emperor. Adjoining were groves and pleasure grounds. At one side was the *bustum*, or place for burning the bodies of the dead, also of white marble, surrounded with a double inclosure, of marble and iron, and planted about with ever-sighing poplars. At the entrance of the mausoleum stood two obelisks, now removed, the one to Santa Maria Maggiore, and the other to the piazza of the Quirinal. There were fourteen chambers ranged round the great rotunda in the interior, the whole diameter being about two hundred and thirty feet.

Whilst dwelling upon the monument, let us spend a few moments upon its occupants. First of all upon him who raised it; for the emperor Augustus was not only himself a remarkable man, but lived in a remarkable era. His age stood exactly between ancient and modern civilizations, the old world and the new, paganism and Christianity. It was distinguished by the noblest intellectual works of antiquity; it has become a proverb for culture and refinement, and perhaps there is no recorded period wherein so much was done destined to exercise so large and abiding an influence on the education of the human race. It brought forth Livy, Virgil, Horace, Ovid, Tibullus and Propertius; but it was marked by a still more important event, and one that has given colour to the whole subsequent history of a large proportion of mankind, and is yet to produce greater and larger results, the birth of Jesus Christ.

There are few characters ancient or modern which have afforded so great a puzzle to historians and biographers, or been the subject of so much discussion and difference of opinion, as that of Augustus the first emperor of Rome. In his own time his true character and disposition appear to have been as little fathomable as they are to us now. He was either one of the noblest and most disinterested of men or the most consummate and successful of actors. He was born in the year sixty-three before Christ: his father was Octavius a senator, and his mother Accia the sister of Julius Cæsar. At the age of twenty he showed the greatest tact and discrimination in affairs. He formed a triumvirate with Antony and Lepidus, but soon found means to shake off his companions in government and occupy the imperial seat alone. This triumvirate had to answer for the blood of three hundred senators and two hundred knights, and the death of the orator Cicero, a professed friend of Augustus; acts of cruelty the odium of which clung to him always afterwards. No sooner however was his rule estab-lished than his policy became one of the utmost mildness combined with the most perfect prudence. Indeed he might

be said to have made himself a lesson to all rulers : true
emperor by prescriptive right ; a man and a king, neither
forgetting the one nor confounding the other. He was
warrior, poet and historian. He was the model of a
dignified and cultivated gentleman. He was at once
courteous and manly, tender and courageous ; his tears
could flow for a friend and his hand be frankly extended to
an enemy. He appeared to be always the servant of his
country and his people, and to have their welfare at heart
more than his own. He never made unnecessary or unjust
war. The temple of Janus was closed thrice in his life-time
—only closed twice before in the whole history of the city.
He once thought of resigning the empire and restoring the
republic, and was only induced to retain his position on the
representation of the general welfare. Many wise and
beneficial measures marked his reign, and many improvements were made in the city. He congratulated himself
that he had found Rome of brick and left it of marble. He
abhorred titles and avoided compliments. When he was
slandered he said, " I too can speak," and when his friends
would have had him take further notice of it, he replied that
" words did no harm." He melted down the silver statues
set up to him, and made of them tripods for the temple of
Apollo. He had a particular aversion to the sumptuousness
of a palace, and always sought a less pretentious residence.
He voted in his tribe as one of the people, and appeared in
a court of justice as witness for an old soldier. He recommended his adopted sons to the people *if they deserved it*,
and though he did not forget his friends, he never bestowed
exclusive privileges on them as such. When he was styled
the Father of his country the tears came to his eyes, as he
said he wished for no other honour than its welfare and the
continuance of his people's affection. His house was frugal,
his table plain to himself, generous to his friends ; his habits
temperate. He educated personally and carefully the
children he had adopted, whom he always liked to have
with him and about him. Shortly before his death, when

at the island of Capri, whither he had gone on account of
his health, he spent his visit in the holiday diversions of the
inhabitants, making scrambles for the boys, joking with the
people and entertaining them.   Arrived at Nola near Naples
he was seized with his mortal illness.   He called for a mirror,
adjusted his person and had his toilette made, asking the
bystanders if he had acted his part well in life, and if so,
requesting that they would applaud him.   He died suddenly
in the arms of his wife Livia, begging her not to forget
their union, and bidding her a tender farewell.*   His body
was carried in the night-time from town to town by the
several magistrates and officers of the places which it had to
traverse, reposing during the heat of the day within some
basilica or temple.   It was met at Bovillæ on the Appian Way
by the equestrian orders, who brought it to Rome by night.
The next morning the magistrates assembled, wearing robes
stripped of their purple trimmings ; Tiberius and Drusus,
foster-sons of the defunct emperor, being clothed in ash-
coloured garments : his will was then read.   The corpse was
laid out and incense burnt before it.   On the day of the
funeral those who were to take part in the ceremony
assembled in the morning.   A designator distributed the
order of the procession ; and soon it began to move to the
sound of horns and flutes, sometimes wailing in the saddest
tones and then swelling into triumphant strains, as if to
bear away the spirit of the dead.   After these followed
women chanting the praises of the departed and mourning
the sad chance that had robbed him of life ; then came
mimes or actors : one of them personating the dead emperor
in his manners and appearance ; then his statue robed
in a triumphal habit, carried by the prospective magistrates
of the following year, this statue being accompanied by
another all of gold, and after that a third in a triumphal
chariot ; these were followed by statues of all his ancestors
and relations, excepting Julius Cæsar who had been deified ;

---

* Suetonius says his last words were, " Livia, conjugii nostri memor, vive
et vale."

then came the images of all the ancient Romans of note from Romulus downwards; then numberless freedmen bearing tablets and other devices on which were inscribed the name and deeds of the emperor, together with tokens and emblems of the provinces he had subdued; last of all the body itself laid upon a bed of gold and ivory, trimmed with purple, covered over with a black pall. On reaching the Forum the corpse was set down, when Drusus read some papers and Tiberius pronounced a funeral oration over it. Then it was carried through the Triumphal gate followed by the senators and knights with their wives, guards, soldiers, in short, the whole inhabitants of Rome, to the *bustum* or inclosed space for burning near the mausoleum in the Campus Martius. Here a funeral pile was erected of fir-wood hung with festoons, tapestry and costly draperies, and planted about with cypress trees. Upon this the body was placed together with the bed upon which it was laid. The eyelids of the corpse were opened that the light of heaven might be mirrored within them. A last kiss from the nearest and dearest was imprinted on the pallid lips. Three times the procession passed round the pile, throwing various precious gifts upon it—oils, odours, and rich ornaments; the soldiers even casting upon it the rewards they had obtained for distinguishing themselves in the service of the state under his generalship. Many of the spectators also threw upon the pile gums, frankincense and valuable offerings of various kinds, together with locks of their own hair. When this was done the centurions set fire to it with averted faces amidst loud wailings and great cries from the whole multitude.* As the flames rose an eagle was seen to soar in the air, which was supposed to carry the soul of the defunct up to heaven.

For five days the desolate Livia, wife of the emperor,

---

* This outcry was raised before lighting the pyre, in order to awaken the corpse if it should be only in a trance. The elder Pliny tells a story of a person waking up by the heat of the flames when the pyre had been kindled, but too late to be saved.

clothed in white and accompanied by a number of knights, watched the expiring flames and crumbling ashes. Then what remained of the dead from the destructive fire was carefully gathered, washed in wine and milk, then dried upon a funeral cloth and finally placed with spices, odours and rich gums, in an urn marked with a pious D.M.—thus consigning him to the care of the deities of the dead—and reverently carried to the mausoleum : after which the priest sprinkled those present with pure water from a laurel bough, and they retired leaving the ashes of the departed to their repose with a mournful " Farewell ! "

The features, form, and bearing of Augustus are all familiar to us through the sculptures still existing of him, from the handsome and refined-looking boy to the commanding general and imperial ruler. He had rather a low forehead, his hair was straight, his nose aquiline, his eye bright, his face and features bearing a look of breeding and culture without any trace of malice, sensuousness, or craft upon them, his figure erect and vigorous—a man looking more like one fitted for command than obedience, but not in anywise harsh or severe.

Tacitus says there were many and various opinions expressed of him after his death. Some extolled him amongst the noblest and most disinterested of the race, others attributed to him an underlying selfishness and politic egotism as the main-spring of his life and actions. Perhaps neither were quite right. He may have begun to some extent as a political egotist and ended with a large patriotism and genuine love of his kind and country. It would be scarcely a wonder if the best of the Romans at that time should have grown up selfish and cruel, educated amidst so much selfishness and cruelty—at least until reason and reflection had asserted their sway with sufficient force to induce individual views and prescribe an independent line of conduct. Augustus may have been schooled into these as we are all of us schooled, through the training of experience and the added thoughtfulness of years.

However this may have been, divine honours were **decreed** to him at his death, the place where he died **was conse-**crated and temples raised to his honour. His memory is preserved to us even to this day in the names of one of the months of our calendar, that of his birth.

Augustus, **however, was not the first to be** placed within the mausoleum. Before him **the** remains of his young **nephew** Marcellus, already mentioned, had been laid there, **the** beloved of all Rome, whose elegy Virgil sings so nobly **in his Æneid.** "My son," he makes Æneas say, "seek not to **learn** your people's boundless woe : him fate shall but show to the world, nor suffer him longer to exist. **Too mighty** had the Roman race appeared **to you,** ye gods of heaven, had these blessings **become its own for** ever . . . **Give me** handfuls of lilies ; **I** would strew bright flowers and plenteously : with these gifts **at least** honour **the spirit of** my descendant, and discharge an unavailing **duty."** *

Here also was laid Octavia, his mother, the long-suffering wife of the ignoble **and** irresolute Antony. **Sister of** Augustus, her marriage with Antony had been but a political **step to** assure good feeling between the emperor and his **colleague.** At first Antony could **not** fail to be attracted by so much beauty and virtue, but he soon forgot her during his service in the East, exposed to the voluptuous blandishments of the Egyptian Cleopatra. Whilst he was giving himself up to a life of effeminating pleasure, she was educating her children and step-children quietly **at home.** When Antony was about to make an expedition **against** Artavasdes, king of Armenia, she set off with troops and money **to** assist **him ; but** on arriving at Athens he sent **her** word to return : she did so, but sent **forward the resources.** When the war was **over, fascinated by the too potent charms** of Cleopatra, he sent his faithful **wife a bill of** divorce. This, together with the death **of the** much-loved Marcellus, off-

* O nate, ingentem **luctum** ne quære tuorum ;
  Ostendent terris hunc **tantum** fata, neque ultra
  Esse sinent, &c. **Æn. vi. 869.**

K

spring of a former marriage, preyed upon her mind. She died. Her funeral was a public one. Her step-sons carried her to her grave, and Augustus himself pronounced her funeral oration.

Another illustrious dweller within the walls of this tomb was Germanicus, the able and accomplished general and fine-spirited gentleman. He was adopted by Tiberius, fought much in the German wars, and was so popular that he aroused the bitter envy of his foster-father. He was distinguished by some of the noblest traits of antique times. He commanded his soldiers faithfully, and knew how to refuse an empire when it was offered to him ; preferring death to treachery or a defalcation from his allegiance. He died from the effects of poison, as was generally supposed, secretly administered at Daphne near Antioch, in the thirty-fourth year of his age. The news of his death was received with the greatest consternation at Rome ; and although Tiberius wished to curtail all demonstration and ceremonial at his funeral, yet Tacitus tells us that "the day on which his remains were deposited in the tomb, at one time exhibited the silence of perfect desolation, at another the uproar of vociferous lamentation ; the streets of the city were crowded, one general blaze of torches glared throughout the Campus Martius ; there the soldiers under arms, the magistrates without the insignia of office, and the people ranged according to their tribes, passionately exclaimed, that the commonwealth was utterly lost, that henceforth there remained no hope, so openly and so boldly that you would have believed they had forgotten those who ruled over them."*

Not less worthy of regret was the fate of his noble-minded wife Agrippina. She was the very model of a Roman matron ; fine of person, severe in morals and character, ambitious, with a largeness of capacity that rendered her equal to the highest emergencies. She was with her husband in Germany during the campaign. In his absence

* The Annals, B. iii.   Translation in Bohn's series.

it was rumoured that the Roman army had been cut off in the country of the enemy, and that a body of Germans was approaching the bridge to invade Gaul. When it was proposed to destroy this bridge, which would effectually have cut off the retreat of the Romans, she manfully withstood the cowardly proposal, herself assuming the command of the forces, assisting the wounded and distributing clothes and other necessaries with her own hands. Her only fault was that of being too much revered by the Roman people, who called her the ornament of her country, the representative of the race of Augustus, the unmatched example of primitive virtue. For this she was banished by the cruel command of Tiberius, to Pandataria, a small barren island in the Gulf of Gaeta, where she lived miserably for three years, and then died, as it was thought, of voluntary starvation ; her ashes being afterwards brought to Rome, and deposited here.

Hither came also the younger Drusus, the son of Tiberius, of whom little more need be said than that Tiberius himself reproved him for his bloodthirsty cruelty to slaves in the arena. He died from the effects of a slow poison administered by an eunuch with the connivance of his wife, at the instigation of Sejanus, a designing favourite of Tiberius, who had been struck by Drusus. He had a great funeral. All his ancestors, real or supposed, from Æneas downwards, were carried in effigy, in a long train. For all that, there is no evidence that his death was a matter of much regret to any one.

Here also were placed the remains of the monster Tiberius. He was the successor to Augustus, by whom he had been adopted and recommended. In early life he distinguished himself as a brave and able general, and his reign was begun with a mild and promising policy. Soon, however, this was lost sight of. Jealous, tyrannical, libidinous and cruel, he finally retired to the island of Capri, where his worst qualities developed themselves from a shameful and unnatural licentiousness to the most horrible and revolting cruelty. The ruins of his palace are yet to be seen on an elevated promontory of the island, and the cliff is still shown whence his miserable victims were hurled down to the beach below, from which the sound of the falling waves is only heard faintly. Nothing was too mean or ignoble for his baseness and brutality; invention could go no farther in abominable lewdness and ferocity. His cruelties and vices have become a proverb; they need not be dwelt on here. Suetonius leaves no part of his character and none of his ill-doings undescribed. He says that when a youth one of his masters used to tell him he was composed of mire mixed with blood. His evil nature never deserted him. He is described as tall, burly and very strong; so strong that he could wound with a flip, and bore an apple with his finger. He had a fair complexion, large eyes, and long hair behind. He walked stiffly and uprightly, spoke very slowly, and with a slight gesticulation of his fingers. There must have been something very repulsive in the latter characteristic, since it was remarked upon and disliked by the senate and people whilst Augustus was yet alive. Augustus, however, excused him, by saying it was his natural manner, and meant no harm. He was not without literary power. He wrote both in his own tongue and in Greek; devoting a certain portion of his time to study. He died at Misenum in the Christian year thirty-seven, and the seventy-eighth of his age, after a reign of a little more than twenty-two years and a half. When his remains were brought to Rome, the people cried out that he should be thrown into the Tiber, praying heaven and earth that he might have no repose for his wickedness. His body, however, underwent the usual rite, and he was placed in the Augustan tomb.

Another iniquitous tyrant entered these precincts in the person of Caius, called Caligula. He was the son of Germanicus. The most charitable supposition is that a severe illness had left him no longer responsible for his actions and behaviour. Nothing was too enormous for him to perpetrate

Once during a fight of wild beasts, when there were no more criminals to be sacrificed, he ordered people taken at random from amongst the spectators, first to have their tongues cut out, and then to be cast into the arena. He had persons tortured for his amusement during meals. At a horse-race, when the people were disposed to favour a competitor more than himself, he is said to have wished that they had all one head, that he might strike it off at a blow. He threw money mixed with iron spikes amongst the populace, by means of which many were wounded, and some killed. He was continually impersonating some fanciful character ; sometimes appearing as Hercules, Juno, Diana, Venus, Bacchus or Neptune, as suited the madness of the moment. But perhaps his crowning folly and insolence was that of building a temple to himself, and furnishing it with his own image. At last one of his servants named Chærea put an end to his miserable life, after he had reigned nearly four years, in the forty-first year of the Christian era.

Next came the weak and characterless emperor Claudius, who nevertheless left some great works behind him. The aqueduct built in his reign still strides in broken but ma- jestic arches across the Campagna of Rome, and traces of his harbour at Ostia are still visible.

Many others helped to fill the walls of this huge sepulchre. The last placed within it was Nerva. He was emperor towards the end of the first Christian century. Dion Cassius gives some fine characteristics of him. On as- suming the government he took an oath never to put a senator to death, and kept it, even to those who had con- spired against his life. When the conspiracy of Calpurnius Crassus came to his ears, he sent some well-sharpened daggers to be placed near him, at the public shows, that he might see he had no fear of him. The captain of his guard made an insurrection amongst those under his command in order to have certain persons put to death. Nerva offered his own head ; but would not comply with their demand. Seeing that his age—he was sixty-five—decreased the respect due to his function as emperor, he ascended the Capitol, proclaiming that, for the good of the empire, he appointed Trajan his successor. He reigned somewhat more than four years. At his death he was carried to the pile on the shoulders of senators in the same manner as Augustus had been.

From the time of Nerva the mausoleum remained closed until it was violated by Alaric at the Gothic invasion, in the hopes of finding a treasure there. In the thirteenth century it became a fortress of the Colonna family during the civil factions by which Rome was torn at that time. The whole internal portion of it was subsequently destroyed by the people, with the exception of some narrow chambers which still remain ; one of them is supposed to belong to a corridor leading to the central hall where the ashes of Augustus were placed. There are also still evidences of abutting halls on the ground-floor.

One more episode in its history should not be forgotten. It is the last tragical act in the career of the spirited reformer Rienzo. After he had been slain and his headless corpse dragged about the streets and then hung from a balcony for two days and a night, pelted with stones and receiving every kind of indignity, it was taken down and dragged to this tomb, where the magistrates assembled, and a great concourse of people. Here it was placed on a huge pile which was set on fire. His corpulence of person, says his biographer, caused him to burn very readily, so that he was soon entirely consumed. Thus perished the great champion of liberty and justice, sacrificed by the ignorance and the cruelty of the people whom he had attempted to serve, who could make no allowance in the splendour of the hero for the imperfections and weaknesses of the man.

After the mausoleum had been abandoned by the Colonna, it became successively a fortress, a garden, and a theatre. It is used in the latter capacity still. On its summit a stage is constructed at one side ; stone seats pass round the

arena, the central space being filled with fashionable crowds
on the summer afternoons who assemble to witness the open
air performance of Alfieri or Goldoni, or to laugh at the last
new farce imported from the French. Sometimes it is used
as an amphitheatre for equestrian performances. What a
moral does it furnish ! Yet how few· of the spectators on
such occasions bestow so much as a thought on the puissant
dust which once reposed beneath and perhaps still moulders
into nothingness amongst the broken ruins ! As I have sat
here sometimes in the warm summer evening when the
sunlight has died on the walls, and the first stars begun to
look forth from the transparent sky, it has seemed as if the
spirits of the old heroes have crept once more from their
hiding places. I have seen the imperial Augustus gather
up his robes in the senate, and the youthful Marcellus
appear—still living in his noble epitaph. I have seen the
dignified and matronly Agrippina standing before me in
all the commanding grace of womanhood. Britannicus, the
innocent victim of the heartless Nero, has looked upon me
with mournful eyes ; and Tiberius with his sinister gestures
and cold tones filled me with a creeping horror. Caligula,
Antonia, Claudius, Nerva, have all appeared before me,
whilst the mimic stage and its counterfeit actors, together
with the whole audience, have vanished, giving place to a
mightier drama with the races of all time as the wondering
spectators.

Leaving the ancient mausoleum, and passing between
open banks, we approach the confines of the city. Over
the meadows to the left the vast range of the Vatican is
exposed in all its length, flanked at one end by the façade
and dome of St. Peter's, perhaps the most imposing of all
the views obtained of it.

In order to take our farewell of the city, I will ask my
readers to accompany me for an evening stroll to the top
of the neighbouring Pincian hill, the last we see of Rome
on this side of it. Crossing the Piazza del Popolo we climb
by steps and shady walks to its lofty summit. The sweet

spring has filled the gardens with flowers. Already the white almond blossoms have fallen, but the billowy acacias of the Villa Borghese are crested with odorous wreaths of snowy foam. Fountains toss up their crystal columns from basins of marble or artificial rock-work, murmuring pleasantly. The sun, not far from his setting, pours a golden flood of light over temple and turret and house-top. Below lies the Piazza del Popolo, marked by all varieties of character and calling; now we see a number of ecclesiastical students in long dark skirts, walking in couples, then a file of soldiers; there a group of countrymen with shaggy goatskins covering their thighs, reminding one of the fabled satyrs of old, carry large cakes of bread slung on a cord over their shoulders; there a wine-cart goes with its jingling bells and tent-like covering for the driver, by whose side a little dog barks vociferously; now a woman lingers by the central fountain, leaning on an elegantly-shaped copper pitcher, and now a sombre procession of monks passes by, each bearing a lighted candle, and chanting the mournful office for the dead.

In the meantime the sun has set. The gay crowds of fashion and pleasure have departed. The city lies steeped in sober grey. Beyond the roofs of the houses and the hidden river a long plain sweeps to the foot of the Vatican and the mighty dome of St. Peter's, which stands in aërial tones against the skirts of the passing day, supported by the serrated line of the Janiculum on the one side, and the plumed heights of Monte Mario on the other. The golden light has faded; only a deep glow of orange fills the horizon. The sky at the zenith begins to assume a deep purple. The crescent moon increases in distinctness: and now begins the solemn pageantry of the night. The air seems to grow in clearness. Glassy abysses are opened, depth beyond depth, until it would seem that the very empyrean must become visible. A few curling clouds lie loosely about the horizon. The evening star burns brightly above it. Dimness creeps amongst the trees. The flutter-

ing bat flits hither and thither as if uncertain of his course.
The owl beats the air, giving forth his solitary cry. The
nightingale begins to sing with a low whisper, growing
louder and louder until the thickets overflow with song.
The beetle booms by with a surly hum ; night moths
flutter ; flowers close ; stars awake one by one till the
whole heavens are robed in sparkling glory. Lights begin
to sprinkle the streets and houses. Hark ! that was the
first stroke of the hour of Ave Maria. For a few moments
the air seems alive with the sound of bells : then all is still.
Moment by moment the heavens grow more tenderly
beautiful. The rose of day has turned into the lily of night ;
who shall say which is the fairest?

THE PINCIO, FROM THE VILLA BORGHESE.

CHAPTER VI.

FROM ROME TO FIDENÆ.

BEFORE leaving Rome I should like to take my reader farther into it. I should like to go with him through its various sculpture and picture galleries. I should like to survey its ancient ruins, quaint gardens and old world nooks in his company. I should like to lead him away from the tide of tourists and casual visitors into the delightful semi-bohemian artist life of some of its more permanent residents :

> A world of beauty
> Where love moves ever hand in hand with duty;
> And life, a long aspiring pilgrimage,
> Makes labour but a pastime of delight.*

But this the limits of my prescribed course forbid. We must leave its dear old walls for " fresh fields and pastures new."

I was once more indebted to Mr. Welby for the opportunity of exploring the navigable portion of the Tiber above Rome. One of his steamers leaves the Ripetta (the smaller quay at the northern end of the city) periodically for the purpose of towing up the charcoal and other barges, which, when laden, return with the stream. He was kind enough not only to permit Mr. Hemans and myself to make use of his steamer, but took pains to have accommodation specially prepared for us, as we should have to spend a night on board ; so that when we went early one brilliant morning with rugs,

---

* 'My Beautiful Lady,' by T Woolner.

wine, provisions, etc., expecting nothing more than a **bed of boards** to lie upon, with no particular convenience of any sort, we were agreeably surprised to find a commodious and comfortable cabin at our disposal, with **seats and sofas in it.** The proposed voyage only **extended** to a distance of about thirty-five miles, but as this would take the whole of the day, heading the stream and towing a number of large hulks **in our wake, on** reaching the highest point attainable the **vessel had to be** moored for the night, dropping down to Rome again the next morning. In describing the various points and places of interest which the Tiber passes I shall **take** them in this upward journey ; but the reader must **be** aware that they were each made the object **of a special** journey (some more than one) from Rome.

Of course there was the usual number of grown men with a good sprinkling of young fry on board the vessel, who, **if** they did no more, enjoyed the trip very much, to judge by their gambols alternating with long **dozes in shady corners,** besides **contributing to keep up** the spirits **of** the ship's **company by a** continual **flow of merriment and good-humour.** Our departure was a very animated **one.** The **sun** shone brilliantly ; the river sparkled as if smiling beneath the **prow of** the vessel ; the old river had put off every forbidding **scowl,** and looked pleasantly under the blue sky.

No sooner is the boundary wall of the city passed than the houses at once cease to occupy the banks, which are left to grazing sheep and the little birds that sing amongst **the** bushes. There is, however, a single villa on the left, **said to** have been once inhabited by Claude the **landscape painter.** Nowhere are the sunsets seen to finer effect. **He may well** have watched them here until they suffused **his soul with** their glory, and **then flung them on to his canvas with the** glow of an inspiration.

Just opposite to this **place, on the other side of the river, with the** old **Via Flaminia** running **between, is** Monte Parioli, **a tufa-formed elevation,** nowise famous or notable excepting **for a** certain **picturesqueness which** it bears.

About a mile from Rome Monte Mario is reached, which
may be considered the most northerly abutment of the
Janiculan range. Its sides are varied by alternate sterility
and culture ; upon its top are gardens, groves of cypresses,
two or three villas, and one tall expansive stone-pine, which
is a beacon to the country round. The views of the river
as seen from its sides and summit, in its numerous windings
along the Campagna, are very charming. Here resided
Julius Martialis, the friend of the Latin epigrammatist
Martial, the latter of whom has left us one of the most
charming descriptions in literature of the view obtained
from its summit. It is as follows :

" On the long ridge of the Janiculan hill lie the few acres
belonging to Julius Martialis ; land more blest than the
gardens of the Hesperides. Secluded retreats are spread over
the hills ; and the smooth summit, with gentle undulations,
enjoys a cloudless sky, and while a mist covers the hollow
valley, shines conspicuous in a light all its own. The graceful turrets of a lofty villa rise gently towards the stars.
Hence you may see the seven hills, rulers of the world, and
contemplate the whole extent of Rome, as well as the
heights of Alba and Tusculum, and every cool retreat that
lies in the suburbs, with old Fidenæ and little Rubra, and
the fruit-bearing grove of Anna Perenna, which delights in
virgin's blood. There may be seen the traveller on the
Flaminian and Salarian roads, while his carriage is unheard,
so that its wheels are no interruption to gentle sleep :
neither is it broken by the cry of the boatswain, or the
noise of hawsers, although the Milvian bridge is near, and
ships are seen gliding swiftly along the sacred Tiber. This
country box, but which ought rather to be called mansion,
is rendered additionally agreeable by the welcome of its
owner ; you would imagine it to be your own ; so ungrudg-
ingly, so liberally is it thrown open to you, and with such
refined hospitality. You would deem it the pious abode of
Alcinous, or of Molorchus recently made rich. You, now,
who think all these attractions insignificant, cultivate with

a hundred spades cool Tivoli or Præneste, and **give the** slopes of Setia to one single husbandman ; whilst **I,** for my part, prefer to all your possessions the few acres of **Julius** Martialis."*

This hill used to be called **the** Clivus Cinnæ. Dante alludes to it by the name of Montemalo. It was changed to Mario, after Mario Mellini, to whom it belonged in the **latter part of the** sixteenth century. It is interesting to **geologists in** that it contains quantities of marine shells of **the pliocene** period ; the beds **in** which these are found are superimposed volcanic strata.

Descending the slopes towards the Ponte Molle is the Villa Madama, **a** somewhat desolate-looking tenement, which takes its name from Margaret of Austria, **natural** daughter of Charles the Fifth, who married into the **Medici** family, for one of whom it was built. It **is** decorated **with** frescoes by Giulio Romano and Giovanni da Udine.

The plain beneath is used as a military exercising ground. **It** was here that the magnanimous and noble-minded Arnoldo da Brescia was made the martyr **to a** wider sense of freedom and a larger disinterestedness than his age could understand or appreciate. He was first hanged, and then his **body** was burnt. His ashes, thrown into the Tiber, have **long** sown themselves on other shores, bringing forth abundant increase. Let the reader, if he will, turn to the life and death of this self-devoted hero ; but here we will rather choose to draw the veil before a painful and disgraceful tragedy, too sickening in its details for our summer's holiday.

It is supposed that the temple **of** Anna Perenna **must** have stood near here, whose festival is so graphically described by Ovid.

" On the Ides " of **March, he says, " is the mirthful festival**

* Juli jugera pauca Martialis,
  Hortis Hesperidum beatiora,
  Longo Janiculi jugo recumbunt, &c.
                                        Ep. iv. 64.

Translation in Bohn's Library.

of Anna Perenna, not far from thy banks, thou Tiber that
flowest from afar.   The common people assemble and
carouse, scattered in every quarter on the green grass; each
with his sweetheart is there reclining.   Some spend their time
in the open air, some pitch their tents ; by some a leafy bower
is formed of branches.   Some when they have fixed up reeds
there in the stead of solid columns, place over them garments spread out.   Yet with the sun and wine do they wax
warm ; they pray for years as many in number as the cups
they quaff, and reckon on as they drink.   There you will
meet with the man who can drink off the years of Nestor ;
the woman who becomes as old as the Sybil by the number
of her cups.   There, too, they sing whatever snatches they
have picked up at the theatres and move their pliant arms in
time to their words.   And now having laid aside the bowl,
they trip the uncouth dance, and many a gaily-dressed
wench skips about with her locks flowing.   When they
return, they stagger and are a gazing sight for the mob, and
the multitude that meets them pronounces them to be
glorious souls.   I myself met them lately ; the procession
seemed to me one that was worthy to be mentioned again.·
A drunken old hag was dragging after her a drunken old
man."*

Here the ancient Pons Milvius (now Ponte Molle) crosses
the river.   A part of it dates from the beginning of the
second century ; though it has suffered many reverses since
that time.   The ambassadors of the Allobroges who were
concerned in the Catiline conspiracy were here arrested by
the order of Cicero.   It was the scene of some of the wild
nocturnal orgies of Nero mentioned by Tacitus ; and it
was from its parapet that the emperor Maxentius lost his
life when fleeing from the battle of the Saxa Rubra.
Modern architecture has not done much to improve it as
far as appearance goes.   It is disfigured by an unsightly
tower built at one end of it, and some very bad statuary.

After passing Ponte Molle the Campagna is fairly entered

* Fas. iii. 523.

upon—that vast tract of almost desert ground that stretches for twenty miles on every side of Rome. Beautiful as it is in the morning hours, when the thin mist lingers in its hollow places and the lark pours forth his rapid notes in the air, it is, perhaps, still more impressive clothed in the sombre hues of the late evening, when the golden sunshine has died from the broken masonry which here and there rises from its sod, and the great mounds loom out and stretch from valley to valley like huge hillocks piled upon the graves of buried giants, and the grey ruins stand like tombstones to mark the places where they lie. It is then that the voices of the past speak loudest from its interminable undulations, and the solitude becomes peopled with the shadowy forms of those who once turned its desolate bluffs and headlands into the seats of human industry, interest and ambition.

As the vessel slowly toiled up the stream I noticed particularly what I had often observed before, that there was a subtlety and peculiarity in the surface colour of the waters of the Tiber which I never saw on any other stream. The blue of the sky reflected in the tawny hue of the eddying water gives an indefinite shimmer, so subtle and delicate, and so difficult to analyse, as almost to defy the skill of the artist in its reproduction. Perhaps this is the reason why one sees it so seldom painted well, or even at all.* To-day it was particularly elusive, tender and bright, as it twirled itself into tiny eddies running into each other with a thousand sparkling dimples, and coursing each other down stream as if in playful rejoicing at the fair morning and the clear sunshine which pervaded the world from earth to sky. The gossamer spider, nothing daunted, crossed the stream on his frail support, and the butterfly flitted from one bank to the other, whilst numerous birds enlivened our way with various songs ; the thrush, the nightingale, and, above our heads, the soaring lark.

After passing some foliage-covered cliffs on the right

* Mr. J. C. Moore, in some of his water-colour drawings, appears to me to have given some of the most satisfactory renderings of it.

and a picturesque round tower on the left, a bend of the
river brings us to Acqua Cetosa, some famous mineral
springs which have been in use since the times of the
ancient Romans ; and immediately afterwards to a long,
elevated mound with a level summit, sloping upwards from
green pasture-grounds.   Although there is not a vestige
of ruin upon it, yet a little observation renders it apparent
that its form has been modified by artificial means.   It was
here that the ancient Sabine city, "towered Antemnæ," once
stood, sung by Virgil, and stated by old historians to have
been no inconsiderable rival of early Rome.   Its site is
unmistakably identified by ancient descriptions, which give
it as lying exactly between the junction of the Anio with
the Tiber.

It was from this city, together with those of Cænina
and Crustumerium, that Rome was partly populated, for
Romulus, finding his newly-founded colony to consist of
little more than a band of warriors, sent embassies to the
neighbouring Sabine cities with proposals for intermarriage,
which were one and all refused.   Upon this Romulus,
smothering his indignation, invited the Sabines from these
towns to witness some athletic games in Rome.   They
came, bringing with them their wives and daughters.   They
were hospitably entertained by the Romans, who, at the
same time, took care to show them all their advantages
of position, together with the fortresses they had built.
Whilst the spectacle was going forward, by a preconcerted
plan, a number of armed Roman youths rushed forwards,
and seizing as many of the younger women as they
could, carried them off by force.   In vain the Antemnates
inveighed against this inhospitable outrage, calling upon
their gods for vengeance.   Whilst the Sabines put on
mourning and tried to rouse the neighbouring states to
revenge, Romulus endeavoured to excuse his conduct, and
appealed to the women taken, who soon began to form
home ties and attachments to their husbands which they
were not desirous of severing.   At last, after numerous

skirmishes, Romulus overtook their army **on a foraging excursion, completely routed them, and gained possession of their** city. At the entreaty of **Hersilia his spouse, who had been one of the previously captured women, he spared them on** condition that Antemnæ **should become a colony of Rome: such of the inhabitants as chose to leave it being allowed to do so, and to reside in Rome with the privilege of citizenship, their lands and** possessions **being retained to them.** Dionysius says **that three thousand men with their wives and families** availed themselves **of** these conditions. The same historian gives a fine description of the **Triumph of the** conqueror on this **occasion, who** followed the procession of spoils and booty, clad **in a purple** robe and crowned **with laurel, in a chariot drawn by four** horses, his army following, infantry **and cavalry ranged in** their several divisions, singing hymns **to the gods and** celebrating their General in extemporary **verses. They** were met by **all the** inhabitants **of the city, who caressed** and praised **them: and on entering** they **found tables spread with viands and bowls of wine, so** that **each** might **eat** and drink what **he chose.   This was the first Triumph of all her many** magnificent **ones that Rome ever saw.**

The summit of this table-land **commands fine views** of **the Campagna on all sides.   There are still** traces of the **ancient** roads which must **have led to** the gate of the city. Archæologists differ **as to the** position which **the arx or** citadel may **have** occupied. The angle **at the** junction of the rivers is perhaps the strongest point, but **there is a** higher elevation **at** the other side. Strabo mentions **it with** some others **as having** become **an insignificant village.** There is **not so much as a** stone **of the ancient city** left. Probably everything **serving** as building **material may have** been long since carried away to Rome.

In the time of Tarquin the combined **Sabines and Etrus-cans** encamped at the confluence of **the rivers, throwing** a wooden bridge **across** the Tiber. Tarquin, by means of **boats** filled with burning combustibles sent down the Anio,

L.

destroyed the bridge, thus being able to attack the dis-jointed armies severally. The Gauls encamped here; perhaps, also, Hannibal when he approached the Porta Collina. We are informed that Antemnæ was so called because it was "ante amnem posita," situated on the river.

Not to diverge too far from the main course of our journey, I shall here ask my readers to leave the Tiber for a little while to take a cursory view of the Anio, which at this spot empties itself into the larger stream. It is marked by a little island, round which the clear cool waters flow almost hidden in the thick bushes which clothe its banks.

Following its course a little way upwards, beyond the hill of Antemnæ is the Ponte Salarò, the ancient Pons Salarus, the tufa piers of which are probably of the earliest period of Roman construction—must, indeed, be coeval with the Via Salara which crosses it. Upon these piers the bridge was subsequently rebuilt by Narses, after having been partly destroyed by the Goths in the sixth century. The more ancient structure was the site of a memorable event in Roman history, before narrating which it is neces-sary to go back a little.

By one of the oldest laws of primitive Rome it was decreed that on the ides of September a nail should be annually driven by the supreme officer of the city into a certain part of the temple of Jupiter: a custom probably arising before the use of writing became general, for the purpose of marking the lapse of time. So important was this ceremony considered in after-times that a dictator was elected for the special purpose of fulfilling it. To this function one Lucius Manlius was appointed, in the year of Rome three hundred and ninety-two, who, extending the privileges of the office, sought to intermeddle with more weighty matters of state, assuming the generalship of the army, and enforcing large levies from the youth of the city with the greatest cruelty and severity. Of a violent temper and inordinate ambition, he took the name of Imperiosus,

and went so far as **to banish his own son** from **the city,**
who, though a youth of good solid power, had not the gift
of oratory—who was, in fact, a **man of** deeds not words,
as will presently appear.   For this **sole crime** his father
condemned him to follow a life of rustic labour, blunting by
his brutality whatever fine feelings the youth might have
possessed.   That he was gifted richly enough in this respect
the following circumstance will show.   For his misuse of
power **and** unnatural conduct towards his son, Manlius,
after having first provoked the people until a threatened
insurrection compelled him to lay down the dictatorship
before the proper term had expired, was arraigned before
the senate amidst much popular indignation by the tribune
of the commons, Marcus Pomponius.   When this **came to**
the ears of Titus the son of Manlius, furnishing himself **with**
a knife, he went to the house of the tribune, and professing
to have business of importance with him, **was** announced
into his presence and **all others** bidden to withdraw.   Approaching the couch **on which** Pomponius lay, **he** held the
knife over him and threatened to kill him on **the** spot if he
did not at once solemnly swear to abandon the prosecution
of his father, which he was accordingly obliged **to** do.
When **this** circumstance became reported abroad, as it
presently did, the accusation against his father was not
only allowed to drop, but Titus himself elected a tribune of
the soldiers without any other merit than his blunt, straight-
forward bravery and powerful physique, an office **which**
he fulfilled so well that he became afterwards dictator.

    Shortly after this the Gauls approached Rome, **encamp-**
ing just on the other side of the Salarian bridge **from the**
city, the Romans in a large army coming forth **to** meet
them.   **Both sides** strove to make themselves master **of**
the bridge, **and** several skirmishes **were fought** without
being decisive.   **At** last a Gaul of gigantic frame and
stature came forth and challenged the Romans to meet
him in single combat with the best man they had in the
army.   For some time no one answered the challenge ; but

after a while Titus Manlius offered to fight the Gallic
champion with the permission of the dictator. Being properly accoutred and stepping on to the bridge, both armies
stood by to watch the issue of the combat, the Gaul regarding Titus with the greatest contempt. After receiving
a tremendous blow on his armour from the sword of the
Gaul, Titus immediately closed with him, and after a short
struggle pierced him several times in the lower part of his
body, so that he died. When he was dead Titus did not
despoil or otherwise maltreat the corpse of his fallen foe,
as was usual, but simply removed from his neck a torc, or
ornament of twisted gold, which he fixed about his own ;
from which circumstance he subsequently obtained the
name of Torquatus, which remained as the surname of his
family always afterwards. So decisive was the death of
their leader considered, that the Gallic army decamped
hastily the same night, leaving the Romans to return unmolested to the city.

Somewhat farther up the stream is the Ponte Nomentano,
built by Narses to replace a more ancient one built by
Totila. It is covered with a picturesque castellated structure added in the eighth century, and subsequently modified. Near this bridge are the ruins of two large tombs of
unknown origin, and a little beyond a large mound or hill,
a spot particularly pointed out by Livy as the Mons Sacer,
or Sacred Hill of the ancient Romans, which obtained its
name in a memorable manner.

After the expulsion of the Tarquins from Rome the
condition of the people under the nobles became an oppressed and suffering one. Compelled to borrow money
from the patricians in order to till their land and prosecute
their business, after the drain on their purses and loss of
time caused by the subsequent wars, they were treated with
the utmost rigour and harshness in case of failure to meet
their engagements from whatever cause—so severely, indeed, as not only to be frequently cast into prison on the
hard fare of bread and water, but also they were liable to

be sold into slavery, or even to lose their lives; or, if there were several creditors, the body of the debtor might be hewn into pieces and distributed amongst them.

One day there appeared in the Forum an emaciated old man of squalid appearance, torn with stripes, clothed in rags and laden with chains. He lifted up his manacled hands and told the people the sad story of his woes. He told them how the enemy had destroyed his house and robbed him of his property, how he had been compelled to borrow money of one of the patricians, how misfortune had prevented him from repaying it, and how he had been cast into prison, scourged and laden with those chains. The appeal was an irresistible one; menacing murmurs arose amongst the people, the low thunders of a coming storm, and shortly afterwards, when Rome was invaded by the Volscian foe, the people in answer to the levy proclaimed by the consuls, one and all refused to be enrolled unless there was a suspension and alteration of the hard laws between debtor and creditor. On promises being made the people were induced to serve; but no sooner were the wars over than the promises were forgotten, matters remaining as they were before. Precisely the same thing took place again shortly afterwards, similar promises being made and as little regarded: but this time the issue was more decided. Whilst still under arms the people elected Junius Brutus and Sicinius Bellutus as their leaders and marched off to this hill, determined to set up a rival colony of their own away from the ancient city. In vain they were besought to return; the people, already too much deceived, would listen to no proposals. It was in this state of matters that an old man named Menenius addressed the people with the fable of the Belly and the Members. "It happened," he said, "in ancient times when each part of the body was endowed with language and a will of its own, that the various members of the body rebelled against the condition of the belly, which they said did no service for the commonwealth, but, having its needs all supplied,

was borne about and attended by the members without
rendering any benefit in return. Accordingly they conspired against it : the hands that they would not feed it,
the mouth that it would not receive its food, and the legs
that they would not bear it. Whilst thus attempting to
subdue the body, however, it was found that there was no
part of the state which did not suffer in consequence—that
the whole system, in fact, was reduced to emaciation and
sickness. It was thus found that the belly was by no means
useless ; and only on the members returning to their several
functions was the commonwealth restored to health and
happiness." Impressed with this fable, the application of
which to their own circumstances was obvious, at last they
agreed to return to Rome on obtaining certain terms ; as
that the debtors who could not pay should have their debts
cancelled, that those who had been enslaved on account of
their debts should be set at liberty, and that two of their
own body should be appointed to watch over their interests.

On the spot where this treaty was made an altar was
built to Jupiter, the Causer and Banisher of Fear ; since
the plebeians had retired thither in fear and returned in
safety. The place was called Mons Sacer, or the Sacred
Hill for ever afterwards, and the laws by which the people's
tribunate was secured were called Leges Sacratæ, the
Sacred Laws, which might be said to constitute the Magna
Charta of Rome.

Following the course of the stream still onwards is
Cervara, where there are immense tufa-quarries cut underground. These quarries are spoken of by Strabo. The
stone has been cut out, forming large chambers and halls,
square columns having been left here and there to support
the roof, with apertures at intervals to admit the light.
The creeping plants which hang through these apertures,
the long ranges of columns, the irregular distribution of the
chambers, and the mysterious gloom with which they are
pervaded, produce a singularly solemn and picturesque
effect. Their very stillness summons to the eye of fancy

hundreds of busy workmen occupied in removing the stone
—slaves under the cruel lash of the overseer falling at their
toil; the noise, the bustle, the activity, both within and
without, as the distant aqueduct crawls slowly, arch by
arch, to its destination, or the temple or palace grows up
day by day within the walls of the city. Not very distant
from the river on the right is the site of the classic city
of Collatia, an ancient Alban colony founded by Latinus
Silvius, where the virtuous Lucretia lived, and the tragical
occurrence took place which drove the Tarquins from
Rome and resulted in the establishment of a republic.
A little more removed from the river in the same direction
is the place where the ancient Volscian city Gabii stood,
the school of Romulus and Remus. Remains of the
temple of Juno mentioned by Virgil are still to be seen.
The lake was drained off some years ago. Farther on, a
somewhat turbid stream of a strong odour pours its waters
into the river. This flows from some sulphur springs
situated about a mile to the north of the stream. They
were the ancient Aquæ Albulæ, and are frequently mentioned by classical writers. They now consist for the most
part of shallow pools overgrown with reeds and rushes
encrusted by petrifactions. Some grey and broken walls
still stand, which once formed baths for the use of the
waters. They were frequented by Augustus and enlarged
by Zenobia. It was to this place that Virgil makes King
Latinus go in order to consult the oracle of Faunus, which
once stood here, concerning some prodigies which had occurred foretelling the coming of Æneas. "These prodigies,"
says Virgil, "disturbed the king, and so he goes to the
oracle of Faunus, his prophetic sire, and consults the
groves beneath high Albunea; which is the greatest of
woods, resounding with the murmur of its holy fountain,
and breathing forth from its dark shade a strong mephitic
exhalation." The grove from which "the nations of Italy
and all the land of Œnotria looked for responses when in
perplexity" is now no more to be seen: only the broken

ruin, the bubbling water springs, the wide Campagna and olive-covered mountains. Still, however, these waters are in use, and are considered to have valuable medicinal properties. Sir Humphry Davy found the waters to register a temperature of eighty degrees Fahrenheit; but I believe it is now nearly ten degrees lower. The water is surcharged with carbonic acid gas and contains sulphuretted hydrogen. It is dangerous to bathe too near the springs on a still morning, when the vapours rest upon the surface. During a summer which I once spent with some friends at Tivoli, we often used to go for a bath, and found the waters highly refreshing and renovating. Here we met cardinals from Rome, and other persons who had driven twelve miles across the dusty Campagna for the purpose of making use of the waters. The baths were nothing but a few wooden sheds temporarily fixed. As in the old Roman days, sometimes the gossip of the day was talked over, archæological and other discussions following, in which we all freely joined, taking advantage of the frank Italian courtesy. But oh, the hot drive along the plain under the mountains on our return, when the sun had well risen! No words can describe the oven-like heat as we crawled up the steep Sabine slopes to the more airy heights upon which stands the temple of Tivoli, glad to hide ourselves at noon in the friendly shelter of our little inn.

Farther on to the right are the wonderful ruins of the Villa of Hadrian. It stands at the foot of the Sabine mountains. Its extent seems perfectly interminable. Some antiquaries consider it to have occupied a space several miles in circumference. In addition to its palatial halls, it embraced theatres, baths, temples, barracks, and vast extents of pleasure ground. Some of the most beautiful of ancient marbles were found amongst its ruins, probably including that of the celebrated Venus de' Medici. Its enormous walls, many of them left in good preservation, its forlorn appearance, its growth of rank vegetation, the numerous large cypresses which have grown about it, its general look of desertion—so much grandeur, so much magnificence, made the prey of decay and oblivion—make it one of the most touching and impressive mementoes of ancient times.

Following the hurrying stream through many a fairily-fringed vale, by many a mossy bank and glimmering nook of hazel and fern, through groves of olive and spreading vineyards, we at last reach the abrupt heights from which it falls, surmounted by the quaint and picturesque town of Tivoli.

Tivoli (called by Ovid, Tiburis udi, *watery* Tivoli), as every one knows who has visited the classic lands of Italy, was the ancient Tibur, the favourite retreat of the Romans during the hot weather. Hither Augustus retired from the toils of state, here Horace wrote some of his best verses, Catullus and Propertius sung its praises, the wealthy Mæcenas had his seat, and many noble and illustrious Romans their villas or summer residences here. According to Dionysius the primitive town was founded by the Siculi, and was called Catilium after a hero of the times of Evander. "You can plant no tree," says Horace to his friend Varus, "preferable to the sacred vine about the genial soil of Tibur and walls of Catilium."* It is first noticed in history as being the place to which Marcus Claudius, claimant, as the instrument of Appius, of the unfortunate Virginia, was banished. It was subsequently implicated in the Gallic invasion of Rome; and after the defeat of the Gauls at the Porta Collina they fled into Tibur for refuge. The Tiburtines afterwards joined the Latin League against the Romans; but were finally sub-dued by the consul Lucius Furius Camillus in the year three hundred and thirty-five before Christ. They were, however, denied the privileges of Roman citizenship, for having taken part against Rome with the Gauls.

* Nullam, Vare, sacra vite prius severis arborem,
    Circa mite solum Tiburis et mœnia Catili. O. I. 18.

An amusing story is told by Livy and Ovid in connection with Tibur, which happened in the year three
hundred and ten before Christ. The Pipers, who constituted a considerable and important body at Rome,
whose services were deemed requisite at every ceremonial
and festival as well as at celebrations of religious worship,
being curtailed, both in number and in their traditional
privileges, by the ædile of that time, went over in a body
to Tibur. In vain they were entreated to return, until a
certain freedman made them a great feast at his farm in
the country, taking care that they should eat and drink
abundantly. At night closed carts were provided, in order,
as they thought, to take them home. Instead of this, they
were driven to Rome, and on awakening in the morning
found themselves in the Forum. In order to avoid the
ridicule of the people, they caused themselves to be disguised in white garments; a dress which they retained
always afterwards, their privileges being re-established.

Tibur was famous for the worship of Hercules. Nibby
believes the vast structure now in ruins, known by the
name of the Villa of Mæcenas, to have been a temple of
that god. Syphax, the king of Numidia, after being
captured by Scipio at the battle of Massinissa, died here.
Here, too, Zenobia, the queen of the East, who united some
of the finest qualities of the general and the scholar, after
her long and valiant resistance to the arms of Aurelian,
ended her days. Strabo says that the Anio was at one
time navigable from Tivoli to the Tiber. It is so no
longer, I believe, even for small boats.

There are still remains of ancient villas left near the bed
of the Anio, where some mosaic floors and broken walls
have been discovered. It is not now considered the
healthiest of localities, owing to its dampness and sudden
changes of the weather, as embodied in the modern rhyme:

> Tivoli di mal conforto,
> O piove, o tira vento, o suona amorto.

(Tivoli of ill comfort—for it either rains, or the wind blows, or the death-bell sounds). It must have obtained this character pretty early; for it is thus mentioned in one of the epigrams of Martial: "Let us in the summer solstice," he says, "retire to Ardea and the country about Pæstum, and to the tract which burns under the Cleonæan constellation; since Curiatius has condemned the air of Tivoli, carried off as he was to the Styx notwithstanding its much-lauded waters. From no place can you shut out fate: when death comes, Sardinia is in the midst of Tivoli itself."*

TIVOLI.

If I might be permitted here to indulge a moment's personal recollection, I would recur to many happy hours

* Ardea solstitio, Castranaque rura petantur,
    Quique Cleonæo sidere fervet ager;
Cum Tiburtinas damnet Curiatius auras,
    Inter laudatas ad Styga missus aquas.
Nullo fata loco possis excludere : cum mors
    Venerit, in medio Tibure Sardinia est.   B. IV. ep. 60.

spent in these delightful shades in the quiet occupation of
my pencil, when the morning mist still lay like a thin veil
on the Campagna, and the lark was loud in the sky, and
shrill cicalas were vocal from many trees.   No words can
express the tenderness and sweetness of these delightful
seasons.   Through vistas of grey olives the vast plain of
the Campagna was seen to stretch away, streaked with
thread-like roads and dim lines of recurrent aqueducts,
spotted with groves of trees and towered mediæval for-
tress-farms, with a little white dwelling here and there,
and, perhaps, a trail of thin, blue smoke curling gradually
into nothingness.   Almost twenty miles away the dome of
St. Peter's, clearly distinguishable in all its outline, though
every other trace of Rome was lost in distance, stood like
the sentinel of this beautiful land ; at the farthest horizon
some faint, faint lines marking the region of far-off mountains.   But if the distant prospect was lovely, not less so
was that immediately surrounding.   A neighbouring fountain, at a turn of the road, which ran by, springing from a
dim, cool grotto half buried in ferns and straggling trailers,
gave refreshment to groups of picturesquely-dressed way-
farers and their well-laden beasts of burden, the travellers
themselves gossiping gaily or singing loudly, inspired with
the delightful season.   Beneath the trees a shepherd
watched his flock, the sheep cropping the nutritious herbage
with now and then a bleat of satisfaction, whilst a tinkling
bell borne by one of them mixed its pleasant ringing with
the rural voices that filled the air, and the gentle murmur
of falling waters.   In a deep ravine at the foot of these
olive-slopes the Anio wound, half hidden in velvet sward
and fringe-like foliage that bordered its course, beyond
which rose terraced gardens and vineyards, crowned by the
romantic buildings of Tivoli, with its frowning castle in
the background, and the round columned temple of the
Sibyl overhanging an abrupt cliff, which has furnished the
subject of so many pictures.   From this steep were poured
down the waters of the "headlong Anio" in many a

whitened wreath, falling slowly, with silvery band on band,
and then distributing themselves in **airy** clouds **of dia**-
phanous vapour : whilst, above it **all, a** sky of amethyst
blue formed a fitting dome to this gorgeous temple of
Nature, every court **and** chamber of which was redolent
with the odorous incense of the morning.

I will detain **the** reader yet a little longer in this fairy-
land of enchantment to take him into the quaint gardens
of the Villa d'Este, that stands on one of those heights ;
for assuredly he will be glad to linger a few moments
within its guardian walls, with their grey old gateways
grown with moss and lichen. It occupies a midway region
between nature and art ; for here Nature, as if jealous of
the interference of man where her own work is so beautiful,
is quick to take back to herself anything of which he may
once have had possession. One might imagine that the
sylvan and the faun had not yet deserted its still ilex-
shades and dilapidated grottos hung with long fronds of
hartstongue **and** delicate maidenhair—that daintily-shaped
dryads might still slip the bark, and flit stealthily between
those ancient boles ; or the glittering naiad, abandoning the
cool depths, sometimes sit sunning herself on the brink of
one of those broken basins dribbling lazy jets of crystal
water, wreathing her moist hair with flowers, and crooning
old-fashioned songs in a soft undertone—nay, even if
tawny-skinned, goat-footed old Pan, with his lofty eye-
brows and shaggy flanks, should be found seated at the
foot of some twisted **root,** piping a rustic melody, it would
scarcely **seem a** matter of surprise ; so congenial **with**
every old-world association does the spot appear. **From**
crumbling terraces mighty cypresses, with split and wrinkled
boles, shoot up thick pillars of gloom, abundant fountains
tossing their silvery columns at their foot. Here the lizard
sleeps all the day, or runs about nimbly in the sun. Tall
clipt hedges enclose plots **of** rank grass and beds of
rampant flowers ; roses reach forth their neglected sweets
with straggling hands ; violets and lilies have offered their

lips in vain, and are now tired of blooming unnoticed and uncared for: only the throstle and the blackbird and the warbling nightingale enliven the solitude, glad to be alone in the sweet hours of morning and eventide.

I might here tell how the beautiful Anio follows the intricate regions of the Sabine mountains, under the cliffs of the picturesque convent of St. Cosimato, through the open fields of Spiaggia, furnishing water supplies to romantically situated towns and villages perched on eyrie-like fastnesses of crag and rock; how graceful and lovely maidens come down from these, bearing chastely-shaped water-vessels on their heads, whilst the older dames, with spool and distaff, stand spinning and gossiping together; how the river winds and wanders until it reaches the wonderful little town of Subiaco, the ancient Sublaqueum, with its quaint towered bridge, its crowning citadel, its narrow crowded streets, its rumbling mills, its sombre arched passages, its curious nooks and corners all dim and grey and fitted to the artist's pencil, with here and there a pious picture and glimmering lamp burning before it; but it would lead us too far out of our way to do more than mention the pleasant regions of this romantic country, with its fresh scenes of beauty at every turn; the olive-groves and vineyards, the wayside shrines garlanded with wreaths and decorated with flowers; the wondrous church of St. Benedict built against the rock, where was the cave he once inhabited, within which the softened light falls between descending arches upon the groups of saints and angels which adorn the spandrils; these we must leave, and let the stream wander at will amongst the blue mountains from its source in the Abruzzi; for our space does not permit us to linger too long in these secluded fastnesses of Nature, where existence itself might well be lost to the outer world in a perpetual dream of beauty and self-contented indolence.

As we again pursue our way along the Tiber from the point where the Anio falls into it, a wide plain extends itself on either hand, through which the river winds and wanders. This plain has been the **scene of a hundred** fights. Over and over again it **has** been deluged with blood in both ancient and modern times. No doubt many an unrecorded struggle has taken place upon it which the pages of history will never know. It is bounded on the left by a not very lofty but abrupt range of rocks called the Saxa Rubra, well sculptured by time, and tinted with **many-coloured** lichens. As we pass along the river, a hollow cave may be seen cut into the face of the escarpment which has a deep interest, in that it has been supposed, with every probability, to have been the burial-place of the family of Ovid **the Latin** poet. It was discovered in sixteen hundred and seventy-four, then covered with elegant paintings, symbolizing the reception of the poet in the spirit-land, with other relevant pictures, as also inscriptions **to** Quintus Ambrosius Naso, his wife and freedmen. **They** have all long since vanished ; **but** the designs of them have been preserved in the drawings and engravings of Santi Bartoli. From these indications it has been inferred that **this** was the burial-place, if not of the poet himself, at **least of his** family and descendants.

Whilst contemplating this tomb, it is melancholy to turn to the poet's long and weary banishment, with the complaints of which his elegies and epistles are so loaded, and **recall** his words as he was perhaps thinking of this dim **cave.** "Shall I then depart," he writes to his wife by the hand of another, "so far away in unknown regions, and will death be embittered by the very spot? Will my body not waste away on my wonted couch? Will there be **no** one to lament my sepulture? And will not a few moments be added to my life as the tears of my wife fall upon my **face**? and shall I give no last injunction? and shall no friendly hand close my failing eyes amid the sobs attending my last moments ; but shall barbarian earth cover this head, unlamented, without funeral rites and **without the honour of a tomb?** . . . Oh, that my soul **would** perish with my body, and that no part of me would escape the consuming pile! For if my immortal spirit soars aloft into the vacant air, and the words of the Samian sage are true, a Roman shade will be wandering amid Sarmatian ghosts, and will ever be a stranger amid uncivilized spirits."[*]

This sad letter concludes with the request that when he is dead his ashes may be taken back in an urn mixed with leaves and powdered amomum, and laid in the ground near the city, with an inscription (though he says his most enduring memorial must be his works) telling who it is that lies there, and calling upon the passer-by for a prayer that he may be allowed to rest in peace.

Beneath these cliffs runs the Via Flaminia, going from Rome in a northerly direction, crossing the Cremera, and passing Prima Porta in the way towards Florence. Many a sturdy fight have these grim rocks witnessed, many a heart has beat thick and fast under their solemn shade, many a dying eye has grown dim with the film of death as it gazed on their stern fronts, unchanged through all the slaughter; many a weeping mother has passed underneath their lowering brows, her heart filled with tears for her life's companion slain; many a newly-made orphan sat at their foot in sadness and desolation. To describe all the known scenes of which they have been the unmoved spectators would fill a volume: let it be enough to give one here, not the least important.

In the early part of the fourth century, the rule of the Roman empire was divided between Constantine and Maxentius; the former holding the Italian, and the latter the transalpine territory. Whilst Constantine fulfilled the duties of a responsible office with tact and vigour, Maxentius, who remained in Italy, gave himself up to the abuse of power and the worst passions of humanity. Selfish, indolent, and unjust, he sought but to support and enlarge a vicious soldiery at the expense of the best and noblest people and sentiments of the state, and last of all, plotted

---

[*] B. iii. el. 3.

to overthrow his coadjutor, **in order to take the reins of full
power** into his own hands. The honest and **fine-spirited**
Constantine, nevertheless, disregarded **as long** as **possible**
every attempt to bring **about a contest ; but finally, com-**
pelled to act, seconded **by the earnest request of the**
Roman **people that he would** help them **to** get **rid of** a
mean and contemptible **tyrant, he** mustered all his available
troops, passing the Alps to meet an enemy whose numerical
force was four times greater than his own. Enervated, **however,** by supineness and the luxuries of southern life, the supe-
rior number of the Italian army did not avail them ; for the
vigorous and active Constantine, after a succession of signal
victories in north Italy, marched rapidly towards Rome **and**
met the army of Maxentius encamped **on the level plain**
stretching from these rocky cliffs (themselves **of an ominous**
red) to the river, distant from half a mile to **a mile from**
their base. Constantine disposed his troops **that the enemy**
might have the river in his rear, himself taking **a prominent**
lead, charging the foe with **his heavy** Gallic **cavalry. The**
defeat of the Maxentian army **was** complete, **in spite of the
bravery of the** prætorians, who perished **to a man** where
they first stood. The army **fled in** wild confusion, driven
by thousands into the Tiber, **whilst** Maxentius himself, attempting to regain the city by the Milvian bridge, was thrust
into the stream in the struggle, and drowned in its waters.

Visitors to the Vatican will recollect the spirited representation of this battle given in Raphael's fine design on **the**
walls of the Stanze. **He** has, however, with the permissible
latitude of art, chosen for the **scene** of the battle **the neigh-**
bourhood **of the** Milvian bridge, three miles **from the spot**
where **it** actually occurred. It **also finds a sculptured**
record on **the arch** of **Constantine near the Coliseum, which**
was built to commemorate **this event.**

On the heights **stretching along the Via** Salara as it
approaches Castel Giubileo, **is a** desolate-looking residence,
called the Villa **Spada. This** is supposed **to** occupy the
site of **the villa of Phaon,** freedman **of Nero** the emperor,

M

who here killed himself. The story of his latter days is told with close circumstantiality by Dion Cassius. After he had enacted every vice and all manner of folly, a Gaul, named Caius Julius Vindex, descended from a royal family, whose father was of the order of senators, got up and denounced him publicly. Nero set a reward of twenty-five millions of drachmas on his head. "I will give my own head," said Vindex, "as a reward to him that shall bring me that of Nero." Vindex shortly afterwards, misunderstanding his colleague Rufus, destroyed himself. Rufus, however, carried out the revolution. At first Nero pretended to despise the movement ; but when he learned that Galba was proclaimed emperor, he was seized with a panic, and then formed a resolution to destroy the senate, set fire to Rome, and retire to Alexandria, saying that he would live there by the practice of music, in which he believed himself to be a proficient ; but when he was deserted by his guards, he disguised himself, mounting a sorry horse, following the Via Salara. Finding, however, that he was known and saluted on the high road, he dismounted, hiding himself amongst the canes and reeds, where the least sound terrified him. Taking refuge in a cave, he was compelled to make a meal of bread and water for the first time in his life. "Is this the delicious drink I was wont to have ?" he asked himself scornfully. In the meantime tidings had reached Rome of his place of concealment. When he heard the approach of the horsemen sent to seek him, he implored the three freedmen who were his sole attendants to kill him, which, when they refused to do, he said, sighing, that he was the only man in the world who had neither friend nor enemy. As the horsemen approached, he thrust his sword into his body, saying, "Gods ! what a master dies to-day." He was the last of the race of emperors who claimed descent from the line of Æneas through Augustus.

A little beyond the Villa Spada, and about five miles from Rome, between the river and the Via Salara, is seen

the somewhat abrupt acclivity of Castel Giubileo, the site
of the ancient Fidenæ ; the "urbs alta et munita"—lofty and
fortified city—of Livy, a bold headland rising from the level
of the plain, its steep side presented to the river.   It obtained its present name from the house on its summit,
which was built in a jubilee year.   Formerly the river, now
some distance from its base (swift and vertiginous still, as
described by Dionysius), may have ran immediately beneath
it.   It would then have been a formidable place of defence,
which might partly account for the success with which it
held out against the more powerful Romans.   On the side
from the river, it gradually slopes down until it joins a
range of hills rising on the north-west, consisting of volcanic
tufa, honeycombed with the tombs of the ancient city.
Some of these remain tolerably perfect, with niches for the
lamps and urns, and seats cut out of the rock.   Whatever
sculptures may have existed on the face of the rock outside
of the tombs have quite vanished.   These tombs have all
the evidences of Etruscan origin.   The city, when at its
largest, must not only have covered the sloping headland
above described, but also have been extended from the
lower part of the promontory to the adjacent range excavated with tombs.   These cliffs would also offer a strong
position in warfare.   Probably the vulnerable point would
be that lying between the two hills, from which its defeats
for the most part may have been accomplished ; although
in the case of its being undermined, as mentioned by Livy,
he tells us that the mine was carried into the arx or citadel,
which might be supposed to have occupied the highest and
steepest part of the promontory.   Nibby, however, thinks
that the arx was placed on the longer range of hills
removed from the river.   The same writer assigns the
fragments of marble and other remains found betwixt
the Villa Spada and this place rather to edifices of
the latter empire, than the primitive Fidenæ.   He even
thinks it probable that some large stones found here may
have formed a part of the walls.

M 2

The history of this city is an eventful one. In giving a sketch of its more noteworthy events, it will be necessary to begin with an old story.

In the early days of regal Rome, Tullus Hostilius was placed upon the throne by election of the people, who confirmed himself in their good graces by abandoning the royal prerogative of certain lands in their favour, with other acts of grace. At that time Rome was growing in splendour and power; so much so, as to fall under the envy of the neighbouring states and towns. Amongst these was Alba Longa, standing by a volcanic lake on an eminence of the mountains to which it gave the name, about fifteen miles from Rome, under the government of a certain Cluilius, who was also possessed of a sentiment of envy towards the sister city, both Rome and Alba being said to own a common ancestry from the Alban kings of Lavinium, descended from Æneas. Not daring to attack Rome without some pretext, Cluilius incited the Albans to petty thefts and pillagings on the Roman territory, thinking by this means to bring himself in contact with the Romans, and accomplish his warlike intentions with a better grace. The Romans, irritated by these marauders, at last made an incursion into the Alban territory, slaying some, and taking others prisoners. This was just what Cluilius wished. He assembled his countrymen, inveighing against the Romans bitterly, requiring that ambassadors should be sent to Rome to demand satisfaction; which was accordingly done. As the two nations were nominally allies according to a treaty entered into in the days of Romulus, by which either city was to sue for justice of its colleague in case of wrong, and war was not to be commenced unless this was refused, neither wished first to break the compact subsisting between them. So when the ambassadors arrived in Rome, Tullus Hostilius caused them to be entertained sumptuously until the following day, but without seeing them; in the meantime sending other, Roman, ambassadors to the Albans, to demand a similar satisfaction from them, in order that the Romans should not be the first called upon to make reparation. On the former stating their ambassage, they were refused on the ground that already their embassy had been anticipated. When they returned to Rome, Tullus summoned the Albans, and informed them of his stratagem, telling them that as he had already been refused reparation at their hands, he declared a just and necessary war against them.

So the two armies were drawn up against each other, and a goodly array they would seem to have presented, since each hesitated to make the attack, even until the warmth of the animosity between them began to diminish. Cluilius at last resolved upon action, but the night before the proposed encounter, was found dead in his tent, apparently from natural causes. In his stead was appointed Mettus Fufetius, accused by the historians of tardiness and incompetency. However that might be, he proposed an armistice, submitting that instead of risking the safety of the two states by a devouring warfare, they should rather appoint certain individuals to fight out the quarrel, and decide by personal combat which of them should rule the other, imforming them that already the Fidenates and Veientes, who under the reign of Numa had pretty well recovered their former reverses, had entered into a secret alliance to break off the Roman yoke by waiting for the day of battle, with the intention of rushing in on its termination, and treating both victor and vanquished as common enemies ; in proof of which he caused letters from his friends in Fidenæ to be read, the contents of which were confirmed by the messenger who bore them. The Romans were, therefore, not unwilling to accede to the proposition of Mettus. But now, whilst every person wished to thrust himself forward as eligible for so honourable an undertaking, arose the question as to who should be entrusted with an enterprise of so momentous an issue. Proposal after proposal was made and discarded ; but circumstances at last decided what counsel and consideration had failed to effect.

In the city of Alba there was a man named Sicinius, father of twin daughters who had been married, the one to an Alban, the other to a Roman. These daughters had each brought into the world three male children at the first birth, who grew up, gifted in beauty and strength, and magnanimity of mind. These were thought to be pointed out by the gods as fit champions for the national supremacy. It is true, that at first there were objections raised on the score of consanguinity, but these were speedily overruled by the youths themselves, who professed themselves willing to forget everything else in the honour and prosperity of their respective countries, without any desire to excuse themselves from the combat. Accordingly, they were placed face to face in front of the two armies, which were drawn up to witness the combat on the confines of the two states. It was a touching sight to see these young men, relatives, with warm and friendly feeling to each other, come to the contest, arrayed in the panoplies of war, but each bearing withal the insignia of death upon him, as if he expected to come out of it no more alive. It was a still more saddening sight when they threw themselves with tears and strong expressions of tenderness into each other's arms, protesting against the hardness of fate that compelled them to stand before each other as enemies. A dead silence prevailed when they first began to fight, but presently the excitement of the contest burst forth ; both armies loudly cheering and inciting the combatants, till the enthusiasm knew no bounds. Long was the strife doubtful ; until, at last, the eldest of the Albans, after giving and receiving many wounds, ran his adversary through the body and killed him. But too soon rose the mighty shout from the Albans, who now considered the victory certain, for one of the Roman brothers fighting near him immediately disengaged himself, and attacking the successful champion, vehemently plunged his sword in his throat, so

that he also died.   This death was again avenged instantly
upon the Roman, who however, before he was slain, ham-
strung the Alban, who, though considerably disabled, yet
managed to rally, in order to assist his remaining brother
against the last of the Roman trio.   The latter now seeing
himself liable to be overpowered, conceived the stratagem
of flight ; and when he had by this means separated his
adversaries, the one already lamed not being able to keep
up with the other, and whilst the whole Roman army was
hooting him as a coward, and the Albans already crowning
themselves with bays, turned round suddenly, first slaying
the foremost one, and then putting an end to his companion.
Thus the field remained to the last of the Roman combatants, who, taking the tokens of victory, hastened to the
city, with the filial sentiments of his time and country, to
convey the joyful intelligence to his father.

Now, as he entered the gates of the city, amongst the
crowds pressing out anxious for news of the contest, he was
much surprised to meet his own sister, who, unattended and
in dishabille, had so far forgotten appearances as to have
set aside those rules which were something more than
matters of etiquette to the Roman maiden.   Willing, however, to put the best construction upon her appearance, he
naturally concluded that anxiety for her brothers' welfare
had brought her out thus inconsiderately.   But there were
other reasons than this.   Unknown to her brother and the
world, she had been already affianced to one of the Alban
youths, and hearing the result of the conflict, had rushed
out of the house despite of all efforts to detain her.   Meeting
her brother, crowned with garlands of victory, and bearing
the spoils of the slain, amongst which was an embroidered
garment which she herself had worked for her lover—perhaps he had worn it tenderly to his heart for that very
reason—all stained with blood ; with many lamentations
she upbraided him in the bitterest terms, asking him of
what wild beast he had the heart, beating her breast, and
tearing her hair violently.   He in his turn replied with the

greatest indignation, that she was not worthy of her name or country, thus to dishonour both, and drawing his sword, pierced her through the body, bidding her go and rejoin her departed lover.

And herein comes out the sturdy stuff of which the old Roman character was made. When the father heard of it, so far was he from disapproving of what had been done, that he would not allow her to be brought to the family tomb, or any funeral ceremony to be used over her ; and, indeed, refused to take any part in her burial at all ; so that the passers-by were fain to cover her with earth and stones where she lay. The same day this iron-hearted father partook of the festivities and rejoicing as though he had no concern whatever with the tragical events that had brought them about.

At that time murder in Rome, especially domestic murder, was most severely punished ; for the murderer was outlawed by the act ; so that he might be put to death without trial. Horatius was brought before the king on the capital charge. But whilst the latter, sorely puzzled, knew not whether to acquit or condemn him, the father came forward, protesting against his accusation, and saying, as the father of both, he had a right to be heard. Tullus, however, not willing to have the responsibility of decision, committed the question to the votes of the people, who acquitted Horatius of murder. The king, nevertheless, scarcely satisfied with this inquisition for blood, caused him to undergo various purifying ceremonies ; the last of which was that he should pass under the yoke (a transverse beam laid across two perpendicular ones) beneath which captives were led, in order to obtain manumission. The one beneath which Horatius passed stood long afterwards, stretched above the altars of one of the streets of Rome, an object of reverence to the citizens, henceforward called Sororium Tigillum, or the Sister's Beam.

No sooner had the Romans consolidated, as they thought, their new union with the Albans, than they declared war a

second time against the Fidenates, in order to **punish them**
for their intrigue. The latter, having obtained **the assist-**
ance of the Veientes, put themselves in **open revolt and**
retired to their city, together with the allied troops. The
king of Rome placing the utmost confidence in the Alban
general, communicated to him all his designs. Fufetius,
however, growing jealous of Roman rule, formed a secret
conspiracy with the Fidenates, promising to turn round on
the Roman army as soon as fortune should favour his
designs. Tullus crossed the Anio, and placed himself on
the plain lying on the southern side of Fidenæ, with the
intention of going to battle the following morning. Fufetius
in the meantime summoned the chief men of the Alban
army, explaining his plans and inciting them to get **rid of**
the Roman yoke. The next day at sunrise the Fidenates
left their camp and ranged themselves **out** for battle.
Tullus also crossed the Anio, and disposing his troops **near**
the banks of the Tiber, stood opposed to the Veientes ;
the Albans facing the Fidenates, away from **the river, at**
the foot of the hills trending towards Fidenæ. **As** the two
armies approached, the Albans, separating themselves from
the Romans, began to ascend **the** heights, thus leaving the
right wing of the latter uncovered and exposing them to
great slaughter. At this moment a horseman rode up,
informing Tullus of the real state of matters. With great
presence of mind he immediately ordered the cavalry **to**
elevate their spears ; by this means concealing the retreat
of the allies from a great proportion of his army ; **calling**
out in a loud voice, that they were taking up that **position**
by his orders so that they might reach **the enemy's rear.**
This being **heard by the** Fidenates, **it caused them to**
misdoubt **the** intention of Fufetius, and giving **way to the**
redoubled efforts of the Romans, they **at** last fled in
confusion into their city. **The following winter** they were
reduced to their **former condition of** dependence after
having been besieged **by** Tullus **and at** last compelled to
submit **to his own terms.** To end the story, Fufetius was

first beaten with many stripes, and afterwards drawn asunder by horses; and Alba finally levelled to the ground, its inhabitants being driven for shelter into Rome.

Without noticing the minor encounters between the Fidenates and the Romans, the next important one was during the consulate of Publius Valerius, surnamed Popli-cola, and Titus Lucretius, in the year four hundred and ninety-six before Christ, when the Sabines made war upon Rome at the instigation of Sextus, son of Tarquinius, allying the Fidenates. There were two camps formed, one in the open field not far from Fidenæ, and the other within the city; the latter both for a guard to the city and a reserve for those without. The Romans marched out to meet them, intending to bring matters to an immediate engagement. The Sabines, on the contrary, fearing the unflinching boldness of the Roman troops, prepared for the surprise of a night attack, rather than face them in the open field. An ambuscade was laid, and everything put in readiness for carrying out this plan, when a deserter from the Sabine camp gave intimation of all that had been done, which was confirmed by some prisoners taken while getting wood. A little before midnight the Sabine general crept stealthily to the Roman camp, shrouded in silence and the darkness of the night, and seeing no lights nor other indications of wakefulness, concluded that the enemy was steeped in slumber, oblivious of danger. Filling up the trenches with the fascines they had prepared, they passed over unopposed, but immediately on entering the camp they were attacked and killed by the Romans who were lying in wait for them. At that moment the moon arose showing the Sabines heaps of their slain companions and their own danger. A great shout was raised by the Romans. In a moment the camps of both generals were in motion, fully armed. On that night there fell of the Sabines and their allies thirteen thousand, four thousand two hundred being made prisoners. In a few days the city of Fidenæ was taken. The principal persons being punished, but the city left to a great extent unmolested, only receiving a garrison of Roman soldiers within it to keep it in subjection.

The last act remains to be told in the changeful history of the city. In the year three hundred and sixteen of Rome, or four hundred and thirty-eight before the Christian era, Fidenæ again rebelled against Roman dominion, placing itself under that of Veii, and, what was worse, by the order of Lars Tolumnus, king of Veii, slew four Roman ambassadors sent to inquire into their disaffection. This was at once cause for war. The Fidenates were not only supported in this struggle by the Veientes, but also were further strengthened by the Falisci, an Etruscan people belonging to a district higher up the river. The two former hoped rather by protracting the war to harass and gain an advantage over the Roman troops, but the Falisci, on the contrary, being some distance from their homes, wished to give battle at once and decide the contest. This Lars concluded to do, and sending a party of Veientes, who were the most numerous of the forces, to attack the rear of the Romans during the heat of battle, at once prepared for the engagement. The Fidenates were placed in the centre, the two allies respectively occupying the lateral wings. For a while all was silent, the Romans awaiting the issue of some auguries before the onset. Presently a loud shout was raised. The armies met with clashing weapons; but everywhere the Romans had the advantage. Lars himself behaved valiantly. Again and again he rallied his cavalry, rushing into the thick of the fight, dealing slaughter on every hand; even when the allied army was giving back from the shock of Roman arms. Whilst matters were in this condition, one Aulus Cornelius Cossus, a tribune of the Roman soldiers, seeing the Roman army driven back by the charge of the Veientine king, whom he recognised by his royal apparel as he flew along the lines of his troops inciting them to action, rode forwards, exclaiming, "Is this the traitor to treaties, and rebel to the law of nations? As a victim he shall now be slain (if the gods desire anything to be kept sacred), a sacrifice to the manes of the murdered ambassadors." Thus saying, he rode at him furiously with level lance, and throwing him upon the ground as he attempted to rise, flung him back with his shield; finally pinning him a corpse to the earth, taking his spoils, decapitating him, and placing his head upon the point of his spear. By this bloody token the whole allied army knew it was beaten, and fled panic-stricken on every side; the Fidenates making the most successful retreat from their knowledge of the country; the Romans, after pursuing them to their intrenchments, crossing the Tiber and returning to their city with much booty from the surrounding territory.

A great triumph was the reward of Cossus, in which he bore the spoils of the slain king, followed by the soldiers, who extolled him in unmeasured verse as being equal with Romulus. These spoils he carried to the temple of Jupiter Feretrius. So much was he praised and honoured that all eyes were drawn from the dictatorial carriage even, and none shared with him the popularity of that day.

The Romans did not immediately follow up their victory, as the surrounding country was devastated by a severe pestilence; but the Fidenates, taking advantage of the lull of hostilities, descended upon the Roman territory, committing great depredations, and being again joined by the Veientes (the Falisci could not be induced to take part in the struggle any more), approached the walls of Rome. The Romans were, however, quickly under arms, and not only repulsed them from the city, but followed them almost to Nomentum, where a great battle was fought, the Romans being victorious as before. The Fidenates took refuge within their city, which, being loftily situated, well fortified and supplied with an abundance of provision, could neither be taken by assault nor blockade. Upon this the Romans determined upon carrying a mine into the citadel. Distracting the people by feints and skirmishes, they were able finally to accomplish their object, emerging into their stronghold, and then making themselves masters of the city.

Fidenæ had scarcely kept truce with Rome ten years after this defeat when it was reported that some Fidenatan youths had joined the Veientes in a marauding party on the Roman territory. Again, however, collision was avoided for the time being in consequence of a severe drought, followed by a dreadful plague in which men and animals suffered alike. Heralds were afterwards sent to Veii and restitution demanded, but in vain. War was declared against Veii, and in an engagement that ensued the Romans were worsted. Dispirited by their defeat, the Romans re-entered their city amidst general mourning, whilst the Veientes sent round to the neighbouring states inviting them to unite in the contest with Rome. The only one, however, which listened to this proposal was Fidenæ. Slaying the Roman settlers who had taken up their abode within their city, they at once allied themselves with the Veientes and prepared for renewed hostilities. It was deliberated which would be the most eligible seat of war, Veii or Fidenæ. At last it was concluded to carry it to the latter place; and once more this fertile plain was destined to be covered with blood for dew and the bodies of slain men for the fruits of the earth.

The Roman camp was pitched at a distance of fifteen hundred paces from Fidenæ, on the Roman side, with a range of hills rising on the right and the Tiber on the left. Mamercus Æmilius was dictator and Aulus Cossus master of the horse. The engagement began. The Roman legions fought impetuously, furiously, calling their enemies murderers, traitors, and truce breakers, bad both as friends and enemies.

From the very first the Romans had the advantage, and pressed their opponents even to the gates of their city. But here the surprise of a new and unusual mode of warfare awaited them. No sooner had the Romans gained the entrance into the city than they were met by a vast multitude of persons rushing out of the gateway, bearing blazing torches and firebrands, who, with wild cries, rushed amongst them, dismaying them with flames of fire and the most furious and frantic gestures and behaviour. At first the Romans were beaten back; but Quintius Pennus, military tribune, rushed forward calling on them to dash out the brands with their weapons, or seize them and burn the city with their own flames, remembering their names and wrongs as Romans. The firebrands were seized, upon which the warfare was redoubled, as the dictator took off the bridle from his horse, bidding his troops do the same, and setting spurs to its flanks determined either to be a conqueror or to perish. The cavalry under his command followed his example, rushing hither and thither and distributing slaughter on every side; leaving their traces marked by the dead and wounded wherever they passed. The Roman reserves had already attacked the enemy in the rear. Thus surrounded, the whole battle became enveloped in smoke and dust. A universal slaughter ensued. The Veientes rushed precipitately to the river, across which their own city lay, where most of them perished, either slain on its banks or else borne down in the water by the weight of their armour. Hotly pursued to the gates, the Fidenates were no longer able to exclude the enemy. The city was entered and pillaged, the inhabitants being carried to Rome and sold as slaves: thus closing the history of Fidenæ as an independent state and people.

Henceforward it fell into decay. It is mentioned by Cicero, Horace, Strabo, and Juvenal, as being a place of insignificant importance in their days, yet it always maintained a municipality. In the reign of Tiberius it was the seat of a disastrous calamity thus related by the historian Tacitus :—

"A sudden calamity occurred in the consulship of Marcus Licinius and Lucius Calpurnius, which equalled the havoc of the most destructive wars; its beginning and end were

simultaneous. One Atilius had undertaken to erect an
amphitheatre at Fidenæ, there to exhibit a combat of
gladiators : he was of the race of freedmen, and as he
engaged in the business from no exuberance of wealth,
nor to acquire popularity amongst the inhabitants, but as
a matter of sordid gain, he neither put it upon solid foundations, nor employed braces to strengthen the wooden fabric
which formed the superstructure. Thither flocked from
Rome persons of either sex and every age, eager for such
shows, as during the reign of Tiberius they were debarred
from diversions at home ; and in greater crowds from the
nearness of the place : hence the calamity was the more
disastrous ; for the theatre being crowded so as to form
a dense mass, and then rent asunder, some portions tumbled
inwards, others bulging towards the outer parts, a countless
number of human beings, either intent upon the spectacle
or standing near around the place, were either borne headlong to the ground or buried under the ruins. Those,
indeed, who were killed by the shock of the first crash,
escaped, as far as was possible in such a disaster, the misery
of torture : much more to be pitied were those who, with
portions of their bodies torn away, were not yet forsaken of
life ; those who by day beheld their wives and children,
and by night distinguished them by their groans and cries.
And now others, summoned to the spot by the sad tidings,
bewailed one his brother, another his kinsman, a third his
parents : even they whose friends or kindred were absent
on a different account, were yet terrified ; for as it was not
as yet distinctly known who had fallen in the calamity,
the alarm spread wider from the uncertainty.

"When the ruins began to be removed, they crowded
around the dead, embracing them and kissing them ;
and frequently there arose a contest about their identity,
where distortion of the features, personal resemblance,
or similarity of age had created a liability to error in
those who claimed them. Fifty thousand souls were
crushed to death or maimed by this sad disaster : it

was therefore for the future provided by a decree of the senate, that no man under the qualification of four hundred thousand sesterces should exhibit the spectacle of gladiators; and no amphitheatre should be founded but upon ground of proved solidity. Atilius was punished with exile. However, immediately upon this destructive calamity, the doors of the great were thrown open; medicines and physicians were furnished to all; and at that juncture the city, though under an aspect of sorrow, presented an image of the public spirit of the ancient Romans; who, after great battles, relieved and sustained the wounded by their liberality and attentions."*

Of Fidenæ itself there is now nothing left; although Cluver, an antiquary of the latter part of the seventeenth century, says that in his time there still existed ruins of considerable importance, partly in the valley and partly on the high ground. Kircher also speaks of the remains of a large city existing at Castel Giubileo, in sixteen hundred and thirty-seven. Now a solitary farm-house crowns the summit of its site, which stands as a beacon to all the country round. It is a sturdy edifice with a large court and a chapel. Probably it may have been built from remains of the ancient city. It is only tenanted by a few peasants, and wears a dreary and forsaken appearance. The noise of a bustling population and the clash of arms have given place to the singing shepherd and bleating flock, or the dead silence of the Campagna. I will ask the reader to climb with me up to the summit in one of several visits I made to it from Rome.

What a prospect lies before us! At our feet a varied and luxuriant plain stretches away through many a sunny upland and sombre hollow. Rich and, at the same time, subdued in colour, the billowy Campagna floats into seas of aerial grey just touched by the far sunlight into little rosy isles of rest. Through this plain, crossed with lines of road and spotted with white houses, with here and

* Ann. iv. 62, 63.

there a cypress or a pine rising beside them, the river
wanders, turning hither and thither as if loth to leave
it.   Its banks are clothed with bursting vegetation, its
tawny bosom taking the silver-broidered shadows, curling
and waving them in its turbid depths.   The farther side of
the plain, dotted over with feeding sheep, was the battle-
field of Maxentius and Constantine before described.   Beyond this runs the range of the Saxa Rubra, now smiling
grimly in the sunshine, to the left of which are seen the
pleasant heights of Monte Mario and the huge dome of
St. Peter's.   Beyond the plain, over an undulating tract of
rising ground, the blue outline of Soracte keeps the horizon.
More to the right, dimly imbedded in a distant hollow, the
Cremera flows and empties itself into the Tiber ; and
farther still, hardly discernible in the trembling summer
air, are the heights of Veii.   Then comes the elevation upon
which stood the villa of Livia.   Nearer, and in the same
direction, a few grey buildings at Marcigliana mark the
conjectured site of the ancient Latin city Crustumerium.
Beneath this hill flows the Allia ; beyond which lies the
battle-field on which the Romans met with their shameful
defeat by the Gauls under Brennus.   Following the same
direction, the Sabine mountains rise, beginning with the
abrupt peaks of Monticelli ; some snowy summits gleam-
ing at the far horizon, fit guardians of so beautiful a territory.   At their foot may be seen the dim sparkle of Tivoli,
St. Angelo the birth-place of Servius Tullius, Palombaro,
and many lesser towns and villages.   Over all this a tender
and luxurious calm broods.   It is impossible to realise the
fact that these desolate heights were once piled with cities
and peopled with an active and bustling humanity, much
less that the plains below were the seat of so much horrible
slaughter and bloodshed.   Now every trace of passion and
ambition has vanished.   Quiet sunshine fills the scene.
Tranquillity reigns once more, and Nature is at peace with
herself.

N

CHAPTER VII.

FROM FIDENÆ TO SCORANO.

AS we passed along the river there was an inexpressible grace and beauty in the shifting lines of the Campagna, bounded by the Tusculan range of hills softened in the warm glow of the bright sunshine ; every moment opening out some new charm in the landscape, each appearing more lovely than the last.

Nearly opposite to Fidenæ, on the left, the Cremera discharges itself into the Tiber ; an inconsiderable stream in itself, but the nurse and companion of the Etruscan city Veii. Following its picturesque bed for about six miles, a romantic valley of deeply-cut gorges and escarped heights is seen in which this city was situated. Its site, long an object of research, was determined by interpreting strictly the descriptions of the old historians, who in regard to its physical features and distance from Rome, appear to have described it very accurately—so accurately and so obviously that it is singular it could have escaped identification so long, especially as its site is definitively marked by traces of human labour in the remains of walls, tombs and other monuments. Its situation is highly romantic, but it can only be appreciated in its immediate vicinity, as its highest point does not rise very much above the level of the surrounding Campagna, which, after the gorges are surmounted, everywhere slopes from it in easy lines. The sides of these ravines are clothed with thick plantations ; over one of which a branch of the Cremera, after turning a picturesquely situated mill, falls, and then flows away deep down, half hidden amongst broad-leaved burs and sapling oaks. Surrounded by these gorges ; the result of volcanic action of enormous force—the ancient city rose upon the steep and lofty rocks, further fortified by massive stone walls, ruins of which still remain.   No wonder that it could stand a ten years' siege ; it would be rather a wonder that, if sufficiently provisioned, it could ever be taken at all from without.

VEII, FROM THE CAMPAGNA.

The importance of Veii was once very great.   It was said to have been as large as Athens.   It was even seriously deliberated after its final reduction by the Romans, when the Gallic invasion under Brennus had produced such serious results to their own city, if it would not be better to transfer Rome altogether to Veii.   It was only on the strong appeal of Camillus to the associations belonging to the city of their forefathers, that the Romans were persuaded to abandon the project.   Dionysius says that " it possessed a large and fruitful territory, partly mountainous and partly in the plain. The air was pure and healthy, the country being free from the vicinity of the marshes, which produce a heavy atmosphere, and without any river which might render the morning air too rigid. Nevertheless there was abundance of water, not artificially conducted, but rising from natural springs, and good to drink."[*]

The first time that Veii appears in history, is when the Fidenates seized on some boats of provisions despatched to Rome by the Crustumerians at a time of famine, drawing upon themselves the enmity of Romulus, who thereupon made himself master of their city, and established a garrison there of three hundred soldiers. The Veientes, looking with jealousy on this advancement of Roman power, requested Romulus to withdraw his troops from Fidenæ, and to restore to the Fidenates the lands he had confiscated. Romulus refusing, they drew up their army in front of Fidenæ, upon which he immediately occupied the city itself. This resulted in a battle, in which the Veientes were discomfited. They then made a truce for a hundred years, the conditions of which were registered on stone columns, ceding to the Romans certain territories on the river, together with the salt flats of Ostia.

Amongst the many subsequent contests between the Romans and Veientes, there are some more important than the rest, which may be here noticed. One of these happened under the joint consulship of Cneius Manlius and Marcus Fabius, when the Veientes declared war against the Romans, largely supported by the Etruscans of the neighbouring country. These consuls marched against Veii, encamping on two adjacent hills before it. The Roman army, however, being greatly inferior in numbers to that of the Veientes, and being, besides, disturbed with disaffection, it was thought better to fortify the encampment, and, by forbearing action as long as possible, increase the ardour of the soldiers for an engagement. Of this the Veientes and

---

[*] In one of the fragments discovered by Cardinal Mai.

their allies being aware, they suffered considerable uneasiness,
and did all that they possibly could to **provoke** a combat
by taunting the Romans with cowardice, **and** challenging
them to come **forth** and fight, approaching the very gates
and ramparts of **their** fortification. This **stratagem of** the
Roman **generals** had its effect upon their troops. The
soldiers came in a body to their tents, entreating them to
be led to battle, in order that they might stop the boasting
of the enemy. The generals, however, refused, and dis-
missed them, cautioning them that whoever raised his arm
against the foe, would be treated as one of them, and immediately put to death. At last the Veientes actually
began to draw a line of circumvallation around the **Roman**
camp, and to cut off their supplies, whereupon the **soldiers**
came once more to the tent of their generals, and **demanded**
that they should be at once led into an engagement. **Their**
enthusiasm was still **more** inflamed by **a** plebeian of **ac-**
credited honour **and** courage, named Marcus **Flavoleius,**
commander of one **of** the legions, who came forward holding
up his sword, and swearing that he would return to Rome
victorious or not at all. Presently the whole **army** followed
his example.

So the battle commenced, and a very sharp engagement
it was for both sides. The Etruscans threw away their
javelins in the confusion of the onset, so that it very soon
became a hand-to-hand fight. Amongst the foremost in
the fight the noble Fabian family were the most conspicuous for their gallantry. One of these, Quintus Fabius,
who had been consul **two years** before, as he was heading
his men in the thick of the fight, was pierced in the **breast**
by the sword of an Etruscan and killed, which **had so** dis-
heartening an effect on the Roman soldiers, **that they were**
beginning to give way before **the redoubled** strokes of the
enemy, when the consul Marcus, leaping over the body as
it lay upon the ground, cried, "Is this your oath, soldiers,
that you would retreat, driven back to your camp? Do you
fear the enemy more than Jupiter and Mars, by whom

you have sworn ?   But I, who have not sworn, will fulfil
your broken vow beside this body." His brother consul
then appearing, bade him leave speech for action ; upon
which, both rushing forward, carried with them the whole
line.

This gallant spirit soon diffused itself throughout the
army.   Various were the fortunes of the fight.   But whilst
it was still raging, the Etruscans, relying on their superior
numbers, had draughted their reserves, and set them to
plunder the Roman camp.   Whilst they were thus occupied,
the veteran troops of the third line, who had been driven
back to the camp during the engagement, now attacked
these on their own account, sending word to the general
what had happened.   Manlius immediately went thither,
and posting his troops at the various entrances, began to
attack them with vigour.   This aroused the fury of the
imprisoned enemy, who, in their desperate attempts to free
themselves from the perilous situation, killed the consul,
which so dismayed the Romans that they began to give
way before them.   This being perceived by the lieutenant-
generals, they immediately opened a way for the Etruscans,
who, rushing out of the camp, were met by the victorious
troops of the Roman army, and at once discomfited by them,
driven before them, together with the whole Etruscan army,
into the city.   The Romans waited in their encampment
for several days ; but as the enemy did not again make its
appearance, and an attack upon the city would have been
quite out of the question, they returned to Rome, rejoicing,
indeed, in their hardly won victory, but full of regrets for
the two illustrious heroes who had paid the forfeit of their
lives as the price of their bravery.   A triumph was decreed
to the consul, who led his victorious troops into Rome ; but
he refused to enter into it in respect and grief for the dead ;
thus, as the historian says, gaining to himself a nobler
triumph.

The war, however, was not over ; for the Veientes and
their allies kept up constant and harassing incursions into

the Roman territory.   At the same time the Romans were
beset with enemies on every hand.   So emboldened were
the Veientes that they had actually advanced as far as the
Janiculum on the other side of the Tiber, menacing Rome
itself.   Whilst the senate was sorely puzzled what course
to take in the midst of so many enemies, with an im-
poverished treasury, the distinguished patrician family of
the Fabii came forwards, and through Cæso as their mouth-
piece, volunteered to go forth against the Veientes, the
expedition being at their own charge and responsibility,·
both of supplies and men, since it was not so much a great
force that was required as a constancy of watchfulness to
withstand the incursions of the foe.   This offer was thank-
fully accepted.   They left the city amidst the acclamations
and benedictions of the people ; three hundred and six
bearing the name of Fabius, but numbering with their
clients and followers from three to four thousand men.
When they came to the river Cremera, not far from Veii,
they built a fortress upon a steep and craggy hill, surrounding it with a double ditch, and fortifying it with
towers ; thence ravaging the country beyond, whither the
Veientes had taken their herds and flocks, thinking, by this
means, to place them out of the reach of the enemy.   They
occupied this position two years.   Their confidence, however, at last proved their ruin.   The astute Veientes soon
perceived that if they were to be overcome, it must be by
taking advantage of their bravery and daring, rather than
opposing them by strength.   An ambuscade was laid ;
herds of cattle were driven within sight of the fortress they
had erected, with a plain lying between ; the Romans
immediately going in pursuit.   Whilst they were dispersed
in securing the cattle, the Veientes rose up on every side of
them, pressing them until the whole band was confined
within a narrow circle, fighting valiantly.   Thus beset, they
formed themselves into the shape of a wedge, and laying
their strength upon one spot, forced their way out, and
ascended a neighbouring acclivity, by this means obtaining

a temporary advantage. Their valour, however, availed them little, for the enemy, sending round large detachments, poured upon them from higher ground ; so that they every one fell, fighting to the last man on the spot they occupied. It is said that the whole family of the Fabii here perished, excepting one youth left in Rome to prolong the race.

After this the Veientes once more occupied the Janiculum, even crossing the Tiber and penetrating as far as the temple of Hope, which stood near the modern Porta Maggiore. They were however eventually driven from their position, and retired to their own city.

The Veientes afterwards allied themselves with the Fidenates, many subsequent engagements occurring between the united armies and the Romans, some of which have already been described, as taking place near Fidenæ.

At last the Romans determined to bring about an ultimate trial, and, if possible, to entirely destroy their city, as they had done the cities of Fidenæ and Alba. This resolution, however, was at first frustrated by a new alliance which the Veientes formed with the Capenates and the Falisci, and the quarrels which took place between the two Roman generals Sergius and Virginius. The antagonistic commanders were recalled and new ones appointed. The object of the Roman army was to cut off all their supplies, as well by keeping a close guard around the city as by depopulating the neighbouring country, and destroying the produce. In this position of affairs, significance was given to a circumstance, the connection of which with the matter in hand is not altogether obvious. The waters of the Alban lake had risen to an unusual height, it was said, without any apparent cause ; no rain having fallen at that time. A commission was sent to the Delphic oracle to learn what might be portended by this extraordinary occurrence. Whilst they were away it was delivered by an old Veientine soothsayer in the form of a prophecy, that Veii could never be taken until the waters of the Alban

lake should find their way by an artificial outlet **to the sea.**
The old man was decoyed from Veii, under pretence **of**
consultation on some other matter, and then carried forcibly
into the Roman camp, where **he** repeated what he **had**
previously disclosed, describing how the desired object was
to be attained.   All that the old seer had uttered was confirmed by the message of the oracle.   The prescribed work
was at once entered upon.   The side of the hill, within
whose hollow basin the lake lay, was pierced with a tunnel,
and the waters drained off to a considerable depth.   The
tunnel remains to this day, still serving the purpose for
which it was first formed.   The significance of the fact may
lie in the suggestion of carrying a mine into Veii.   It **could**
hardly, however, have taught the Romans the first use **of**
such an expedient, since they had already taken **Fidenæ by**
the same means.

A new impetus was given to the war by **the** appointment
of Marcus Furius Camillus to the dictatorship.   **His** popularity and energy at once organised the whole proceeding.
He made fresh levies of troops at Rome, doing away with
the harassing and random skirmishes in which the Romans
had been in the habit of engaging, concentrating the whole
forces of **the army to** the special object in view.   A mine
was commenced at some distance from the city.   The
pioneers were divided into six companies, working night
and day, six hours, consecutive labour allotted to **each**
company in rotation.

When the city was on the point of being taken, Camillus
sent to Rome to know what was to be done with the spoil.
After many differences of opinion, it was finally proclaimed
through the streets of Rome that such **of the inhabitants as**
wished to **share the** plunder **of the city about to fall into**
their hands might go to the camp for that purpose.   When
all was in readiness, Camillus vowed a tenth part of the spoil
to the god Apollo, and making a feint of attacking the city
on various sides, as **the soldiers ran** to the walls, the mine
was suddenly burst open in the very heart of the citadel,

and as was said, within the temple of Juno.   An incident is added, for the truth of which, however, the old historians do not vouch.   At the moment of bursting up the mine the king of Veii stood about to offer up the entrails of a certain animal on the altar of Juno, when it was declared that whoever should make that offering should be victorious over the enemy.   The Roman soldiers, hearing this, suddenly emerged, and seizing the sacrifice, themselves placed it upon the altar ; thus assuring themselves the victory. Immediately the whole city was in an uproar.   Armed men poured in on every hand.   Fire and slaughter did their fearful work, until the dictator caused it to be proclaimed that those who laid down their arms would be spared. Every article of value was seized by the Romans, and the inhabitants sold into slavery, the money being applied to the public treasury.   Youths selected from the army, purified and arrayed in white, were appointed to lay reverential hands on the sacred images and bear them carefully away with much ceremony.   When they came to the statue of Juno, which occupied the temple, she was asked if she were willing to go to Rome, when, it was said, she bowed her head in token of assent.   This statue was taken to the Aventine hill, where Juno held " her eternal seat ;" Camillus subsequently raising there a temple to her honour.

Thus fell the great city of Veii, the wealthiest of the Etruscan nation, three hundred and ninety-six years before the birth of Christ, impregnable by attack from without, after a long ten years' siege of summers and winters, during which time its enemy always suffered more than itself, art and not force having been its final overthrow.

Great was the joy at Rome on the destruction of the old enemy.   Before the senate could prescribe any religious ceremonial the temples were crowded with matrons pouring out their thanksgivings to the gods for the great victory.   A four days' supplication was appointed—more than had been decreed at any other war.   The whole city went forth to meet Camillus with the highest demonstrations of joy.

His triumph was an honourable one : though there arose some difficulty afterwards about the fulfilment of **the vow** Camillus had made of the dedication **of** the tenth part of the spoils to Apollo, since it was found hard to force the people to give up **from what they had taken** that which was necessary to acquit the sacred promise.

From that time Veii became lost as an independent city —indeed could be scarcely said to survive as a city at all— **serving only as** an unimportant Roman colony. It had been **proposed,** as already stated, after the disastrous battle of **the Allia** that Rome itself should be transferred thither, **in** order to save the rebuilding **of** the houses and other **struc-** tures destroyed at that time ; from which circumstance **one** may gain some idea of the importance of the Etruscan city. Many families indeed had already established themselves there, but they were afterwards recalled by **decree of the** senate, which made it an offence punishable **with death for** any Roman to remain at Veii beyond a prescribed **period.** Gradually it fell into decay, without any subsequent history of importance.

There is now very little of it left, but that little is full of interest and significance. The position in **itself** is so re- **markable as** to make a great deal apparent as to its ancient **condition,** whilst it is interesting to trace out, partly by speculation and partly **by** description, much of which there **are** only left obscure indications. The roads by which it **was** reached are still to be seen cut deep down into **the** solid rock so as to form lofty escarpments on each side. **The** rock itself is of distinctive volcanic origin, consisting **of masses of black** pumice reposing **on an aqueous deposit of** ashes ; **the former** bearing **all** the **appearance of** a fresh eruption. Ruts are traceable **at the sides of** some of these roads, which are very narrow ; only capable of admitting one vehicle at a time. The positions of the gateways are also still to be discerned by grooves and other marks **in the rock.** **The arx,** or main citadel, has been supposed by most archæ- **ologists to** have occupied the position of the modern hamlet of Isola Farnese, which is the most elevated part of the whole area, and nearly inclosed by the two streams flowing into the Due Fossi ; its precipitous sides having been cut away to form the sole road up to it. Sir William Gell, however, and Canina, the celebrated Italian archæologist, place it at the western extremity. Both of these are strong positions, but it seems to me that the former is rather more so than the latter. Sir William Gell's theory of the exclusion of this part from the city on account of the tombs found excavated in its sides, neither the Etruscans nor the Romans being accustomed to bury their dead within their cities, has been generally rejected, since it is not likely that the Veientes would have allowed so impregnable a point in so close proximity to the city to be exposed to the occupation of an enemy.

Passing round the city by the mill before mentioned we come to the spot where were found the columns which now ornament the front of the post-office in the Piazza Colonna at Rome, and some others placed in the basilica of St. Paul outside the walls. It is conjectured that they formed a part of the Forum. Still farther, we arrive at the Ponte Sodo, a tunnelled cutting made through the rock in order to admit the passage of the river. Following the same direction, one of the finest known Etruscan tombs is to be seen excavated in the rock. It was discovered by Campana in eighteen hundred and forty-two, being left pretty much as it was found, some gold fillets only having been carried away from it. It is entered by a passage cut into the rock, guarded by two lions in marble : two more keep the door. The tomb consists of a double chamber, which is supposed to represent more or less accurately the form of an Etruscan house. The walls are painted in grotesque forms of men and animals, the roof being shaped into imitation beams and rafters. Vases and other vessels are set about, some of them painted with curious caricature figures. Most interesting of all, on shelves or couches cut in the rock on either side of the door, when it was first opened, lay a human skeleton, which the air soon

crumbled into dust.   One of them wore a helmet—there it
lies yet—pierced by a lance-thrust ; doubtless the death-
blow to him who **wore it**.   It is strange that there was **no**
name **or** indication in any part of the tomb which might
attach a personality to these dusty children of oblivion, who
must nevertheless have **been** of some distinction in their
time.   **Remains of** other sepulchres are found in its neighbourhood, which probably constituted the chief necropolis of
the city.   But, indeed, there are many of them in various
parts of the outer city, some of which are utilised as sheep-
cotes and cellars, on the ceilings of which can be generally
discerned the form of beam and rafter which characterises
these strange habitations of the dead.   Passing onwards,
fragments of the walls of the old city are seen here and there,
consisting of huge blocks of tufa.   A little farther we come
to the remains of the Roman municipium or colony founded
after the subjugation of Veii, which only covered a moiety
of the site of the Etruscan city.   Here were found colossal
heads of Augustus and Tiberius, together with a large statue
of the latter crowned with oak ; now in the Vatican museum.
The Roman character of this part of the **city** is distinguishable by the grey walls of some columbaria which rise out of
the tangled brushwood, their empty recesses exposed to
the full glare of the sun.   These once contained the ashes
of the dead, mourned over, wept over, prayed over ; but
oblivion has long since sealed them his own, not even **re-**
garding the pious D.M. that consigned them to the keeping
of the divinities of the dead, nor leaving any record of where
they are sown except the summer flowers which **bloom from**
their dust.   These grow in luxuriant beauty **from every**
crevice, **and lay** their tender faces against **the** crumbling
stone, as if witnesses of the frailty of **humanity.**

It is perhaps no **wonder that there should be so**
little of this city of three **thousand** years ago **left** to us.
Propertius tells us that at the commencement of the Christian era it was a half-obliterated ruin.   " O, ancient Veii,"
he says, apostrophising it in the spirit of ancient times,

"thou also wert then a city, and the golden chair of state was set within thy forum. Now within your walls the shepherd gently winds his horn and harvests are reaped among your bones."[*] Also Lucan tells us in the first Christian century, "All the name of Latium has become a fable; hardly can the dust-covered ruins point out to us Gabii, Veii and Cora."[†]

Previously to our journey up the river, Mr. Hemans and I had spent a few days at La Storta; a little roadside inn, on the ancient Via Cassia, a short distance from Veii, which is now called Isola Farnese. The elevated position generally supposed to have been that of the citadel of the ancient city is now occupied by an old baronial mansion built in the fifteenth century by the Colonna family in their contentions with the Orsini. It is a dreary-looking tenement, and appears to be fast falling to decay. It is spotted with putlog holes, pierced with unglazed windows, and hung with forlorn wreaths of dark green ivy and a rank growth of pellitory-of-the-wall. It includes a large court which constitutes for the most part the modern hamlet, than which nothing can be more miserable. The houses are of the worst ever seen even in Italy, and they are shared by pigs, hens, and dogs. The misery and wretchedness of the place is oppressive. Just outside of the walls is a chapel, the service of which is supplied by some distant priest or friar in orders: and even the sanctuary of their religion, generally cared for more or less scrupulously, is here filled with the accumulated dust and dirt of years. The people seem to be living without a thought of anything better, in absolute ignorance, neglect and misery.

[*] Et Veii veteres et vos tum regna fuistis,
    Et vestro posita est aurea sella foro.
  Nunc intra muros pastoris buccina lenti
    Cantat, et in vestris ossibus arva metunt.
                                        Lib. iv. el. 10.

[†] Tunc omne Latinum
  Fabula nomen erit: Gabios, Veiosque, Coramque
  Pulvere vix tectæ poterunt monstrare ruinæ.
                                        Phar. vii. 391.

To go over the ground once occupied by this important city is almost like traversing a grave-yard. Where strongholds arose and a powerful people found their dwelling the dog-rose and the red poppy bloom uncropped ; yellow broom grows where once have been streets and centres of business and gossip ; the wild fig splits the crumbling wall ; the untrained and wasted vine, whose ancestral grape may have given heart to the Veientine soldier against his Roman foe, straggles hither and thither at will. As we forced our way through the tangled brushwood and over hillocks that marked the place of buried ruins, I saw a fox stealing by the woodside. The only sounds that met our ears were the cry of the quail, the shriek of the grasshopper, and the melody of the song bird undisturbed in these secluded regions ; but all seemed to be tinged with a melancholy tone, made sadder by the hoot of an owl, which from the recesses in the wood, forgetting his proper season in the gloom by which he was surrounded, awoke the sleeping sunshine of mid-day with a loud "to-whoo !"

And yet one scarcely knew why it should have appeared so melancholy ; for it was beautiful—intensely beautiful. The feathery foliage clomb the steep bank, taking a silvery aureole from the sun ; larks were loud in the sky ; the sound of falling waters came to us, murmuring pleasantly ; the earth opened its most brilliantly coloured flowers ; butterflies fluttered everywhere ; the rocky shelves were as green as garden terraces, whilst picturesque-looking maidens went down to the fountain with quaint pitchers balanced sidelong on their heads—the fountain a cool and mossy nook of flickering lights and shadows. But the past lay upon it all—the tale of glory departed—the harvest of time reaped in overgrown heaps of wasting stone and barren hillocks of nameless dust.

Returning once more to the Tiber, and pursuing our way upwards, a little past Fidenæ and on the same side of the river, the stream of the Allia flows into it. It is famous as marking the site of an important engagement between the Romans and the Gauls which took place upon its banks.

Up to about three hundred and sixty years from the foundation of the city of Rome, or three hundred and ninety years before the birth of Christ, the republic had been steadily increasing in power without having received any absolutely disastrous reverses ; but at this time, whether from the over-population of their own territory, or, as some say, the inducement of the wine, or for whatever other reason, Italy became overrun by the Gauls, a half-civilized, transalpine race, who poured upon the country, producing confusion and ruin wherever they passed. After having devastated many parts of north Italy, they reached so far south as Clusium, the modern Chiusi, a city of Etruria, between Siena and Orvieto. Beset by an enemy so numerous and formidable, bearing strange arms and of unaccustomed aspect, the terrified Clusians sought to obtain the aid of Rome against their unknown foe. Negotiations with the Gauls were entered into ; but on their requiring land to be given to them for a colonial settlement, diplomacy was broken off with mutual reprisals, finally ending in an appeal to the sword. At once they started for Rome, without stopping to commit any depredations by the way. It was only at the eleventh milestone from the city, where the river Allia, descending from the Crustumerian hills in a very deep channel, joins the Tiber, not far from the road, that the Romans thought of opposing them. It would appear that they looked upon the circumstance with the most imprudent indifference ; not regarding the large force of the enemy, nor their ardour in fighting, nor their desperate ferocity. The Roman army was drawn up in the face of the enemy, the reserves being placed on a small eminence at the right. The Gauls, instead of meeting the body of the army in the open plain, at once attacked the reserves and routed them, which had such an effect upon the other troops that they were seized with a panic, and at once took to flight almost without striking a blow, some of them swimming the Tiber and taking refuge even in the inimical Veii, some being drowned in its waters ; such of the rest who were

fortunate enough **to** escape with **their lives, hurrying to**
Rome the nearest way ; large numbers **of slain being left**
on the field.   The Romans **and their allies in** this **fight**
numbered **forty thousand,** whilst **their** enemies cou. .ed **as**
many **as seventy thousand.**

At this **sudden stroke of** fortune the Gauls themselves
wondered, and could hardly believe that **it** was not some
feint on the part of the Romans to entrap them into further
danger : but at last seeing that no one· returned to molest
them, they began to collect the **arms and spoils of the slain
and to** think of going to Rome.

Here the local narrative might terminate with the ghastly
spectacle the round midsummer moon saw that night **as it**
rose over the groaning plains, but it will **be scarcely out of**
place **to** follow it a little **farther.**

On reaching Rome, which they did **the same evening,**
the Gauls were **still more amazed to** find **the** gates **left**
open, and no apparent preparation of defence made against
them.   Dreading **an ambuscade,** they encamped beneath
the walls that night and **the** following **day,** endeavouring
to frighten the inhabitants of the city by **loud** cries and
discordant noises. The senate, seeing the imminence of the
danger, withdrew the fighting population, together with
what stores and munition could **be** procured, to the citadel
of the Capitol, there **entrenching** themselves **in the** best
manner **they were able,** leaving **the** non-warlike and the
aged **to do the** best they could ; the **latter,** who themselves
had borne honours and occupied important and **elevated**
positions, consoling the people with their **own willingness**
to suffer **anything rather** than that **the whole city and
nation should be destroyed.** One may picture the misery
and **confusion of this moment : the entire** population,
including **women** and **children, rushing about** hither and
thither ; the vestal virgins **bearing** away the sacred relics ;
the ex-officials arranging themselves in the dignity of **their
disused robes and** calmly awaiting the advent of the enemy.
In the meantime the Gauls began **to** distribute themselves

throughout the city, but with mistrust and timidity, afraid to enter even the open doors of the houses, and awed by the venerable and majestic figures of the aged patricians sitting in the porches of their palaces, until a Gaul, bolder than the rest, stretching forth his hand and stroking the white beard of one of them, as if to assure himself of his reality, was immediately struck with the ivory staff he held in his hand. This was the signal for an immediate slaughter. All suffered that came under the sword; the houses were plundered and set on fire; devastation and terror reigned everywhere. For several days the defenders of the citadel watched the burning of their houses and the slaughter of their wives and children with distracted hearts, but still maintained their guard manfully, and when at last the Gauls, wearied with the work of destruction, attacked the citadel itself, they were defeated with dreadful losses; so that they dared not repeat the attempt. Neither, indeed, durst the Romans emerge to fight in the open. Thus worsted, and much in want of supplies, the Gallic army divided itself; the one half remaining to besiege the citadel, and the other roaming the surrounding country in search of plunder.

Now it happened in the course of this marauding expedition that amongst other places they lighted on the city of Ardea, the capital of the Rutulian territory, not far from the sea-coast, about twenty miles south of Rome, to which place Camillus had been driven under the accusation of having personally appropriated certain Etruscan spoils, but really for his humanity and justice towards the conquered Falisci, whose city he would not allow to be sacked. Fired with the indignities his people were suffering, and magnanimously forgetful of his own wrongs, the exiled hero strove to incite the Ardeates to emulate the prowess of Rome, and build up to themselves an honourable name by rescuing it from its present dire calamities. His appeal was not disregarded. Issuing from the gates at night under his direction they found the Gallic troops lying in

unguarded sleep, gorged with wine and victuals, the fruits
of spoliation and pillage.   Attacking them thus, supine and
defenceless, they were very easily defeated, fleeing to all
parts of the surrounding country, some to Antium, where
they were cut off from their comrades and slaughtered by
the inhabitants; others to the Veientine territory: these,
however, being not only unmolested but succoured by the
Veientes, who took the opportunity of revenging themselves
on Rome in this its sore extremity, attacking the Ardeian
troops, and then returning to Veii with much satisfaction
and a great deal of noisy rejoicing.

But when the Romans who had fled from the battle of
the Allia and were now detained as prisoners in Veii heard
of the success which Camillus had had against the Gauls,
they began greatly to bewail their own and their fellow-
citizens' folly in having banished so able a general and
upright a man from Rome, lamenting that he was not once
more at their head, when they felt assured that a master-
stroke might be made in their favour.   Their desire was
not allowed to waste itself in idle complaints.   They
contrived means to have a proposition conveyed to Camillus
that he should place himself at their head as commander.
He, however, refused to undertake the office excepting by
special appointment of the senate of Rome.   In this
difficulty a young man named Pontius Cominius came
forward, proffering his services to go to Rome to obtain it.
Disguising himself as a peasant, on arriving at the gates he
cast himself into the river, sustained by corks, and swimming to the Capitol, climbed up the steep side of it with
great difficulty, and then, after stating his errand and
witnessing the appointment of Camillus as dictator, returned
in the same manner.

In the morning some Gauls passing round the base of
the Capitol saw traces of footmarks, and after proving the
practicability of the ascent, a party was organised to attempt
the citadel on the following night.   Already had they
reached the summit without any alarm, when the sacred

geese kept at the temple of Juno, prowling about half-starved, hissing and cackling, awoke the whole camp, who, falling upon the Gauls, quickly routed them, killing some and throwing others down the rock.

In the meantime Camillus busied himself in organising his army, matters growing worse and worse with the Romans. Famine looked them in the face and sickness and weakness seized them for a prey. Neither were the besiegers much better off. The burnt and burning ashes of the houses blown into their camp almost suffocated them, fever raged in their midst; so dreadful, indeed, was the mortality on this occasion that the heaped remains of their dead, after being partially consumed by fire, remained in the form of a large mound which subsequently gave a name to that part of the city.

At last, when endurance could hold out no longer on either side, an armistice was proposed and arrangements for peace entered upon. The Gauls demanded a thousand pounds weight of gold as requisition. As it was being weighed it was found that the besiegers had furnished false weights for the purpose. On the Romans remonstrating against this perfidy it is said that Brennus the Gallic chief scornfully flung his sword into the balance, proclaiming, "Woe to the vanquished." At this precise juncture, Camillus and his troops arrived on the scene. Camillus immediately seized the gold in the scales and handed it to the senators, saying that Rome was accustomed to redeem itself with iron and not with gold. When told that he was breaking a compact already concluded, he replied that he alone by right of his office of dictator had power to enter upon such an engagement, and that by his permission it had never been made. A sharp conflict immediately ensued in which the Gauls suffered severe losses, decamping the same night and leaving the city. The next morning Camillus followed and routed the invaders, whose destruction was completed by the peasants and other inhabitants of the surrounding country, who all rose up against them.

Livy says that Camillus saved Rome twice in **dissuading** the inhabitants from abandoning it altogether **for Veii after** this terrible invasion.

Near this spot was **also fought a** subsequent battle between the Romans and the **inhabitants** of Præneste, in which the latter were defeated.

A little distance past the junction of the Cremera with the Tiber, somewhat removed from the left bank, is the **villa** of Livia, the dignified and matronly wife of Augustus. **Her** real character is almost as inscrutable as was that of her imperial husband. It is thus given by the historian Tacitus. "In her domestic deportment she was formed after the model of primitive sanctity, but with more **affa**bility than was allowed by ladies of old: **as a mother** zealous and determined; **as a** wife kind and indulgent; well adapted to the fastidious and complex character **of** her husband, and the subtle nature of her son" [Tiberius]. Doubtless **here** she spent many hours of pleasant leisure in the company of Augustus **in** his holiday retirements from the cares of state. It is within easy reach of Rome, about seven miles from the Flaminian Gate. The place was called Prima Porta, being the first halting-place from Rome : nine miles distant from the Golden Milestone at the foot of the **Capitol.** Suetonius gives a whimsical story of the original foundation of this villa in his life of Galba. He says that soon after her marriage with Augustus, Livia once went to visit this estate, situated in the Veientine territory, when **an** eagle let fall a white chicken into her lap, carrying a sprig of laurel **in** its mouth. She planted the laurel, which grew and flourished. From the progeny of this sprig the **crowns of** the Cæsars were subsequently **woven** for **festivals, its** growth corresponding with their welfare. **The** fowl, too, was prolific. Dion Cassius says that the death of Nero, who was the last of the Augustan race descended from Æneas, was presaged by the withering away of the laurels, and the extinction of the race of fowls.

When **H. and** I visited this place from **Rome,** whilst

we were reposing in the *osteria* after a warm walk, we sent to inquire if we could have the key to inspect the villa, which was in the keeping of the parish priest. Presently the messenger came back to say that the priest was ill in bed, and that we could not have the key. Upon this we went ourselves to the house where he lived. The door was opened by a girl, who began to tell the same story. The priest, however, hearing our voices, made his appearance fully dressed, at the top of the stairs, and said that there had been some Germans there a few days before, who would only give half a franc for having the door of the villa opened. "Now," he said, "it is a very unreasonable thing that a person should go into those damp chambers and take a fever for so small a consideration as half a franc." H. and I both agreed that it was highly unreasonable under the circumstances; and promising to satisfy the bearer of the key with a sufficient donation, a man was sent to accompany us.

At present there is but a small portion of the villa excavated. On the walls of one of the chambers, thickly leaved branches, intermingled with fruit and flowers and birds, are painted in distemper. They are executed with much spirit and power from a realistic point of view, so as to form a very refreshing and beautiful series of objects for the eye to rest upon. Many valuable works of art were found here, the most important of which was the fine statue of Augustus now forming one of the treasures of the Vatican museum. The villa stands upon an eminence commanding a charming view of the surrounding country. At its foot the river winds through green banks bordered with delicate foliage. Beyond are seen the bare slopes of Antemnæ, and more to the north the solitary old feudal tenement that marks the site of Fidenæ, standing where once the formidable Acropolis shone in the light of the morning sun, or burned like a flame in the glow of the evening red. On the other side, the Via Flaminia wanders towards Rome under the bare, blank bluffs of the Saxa Rubra.

About two miles beyond Fidenæ, on the same side of the river, is a group of farm-buildings, bearing the name of Marcigliana, which look more like some sturdy mediæval fortress than the centre of quiet agricultural labour. They are situated at a considerable elevation, and inclose a spacious court, whose grass-grown pavement and wasted walls give an eery aspect of desolation to the place. It has been surmised that the ancient Latian city, Crustumerium, once occupied this height. It is true that Sir William Gell and some others have fixed upon Monte Rotondo as being the more probable site ; but the proximity of that town to Mentana, the undoubted position of the ancient Nomentum, and its more remote distance from the river, have caused other archæologists to give this the preference. Besides, Kircher, in his Latium Vetus, published in sixteen hundred and seventy, says that it was noticeable for its remains of ancient edifices, and though few or no traces of these are left, they may have been used in the fabrication of the building which now occupies the summit.

Crustumerium was one of the most ancient cities of Latium, said to have been founded by the Alban king Silvius Latinus, who opposed Æneas on his first arrival in that part of Italy. It is mentioned by Virgil as one of the first cities which forged arms for the war.[*] The Latin poet Silius Italicus speaks of it as being of later origin than Antemnæ.[†] It is first heard of in history as being one of the allies against Romulus after the rape of the Sabine women, when it was conquered by him, and made a Roman colony. It scarcely appears to have had an independent existence afterwards, and probably soon fell into decay, since it is mentioned by Pliny as one of the extinct cities of Latium. It, however, gave the name to a district and to a Roman tribe. Its territory was very fruitful, rich

---

[*] Quinque adeo magnæ positis incudibus urbes
Tela novant, Atina potens, Tiburque superbum,
Ardea, Crustumerique, et turrigeræ Antemnæ. Æn. vii. 631.
       [†] Antemnaque prisco
Crustumio prior.

in corn, and famous for its pears. It sent supplies of the former in boats to Rome during a famine, which being detained and pillaged by the Fidenates, caused the Romans to make their first war against them.

Marcigliana is a large farm, chiefly dairy. The agricultural implements lying about could not have been simpler or ruder if they had belonged to the days of Virgil. So unprogressive is the Italian mind, so indifferent or incapable in all arts of contrivance, that as we were going by one of the outbuildings, we saw some men actually making butter in large mugs by stirring the cream about with unwashed hands. This was not, it must be recollected, at a mountain hovel, where a miserable cow might eke out the scant subsistence of a few poverty-stricken wretches shut out from intercourse with the rest of the world, but on one of the largest farms of the Campagna, almost within sight of the walls of Rome, belonging, I believe, to one of its noblest families, and managed, I suppose, by the professed *mercante di Campagna.* Amidst such a condition of things, of which this is only a sample, one would naturally ask, what is the meaning of the word proprietorship in Italy, or if such a term as Useful Arts is to be found in their dictionary.

From Marcigliana, the river-country presents soft, well-wooded slopes, whose delicately-pencilled outlines, changing every moment in the upward passage of the stream, undergo a thousand variations, each more beautiful than the other. The banks are fired with yellow broom. The tortuous sweeps of the river present broad flat surfaces to the sky, mingling its reflected azure with the hue of its yellow waters. Long-horned cattle stand upon the banks, gazing curiously. One turn after another goes by, until we reach the mediæval town of Monte Rotondo.

Monte Rotondo is about fifteen miles from Rome. It offers no particular point of interest excepting its picturesque situation and old baronial residence, so large in its proportions as to appear to compose a considerable part of the town. It would seem that the lord of the manor in Italy always considered himself bound to raise a huge pile of buildings on his territory, dignified by the name of **palace**, as an evidence of, and testimony to, his title of possession, afterwards to be allowed to fall into decay, a tenement for owls and rats. We are accustomed in England to associate such residences with the occupation of the owners for at **least** a part of the year, and to see them surrounded with some little tokens of care for the tenantry and neighbours. **Here it** is different. A landlord scarcely ever delights in **the** improvement of his estate, but simply sets it under a management interesting and curious as a relic of mediæval practice, being content to receive the emolument **from it** without further trouble. There are not the least indications of the slightest care or attention bestowed on dependents **in** the neighbourhood of such central mansions. Often **enough** their courts are the dirtiest parts of the whole town, **and** the beggar sits on their door-steps. It is pitiable, **where so** much that is required might be done, to see nothing **what-**ever attempted. Perhaps the friar of a neighbouring **con-**vent may give some desultory instruction **to the** miserable people, himself scarcely less unlearned; but by those who **ought to** take an interest in the welfare of their fellow-creatures, **from** whom they reap the means to live above **the** fatigues of labour, nothing whatever appears to be done. No legislation nor any appointed system of public educa-tion can compensate for the social defect of the mutual influences of the classes. It is not in the least the **result** of pride or superciliousness. These are quite unknown **in Italy as they exist** in England. It is pure indifference. There **is** money in Italy, there is time **in Italy, there is** good sound **common** sense and plenty **of good feeling in** Italy; **but who shall arouse the Italian mind from** the apathy and indifference **in regard to social elevation** in which it lies? Who shall show it **that the most** ignoble slavery may subsist beneath the **very** flag of Freedom—the **slavery** of Ignorance, Dirt, **and** Idleness? Well, indeed, **has the wise Massimo d'Azeglio** said, the enemies of Italy have not been those of Austria and France, but rather those within her own shores, and in her own bosom. A natural politeness, that crowning grace of Christian breeding, a sweetness of manner and amiability of disposition beyond parallel in any of the nations of Europe with which I am acquainted, a kindliness and warmth of feeling quite exemplary, a sharpness and aptitude of perception and judgment not infrequently reaching to a very large wisdom, make the absence of energy and enthusiasm in what is true and right, the want of thoroughness, transparency, and self-respect, all the more bitterly felt and keenly regretted. This regret becomes a wonder when one remembers such names as Carlo Borromeo, Gregory the Great, Savonarola, Arnoldo di Brescia and a few others of more modern times, to whom a pure and energetic individual life and the enlargement and elevation of the human race were the crown and aim of all their desires and labours. To every philanthropist it must be a matter of deep pain to see how much young Italy has in its power : how little it uses its capabilities and opportunities in living in and teaching the great law that the only way to moral and social elevation and national greatness lies in an absolutely ruling and entirely uncompromising personal self-respect—a love of right for right's sake and of truth because it is true.

This is a digression ; but Monte Rotondo must be answerable for the delinquency. It unavoidably points to some such reflections. They belong to it as much as its history, although it is by no means unique in the characteristics here dwelt upon.

Its history is not a remarkable one, though eventful enough. The town is first mentioned in a papal bull of the year one thousand and seventy-four. It went through the usual mediæval sieges, burnings and outrages. It was closely implicated in the quarrels of the Orsini and Colonni—those public brawlers of the middle ages—of the former of whom it was a stronghold ; and thence, after several changes, passed under the rule of the Church. It was between here and Mentana that the conflict between the papal troops, assisted by the French, and the Garibaldians took place in eighteen hundred and sixty-seven, when the latter were defeated. The baronial palace of the Orsini mentioned above is a fine example of the ancient fortified mansion of more disturbed times. It is surmounted by a lofty square tower, overlooking a vast extent of the Campagna; its old turrets and walls crumbling to decay with damp and neglect.

Somewhat more than a mile to the south-west of Monte Rotondo is Mentana, the ancient Nomentum. Dionysius says that it was founded at the same time with Crustumerium and Fidenæ. Virgil, also, in the meeting of Æneas with his father in the Elysian fields makes Anchises say, "What youths are there! See what mighty vigour they display, and bear brows shaded with the civic oak! These for your posterity shall build Nomentum, and Gabii, and the city of Fidenæ."[*] Thus it may be considered to have been one of the earliest colonial cities founded by the Alban kings. It was subjected to Rome by Tarquinius Priscus; but afterwards joined the cities of the Latin League (of which there were thirty, including this), in the endeavour to reinstate the banished Tarquins on the throne of Rome. It is the only one of those ancient cities still left inhabited. Once, when Rome was hard beset with pestilence, and many earthquakes had occurred to affright and dispirit the inhabitants, its old enemies seized the opportunity of making incursions into its territory, committing great depredations. Aulus Servilius being appointed dictator, called all those to arms who were able to bear them; and attacking the Etrurians on the high ground of Nomentum, routed them and drove them into the city of Fidenæ, which resulted in its final capture

---

[*] Qui juvenes quantas ostentant, aspice, vires!
   At, qui umbrata gerunt civili tempora quercu,
   Hi tibi Nomentum, et Gabios, urbemque Fidenam,
   Hi Collatinas imponent montibus arces.
                Æn. vi. 771.

by means of a mine, as already related. It finds no
mention in the later periods of history. It is, however,
frequently named by classical writers. Strabo alludes to
it as the "small city of Nomentum." Ovid, at the end of
the fourth book of the Fasti, describes a curious procession
of persons arrayed in white that he met as he was returning from the city, who with great ceremony were
going to offer the entrails of a dog to the dog-star in
propitiation for a blight at that time ravaging the produce
of the fields. It is several times mentioned by Martial.
"Do you ask me what profit my Nomentum estate brings
me, Linus?" he asks, with biting sarcasm, either in joke or
in earnest. "My estate brings me this profit—that I do
not see you, Linus."* He gives a pleasant picture of its
rurality and retirement in another of his pieces addressed
to Castricus at the voluptuous seaside town of Baiæ.
"Whilst happy Baiæ, Castricus," he says, "is showering its
favours upon you, and its fair nymph receives you to swim
in its sulphureous waters, I am strengthened by the repose
of my Nomentan farm in a cottage which gives me no
trouble with its numerous acres. Here is my Baian sunshine and the sweet Lucrine lake; here have I, Castricus,
all such riches as you are enjoying. Time was when I
betook myself at pleasure to any of the far-famed watering-
places, and felt no apprehension of long journeys. Now
spots near town and retreats of easy access are my delight;
and I am content if permitted to be idle."† Seneca also
had a villa here. It had a fertile and productive territory,
much famed for its wines; a characteristic which it still
preserves.

In mediæval times it is noticeable from its having been
the meeting-place of Charlemagne and Pope Leo the Third,
accompanied by the senate of Rome, in the year eight

---

* Quid mihi reddat ager quæris, Line, Nomentanus?
  Hoc mihi reddit ager: te, Line, non video.
                                                        Ep. ii. 38.

† Ep. vi. 43.

hundred, when the former went to receive the imperial crown in that city. This meeting was celebrated by a sumptuous feast, combining all the profusion, pomp and splendour which characterised such occasions in former times. The ceremonial of his subsequent coronation at Rome is thus described by Gibbon :

"In his fourth and last pilgrimage, he was received at Rome with the due honours of king and patrician . . . . . On the festival of Christmas, the last year of the eighth century, Charlemagne appeared in the church of St. Peter ; and to gratify the vanity of Rome, he had exchanged the simple dress of his country for the habit of a patrician. After the celebration of the holy mysteries, Leo suddenly placed a precious crown on his head, and the dome resounded with the shouts of the people, 'Long life and victory to Charles the most pious Augustus, crowned by God the great and pacific emperor of the Romans!' The head and body of Charlemagne were consecrated by the royal unction ; after the example of the Cæsars, he was saluted or adored by the pontiff ; his coronation oath represents a promise to maintain the faith and privileges of the Church ; and the first-fruits were paid in his rich offerings to the shrine of the apostle. In his familiar conversation the emperor protested he was ignorant of the intentions of Leo, or he would have disappointed them on that memorable day. But the preparations for the ceremony must have disclosed the secret ; and the journey of Charlemagne reveals his knowledge and expectation. He had acknowledged that the imperial title was the object of his ambition, and a Roman synod had pronounced that it was the only adequate reward of his merits and services."[*]

Here was born the famous Crescenzio Nomentano, who for some time ruled the destinies of Rome during his occupation of the fortress of St. Angelo, as already mentioned.

The modern Mentana is a miserable little town, consisting of one long street. Its mediæval castle still frowns

* Dec. and Fall, chap. 49.

at one end of it, shorn of its warlike character, hanging out
forlorn flags of surrender to all-conquering Time in the
shape of tattered fronds of maidenhair and other parasitic
plants that find an undisturbed rooting on its walls. Some
old sarcophagi reversed, with the inscriptions still legible,
form seats under the church tower for evening gossipers.
A few fragments of old marbles are here and there built
into the walls or reared against them ; but no recording
monument remains to testify of its former importance.

Whilst we were passing along the street, we met a
benevolent-looking priest, who seemed to be the essence of
geniality and blandness, friendly smiles beaming all over
his face. He appeared to be on such terms of good-nature
with his parishioners that he might have been a sort of
Vicar of Wakefield in his little territory. As we stopped
to sketch the old castle, a little boy came and stood
beside us, whom I began to question as to his education.
He said he knew almost nothing, and that there was
no school in the place. "But," I said, "does not the
good father priest whom I saw in the street teach you
anything ?" "When he first came," he said, "he tried very
hard to do so ; but we were all so stupid we could not
learn anything whatever, so he gave it up." "And how
does he occupy himself now ?" I asked. "Now," said the
boy, "he goes to sleep."

The highest navigable point of the river at present for
large vessels is at a place called Scorano, which is about
twenty miles from Rome by land, and five and thirty by
the river. It is represented by a wide undulating plain,
marked by a few of the conical shepherds' huts which form
so characteristic an object on the Campagna. Once there was
a regular boat service as far as Ponte Felice ; but since the
opening of the railway the river has been allowed to fall into
neglect, so that what little traffic there is beyond Scorano has
to be carried on by means of small boats dragged by buffaloes.

As our vessel laboured and panted up the stream with
its string of barges behind it the day began to wane. The

mountains clothed in their purple hues seemed to be removed
to another world of unearthly splendour. The banks of
the river were dashed with glowing streaks of crimson as if
spilt with ruby-coloured wine. One by one the birds retired
to rest, all but the nightingale, who continued his sweet
strain into the night. A glassy calm settled on the river
except for the tortuous vortices that vexed its liquid surface,
shattering the pale reflection of the crescent moon, which
with the first star of evening came out in the sky. Soon
the mighty constellations began to wheel and burn above
us. The fitful firefly glanced in and out amongst the
bushes as the dews began to fall. When the daylight was
quite gone the prow of the vessel was thrust into the bushes
of a little bay, and soon a deep silence reigned around only
broken now and then by the hooting owl as he mixed
his note with the sovereign nightingale, the croak of a frog,
or the distant cry of the cicala, whilst the gliding water
gave a thin faint murmur from time to time, as if whispering in a dream. It was long before I could tear myself
away from the prospect. The vast Campagna was spread
in solemn gloom around. Those very stars lighted it in
the days of its olden glory. I watched the solitary lamp
of a far-off *tenuta* as it glimmered through the night. A
wood-laden bark floated slowly down the stream with a
blazing fire at its stern to light its wandering way. When
it had vanished in the windings of the river, I too, rolling myself in a rug in the cabin, was soon involved in a deep sleep.

I was wakened at the first streak of dawn by a bird in
the bushes, which must have sat close to my ear, though I
did not see him. First a little broken chirrup, and then a
full tide of flowing, gurgling song, as if his heart had been
burthened with music and it had overflowed in a joyous
melody. Note after note came pouring out of his mellow bill,
till the cabin seemed filled with his warbling. I arose with a
sense of chilliness, noticing for the first time that all the
apertures of the cabin had been left unclosed. I went on
deck. One by one the sleepy crew mustered. The hollows

of the Campagna were hid in mist, out of which here and there peeped a conical shepherd's hut. The river presented a very remarkable spectacle. It was covered with wreaths or pillars of mist, which stood in compacted forms on the surface of the water like spirits of the night surprised by the coming of day. Presently, as some insensible air was breathed about them, they began to move slowly up and down, sometimes approaching each other as if to whisper mysterious secrets, then gliding along in crowds, but without breaking or intermingling their forms ; then they would appear to be animated with the sober movements of a solemn dance, bending and wavering, turning leisurely by the bushes on the banks. Soon some large boats began to loom through their substance, bringing to mind the spectral vessels that bear the death-freed souls across the fabled Styx or Acheron. But now our vessel began to pant and groan, and being liberated from the moorings, we were soon steaming rapidly down the river. I stood on the captain's deck chilled with cold, straining my eyes uneasily in the direction of sunrise. As it grew redder and redder the lark flew up into the sky singing loudly. Soon a golden rim rose above the mountain tops and the silent beams glided along the pearly plain, bringing a new day to the world, so brilliant, so glorious, that one longed to run to every sleeper and wake him with the tidings that the sun had risen.

Our downward journey was enlivened by a very interesting conversation with an assistant engineer or stoker on the vessel, whose services were not required below. He was full of intelligence, looked hopefully to the future of Italy, reasoning soundly upon matters of national progress and personal development, in a manner that would have done honour to any social institute in England.

In two hours we accomplished what had taken us a long day in the upward course of the stream ; and Rome had scarcely risen from its bed when we found ourselves once more landed on the steps of the Ripetta.

CHAPTER VIII.

I PURPOSE here to interrupt the course of our journey for the length of a chapter in order to give my readers some account of a little-known class of literature (if that may be called literature which has been composed in a great measure without the use of letters, and is only now imperfectly in print), the popular songs of the people of Italy inhabiting the region of the Tiber: beginning with the Campagna of Rome and ending with those of Umbria.

It is a thing hardly to be believed that in the heart of a rude and uncultivated peasantry, incapable, for the most part, of either reading or writing, there should exist one of the noblest and purest fountains of lyrical inspiration and composition, a faculty so delicate and refined as very often to produce, I will not say rivals to Horace and Catullus, but something which often matches them, in subtlety of rendering, in neatness of form and finish, breathing a fragrance and delicacy of sentiment quite unknown to their time and age. By far the greater part of these are on the universal subject : they are love songs ; they treat of lovers' joys and lovers' woes, with old tales of devotion and insepararable attachment. One of their most remarkable features is their thorough wholesomeness and purity. They are darkened by no shade of coarseness, nor by any touch of sensuality. They are pure as the sunshine, the wind, the fresh flowers—as the simple affections of which they are

P

the offspring.   They reflect no traces of bad passions, they
harbour no brood of dissoluteness or vice ; they are without
affectation, prudery, or license, bird-like and self-unconscious
in their utterance, as such songs should be.   Many of them
embalm the relics of knightly chivalry, in which the beloved
one is addressed as *dama* (or dame) and the lover is called
servente amoroso (loving servant).   It is from the mountainous
districts that these sweet songs have emanated in their
purest form, and in which they have been best preserved :
where the invader has seldom come, and where robust
habits and a remote locality have placed the people out of
the reach of social corruptions and depreciating tendencies.
There is a perceptible difference between the language of
the mountains and that of the plains ; the latter being
mixed with Gallic phrases or corrupted by Spanish influences.   The same holds good also of the moral tone of
the people and their compositions, the former being loftier,
purer, and distinguished by a higher social sentiment and
a more domestic character.   Even where these verses
contain technical defects of construction they breathe a
music and fitness of sound to sense, and embody an artless
grace of expression often denied to culture and more
elaborate literary means.   Sometimes they are jocular,
sometimes smart, sometimes homely, sad, or sorrowful,
as suits the humour of the composer.   Many of them
might have been written by Dante or his friend Cino
da Pistoia.   They are full of allusions to natural things.
The stars, winds, birds, fruits, or flowers, furnish inexhaust-
ible images, and are frequently personified to symbolize the
sentiments of the composer.   Here is one in which the
lover apostrophizes his mistress's affection under the emblem
of a dove.

> Vola, palomba, quanto puoi volare,
> Salisci in alto quanto puoi salire,
> Gira lo mondo quanto puoi girare :
> Un giorno alle mie mani hai da venire.*

---

* This and several others here quoted are from the ‘ Canti Popolari

Which may be translated :

> Fly, fly, wild dove, as far as thou canst go;
> Rise in the air as high, as high can be;
> Sweep round the world wherever winds may blow:
> One day, where'er thou go, thou must return to me.

Here is another of a similar order, full of exquisite symbolism.

> Un garofano ho visto da una banda,
> Dall'altra parte un generoso fiore;
> E passa il vostro amore, e mi domanda:
> Chi ha donato a voi questo bel fiore?
> Rispondo: È nato nel giardin dell'alma,
> Dove si leva la spera del sole:
> Dove si leva e dove si riposa;
> Vóltati verso me, candida rosa:
> Dove si leva e dove si ripone;
> Vóltati verso me, candido fiore.

For which the English reader must accept this.

> A pink opens out on one hand,
> On the other an exquisite flower;
> And your love passing by doth demand,
> Who gave you this beautiful flower?
> I reply, It was born in the land
> Of the soul, where the sun rules the hour—
> Where he rises and sinks to repose—
> Turn towards me, immaculate rose—
> Where he rises and where he reposes—
> Turn towards me, pure rose of all roses.

Almost all of the Tuscan songs are love songs, partly based upon Latin traditions; possibly some of them may have even retained an Etruscan character. They have, however, been largely influenced by the troubadour element

Toscani,' collected and annotated by Giuseppe Tigri, and published at Florence by Barbèra. I am also further indebted for some of the information conveyed in this chapter to his introductory essay attached to the same. It will be needless to point out to the reader of the Italian language the little peculiarities of dialect here and there made use of, as their meaning is always apparent.

of the thirteenth and fourteenth centuries, when every one used "sweet and airy rhymes of love ;" doubtless many of them had their origin at that time. They follow endless. modulations and modifications ; so that the same song is often reproduced, wholly or in part, in divers forms ; but their main traits are never lost : they are always subtle and delicate, reflecting the manifold aspects and idiosyncrasies of the various minstrels by whom they are adapted.

As regards the tunes or chants to which these songs are sung I cannot give a very definite account. They are all in a minor key, of course, as the music of nature always, or nearly always is ; their rhythm very difficult to make out ; many of them giving the idea of the wail of some wild bird or animal more than the ordered melody of the human voice. They are probably to be resolved into a few and very simple elements originating in remote ages, it may be in the days of Catullus and Virgil, or even earlier still.

The songs of the Campagna and region about Rome possess distinctive characteristics. They are almost invariably composed of eight lines or verses, of eleven syllables each, rhymed alternately, the first two lines generally containing some picturesque conceit to seize the attention, which is repeated at the end of the song. In these songs the people embalm their most sacred emotions, showing the greatest unwillingness to expose them to strangers. Visconti (who was one of the first collectors of these little lyrics) had much difficulty in persuading them to repeat them to him. In some cases he failed altogether, and in others they were not able to do it excepting by singing. It is to the intrinsic and personal nature of these songs that Visconti attributes their nerve and force ; being usually composed for a special end without any reference to a wider appeal, just as a love-letter might be. Though they sometimes contain archaisms, yet they are always composed with great purity of diction and without the least vulgarity. What neatly-turned strain of Tasso or other most cultivated Italian poet, for instance, could be more exquisite than this charming little lyric?

> Rosa gentil nel giardin d' Amore,
>   Vaga comparsa fai tra verdi foglie,
> Il tuo purpureo e candido colore
>   Luce da l'occhi e pace a l'alma toglie;
> Intorno spandi sì soave odore,
>   Ch' ogni maggiore piacere in sè raccoglie;
> Punto da le tue spine questo core
>   Di dolor morirà se non ti coglie:
> Rosa gentil, che nel giardin d' Amore
>   Vaga comparsa fai tra verdi foglie.*

Which may be thus rendered into English.

> Dainty sweet Rose, who in Love's garden-ground
>   Amidst green leaves thy face dost half reveal,
> Thy white and red in subtle mixture bound,
>   Light from the eye, peace from the soul do steal:
> Such tender odour thou dost scatter round,
>   That every joy in thee hath end and seal;
> This heart must die pierced by thy thorn's sharp wound,
>   If thy ungathered balms refuse to heal:
> Dainty sweet Rose, who in Love's garden-ground
>   Amidst green leaves thy face dost half reveal.

There is another characteristic of these songs of the Campagna I believe quite peculiar to them. It is that all the lines have very often the same terminal consonant, the variation of the rhymes being got by a simple change of the penultimate vowel, by which a very smooth and flowing effect is obtained. Here is a sample of this kind of composition.

> Lucentissima stella mattutina,
>   Vaga ninfa d' Amore, dea serena,
> Non ci passa nè sera nè mattina,
>   Che non rimira la bellezza tena;

---

* This and several of the following songs are taken from a little *brochure* entitled "Saggio de' Canti Popolari della Provincia di Marittima e Campagna," by the late Commendatore P. E. Visconti. It was printed in Rome in eighteen hundred and thirty, but is now very rare, and difficult to be met with.

Chi la rimira sà faccia divina
  L' aria se ce và nuvola serena ;
Quando esce lo sole a lei s' inchina,
  Credendo che ce sia la Maddalena :
Lucentissima stella mattutina,
  Vaga ninfa d' Amore, dea serena.

It will be seen that in these verses the penultimate syllable has only been changed throughout in one particular. I have indicated it in the following translation ; though, of course, it would be impossible to follow it accurately in the English language.

Clear morning star, whose beams do brightly shine,
  Sweet nymph of Love, divinity serene,
No morn or eve may meet these eyes of mine,
  Wherein thy fair-like beauty is not seen :
Who sees thy face beholds a face divine,
  Makes heaven of every sullen vapour clean ;
The rising sun to thee doth first incline,
  Believing thee the beauteous Magdalene :
Clear morning star, whose beams do brightly shine,
  Sweet nymph of Love, divinity serene.

Here is another, containing a lover's protestation worth transcribing.

Prima ch' io lasci te, gentil signora,
  I duri sassi si faranno cera,
Madre dell' ombre diverrà l' aurora,
  Il mezzogiorno sonerà la sera,
Saranno il foco e l' acqua uniti ancora,
  Eterna durerà la primavera ;
I nostri amori finiranno allora
  Quando 'l mondo ritorni a quel che era.
Prima ch' io lasci te, gentil signora,
  I duri sassi si faranno cera.

Ere I do leave thee, gentle lady bright,
  The solid stones shall melt like wax away,
The mother of shadows quench the morning light,
  And eve proclaim the tidings of midday,
Fire and water in one bond unite,
  And spring unchanged for ever hold his sway :
Then shall our ended loves be finished quite,
  When earth its primal chaos shall display.
Ere I do leave thee, gentle lady bright,
  The solid stones shall melt like wax away.

Here the singer has evidently met with reverses.

> Misero chi confida a la fortuna,
>   Pazzo chi crede in amicizia umana :
> Nel mondo non si dà fede veruna ;
>   L' amante più fedele s'allontana.
> Le donne sono simili a la luna,
>   Fanno li quarti ad ogni settimana ;
> Meglio è lasciarle andare a una a una,
>   E vivere con tutte a la lontana.
> Misero chi confida a la fortuna,
>   Pazzo chi crede in amicizia umana.

> A fool is he who waits on fortune's boon,
>   Mad he who counts on friendship's* fickleness ;
> The truest trust is bent and broken soon ;
>   In this world is no certain steadfastness :
> For women vary as the varying moon,
>   Which every week a different face doth dress :
> Better to pass them by thee one by one,
>   And bide away from them in singleness.
> A fool is he who waits on fortune's boon,
>   Mad he who counts on friendship's fickleness.

The next I shall quote has an air so delicately sad and tender in its expression, so refined and pensive in its low-breathed sorrow, that I scarcely know where to place it amongst all the erotic lyrics with which I am acquainted.

> Vanne, sospiro mio, vanne a trovare
>   Quella che doglia sol me reca al core !
> Giunto dinanzi a lei, fatte a parlare ;
>   Racconta le mie pene, 'l mio dolore ;
> Dicce che peno sempre, e che me pare
>   De vederme ridotto all' ultime ore ;
> Dì, che quantunque me faccia penare,
>   Costante sono sempre nel suo amore—
> E se la trovi sorda a li lamenti,
> Povero mio sospir, te spargo ai venti.

I cannot hope to have translated with anything like the sentiment of the original this fragile little lyric, exhaling the very aroma of the soul's tenderness. It would require a Shakespeare, a Fletcher, or a Ben Jonson to do it justice.

---

* *Amicizia,* however, in Italian, means rather more than "friendship" in English.

Here is the best representative that I can give my English readers for it.

> Go forth, my sigh, go sadly forth, and find
>   Her who doth feed my heart with sorrow's flow;
> And if thou reach her tell her all my mind,
>   Recount my griefs and paint my wasting woe;
> Tell her I suffer still—through her, unkind,
>   My life's last hour in anguish seems to go;
> Tell her that though she scorn me, still I bind
>   My soul to hers with love no change can know—
> And if, sad sigh, thou find her unrelenting,
> Then die upon the air in vain lamenting.

The following little song is of another order, but scarcely less charming in its way than some of the foregoing. It was taken down from the mouth of a peasant at Castel Gandolfo, at the foot of the Sabine mountains.*

> La prima volta che m'innamorai
> Piantai lo dolce persico alla vigna,
> E poi gli dissi, Persico benigno,
> S'amor mi lassa, ti possi seccare!
>
> A capo all'anno ritornai alla vigna;
> Trovai lo dolce persico seccato;
> Mi butto in terra e tutta scapiglio:
> Questo è segno ch'amore m'ha lassato.
>
> Albero che t'avevo tanto a caro,
> E t'innaquavo co li miei sudore,
> Si son seccate le cime e le rame
> I frutti han perso lo dolce sapore.
>
> Morte vieni da me quando ti pare,
> Giacchè il mio bene ha mutato pensare.

> When first the sweet pleasure of loving I knew
>   I planted a peach in my vineyard one day,
> And prayed, if my loved one should e'er prove untrue,
>   My beautiful peach tree might wither away.

* By my friend, Signor Ettore Ferrari, a young Roman sculptor, who adds a wide literary culture to his professional abilities. I may take this opportunity of acknowledging my obligations to him also in other respects in the compilation of this portion of my volume.

In the spring I returned to my vineyard, and found
  My peach tree was drooping, all faded and dried;
Then weeping, I threw myself down **on the ground**;
  For this is a sign she is faithless, I **cried.**

My beautiful peach that **to** me was so dear,
  So anxiously tended **and** nourished with pain,
Its branches are withered, its leaves are grown sere,
  Its fruits their sweet savour no longer retain.

Come, Death, when thou wilt; all my pleasures are o'er,
Since she who once loved me now loves me no more.

As we leave the Campagna of Rome and enter into **the** districts of Umbria these songs assume **a** rather different form, though the character of them is very much the **same.** They are for the most **part** designated **by** the term Rispetti (or respects). They are short **poems,** wherein **the** lover addresses his mistress with compliments or salutations. They are usually composed **in from six to ten lines or** verses; those of eight lines generally interrhyming **the first six, and closing** with a **couplet** conveyed **almost** always with great point **and** force, gracefully inverting and repeating the previous subject. Their conceptive treatment is sometimes sententious, and then the principal sentence **is** first **laid** down, and the corollary follows by way of deduction **from it,** or else the subject to be enforced is first **stated, and** the example or apology used by way of illustration. Here **is** one of this class of poems in which the Muse has tried her hand on the old problem.

O Dio del cielo, o Dio del ciel benigno,
Perchè tu non facesti il mondo paro?
Tu facesti chi ricco e chi meschino,
A chi donasti il dolce, **a** chi l'amaro,
A chi tu desti l'oro, **a** chi **lo** piombo:
Non è nessun contento **in** questo mondo.
A chi tu desti l'oro, **a** chi l'argento:
In **questo mondo 'n** è nissun contento.

O God of heaven, **O God of heaven benign,**
  Why mad'st thou **not this** hapless **world more even?**
For one is rich, and one in want doth pine;
  To one is sweet, to one is bitter given;

And one to lead, and one to gold hath birth:
There is no one content upon the earth:—
To one is gold, to one is silver sent:
Upon the earth there is no one content.

Here is another of the sententious order.

Simile è l' uomo all' uccelletto in gabbia;
Non canta per amore, ma per rabbia.
Così son io quando vedo tene;
Canto, ma il mio cantar m' accresce pene.

Man, like a bird shut up within a cage,
Sings not for love, but rapt with sorrow's rage;
So I, when thou dost pass beside my door,
Sing, but my singing makes the pain the more.

What shall we say of the peasant's wife or *innamorata* who can address him on the eve of a journey in such terms as these ?—

O bocca d' oro fra pomi d' argento,
Ora lo vedo che tu vuoi partire.
Pártine pure, e vattene contento;
Ricórdati, idol mio, del ben servire:
E per la via troverai dell' erbe;
Ricórdati, idol mio, di chi ti serve:
E per la via troverai dei fiori;
Ricórdati, idol mio, di chi abbandoni:
E per la via troverai dei sassi;
Ricórdati, idol mio, di chi tu lassi.

O golden mouth in silver apples set,
I know the time is come when you must go.
Go, then; your parting with contentment met;
  Remember, dear, the service that you owe:
And by the way green herbage you will find;
Remember, dearest, whom you leave behind:
And by the way bright blossoms will enweave;
Remember, my sweet idol, her you leave:
And by the way hard rocks and stones will lie;
Remember her to whom you say good-bye.

This was probably given forth on the occasion of the lover's departure to the lowlands, where many of the peasants go at certain seasons of the year to assist in the labours of agriculture. The allusion to the temptations, troubles and difficulties with which he may meet, and through which he is to be protected by the guardian thought of the loved one, is beautifully conveyed. It will hardly be believed that such songs as these should be the composition of totally uneducated persons, as far as literary culture goes. Still more amazing is it that such elegant strains should be frequently given forth impromptu—the offspring of the moment without any premeditation. Tigri, in the introduction to his collection of Tuscan popular songs, gives some interesting particulars regarding the faculty of improvising amongst the peasantry, from which I will make a few extracts.

"The countryman," he says, "both in the mountains and on the plains, is accustomed to sing at every age and at all hours. Singing, he feels his labour grow the lighter, whether it be domestic or that of the fields. The old man sings at the loom, or as he sits by the fire, and his songs, always seasoned with some good and sentential matter, are learnt by his children and grandchildren. If to the exercise of the faculty of song is adjoined the advantage of having read or heard some poetical composition, 'the Royal Race of France' (I Reali di Francia), or the verses of Tasso, for example, it will be scarcely surprising when I say that these songs transmitted from family to family not only originated with themselves, but that exquisitely beautiful ones are being composed in the same manner by the men and women of to-day. I myself knew a girl of our mountains from the hamlet of Stazzana, named Maria, an authoress of much spirit, who, although, she told me, she had never read a single book of poetry, yet knowing by heart an infinite number of these songs—just as a youth newly emerged from his rhetorical exercises with the ring of classic verses still in his mind would, by recurring to them, be able to frame good ones—with a natural aptitude for making verses, readily succeeded in composing harmonious and effective lyrics. The same thing was the case with a young shepherdess called Cherubina, whom I also met. This young girl, of a pleasing person, full of spirit and good sense, showed me, after many entreaties and pretty excuses, some verses on the Passion of our Lord, which she had composed without any other help than that of nature and two little books of devotion from which she had taken the subject, which she carried with her every day when she went to tend the sheep.   When I asked her to repeat to me some Rispetti, she excused herself by saying, 'Oh, sir, I can repeat ever so many when I sing—but now—unless they came clearly before me, indeed I cannot.'   So true is it that they do not conceive of poetry without song ; in fact they never speak of *improvising*, but of *singing* poetry.   This I can confirm with the example of a well-known improvisatrice of the Pistoian Apennines, Beatrice di Pian degli Ontani, of whom Tommasèo thus writes in the preface to his 'Canti Popolari.' 'At Cutigliano I found a rich vein of song which I was not able to exhaust in a whole day.   I caused to come from Pian degli Ontani, about three miles distant, a certain Beatrice, the wife of a shepherd, herself also a tender of flocks, who did not know how to read, but could im- provise in octaves [stanzas of six interrhymed lines and a couplet]. . . Beatrice warmed in a trial of skill with a respondent, singing for a whole hour in elegant and refined terms, with the few ideas which had been bestowed upon her ; always taking up the rhymes of the two last verses sung by her companion.'   I may add that from that time she has been constantly in the habit of singing impromptu ; and that during the last Italian events of eighteen hundred and forty-eight, often called to Cutigliano to improvise before various persons, she was not in the habit of refusing ; but without any preparation, only asked to be made ac- quainted with the incidents (which were those of the time) upon which they desired her to improvise, when in the midst of a circle of the peasantry of the district, she in a moment commenced to sing the most beautiful octave verses."

As an illustration of the faculty possessed by this gifted

woman, as well as for its good, wholesome teaching, I will
here give one of her little lyrics, also made impromptu.

> Non vi maravigliate, **giovanetti,**
> Se non sapessi troppo **ben** cantare.
> In casa mia **non** ci è **nato** maestri,
> **E manco a** scuola **son** ita a imparare.
> **Se voi volete** intender la mia scuola,
> **Su questi** poggi all'acqua e alla gragnuola.
> **Volete** intender lo mio imparare?
> Andar per legna, o starmene a zappare.

Perhaps I have scarcely got the simplicity of the original
in this translation ; but here **is** the sense of it.

> It is no marvel, youths, your song is shorn
>   Of that fine tone which makes the poet **burn.**
> Within my house there is no master born,
>   Nor any school where I my task might learn.
> If you would go to school where I did gain
> My power, mount yonder crags through hail **and rain:**
> If you would read, as I, the muse's tome,
> **Go** dig the ground and fetch **the fuel home.***

I shall here give a few examples from the Umbrian or

---

* It is interesting to compare this with one of Wordsworth's sonnets,
in which he **seems** dimly to have perceived, as a thesis, from the side of
reflection and culture, what has here become a resultant and experimental
fact to the mind of the poetess-improvisatrice.

> Enough of garlands, of the Arcadian crook,
> And all that Greece and Italy have sung,
> Of swains reposing myrtle groves among !
> Ours couch on native rocks, will cross a brook
> **Swoln** with chill rains, nor ever cast a look
> **This way or** that, **or** give it even a thought
> **More than** by smoothest pathway may be brought
> **Into** a vacant mind. Can written book
> Teach what *they* **learn?** Up, hardy mountaineer !
> And guide the Bard, ambitious to be one
> Of Nature's privy **council as** thou **art**
> **On** cloud-sequestered heights, that **see** and **hear**
> **To** what dread Power He delegates his part
> On earth, who works in **the heaven** of heavens, alone.

Tuscan songs of Tigri's collection.   Here is one put
together with considerable grace and poetic perceptiveness.

> La luna s' è venuta a lamentare
> Inde la faccia del divino Amore:
> Dice che in cielo non ci vuol più stare;
> Chè tolto gliel' avete lo splendore.
> E si lamenta, e si lamenta forte;
> L' ha conto le sue stelle, non son tutte
> E gliene manca due, e voi l' avete:
> Son que' du' occhi che in fronte tenete.

> The moon arises in the midnight sky,
>   And thus to Love Divine she makes her moan;
> She says she can no longer stay thereby,
>   Because its splendour, rapt by you, is gone:
> Full sadly she complains, and sadly sighs:
> She counts her stars, and finds the tale is short—
> Two lost for all her searching; they are those
> That shine beneath the bending of your brows.

Here is a gallant little strain, probably the impromptu
of a moment.

> Avete un crine inanellato e biondo,
> C' ha fortemente legato il mio core:
> Ete un par d' occhi danno luce al mondo,
> E mi tengon soggetto a tutte l' ore.

> With many a bright ringlet thy blonde hair so curled
>   Has bound in immovable fetters my heart;
> Those two bonny eyes which illumine the world
>   Still hold me thy subject wherever thou art.

Another on the same subject.

> E son venuto, bella, per comprare
> Questi due occhi che in fronte tenete.
> Non ho portato somma di danaro,
> Che non sapevo il prezzo che chiedete:
> Non ho portato nè oro nè argento;
> Vi lascio lo mio cor per pagamento:
> Non ho portato nè argento nè oro;
> Vi lascio lo mio cor, ricco tesoro.

> I would buy those eyes of thine,
>   Shining bright in beauty's mask,
> But have no gold—could not divine
>   What the price that you might ask

> Gold and silver—failing both,
> Take for pay my heart in troth:
> Neither silver, neither gold,
> Take my heart's rich wealth untold.

Here is a pretty, sad one.

> Rondinella, che passi monti e colli,
> Se trovi l'amor mio, digli che venga;
> E digli, son rimasta in questi poggi,
> Come rimane la smarrita agnella;
> E digli son rimasta senza nimo,
> Come l'albero secco senza il ramo,
> E digli, son rimasta abbandonata,
> Come l'erbetta secca in sulle prata.

> O swallow, flying o'er those rugged places,
> If you find my loved one, bid him come;
> And tell him, here amongst these mountain mazes
> I wander like a lamb bereft of home;
> And tell him, here I live and make my moan,
> Like a withered tree whose top is gone;
> And tell him, here I live without a lover,
> Like a tree whose summer green is over;
> And tell him, here I live abandonëd,
> Like a droughted mead whose grass is dead.

Here is one in a livelier strain, composed also in absence; or, it may be, a half serious little conceit thrown after a faithless one.

> Cupido mio, Cupido marinaro,
> Mi presteresti un po' la tua galera?
> Ch'io me ne vada a spasso per il mare
> A ritrovar la mia dama che era.
> E se la trovo, la vo' imprigionare;
> Metter li voglio al collo una catena:
> Metter li voglio al collo cose belle,
> Un giglio, un bel diamante e quattro stelle.

> Cupid sailor, Cupid mine,
> Lend me but that bark of thine.
> I would sail across the sea,
> To bring my fair one back to me;
> And if I find her, to detain her,
> Round her pretty neck would chain her—
> Would hang about that neck of hers
> A lily, a fine diamond, and four bright stars.

Sometimes they are humorous, as in the following.

> Oh! come fa la donna contadina
> Quando le' vede l'amante passare!
> E va sull' uscio, e chiama la gallina,
> Finchè l'amante si venga a voltare.
> Quando l'amante poi s'è rivoltato,
> Sciò, sciò, gallina, che non t'ho chiamato!

> These country girls are mighty sly:
>   For when they see their lovers' faces,
> Chuck, chuck! as to the fowls, they cry,
>   Until their lover turns and gazes:
> Then call, as if they meant no other,
> Shoo, shoo! these fowls are quite a bother.

Here is one of some newly-bereaved Chloe, almost as pungent as Martial, which says more for her philosophy than her constancy. We will, however, suppose that it is a mere *jeu d'esprit.*

> È morto lo mio amore, e non ho pianto:
> Credevo ben che fusse altro dolore:
> È morto il papa, e se n' è fatto un altro,
> E così farò io un altro amore.

> My sweetheart is dead, but I make no pother,
>   For in life there is too much sorrow:
> When the good pope dies they will find another,
>   And I a sweetheart to-morrow.

Sometimes lines of the very highest order are met with in these lyrics. These, for example, would match with some of the best of Petrarch or our own Marlowe. They are conceived in the finest spirit of true poetry.

> Oh quanto vi sta ben la gentilezza,
> Come ad un prato un bel manto di fiori.

> How do thy dainty graces fit thee well,
> As to a mead a mantle of fair flowers!

Or this one.

> Vi ride prima gli occhi che la bocca.

> Your eyes are seen to smile before your mouth.

It is probable that the great revival of Italian letters in

the latter half of the thirteenth century was in a great
measure based upon these native little lyrics which floated
about everywhere, as a comparison with the poems of Cino
da Pistoia, Dante da Maiano, Guido Cavalcanti, and others,
will render apparent. The resemblance is not only perceptible in the sentiment of many of them, but also in their
construction, particularly in the opening phrase and its
repetition in similar rhymes at the end of the piece, which,
as has been seen, is a characteristic of many of the surviving popular lyrics, being, probably, in the first instance,
an adaptation of the Tuscan and Umbrian *stornello*. These
stornelli are short little interlocutory songs, sometimes
strung together and sung alternately, and sometimes used
as the chorus or refrain to other songs. They generally
commence with the name of a fruit or flower, giving the
motive to the two following lines, with which the latter
rhymes, these constituting the whole of the piece. Here
is a sample of these little productions.

> Foglia d'aprile.
> Ora che me lo hai fatto licenziare,
> E notte e giorno mi farai morire.

> April leaves.
> Now thou hast rejected me, faithless lover,
> I die night and day, my heart so grieves.

Sometimes they vary the apostrophe to some other
object, as in this.

> O luna, O sole!
> O stella Diana, non mi abbandonare
> Fammi rifar la pace col mio amore.

> O sun, O moon!
> O star of Diana, do not forsake me;
> But make my peace with my lover full soon.

Besides these there is another class of songs which constitute a sort of ballad literature to be found in print, which
have nothing whatever of the tenderness, grace, and sentiment of these little lyrics in their composition. They are
mostly vulgar recitals of adventure or crime, sold as half-

Q

penny ballads on the stalls at fairs and festivals. But these are certainly not to be considered indigenous. They are generally either imported from other languages, or are the composition of literary hacks of the cities. How far a larger education might improve or destroy this sweet fountain of native song is a question which experience alone can decide. Very probably, where the touch is so delicate, so instinctively fine and right, education would rather tend to its destruction by substituting other trains of thought and wider intellectual ranges for the simplicity which goes straight to its subject from purely artistic feeling. Fortunately, the Italians are now fully alive to the importance of collecting and preserving these charming effusions, which begin to form one of the most valuable and beautiful pages of all their literary treasures. The work should be proceeded with promptly, before the tide of change and more extended interests shall have swept them ruthlessly out of memory.

SORACTE.

CHAPTER IX.

FROM SCORANO TO TODI.

A S the not very important length of the river between Scorano and Borghetto is traversed by the railway, and I had already passed it several times before, being thus familiarised with the aspects of the river between these points, I thought it sufficient to take the train from Rome to Borghetto in company with Mr. Hemans, who had specially visited many of the localities, so as to be able to indicate any point of particular interest. Accordingly, Mr. Hemans, myself, and Mr. Barclay, who joined us for the purpose of exercising his pencil and studying the valuable works of art that we should meet with, one morning took train from Rome to Borghetto. It will be sufficient to notice the chief features of the country and landscape in passing.

For some distance beyond Scorano the little-cultivated Campagna passes into well-cared-for plains of pasture and arable land, varied with wide patches of sombre woodland. Presently, these plains rise into sloping hills, until they attain a considerable elevation, the summits of which are picturesquely crowned at intervals with towns and villages that seem to belong to the kingdom of the air more than the earth, each with its graceful campanile and perhaps a grey tower or two, bearing on its battered walls memorials of the feudal past. Nothing could be more charming than the situation of these miniature citadels, sometimes built upon a shelf of rock, sometimes rising from groves and trees, sometimes having their foundations laid in slopes of emerald grass. The hills also are very lovely. Their sides are clothed with varied tints of vegetation, broken with soft grey patches of lichened rock. Through this delightful region the river flows, wandering hither and thither, as if to leave no beauty unexplored, no nook, however remote and secluded, unvisited, fed from time to time in his course by the tiny tributaries of meadow-brook or hillside torrent running down joyfully to greet him. At every turn Mount Soracte (now called St. Oreste) presents its majestic outline and torn peak with still clearer distinctness, the tiny convent at its summit like a speck against the sky. This classic mountain properly belongs to the Apennine limestone range, though situated in the midst of a volcanic country. Its name is frequently met with in ancient writers. "Dost thou see how high Soracte stands," says Horace, in his well-known winter piece, "white with deep snow, whilst the labouring woods are crushed beneath their load?"* It was once famous as the site of a temple dedicated to Apollo, whose priests were supposed to possess miraculous powers over the element of fire, which it was believed could not injure them. Virgil alludes to this in the prayer of Aruns before slaying Camilla, when he makes him exclaim, "Highest of the gods to me, Apollo, guardian of holy Soracte, whom first we honour for whom is fed the blaze of pines piled up, whose votaries we, passing through the fire in the strength of our piety, press the soles of our feet on many a burning coal, grant, almighty Father, that by my arms may be abolished our dishonour."†

* Vides ut alta stet nive candidum
 Soracte, nec jam sustineant onus
  Silvæ laborantes geluque
  Flumina constiterint acuto.

    O. i. 9.

† Summe Deûm, sancti custos Soractis Apollo, &c.

    Æn. xi. 785.

To face page 217.

BORGHETTO.

About twenty-four miles from Rome, on the right, is the little town of Correse, which represents the ancient Cures, a celebrated city of the Sabine territory. The earliest notice of it in history is when Romulus, after the subjugation of Antemnæ, Cænina, and Crustumerium, advanced so nearly to the Sabine borders that the nation became alarmed, and joining themselves in league against him under Tatius, the king of Cures, prepared to withstand his progress. Dionysius says it was one of the greatest of the Sabine cities. It is also mentioned by Strabo as having been once important, though a mere village in his day. From this town Numa Pompilius, the early priest-king, went to Rome, from which circumstance the Roman and Sabine people gave themselves the joint name of Quirites. Antique remains are still to be seen in its neighbourhood, though not very numerous or important.

Somewhat removed from the river on the left is Fiano, probably the ancient Flavina or Flavinium mentioned by Virgil and Silius Italicus.* A few miles beyond this point the river is spanned by the Ponte Felice, first built by Augustus, connecting Umbria with Etruria, near which is the picturesque village of Borghetto, whose broken old castle forms so conspicuous an object from the plain. This plain was the seat of a somewhat memorable engagement at the end of the last century. When Napoleon Bonaparte had withdrawn the flower of his army into Egypt, the Neapolitans thought it a good opportunity to attempt to rid their country of the French altogether, who were at that time in the occupation of Rome. On the king entering Rome with his army, under General Mack, who had come from Germany at the king's request, the enemy abandoned it. They, however, soon rallied, and meeting the Neapolitans in this place, defeated them with great slaughter ; so that General Mack with the remnant of his army was driven back to Naples.

Leaving the railway at Borghetto, we got into a vehicle

* Æn. vii. 696.   Sil. viii. 492.

of the country serving as a very limited order of omnibus,
into which four persons might squeeze themselves with
difficulty. At the same time there entered it a portly and
respectable middle-aged gentleman, who devoutly crossed
himself before doing so—the pious prelude of old-fashioned
travellers to any undertaking in which there may be risk or
danger. We had some conversation with him. He spoke
with severity against the new government of the Roman
territory. Under papal rule he had been general of the
fortress of Civita Castellana, which is a considerable one ;
but on its annexation to the kingdom of Italy he had, of
course, been dispossessed. Whilst we were talking, there
came on a heavy shower of rain ; the wretched old sun-
cracked covering of the vehicle allowing the water to pour
upon us in streams from every part of it, so that we were
soon wet through. By the roadside we saw some cloaked
and cowled figures watching over the body of a shepherd who
had been found dead the day before, probably from natural
causes, as we were told there was no mark of violence upon
him. The ex-general made it a ground of bitter complaint
against the new régime that the poor fellow had lain there
so long pending the official inquiry ; for by the law it is
necessary that any one meeting with death in any extraordinary manner must be left in the same place and
position until inquiry has been made. By the time we had
got to Civita Castellana the rain cleared off and the sun
shone brightly. Bidding farewell to our fellow-traveller,
with many offers of civility and politeness on his part to
afford us any assistance that he might be able to render,
we entered our *albergo*, one of the better kinds of inns of
the Roman territory.

Whilst we were sitting after dinner, an interesting-
looking lad came into the room, dusty and apparently
tired. He brought with him a violin, and, after saluting
us, began to play upon it, resting it on his knee, in the
manner which one frequently sees represented in old
pictures. There was a touch of pathos in his appearance ;

he looked thin and worn. Presently, at the request of an Italian who sat at table with us, he commenced to sing a Neapolitan song called " Mastro Raffaello," in a somewhat rough voice. I asked where he came from. " Quite un-necessary to ask," anticipated our companion at table ; " of course he comes from Viggiano ; *non è vero, raggazzino ?*" (is it not true, my boy ?) he said, turning to the young musician. " *'Ngnor, sì,*" (yes, sir), he answered in the manner of the Neapolitans. " It is a most wonderful little town, that of Viggiano," pursued our companion ; "there is scarcely a man, woman, or child in it who does not play some musical instrument, generally the violin, very often with taste and feeling. I have seen a little child," he added, "of three years old take the violin upon its knee and play, not merely with accuracy, but with a style and manner quite surprising." It would appear as if this talent were quite innate, since no one teaches the people, but they seem to grow naturally into it.

Civita Castellana is a few miles to the west of the Tiber, with which it is connected by a small tributary called the Treja. It is situated upon an undulating plateau, but, like Veii, is environed by deep ravines, which entrench it on all sides excepting the south, where it subsides into the plain or table-land towards Nepi and Monterosi. The ravines are doubtless the result of volcanic disturbances which have torn the tufaceous rock into these enormous rents, at the bottom of which streams of water run, turning several picturesque mills in their course. The sides of the cliffs are excavated in many places by numerous Etruscan tombs. The chasms are crossed by two lofty modern bridges leading into the town. The town itself is not remarkable, except for that quaintness and irregu-larity of structure so frequently met with in Italy. It has a fine cathedral front or portico of delicate and graceful architecture, with mosaics by the Cosmati, the celebrated mosaic workers of the thirteenth century. Various remains of ancient Roman marbles are built into the walls of the

houses here and there.   Its mediæval history is embodied
in the sturdy old fortress built by San Gallo for Pope
Alexander the Sixth, still maintained, as has been said, as
a garrison.   Not only is the situation of the town romantic
and beautiful in itself, but it is surrounded by a country
which embraces every variety of spreading champaign,
deep-green woods and far-away hillside slopes spotted
with towns and villages—all overlooked by the towering
Soracte and the more distant mountains of Sabina.

Here stood Falerii, one of the oldest and most powerful
cities of Etruria.   Its origin is involved in obscurity.   The
peculiar character of its position would doubtless cause it
to be chosen as one of the first settlements in this part of
Italy.   It is first mentioned as having united arms with
the Veientes and Fidenates against Rome in the year four
hundred and thirty-seven before Christ, when the allied
forces were defeated by Cornelius Cossus under the walls
of Fidenæ, as already narrated.   Still maintaining the
strongest enmity against Rome, the Falisci did their best
to induce the inhabitants of the surrounding country to assist
the Veientes in their last struggle against their powerful
enemies.   This brought upon them the vengeance of the
Romans.   After the fall of Veii, Camillus led his army
into the territory of the Falisci, who, witnessing from their
walls the slaughter and depredations committed around
them, issued from the city, establishing themselves on the
summit of a steep place of difficult access, about a mile
distant.   Camillus, however, succeeded in obtaining possession of a situation which commanded theirs, and thence
making an onslaught upon them, drove them back with
considerable losses into the city, which was then besieged ;
but its reduction might have been as protracted an undertaking as that of Veii had not a fortunate chance occurred
to further the cause of the Romans.

A schoolmaster, having under his care the children of
some of the chief families at Falerii, was accustomed to
take them for recreation without the walls of the city.

One day he led them gradually nearer to the **enemies'** circumvallations, until they had overpassed the **boundary** and found themselves at the door of Camillus' **tent.** The schoolmaster then delivered the children into the hands of Camillus, telling him that by this means he gave him the power to make his own terms with the besieged city. Camillus, however, rejected the proposal with great scorn, saying that the Romans fought as men and soldiers, not as robbers and traitors ; and placing rods in the hands of the youths, stripped their schoolmaster, and bade them drive him back to the city to receive the reward of his treachery. This piece of good faith on the part of the Romans so affected their enemies that they **at** once entered into **an** armistice, and finally yielded themselves in allegiance to Rome.

The peace, however, was not **a permanent one.   Many** subsequent collisions took place.   The last was in the year two hundred and forty-one before Christ.   **This** rebellion was punished by the **Falisci** being driven **from** the stronghold of their city, and compelled to establish themselves on a plain four miles away, only protected on one side by a deep gorge ; all the **other** parts of their colony being left exposed to an easy attack from without ; the new city losing its Etruscan character, and becoming a Roman **settlement.**

A few fragments of primitive mural structure and the above-mentioned tombs which perforate the rocks **are** almost all the substantial indications left of **the earlier** city ; and yet **it** seems filled with an indefinite atmosphere of the past—those vague **intimations of a former** greatness and vitality which sometimes crowd **the mind** with mysterious surmisings in visiting spots known to have been the theatre of great doings, or the scenes of important events to the human race.   As I stood at my window at night just before retiring to rest, and every sound was hushed but the murmur of the stream deep down in the ravine, and the pale half-moon illuminated the cleft here and there, leaving a dark shadow at the bottom, and the far Ciminian range steeped in spectral light seemed yet to retain the eeriness with which superstition once invested it, the boastful Roman appeared to my mind's eye standing across the hollow gulf, taunting his foe with gestures and contumelious reproaches to come forth and fight, whilst in the town the people ran hither and thither, uncertain what might be the issue of the conflict.

The next morning we went in search of the new city, the Roman Falerii. Our way lay along a pleasant road of three or four miles through flowery pastures, extensive corn-fields, and dwarfed plantations. The harvest was everywhere being gathered in, although it was only the month of June. Bands of reapers were singing merrily at their toil, followed by gleaners in true pastoral fashion. Doubtless, as they went, the reapers would now and then drop an ear or two for the old women and girls, who promptly answered their songs in their rear. At a neighbouring encampment some refreshed themselves upon rustic fare, or laughed and chatted in the shade. The reapers and gleaners were followed by ploughmen, in ranks of ten or a dozen, whose implements were of the rudest possible construction. They were drawn by sturdy yokes of grey oxen, whose ponderous force slowly turned up the furrows to the sun as they received the shouts of their drivers with stolid indifference. Occasionally we met flocks of goats, or droves of oxen, leisurely booming their bells along the dusty road, driven by a man or boy or young girl, looking so charmingly rustic, so much removed from every influence but that of the sun, the fresh air, and simple country experiences, that it seemed as if Chloe and Corydon were once more amongst us, and the idyllic Arcadia returned to protest against modern improvements and the revolutions of ages. It was almost quite suddenly that we came upon Falerii. The effect upon the mind was startling. A turn of the road brought the walls of the city full into view. They stand almost as complete as when they were put together. They are of massive construction, consisting of great blocks of the red tufa of the country adjusted with the utmost care and nicety. In one place they reach a height of thirty-two feet from the bottom of a hollow. At intervals square towers occur all round the city. Two arched gateways still remain, the one surmounted at the keystone by a time-worn head, which is supposed to have represented that of Jupiter, and the other by the head of an ox. Here and there the walls are hung with ivy, or plumed with straggling shrubs, but for the most part they stand naked to the sun, rising out of the rank tangled growth at their feet in desolate grandeur. There is something very affecting in the loneliness of these walls that once inclosed a city of which scarcely a vestige remains. I could well understand what an acquaintance once told me,—that the sight drew tears from his eyes. An intense stillness prevailed around ; not even a breath disturbed the air as we entered the limits of the vanished city. The undulating plain upon which once stood theatre and forum and piscina, is now covered with waving grain, here and there surmounted by the fragment of some broken ruin that tells no tale of its former purpose. At the western extremity of the ancient town there is a church, together with an old monastery, which has been utilized for the residence of farm labourers. It is called Santa Maria di Falleri. The church is of the Lombard style, twelfth century, of very beautiful construction. It is fast falling to decay, though it wants little more than the roof (which fell in eighteen hundred and twenty-nine) to preserve it for many years to come. It consists of a nave, aisle, and transept, containing five apses. Several of the columns, which must formerly have supported some temple of the ancient city, are of fluted marble. Blocks of antique Roman ornament are also let into the walls. But the most valuable part of it is a fine white marble portico by the Cosmati. It is composed of four graceful Corinthian columns, two on each side, and a series of clustering arches. In the highest

point of one of these a mosaic cross has been inserted
which is now destroyed. It is deplorable that so beautiful
a monument of the taste and skill of these accomplished
artists should be lost in ruin, which it assuredly will be
unless the portal be carried away within a few years.
There is something saddening in the juxtaposition of this
Christian temple with the remains of a worn-out age : the
symbols of paganism and Christianity both mingling their
dust in a common decay.

To the botanist and lover of Nature the neighbourhood
of this old city during the summer months presents an
endless variety of interest. It is everywhere surrounded
with the most luxuriant growth of wild plants and flowers,
which burst from the soil in the most brilliant profusion, as
if vying with each other which should make the greatest
show. The ravine that lies under the walls to the south is
quite a galaxy of glories, peopled by tribes of many-coloured
butterflies, that disport themselves gaily up and down these
glittering parterres of Nature's sowing, whilst the old walls
stand round gloomily, as if deploring the changes they have
witnessed.

As we stood examining some ruins outside the walls,
we were civilly accosted by a handsome-looking man on
horseback, dressed in white tights and a short jacket. He
carried a gun in his hand, having an air of energy and
spirit that, in spite of his rustic garments, proclaimed him
to be one more accustomed to command than obey. Indeed
he was the lord of the manor, and proprietor of the surrounding territory. We entered into conversation with
him. He answered all our questions with much politeness,
and pointed out the supposed more important sites of the
ancient city. He said that of late years decay had made
large ravages, so that what little there was within his
recollection was fast passing away. After an interchange
of civilities, he rode off at a brisk pace to superintend the
labours of his estate, and we retraced our way along the
road, always with the grand view of Soracte before us,

which, with a mighty sweep, rose from the **spreading plain,** soft and bright in the brilliant sunshine.

From Civita Castellana **we once more** took the **train for** a short distance, as the railway still follows the course **of** the river. The **country it passes** through is of a quiet pastoral order ; **a kind of** valley, in which are heard the bells of pasturing cattle, pleasant human voices, and songs of birds. On each side the hills rise with various acclivities, **chequered** with fields **and** trees, and surmounted by the same citadel-like towns. Every moment brought into view **a** fresh panorama, always with the river flowing through it ; sometimes rippling over pebbly shallows by groves of white-stemmed poplars, sometimes laving the borders of the vine-yards, in which the vines hung **from** tree to tree **in long** festoons, sometimes singing amongst the stooks **of reaped** corn, or creeping round the spurs of the hills, **like fragments** of amethyst set amongst the stones.

About five miles from Borghetto, on **the right, is the** little village of Otricoli which represents Ocriculum, **a** municipal town of some importance under the ancient Romans. **About the** same distance from Otricoli, **the Nar** joins the Tiber, one of its most important tributaries. Although on this occasion we did not deviate from our direct route to **follow this** stream, yet as I had previously passed along it **as** far as Terni, I shall here give some little sketch of its course in the neighbourhood of the Tiber.

The Nar rises in the Eastern Apennines, at the foot **of** Monte Sibilla (the Mons Fiscellus of Pliny), to the **north of** Norcia. It is about forty miles in length. For **the first** ten miles from its confluence with the Tiber **it follows a** rocky gorge between the mountains, **boiling and roaring** from rock to rock like a seething caldron.

The first **town** met with **on its** banks is that **of** Narnia, built upon the precipice **of a** high hill, beneath which the **boisterous** river pursues **its course.** This town is situated **on the** Flaminian Way, fifty-six miles **from Rome, and** **eight from** the **mouth of** the stream from which it takes its

name.   Before it came into the occupation of the Romans
it was called Nequinum.   Three hundred years before the
Christian era, it was besieged by the consul Apuleius.
Whilst the siege was going on, two inhabitants of the
town, whose residences were near the wall, formed a
subterranean passage, and presented themselves before
the advanced guard of the Romans.   They were taken to
the consul, to whom they made an offer of opening a way
for his army into the town.   One of these men being detained as hostage, the other was sent with two spies to
reconnoitre.   Three hundred armed soldiers were then
introduced into the city by night, who, breaking open the
nearest gate, allowed the Roman army to enter the town,
of which they presently took undisputed possession.   A
colony of Romans was afterwards established here in order
to protect the Umbrian border, the town taking the name
of Narnia from the river.   It would appear henceforward to
have been a tolerably flourishing municipal town under
Roman rule.   It was the birthplace of the Roman emperor
Nerva.   The most remarkable of its antiquities is the celebrated bridge now in ruins, which was built by Augustus
for the purpose of carrying the Flaminian Way across the
river.   From the fragments of it which remain, it is evident
that it must have been a noble structure.   Martial alludes
to it in one of his epigrams addressed to Narnia, the residence of his friend Quintus Ovidius.   " Narnia," he says,
"surrounded by the river Nar with its sulphureous waters,
thou whom thy double heights render almost inaccessible,
why does it please thee so often to take from me and
detain with wearisome delay my friend Quintus?   Why
dost thou lessen the attractions of my Nomentan farm,
which was valued by me because he was my neighbour
there?   Have pity on me at length, Narnia, and abuse
not thy possession of Quintus, so mayest thou delight in
thy bridge for ever." *

* Narnia, sulfureo quam gurgite candidus amnis
   Circuit, &c.—vii. 93.

Following the course of the Nar to where it is joined by the Velino, we reach Terni, the ancient flourishing municipality of Interamna, formerly an Umbrian city of high antiquity. It was once proposed by the Roman senate to divert the waters of the Nar from the Tiber in order to lessen the overflowings of the latter. This, however, was protested against by the Interamnates, who urged that if such were to be the case, some of the most fruitful territories of Italy would be submerged at times of flood. The plan was afterwards abandoned. So fertile was the country, that Pliny says it gave four crops of grass in the year. It was occupied by the troops of Vitellius in the civil war with Vespasian. About three miles above Terni are the falls of the Velino. They are formed by an artificial cutting made by the Roman consul Marcus Curius Dentatus to draw off

THE FALLS OF TERNI.

the waters of a lake which is above them. It is useless to

add to the much that has been said and written about these falls. Nothing could be finer or more romantic than this noble sheet of water falling over the rocks, nor the scenery by which it is surrounded.

Rejoining the Tiber, just below Orte, the landscape is diversified by numerous square mediæval towers, which stand upon the hills like recording pillars of Time, marking its lapse by their still decay. Presently the heights of Orte are seen to rise in solemn majesty. It is built upon an abrupt and lofty cliff, its long line of irregularly constructed houses broken by a campanile with perforated arcade windows and a low dome. As we approached it, the setting sun shone through the arches of a long aqueduct that stretches on one side of it, whilst purple mists began to line the valley.

Before leaving Rome I had been fortunate enough to have made the acquaintance of a doctor who combined the accomplishments of an artist and scholar with those of his profession. He was a native of Orte; and when I told him of my proposed visit to that town he at once promised to write to his father, resident there, and also gave me a letter. He told me that there was no good inn there, but that either his father would himself receive me and my friends or else he would be able to find us a domicile. Accordingly, on arriving at the railway station, which is not very distant from the town, we requested to be driven to the house of the gentleman to whom we had the introduction. Ascending the lofty elevation upon which the town is placed, we were filled with wonder at the quaint houses which hung above the precipice as if a breath would blow them over. It was not easy to see where man had begun his work or nature ceased, so brown, so old, so native to the rock did these quaint houses appear. As we entered the town the narrow streets, the gloomy corners, the arched and rearched passages, through which the light fell on Rembrandt-like figures, the winding steps, the pretty shrines, each with its little lamp, behind which the face of the Madonna was seen looking through festoons of hanging foliage, the curious old-world aspect of everything, seemed to transport one into the land of antique romance, the dream of some mediæval poet or painter.

The house of our destination was entered at the back by a narrow passage. On presenting myself I was met by a venerable-looking gentleman in a long coat, and wearing a *berretta* or cap of dark velvet on his head. He had a long grey beard, a mild expression of countenance, an eye undimmed by age, and that gentleness and repose of manner and demeanor which is the proper heritage of ages of culture and refinement. At the same time his daughter came forwards with a pleasant smile. She had passed the age of girlhood, but was still young. With considerable claims to good looks, she was something better than good-looking. Her smile was as open as sunshine, her manner easy and elegant. She welcomed me as the lady of the house, and said that they had provided accommodation for us with them. In vain I protested against the inconvenience that three guests, and those strangers, must make in their quiet household. No 'nay' would be allowed ; everything had been prepared, and we must come. The warmth and generosity of our reception, than which nothing could have been more friendly or homelike, soon put us at our ease. The house was a very old-fashioned one, built of good solid mediæval stone. It was one of those situated on the edge of the precipice, overlooking the picturesque, winding valley through which the yellow river flowed in sweeping curves and long-tracked lines. The interior consisted of a central hall, in which was a ponderous fire-place surmounted by a heavy stone cornice, something like our English residences of three hundred years ago. Out of this central hall the bed-chambers opened. The room was ornamented with some very creditable oil paintings from the hand of our accomplished hostess. A guitar with some music lay upon the table ; other signs of cultivated occupation being visible. What was not the least remarkable was that in one of the

R

dirtiest towns of Italy, apparently with no underground

THE TIBER, FROM ORTE.

drainage, and amidst so much that was squalid and filthy, here the most perfect and scrupulous cleanliness reigned throughout, from speckless linen to well-washed floors and walls. All this was refreshing to find in a place where we had expected to find nothing ; for although Orte is within two miles of a railway, yet very few strangers think of visiting it, and none of remaining there any length of time. Our host was what is called a *possedente*, a holder of property in the town, living in that kind of generous simplicity which, without being profuse, is sufficiently abundant. Presently he and I turned out for a ramble together. He pointed out the notables of the place ; professing that there was little in the town to interest a stranger, at the same time giving me little peeps into the social and domestic life of the place, which I found very amusing.

The town is Etruscan in its origin. Many cave-like excavations are to be seen in the rocks, which have probably served for tombs, possibly for residences. In some of the oldest houses it would almost appear as if traces of the Etruscan manner were retained in the depressed pointed arches formed of solid blocks of tufa above the doors and windows. The town was called Horta by the ancient Romans, probably from the name of an Etruscan goddess. It became a military colony in the time of Augustus. The road from Falerii to Ameria crossed the river just below the town by a bridge, the remains of which are still left standing.

Modern Orte of course has its head caffè, where the loiterers and gossipers assemble in the evening, some of them even during the day (for there is little business of any kind transacted in the smaller Italian towns), for the purposes of discussion and fellowship. One very characteristic sight struck me here ; not, by the way, the only town in Italy where the same thing may be seen. Giving on to the Piazza there was a low unglazed window protected by a stout iron grating, which lighted a small cell or chamber—the prison of the town—in which there was a young man with matted hair and otherwise neglected toilette walking uneasily to and fro like a caged lion. As I paused to look in at his window he came and put his hand through the grate, asking me to give him something. He could see all that went on in the Piazza, and now and then a friendly gossip would come and entertain him with a little chat.

Whilst we were thus walking about the town I began to talk of my proposed expedition, asking Signor F— as to the best means of making the journey to Orvieto along the course of the river, when an honest-looking young man, who had heard a part of our conversation, came forward, and asked if he had heard aright, that I wanted to go to Orvieto, and then proceeded to say that as he knew the road very well, having frequently passed to and fro in his capacity of miller with corn and flour, perhaps he could assist the gentleman. As he was known to Signor F—, I finally concluded a bargain with him to accompany us, stating

my desire to follow as nearly as possible the course of the
river the whole way.   He said he could not leave his occupation the following day, nor indeed would he be able to find
horses, which were the only means of making the journey, at
so short a notice.   I was unwilling to make this delay if
possible, for I felt that we might be trespassing upon the
hospitality of our host.   My objections, however, were overruled by Signor F—, and as nothing else so satisfactory
could be arranged, I at last consented to remain.

When we returned to the house the active hands of our
hostess and the cook had prepared for us a most abundant
and excellent supper in an upper chamber, for which the
politeness of our entertainers made many unnecessary
apologies.   As we sat over our wine, which was of the best,
we had much conversation, finding our entertainers as intel-
ligent as they were kind and agreeable.   The discourse of
Signor F— was marked by a philosophic breadth and
temperance of view on subjects about which men often
dispute and wrangle, as religion and politics, which are
amongst the noblest fruits of years and experience.   After
supper we returned to the general sitting-room or hall
before described.   The moon was shining over the dim
valley, through which the river winded like a silver serpent.
A profound stillness reigned in the air.   Here and there a
little light glittered amongst the hills.   The moment was an
impressive one.   At our request the Signorina took up her
guitar, singing us some very delightful songs, some of them
specially belonging to the district where she resided ; and
then we retired to rest, happy at the close of a happy day.

The next day was chiefly spent in wandering about the
town and sketching, material for which is here abundant.
Whilst we were sitting in the house in the evening Basileo,
our promised guide, came in, drew a chair into the
circle, and joined in the conversation.   Here, indeed, the
kind of sacredness which belongs to the English household
did not appear to be at all understood, for presently a
woman with a child on some little errand entered in the
same unceremonious manner, as if the privilege of the house

were free to all. Basileo told us that the nearest place where we should be able to spend the night in our forward journey was Bagnorea, at a distance of about twenty-five miles from Orte. At this place Signor F— had a friend, to whom he gave us a letter, sending also a little barrel of wine as an additional recommendation. It was finally arranged that Basileo should be ready the following morning with four horses at daybreak.

Accordingly, with many farewells to our kind host and hostess, the next morning we departed after the usual number of delays, and a great deal of fumbling to attach our travelling-bags to the horses. As we left Orte the morning was slowly unfolding—bands of vapour clinging to the hills, or reposing in the mountain hollows. At intervals broken mediæval towers rose from the rocks, every one of which had its history in the belligerent ages, the river mists creeping about their forlorn walls as if to hide their nakedness and ruin. Underneath the dusty grey olives shepherds rested on their staves, as their flocks strayed on the newly-shorn stubble amidst the gentle tinkling of fitful bells. On a lofty elevation the town of Bassano rose on our left, whilst at our right the river wandered away in whispering shallows or slumbered in silent pools ; groves of poplars lining its wide banks, and casting tremulous reflections into the water. Spreading fields of grain or pulse intermingled with orchards and groves, on which yet lay the silence of the morning, made up the scene—a very soothing and tranquillizing one. Presently we entered a thick wood of fin old trees echoing with the songs of hundreds of birds, amongst which the *chu chu* of the nightingale was particularly distinguishable. As each embowered ravine was passed the eye was carried into endless vistas of dim foliage, over which was drawn a thin blue veil of subtle vapour. Several quaint towns or villages shone down upon us from their heights as we passed beneath them, some of which we should have been glad to explore pencil in hand, if time had allowed. We had several small streams to cross. After passing one of these we were alarmed by cries of distress.

On turning round I saw H. seated, not very comfortably, on the ground, his horse quietly stalking away without him. The animal had put his foot into a hole and fallen, fortunately just after having passed the stream. The rider, however, was soon reinstated, and no particular damage done. About noon we reached our resting-place, more than midway of the journey, at a little town called San Michele, where our guide had some acquaintances, and promised us *un buon pranzo* (a good dinner). Unfortunately, however, no place could be found for our horses. In vain we passed and repassed the burning street to find so much as a shed or sheltered corner where the poor beasts could be protected from the rays of the sun. There was no such thing in the whole place. At last we were permitted to tie them in a little court, and after much trouble found a bundle or two of dry stalks which was called hay. Here they amused themselves by creeping as near to each other as possible, as if with the friendliest intentions, and then viciously kicking each other. In the attempt to separate them during one of these skirmishes I received a violent kick myself on the thigh; fortunately I was too near the heels of the brute to suffer any serious injury. Basileo in the meantime talked, talked loudly and constantly, over all the plans in the world to secure the horses, but did nothing, being evidently about as great an adept in regard to horses as Mr. Charles Swidger junior was in the art of navigation— "which knew nothing of boats whatever." Certainly the poor horses, in spite of their exciting and animated proclivities, had the worst of it; for we were taken to the doctor of the place, where an abundant and sufficiently good dinner was found for us, to which we did ample justice. After dinner we were allowed to doze for half an hour in the doctor's bedchamber. I occupied myself with examining his library, which was of a rather miscellaneous sort, on a little side table. The only medical books I observed had at least the weight of antiquity to recommend them; though I confess I was irreverent enough to hope that I might be preserved from the medical treatment of Hippocrates and

Galen. Scarcely had our eyes been closed in a comfortable
nap before Basileo knocked at the door, saying it was time
to go forwards. Presently we were equipped and again on
our way. Passing through wide districts of waving corn we
entered an oak wood, offering exquisite vignettes of forest
pastoral scenery. The ground was covered with soft green
turf. The trees were embowered high above us, through the
thick foliage of which the sun here and there fell, enamelling
the sward with patches of glittering gold. Thus pursuing our
way Basileo entertained H. with an account of the maraud-
ings of some *malviventi*, or, in plain English, brigands, who
had infested the wood a few days before. We, however,
presently emerged into the open, and after a while entered
upon a high-road, which soon brought us within sight of our
destination.

It was on one of those golden evenings so common in
Italy, but which are never seen in northern latitudes, that
the first view of the town of Bagnorea met us across a deep
ravine, its row of white houses enriched with the gorgeous
hues of the setting sun. Up and down our way led us,
until we entered the town. As soon as we did so, and
Basileo had signified his desire to find a place of lodging
for his horses, a crowd of gabblers came round us, all speaking at once. Presently we dismounted, the horses being led
off in triumph by the vociferous multitude. Curiosity, or
rather humanity, prompted me to see what might be their
future condition. I found them at the far end of a black-
smith's shop without any straw or other accommodation.
In vain we pointed out that there were proper stables, as
set forth in an advertisement over the door, a little lower
down the street. We were compelled at last to leave the
matter in the hands of Basileo, who flew hither and thither
in the hubbub, too excited to listen to anything.

It was suggested by my friends that instead of troubling
the friend of our host at Orvieto we might very well find out
the best inn in the place and go to it at once. I agreed, but
with misgivings. It turned out that there was only one
establishment in the whole place bearing the name of

osteria, and thither we went.   Its first appearance was not
promising ; but things might be somewhat better than they
looked ; they often are in Italy.   On inquiry, we found
there was but one bedchamber, but it was large, and
had several beds in it, if the gentlemen could accommodate
themselves.   H. went to see it ; but the horrors of that
prison-house were never completely unfolded.   Enough.
We at once bore our note and the barrel of wine to
Signor M—.

Signor M— was a young married man, a half-pay in
the pope's service, having held a position under the pontifical government, living under the expectation that the old
dominion would reassert its sway.   He received us very
kindly, and was sorry that his establishment did not allow
him to offer us accommodation in his own house.   Indeed,
it was with great difficulty that we obtained lodgment at
all ; for although Bagnorea is by no means an insignificant
town in regard to size, we were told that so few strangers
came there, that the inhabitants never thought of providing
anything more than they wanted themselves.   At last we
found two rooms in separate houses, where we were lodged
decently, and fed tolerably— quite as well, perhaps, as we
might expect of a place so much out of the world.

Bagnorea was the Balneum Regis of the ancients, formerly
celebrated for its hot-water springs, which have now ceased
to flow in consequence of the earthquakes to which the
town and its neighbourhood have been subjected.   In the
year sixteen hundred and ninety-five a great part of the
town was destroyed by one.   It was conquered by the
Longobards in six hundred and six, and afterwards restored
to the papacy, first by Charlemagne and then by Otho
the Second, in the tenth century.   It was once under the
government of cardinal legates, together with the provinces
of Viterbo.   One of these legates was Cardinal Pole,
cousin to Henry the Eighth of England.   The town consists
of one long street that runs to the edge of an enormous
volcanic basin, perhaps a couple of miles in diameter, from
the centre of which rises a lofty cone, composed of striated

volcanic matter, upon which stands an almost deserted grey
mediæval town, called Civita Bagnorea, overtopped by a tall
square-built campanile. The picturesqueness of the latter
place, both externally and in the rambling windings of its
narrow lanes, is wonderful. Many architectural fragments of
antique Roman workmanship lie scattered about, or are built
into the walls, and several ancient columns are set up in front
of the cathedral. The approach to this little town is still more
marvellous. It is only accessible by narrow ridges or walls
with abrupt sides left in the gradual falling away of the
volcanic matter of which the stratum of this district is
composed. These traverse the profound gulf from the
table-land by which it is surrounded like narrow walls
stretched across abysses which make one giddy to look at,
much less pass over. The one adjoining Bagnorea furnishes
a somewhat nervous pathway ; but those on the other side
of the basin are much narrower and loftier ; so that the
groups of peasantry with their donkeys as they follow their
course seem suspended in the air. During a high wind
these pathways, which I was told are not more than three
feet wide in many places, are particularly perilous ; cases
have been known of persons having been blown from them
into the abyss beneath.

It was the day of a *festa* whilst we were there ; all the
characteristic finery of the townsfolk and surrounding
country being brought out for the occasion. The dress of
the women was particularly picturesque. It consisted of a
snow-white linen head-dress, a low, coloured, stiff boddice,
a gay handkerchief over the shoulders, and a coloured skirt,
most commonly blue.

The quaint little town of Civita Bagnorea was the birthplace of St. Bonaventure, for his piety and learning called
the ' seraphic doctor ;' a man so remarkable in his day, and
now so lost sight of beneath the accumulation of centuries,
that a few words on his life and character may not be
unwelcome.

He was born of pious parents in the year one thousand
two hundred and twenty-one. His proper name was John

of Fidanza. It is said that St. Francis of Assisi, when
dying, exclaimed of Giovanni, who had been healed by his
prayers of a severe illness in infancy, " O buona ventura !"
(O happy fortune !), from which circumstance he took the
name by which he was afterwards generally known. At the
age of twenty-two he assumed the Franciscan habit, and
afterwards became the first general of the order. He was
sent to Paris, where he studied under John of Hales, an
Englishman, who used to say of him, that in Bonaventure
the sin of Adam was not discernible. The legates of Pope
Gregory the Tenth brought him the cardinal's hat during his
stay at a convent a few leagues from Florence, where they
found him occupied in washing the dishes of the convent.
Without ceasing his task, he bade them hang it on a
neighbouring tree until he had finished. His humility
and activity for the good of others knew no bounds.
He died in one thousand two hundred and seventy-four,
in his fifty-third year, and was canonized by Sixtus the
Fifth five centuries afterwards. He left numerous works
behind him written in Latin, all of them distinguished
by a profound spiritual mysticism, great fervency, and an
irresistible incisiveness and penetration of style. He was
possessed of a large vein of poetry—implied even in the
names of some of the works he wrote, as " The Nightingale
of the Passion of our Lord fitted to the Seven Hours,"
" The Six Wings of the Cherubim and the Six Wings of the
Seraphim," " The Soul's Journey to God." The theologic,
or, perhaps, it should rather be called the theosophic,
philosophy of St. Bonaventure is founded upon the principles of a very solid induction, a substantial positivism,
which is the only true basis of theology, as it is of every
other science. He proceeds from the known to the unknown, from sense to spirit. He carries the mortal and
sensible up to the Divine rather than attempts to bring
the Divine down to the human level. His doctrine is
eminently one of development and progress based upon
actual experience ; each state or condition of the graduating
soul being generated by the antecedent one, and producing

another still more elevated to succeed it.   One of the best
representative and most characteristic of his works is, "The
Soul's Journey to God," **Itinerarium** Mentis in Deum.[*]   It
is a mystical and semi-philosophical disquisition on the
Highest Good, which he **makes to** consist **in** the soul's union
with its Creator attained through six steps or grades, as
follows : First, By means of the vestiges of God in the
outward world **of** creation ; second, By the same world of
sense as the habitation of God in essence and presence ;
third, By the mind as made in his image ; fourth, By faith
in the transforming power of Christ ; fifth, By the light of
the Holy Spirit ; sixth, By the contemplation of the
Blessed Trinity, in which is contained the sum **of perfect**
good.   **These** steps he makes **to** correspond to the **senses,**
the imagination, reason, intellect, intelligence, **and the**
elevation of the mind **in** the apprehension **of** Truth ; and
again, to the six **days** of the week, **the seventh being the**
sabbath **of rest** attained in the condition **of a divine ecstasy.**
I will give **a** short extract from this **work, to make his**
system **or** mode of view the more clear.

"Happiness," **he** says, "being nothing else than the
fruition of the highest **good,** and **the** highest good being
above **us, no one can become** happy and blessed excepting
by raising himself **above** himself, **not in** bodily ascension,
but in the elevation of **the heart.   To** attain the first
principle, which is spiritual **and** eternal, and above us, **it**
is necessary to pass through **the** corporal and temporal ;
which **is** outside of us: this **is to be** led **in the way of**
God.   We must also enter into **our** own minds, **which are**
the image of God, eternal and **spiritual** within **us : this is to**
walk in the truth **of God.**   Moreover **we must pass to the**

* Amédée de Margerie, in his essay on the Philosophy **of St.** Bonaventure,
says: "Nous n'hésiterons pas à le dire: si l'*Itinerarium Mentis in Deum*
est une des plus belles consécrations que la philosophie **ait** faites à Dieu de
toutes les facultés humaines, *le Commentaire sur le livre des Sentences*
contient une des plus excellentes théodicées qu'ait produites jusqu'ici
l'**alliance de la foi** et de la raison, une des plus victorieuses réponses qu'on
puisse donner à ceux qui nient l'influence du christianisme pour élever et
transformer la raison humaine."

eternal Spirit, regarding the First Principle : this is to rejoice
in the tidings of God and in the reverence of his majesty."

In his Soliloquies he says, "I will return from the external to the internal, and from the internal I will ascend to
the supernal, that I may know whence I came and whither
I go, wherefore I am and what I am ; and so by the knowledge of myself I may ascend to the knowledge of God."

Dante introduces Bonaventure in the ' Paradiso' as singing
the praises of St. Dominic.

> Of Bonaventure I the vital part,
> From Bagnoregio, who always set
> The meaner for the nobler cares aside.*

He is also conspicuously represented in Raphael's fresco
of the Disputa in the Vatican.

The next stage of our journey was from Bagnorea to
Orvieto, a distance of about ten miles.   This we performed
partly on foot and partly on the backs of asses, accompanied
by a cheery and astute countryman of a good manly type,
who entertained us on the way with some racy information
concerning his country and people, touched now and then
with that good-natured and sceptical kind of sarcasm which
has obtained the name of Macchiavelism.   The country was
very peaceful and quiet—the very ideal of the 'Golden
Age,' when everybody was occupied in rural pursuits, and
the simplest form of agricultural practice was the traditional
heritage from father to son.   Shepherds, leaning upon their
staves beneath the shade of the brown olive, watched their
flocks all day.   The swineherd tended his swarthy multitude.   Bullocks in affectionate pairs drew loads of corn and
other produce on sledges along the worst of roads ; the use
of wheels being apparently unknown, or perhaps set aside
as a useless modern invention calculated to destroy the
severe simplicity of the pastoral life.   The bullocks accustomed to be yoked together, our guide told us, sometimes
grew so affectionate to each other that it was difficult to

> * Io son la vita di Bonaventure
> Da Bagnoregio, che ne' grandi uffici
> Sempre posposi la sinistra cura.
>
>   c. xii. 127.

separate them : neither the one nor the other would allow a
rival in the affections of his companion without showing the
utmost jealousy and uneasiness.   In spite of the primitive-
ness of agricultural operations, the country did not appear to
be wanting in wealth, judging from the not infrequent villas
and large houses surrounded by groves and orchards which
were scattered at intervals on our way ; looking, it is true,
as if uninhabited ; for never a living soul was seen about
them, as they blinked, bare and white, with closed jalousies
in the hot sunshine.   Then there were deep and shady
lanes bordered with hazels and feathery ferns, through
which the sun, here and there, shot bright shafts of light,
making glad the hearts of joyful birds ; there were hedge-
rows garlanded with white roses fencing in the green vineyards ; there were tall palmy-leaved chestnuts showing an
abundance of bristly fruit fast ripening in the heat of
summer, and then beautiful upland slopes of corn waving
in the wind, and yellow for the sickle of the reaper.   At
last we reached a quaint mediæval village or little town
called Porano, girt about with sturdy walls, and having a
massive old towered gateway for entrance.   Amidst the
wonder of the inhabitants we traversed the narrow street,
and entering the back-room of an *osteria*, the walls of which
were decorated with landscapes in distemper of the usual
order, found a welcome refreshment in some tolerable wine.
A few miles more, and we came upon the valley of the
Paglia—a tributary of the Tiber, which it joins three or
four miles lower down—and after pausing a few minutes to
examine the ruins of an old abbey, of which strange stories
are told, we crossed the river and ascended the height upon
which Orvieto is built

> Remote and high,
> Which from the ancient Romans had its name,
> Who thither went because the air is pure.*

---

* La città d'Urbivieto è alta e strana:
  Questa da' Roman vecchi il nome prese,
  Ch'andavan là perchè l'aere v'è sana.
    FAZIO DEGLI UBERTI, *Il Dittamondo.*

Orvieto is the ancient Etruscan town Herbanum, mentioned by Pliny. It afterwards appears to have borne the name of Urbs Vetus, of which its modern one is a corruption. Long before Roman rule, however, it must have been an important Etruscan town or city. Numerous tombs of very ancient origin were discovered in eighteen hundred and sixty-three on the opposite side of the valley across the river, two of which still remain open. They are, like many other Etruscan tombs, placed at the end of long galleries cut into the rock, the galleries or passages being about thirty-five yards long. They have arched ceilings cut into the shape of planks sloping from a transverse beam, the sides being decorated with very beautiful paintings of men and animals, the former almost Phœnician in type. Numbers of figures are seated at a banquet, or perhaps a funeral feast, which is pictured in all its stages, from the kitchen where the slaves are busied in the offices of cooking, to its being served on the table. In one of them is a plain sarcophagus of arenaceous tufa. There are several Etruscan inscriptions on the walls. Numerous others have been opened in the same cliff, some of them containing articles of jewelry, utensils, etc., but none of them painted, with the exception of these two.

The situation of the town is extremely picturesque. It is built on a steep table-rock rising from the valley of the Paglia, whose boundaries are penetrated by the ravines of tiny streams which course the hills to reach the river. The view of the city from beneath is particularly imposing, its lofty line drawn across the sky conspicuously broken by the tall façade of the cathedral, which is everywhere visible. Inside it still retains traces of mediæval habitudes in its narrow streets, quaint architecture, and half-ruined old moated castle at the eastern extremity of the hill.

The name of England or Englishman figures more than once in the history of Orvieto: first in thirteen hundred and sixty-five, when a certain Andrew Belmont, who was probably an English adventurer or *condottiere*, with a company of his countrymen, in the interests of the Church,

opposed Annechino di Rougardo, head of the German
forces. The former were, however, worsted ; the Germans
leaving the country on payment of a subsidy. Belmont
had afterwards a quarrel with Gomez, the nephew of the
pope's legate, who left the English camp secretly by night,
and went to Orvieto. The English, however, immediately
encamped on the plains of the Paglia, beneath the town,
awaiting payment for their services to the Church, committing great havoc and depredations in the surrounding
territory in the meantime. The deputy legate Gomez upon
this recalled to him the successful Annechino, together
with other allies, who drove the English, bitterly complain-
ing of their unfair treatment, in the direction of Perugia.
When they arrived at a place called Santo Mariano a
battle took place, the Perugians joining the forces of the
Church, many English being slain and two hundred taken
prisoners to Perugia. They were afterwards liberated
under certain conditions ; but they quickly rallied, and
being joined by numerous other marauders, both Italian
and German, they defeated the Perugians in an engagement, and then set themselves to ravage the country as
before.*

The name of Orvieto appears again in English history in
fifteen hundred and twenty-eight, when Dr. Stephen
Gardiner, Wolsey's secretary, and Dr. Edward Fox, almoner
to Henry the Eighth, were sent on an embassy to Pope
Clement the Seventh, at that time a refugee in Orvieto after
the siege and sack of Rome already described, in order to
obtain his permission for the king's divorce from Catherine
of Aragon. A letter written by them during their stay at
Orvieto is so characteristic and graphic in its details, that I
shall here transcribe it. It is dated the twenty-third of
March.

" Pleaseth it your grace to understand that we arrived
here at Orviett upon Saturday last past, in the morning,
and having no garments ne apparel other than the coats
we did ride in, being much worn and defaced by reason of

* See Cronaca d'Orvieto dal 1342 al 1368. Milano, 1845.

the foul weather; advertising the pope's holiness of our coming by Mr. Gregorie, we were compelled to tarry all that day and the next day within the house whiles our garments were at the making; wherein we thought very great difficulty, all things here being in such a scarcity and dearth as we think hath not been seen in no place; and that not only in victual, which cannot be brought into the town, in no great quantity, by reason that all things is conveyed by asses and mules, but also in other necessaries, so as that cloth, chamlett, or such like merchandises, which in England is worth twenty shillings is here worth six pound, and yet not to be had in any quantity; and had we not made provision for our gowns at Luke [Lucca] we must of necessity have gone in Spanish cloaks, such as we could have borrowed of the pope's servants, wherein per-adventure should have been found some difficulty, foras-much, as far as we can perceive, few men here have more garments than one. And had not Mr. Gregorie resided here, and, advertised of our coming, made preparation for our lodging, borrowing, as he said, of divers men so much as might furnish us three beds, we had been [in ill case]* at our coming into this town, being a very foul day, as hath been seen, and we within a mile of the town compelled to pass a river on horseback, wherein we rode so deep as the water came almost to our girdelseed, and so wet us, as upon that surfeit one of our servants is at this house in extreme danger of life, and rather like to die than live, whose death should be as great loss as can be in a young man, being himself singularly well learned in physic, in the Greek and Latin tongues, as any we know. We suppose you know him well; his name is Richard Herde. He was wont to resort much to me, Stephyn Gardyner, there, and dwelleth with Master Chancellor of Duchie. If he skape

---

* I have conjecturally supplied this lacuna. I found the letter, in the first instance, in Mr. Pocock's edited "Records of the Reformation." On referring to the original, in the library of the British Museum [Harl. 419, fol. 72] in order to supply, if possible, what might here have been left out, I found Mr. Pocock had printed the letter exactly as he had found it.

it, the physicians here think it a great matter. Mr. Gregorie shewed us that midsummer there cometh a wind *ab Austro* which infecteth all men being in this city and not borne in these parts, *pestilente morbo*, by reason of a river coming within a mile of the city. It may well be called *Urbs vetus*, for every man in all languages would give it none other name. We cannot well tell how the pope should be noted in liberty, being here where scarcity, ill-favoured lodging, ill-air, and many other incommodities, keep him and all his as straightly as he was ever kept in Castel Angel. It is *aliqua mutacio soli, sed nulla libertatis*, and in manner the pope could not deny to Mr. Gregory, but it were better to be in captivity at Rome than here at liberty. The pope lieth in an old palace of the bishops of this city, ruinous and decayed, where, or we come to his pryvey chamber, we pass three chambers, all naked and unhanged, the roofs fallen down, and as we can guess thirty persons, rif raf and other, standing in the chambers for a garnishment. And as for the pope's bed-chamber, all the apparel in it was not worth twenty nobles, bed and all. It is a fall from the top of the hill to the lowliest part of the mountain, where was *primus assensus*, which every man in manner useth for his commodity. For besides that the Venecians, Duke of Ferrare and Florentynes have done, they of Viterbe rebell, and kepe off the city from the pope for their use, trusting that the Spaniards shall have the victory. Also Sigismundus de Maltesta hath entered again into Ariminum, which Monsieur de Lautreke restored to the pope, and keepeth it. The pope is determined by the advice of such as he has about him to make two or three thousand of soteme* to expugne them of Viterbe to the intent he may have access at his pleasure to Rome, which now is letted by them. The victory in Naples is yet ambiguous, and here no certainty what they will do there ; some say they intend to strike battle—some nay."

Some curious pictures of mediæval life in Orvieto are presented to us in an old chronicle of the fourteenth

* I do not know the meaning of this term.

S

century,* from which I will translate a few passages.   The
strong party spirit, remorseless cruelty, and vindictive ferocity
of the time are well illustrated by the following extract.

"On Wednesday, the twenty-second of February, one
thousand three hundred and forty-six, in the third hour—
that is, on the festival of the Chair of St. Peter, a disturbance was raised by Benedetto di Bonconte and all the
Guelphs of Orvieto with him crying, 'Success to the
Guelphs and death to the Ghibellines!'   Presently a part of
them went to the house of Leonardo and another part to the
Piazza del Popolo to encounter the captain.   The captain fled,
seeking shelter in the church of St. Dominic, the Ghibellines
not being able to unite themselves nor to succour Leonardo ;
and so they were discomfited and driven away, and Leonardo was besieged in his stronghold and kept there until
the first sleep, and then it was given up to Benedetto di
Bonconte ; and Benedetto took Leonardo and led him away
prisoner to the fortress of the Sberni, which belonged to
Benedetto.   After this there came many horse and foot
from the country of Perugia in aid of the Guelph party.
Leonardo was kept prisoner at the fortress until the twenty-
seventh of March, and on that day was given up to master
Matteo degli Orsini, who took him to Mugnano, and then
from Mugnano to Rome, where he arrived on the eighth of
April, that is to say the eve of Palm Sunday ; and on the
Monday of Holy Week, which was the tenth of April,
the son of master Matteo caused a carriage of wood
to be made and Leonardo to be placed upon it naked,
bound to a post, and to be wrung with heated pincers in
various parts of Rome, and then to be cut all to pieces
in the piazza before the castle of St. Angelo, the fragments
being afterwards gathered and thrown piece by piece into
the Tiber.   So Leonardo died ; and it was said in Orvieto
that Benedetto had money sent to him from Rome for
giving up Leonardo.   And so Benedetto remained lord of

* Cronaca d' Orvieto dal 1342 al 1363. Già publicato da Ludovico
Antonio Muratori, ed ora in più comoda forma ridotta e diligentemente
corretta. Milano. 1845.

Orvieto, and he caused the stronghold of Leonardo to be pulled down, and denounced many Ghibellines. Thus was accomplished the vengeance of master Matteo degli Orsini."

Although the old chronicle above quoted only goes over a period of twenty-one years, the number of misfortunes and disasters which are noted as having occurred during that time are something incredible. It would seem as if all the powers of nature and all the adverse forces of social dislocation had conspired against the miserable inhabitants of the city : and yet it does not appear that they were worse off than those of other Italian cities of the same period. Here is a sad picture—more sad, perhaps, than wonderful to those who know the condition of some modern Italian towns even, in which the traditional slovenliness of the middle ages as to drainage and other conveniences is probably very faithfully preserved.

" In the calends of May, in the year one thousand three hundred and forty, there began to be a great mortality amongst the inhabitants of Orvieto, which went on increasing day by day until the months of June and July, when there had died five hundred Christians between great and small, male and female. The mortality was so great and the fear of it so strong amongst the people that they died quite suddenly : one morning they were well and the next dead. All work was suspended. This mortality lasted until the calends of September, whence many families and houses perished, it being calculated that by the time it had ceased, a ninth part of the inhabitants had died, those that were left remaining infirm and terrified, abandoning their houses to the dead."

Not very long afterwards an earthquake was added to their list of misfortunes :

"On Wednesday before the third hour, that is on the ninth of September, in the year one thousand three hundred and forty-nine, there was a great earthquake which threw down many walls and large edifices, towers and residences : also the water of the fountains of Orvieto became so turbid as to present the appearance of milk and earth mixed

S 2

together ; and so it remained for more than twelve days. And as it was in Orvieto so was it also in many other towns and villages, whence the people became alarmed ; no labour being followed for more than six days ; and every day there were processions and discipline."

They had scarcely recovered from the earthquake before the city was wasted by a dreadful famine.

In the year one thousand three hundred and fifty-one there arose a great civil contention, a part of the inhabitants of Orvieto and its territory being without the city and opposing those within. The commune of Perugia was called upon to mediate between them. The contending parties were at last brought together, and it was finally concluded that the magistracy of Perugia should be established in Orvieto. It was, however, quite insufficient to maintain order and justice ; robbery and violence continally occurring in the city. " Before the agreement was made between the belligerents by this intervention, you must know," says the historian, "there was the greatest scarcity of every kind of provision ; for nothing to support life was allowed to enter the city. Flour was not to be had because the mills were ruined and no one was permitted to go out to repair them ; so that the people had to grind their corn with handmills within the city, neither in this were they altogether successful, since only a part of them had the means to accomplish it. Pork was very dear, being three soldi the pound ; lamb three soldi ; and mutton three soldi and a half, and this very bad ; and sometimes it happened that none at all could be had. There was no water but that from the cisterns, which was little enough, besides being putrescent, muddy, and rank, so that many persons strained it for cookery and drinking. Of vegetables there were scarcely any, and those who were able to buy them could hardly have enough for four persons for four soldi which were fit to eat ; and frequently such were eaten as would not have been looked at in more prosperous times. Wood was dear, and none could be obtained excepting from the houses which were ruined throughout the city. Of salt there was little, and those who had it would not sell it for less than at the rate of twenty lire the quartengo. In this condition the city stood ; so that every Orvietan was badly off ; those within not being able to go out to their farms and estates with security, neither could those without return to their houses ; for Benedetto di Bonconte and the sons of Pepo with their families and friends drove them away with injury, doing them every possible outrage ; each party striving to gain an advantage over its adversary by taking possession of the castles and strongholds ; those without endeavouring to enter the city by force, those within keeping watch and ward day and night : and in this manner they remained for the space of three months, each attacking the other as he saw his advantage."

One more extract from the history of Ciprian Manente shall complete our illustration of its mediæval condition.

"In the year one thousand four hundred and forty-nine Orvieto was under the government of Arrigo, brother of Gentile di Monaldeschi della Vipera, who was called Gentile della Scala from being the proprietor of that place. During the fourteen years that he had been in possession of Orvieto he had prevented the Monaldeschi of Cervara with other nobles and citizens of the Beffati faction from entering the city, without recognising the pontificate of Rome ; although the pope as well as the Beffati had tried more than once to take the city from his tyrannical hands : to which end many secret meetings between the Monaldeschi and others had been convened at Bolsena, but without finding any way to accomplish their purpose, the city being always well guarded, although it had been brought to a state of great calamity by reason of a pestilence of which a great many of the inhabitants had died. But, as God pleased, it happened that a mode of operation was offered by Gualtieri, a poor man of Porano, small of stature, but astute, who entering Orvieto ill-clothed, and as a mendicant, went to the hospital, and in the morning stood at the door of the cathedral asking alms, in order that he might see the people and observe how things were going. Also during the day he went through the city and round the fortifications, begging in the same manner, but taking all the notice he could of the persons he met and their procedure ; then after having observed everything, he left the city and went to the Beffati, showing them everything and arranging what it was desirable to do. Accordingly, one evening, Gualtieri returned to Orvieto with an iron nail of a pound and a half weight, together with a long cord, concealed in a bundle of wood, and went to the hospital without exciting the suspicion of any one. When he saw the opportunity, having privately taken away a hammer from the workshop of Santa Maria, he fixed the nail to the projection of the fortification under the guard-house of San Francesco, and then hid the hammer ; doing all with so much dexterity that the guard perceived nothing of it. He then gave a sign to the Beffati, who were hidden in a neighbouring orchard. On the night of Santa Lucia, the thirteenth of December, the guard was changed, and when the patrol was past, Gualtieri went to the place where he had fixed the nail, and throwing down the cord, drew up a ladder of ropes which the Beffati had brought, by means of which Signor Corrado with seventy men of the Beffati faction quickly mounted the defences, seizing the guard and other patrols which were around, preventing them from crying out or uttering a word by holding them bound in the guardhouse with the sword at their throats. As Signor Corrado and his followers were going by the street of San Francesco, they met a tame deer, which had been reared in the house of Signor Gentile, which, having bells about its neck, and returning towards the house along the street in front of the Beffati, was in a great measure the reason of their not being heard at first by Signor Arrigone. This was taken as a fresh augury by Monaldeschi della Cervara.* Then all of them went to Santa Maria, and flinging themselves on their knees on the steps, vowed to deliver the city from

* Cervara is derived from Cerva, which means a deer. Probably the family device corresponded with the name.

the tyrant, as far as possible without injury to any one.
Then they went to the house of Arrigo (now belonging to
Petrucci) who hearing the noise, without waiting for help
from his people, who had not yet risen, rushed out with
a pike, and although he was warned if he did not retire
he would be killed, paying no heed to the warning, he
was immediately slain. The Beffati then hastened to the
principal piazza, where there was a body of guards, with
whom an encounter took place. Tomasso di Francesco
Mazzochi, the head of the guard, being killed. The rest
were put to flight and made prisoners ; which being done,
the Beffati immediately rang the great bell of the church
of Sant Andrea, upon which Paolpietro, together with
many others from the neighbouring territories, and fifty
bowmen, broke down the gates with the help of those
already within the city, entering the city at dawn amidst
cries of Peace, peace ! the which being heard by the Mal-
corini, as they perceived their leader dead, they made no
further movement. Thus was Orvieto retaken by the
Beffati and consigned to the rule of Pope Nicholas the
fifth ; the news being sent quickly to Rome."

By far the most interesting object in Orvieto is the cathedral, built in alternate courses of the dark-coloured basaltic
lava and yellowish limestone which is found in the neighbourhood. Tradition assigns its origin to a miracle which occurred near the lake of Bolsena : the same that has been
represented by Raphael on the walls of the Vatican. A
German priest who had disbelieved in the Real Presence, was
convinced by the host in his hands dropping blood. The
elements and other relics were then brought to the pope,
Urban the fourth, at that time resident at Orvieto, who
met them on the way ; the cathedral being afterwards
commenced to enshrine them, towards the end of the
thirteenth century. Mr. Hemans, in his "Mediæval Christianity and Sacred Art in Italy," gives some interesting
particulars relative to the building of this cathedral. He
says : "Pope Clement the sixth granted an indulgence to
all who should visit Orvieto for devotional purposes ; which

spiritual favours were doubled in an indulgence from Gregory the ninth, obtainable by all who should assist at the works for this new cathedral.   Then were seen citizens of all classes co-operating, besides multitudes of pilgrims, who, after attending religious services, would spend the rest of the day in doing what they could to help the masons, stone-cutters, or other artizans at the sacred building.   Persons of good condition carried burdens on their shoulders ; and those who could not do rough work brought drink or food to the labourers, enabling them to refresh themselves without leaving the spot.   It is one of the proofs how utterly were Sabbatarian notions foreign to the mediæval mind, even while religious influences were at the greatest height, that Sundays and other festivals were marked by special activity (in the hours, namely, after the principal rites were over) during the progress of these labours.   Companies of artists were sent to seek and to work the most suitable marbles at Rome, Siena, and Corneto ; and such prepared material used to be brought to Orvieto by buffaloes, or (if from Rome) up the Tiber as far as Orte." *

Amongst the artists deputed to embellish the cathedral was Luca d' Egidio Ventura, or Luca Signorelli, as he is generally called, born at Cortona in the year one thousand four hundred and forty-one.   He was the connecting link between the Umbrian school of Piero della Francesca, and the higher development of the Florentine manner under Michael Angelo.   Vasari says that he awoke the minds of all those who came after him, and that Michael Angelo was much indebted to him.   With as much power and greatness of conception as Michael Angelo, he had a narrower field of expression.   The artistic means at his disposal were fewer, owing to his priority in time ; but he had within him wells of tenderness and sweetness never touched by the great Florentine, as witness the beatified spirits in his Paradise, one of the frescoes on these walls,

* A History of Mediæval Christianity and Sacred Art in Italy A.D. 900 —1350, by C. I. Hemans.   Williams and Norgate, 1869.

and the Santa Cecilia at Città di Castello. It is a pity
that the remoteness and diffusion of his works make a
comparative study of them difficult to most art students.*
His greatest, and, indeed, his representative, works are,
however, here.

These frescoes rank with the world's epics. There is
nothing in art more nobly conceived, more powerfully and
grandly expressed. They stand out with life-like freshness on the pages of Time, and their story is one which can
never lose its interest so long as men and women are born
to sin and sorrow, and with the desire to soar above themselves in the power of a diviner nature. They treat of the
great subjects—Good and Evil and their consequences. The
first is the Fall of Antichrist, which for subtilty of rendering
and manly vigour is unsurpassed in the history of art.
Antichrist, the great power of Evil, falls amongst a group
of persons to the left, striking some of them dead. The
picture embraces many episodes ; but, perhaps, the most
wonderful of all is the great group of the foreground, in the
midst of which Antichrist stands upon a pedestal or altar,
preaching to the people ; a horned fiend behind him, whispering in his ear. At his feet are laid bags of money, gold
and silver vessels, with other worldly treasures. The type
of his countenance and the foldings of his drapery are based
upon the traditional form and manner in which our Lord is
commonly represented. But what a difference ! Instead
of the usual freely flowing wavy hair, this of Antichrist is
carefully parted down the middle, oiled and curled with the
utmost fastidiousness. The folds of his dress, too, and his
attitude are both disposed in the most studied manner. In
the face seem to be written in subtle and delicate characters
the long results of selfishness, evil lusts and heartlessness ;

* There is a picture by him (figured in Crowe and Cavalcaselle's work)
in private keeping at Florence, discovered of late years, which has been
called the "School of Pan," once offered, I believe, to our National
Gallery Commission at a price far from exorbitant. How it is possible
that such a picture should have been resigned is beyond comprehension.
It is an epitome of all that is great and noble in art—sufficient in itself to
enrich a gallery and make a nation proud in its possession.

a face one could not trust : full of the wisdom which comes of sin and worldly prejudice, but all glozed over with an almost dainty speciousness, the bad marks in it being half overlaid without being entirely concealed. All this is visible enough. Never did satire wield a sharper weapon, never did it cut so deep or wear a more serious dress. Of the group around him it would be long to tell. Here a young man in courtly garb sets his arms akimbo, and listens with a self-gratulatory satisfaction ; there a stalwart fellow, the very embodiment of brute power, stands with legs apart, turning his head to a neighbouring friar, evidently prepared for hot work if it should be required. Here a woman is receiving a bribe from the purse of a well-dressed citizen, and there schoolmen and philosophers dispute on the doctrines they hear. On the left a deed of martyrdom and bloodshed is being perpetrated, near to which stand the portrait figures of Luca Signorelli and Fra Angelico, both robed in black, as spectators. No description can give any idea of the vast scenic power and intensity of this noble work. It speaks with a thousand tongues.

Another of these wonderful frescoes represents the Resurrection. Two angels standing upon the clouds, surrounded by cherubs, blow their trumpets over the world. The souls of men and women rise at the sound, some with their bodies, as in life, others as skeletons. One of the most powerful of these is that of a man who lifts himself out of the ground by pressing one hand upon the surface of the soil, and another upon the knee of his liberated leg. Another is being drawn up out of the ground by his two hands by a companion already risen ; others stand about in adoring gratitude, or embrace each other with raptures of overflowing joy.

A third of these paintings symbolizes the Torments of the Condemned. It is something almost too frightfully horrible to contemplate, so intensely realistic is it in its representation. The avenging angels stand above, whilst grisly fiends torment their miserable victims below. One of the most astounding of these groups is that of a hideous monster, who bears a woman on his back through the air, and turns up his face into hers with a diabolical grin. **But** perhaps the utmost power of the artist culminates in **the** figure of a man at the left, who is being thrust head foremost into raging flames. **As** he gasps **with** head thrown back, and an expression of anguish **on his face** that is absolutely appalling, he presses his hands convulsively to his eyes, to protect himself from even the sight of the horrors which he is condemned to endure.

One more picture completes the series. It is the Reward **of the Just.** Newly risen spirits garlanded with flowers look up with a divine rapture, whilst angels place crowns of glory upon their heads, or floating in the sky strew them with showers of flowers. Through some of their faces the very soul seems to glow out in wells of living **emotion.** Angels above them play musical instruments. **Life, joy,** and animation are visible everywhere.

Art can do no more than has been done in these pictures. They embrace all the **tides** of humanity ; they sound the full chord of its emotions ; they reach its deepest springs ; they touch its loftiest ascensions and elevations. Time only tells the old story over and over again : it will never be interpreted in a nobler or more comprehensive language than that in which it has found expression **here.**

I shall not detain the reader any longer over this magnificent cathedral with its mosaic façade and grotesque carvings, nor over the many interesting and valuable works of art it contains. Neither shall I ask him to go to the vast well of St. Patrick, which marks the engineering skill **of** San Gallo : **nor even to** explore any more of the **stream** which has brought us from the main object of our journey.

Along the whole course of the river **Tiber, perhaps that** part of its territory is the **least known and most rarely** traversed which lies between Orvieto and Todi—a distance of somewhat more than twenty miles following the course **of the** stream ; and this **was** to me a somewhat anxious **part of the journey.** In vain I inquired of the landlord of the **hotel,** the waiters, and at the caffè. Nobody knew if there was a practicable road or **not** anywhere within sight of the stream. At last a peasant was found—and a rough-looking fellow he was—who belonged to some part of the intervening country. So he was summoned to a colloquy. When I told him my wish to make the journey to Todi, skirting the banks of the river, of course, the first thing he suggested was that there was a good high-road on the other side of the mountains, almost new, by which I might arrive there with ease and comfort much sooner. Persisting in my intention to follow the course of the river, he said that it was quite impossible, that it was a *strada orribile*, a horrible road : in fact that there was no road at all, but rocks and precipices, impenetrable woods, and dangerous streams —difficulties which it would be quite impossible to over-come. Did no one pass there ? I asked. No one, no one, he assured me ; unless it might be the peasants and charcoal burners here and there. Did he think he could find his way anywhere within sight of the river ? Well, perhaps he might, but it was quite impossible to approach it nearer than two or three miles. Finally I asked if he were willing to undertake the journey and make the best of it ; that is to say, to follow the banks of the river as nearly as might be practicable. This he agreed to do, promising to bring a couple of horses at daybreak the next morning, upon which to perform the journey. My friends would willingly have accompanied me during this stage also, but it was found that no more than a couple of saddle-horses could be obtained, owing to the harvest season ; so they undertook to follow the high road in a carriage, and rejoin me at Todi.

Accordingly, the next morning my guide appeared ; and bidding farewell to my friends, after the usual adjustment of incompetent trappings, we started on our journey. As we passed through the town a sombre grey pervaded the still streets and houses, now and then a resounding footfall, besides those of our horses, waking a sleepy echo. After descending the hill upon which the town stands, we forded the Paglia a short distance down the stream, and were presently threading our upwards way along the left bank

of the Tiber. At first we passed by rustic homesteads and
noisy mills, amongst fields of hemp and Indian corn ; but
soon the scenery became highly romantic, quite justi-
fying the account given of it by my guide. For long
distances no human voice was heard, no human face seen.
Awful shades seemed to brood from ledge and precipice,
whilst below them the river muttered and whispered in his
course, the shadows of tall poplars streaking the pebbly
banks, which were bleached to a ghastly whiteness with the
wrath of many a winter's torrent. After a while we passed
the walls of a desolate little village called Corbaro, once
the stronghold of a powerful mediæval family, and still
retaining a warlike appearance. As it glared down from
its barren shelf of rock it looked as if it might have been
the residence of the genius of this weird territory. Grim
and stern one might have imagined the knight-errant of
old cautiously tracking his way in such a spot filled with
vague fears of enchantment and treachery, scarcely daring
to turn his head at the hoarse cawing of the crow or the
scared cry of the magpie. He would certainly have muttered a paternoster and have grasped his lance more firmly
amidst these lonely shades and unfriendly steeps as the
river filled his ear with ominous murmurs and the poplars
whispered to each other as if untoward spirits had found
a place amongst their boughs and were plotting evil things
against him. For some time the river was the sole clue
to our course ; but presently we were obliged to diverge
from its banks where the ground was cut with deep ravines
by the torrents which in winter time pour from the hills.
Plunging into a wilderness of stunted trees and brushwood,
my guide confessed himself at fault, and there was nothing
for it but to follow the direction as nearly as possible
through the immense forests which here covered the valley
and stretched up the sides of the mountains. Fortunately,
after forcing our way through the brushwood without being
able to see more than a few yards before and around us,
we stumbled on a little patch of cultivated ground, where,
not far from a cottage, a man was occupied in ploughing

with a couple of oxen. We entreated his services to put us on some track which might lead us in the direction of our route, when he immediately left his plough, and accompanying us a distance of two or three miles, gave directions to my companion by which we might be enabled to follow the right course. Soon the scene changed as if by the touch of magic. The village of Civitella de' Pazzi was seen to crown a distant summit. Soft and feathery foliage covered the hill-sides. The severe mountain forms moved into softer lines. A rich green mantled the rising heights upon which light and shadow lay mingled in masses of tender repose. Culture had half withdrawn the natural wildness of the landscape. Gorge beyond gorge the mountains opened their recesses. Undulating plains of grass were spotted with clumps of trees. The labourer sang at his toil. The sheep-bell mixed its sound with the gentle roar of the river. All was peace and intense loveliness. It seemed as if nature, friendly to the labours of man, smiled contentment on the scene in her happiest mood, weaving herself garlands of leaves and flowers all day long. Thus following its course by many a willowy bend and poplared shade the river led us from valley to valley, until the banks becoming more contracted, steeper, and still more gloomy, it began to complain in angry tones at its closer imprisonment. Finally abysmal gorges dropped sheer down through unmeasured depths to its dark bed, wherefrom the moon might be seen at noon between black plumes of ancestral pines, and then it took a wide sweep to the right, and plunged between two narrow walls where no road lay for mortal foot to follow it.

Leaving its companionship for the moment we began to ascend the sides of the valley, through vast fragments of broken rock scattered about as if in mockery of order and law—up, up, until the sky seemed nearer and the sharp mountain breeze blew keenly on our foreheads, drawing the dust into little eddies with a feeble wail. Then what a panorama lay beneath! The long winding valley whose extent we had traversed lay below us like a map. Rocks, groves, farms, fields, villages, all giving variety to its **area** —a miniature world through which the serpentine **river** went from side to side, distributing greenness and **fertility** wherever its course lay.

After riding some little distance across the mountain table-land we struck **once more** into a high road, and I was astonished **to** find my friends H. and B. comfortably seated **at** the **door of a** little *osteria*, where they had just finished **such a meal as** the place afforded. Whatever **it had** been, **there was no** great abundance, for my rustic companion **and I had to** be contented with some dark bread and hard **cheese** with a *foglietta* of indifferent **wine.** It seemed on this spot our roads met, and though my friends had never seen the Tiber for the mountains that lay between, they described the scenery they had passed through as of a very **magni**-ficent and romantic **order.** Presently **we** remounted **our** horses, and striking **off** the road to the right I endeavoured to regain the river, **whilst my** companions **pursued their** journey by the high road. The descent **towards the** river-valley beneath Todi was extremely picturesque. The sun **had** already passed the hour **of** noon. A soft blue haze overspread **the landscape,** which was **seen in** vignette-like glimpses through the branches of motionless trees. Nume-**rous reapers** were passing **from** farm to farm ; the whole **valley vocal with** their strange songs. Crossing the river by **a** handsome bridge **we** commenced the ascent to Todi, which was seen to lift its low-spired campanile into the air, commanding the whole country round. The ascent **to** the town from the bottom occupies more than **an hour,** owing to the windings of the road up the steep sides of **the** elevation upon which it stands. **Circling the old town the** first object **that** meets the eye is a **singular church of** clustered domes, the masterpiece of Bramante. Wearily **we** rode along the lengthy principal street **of** the town without being able to find the inn we sought, which, it **seemed,** had either changed its name or vanished altogether. At last, as no inquiries availed, **we** were on the point of seeking **another, when** H. **and** B. looking **from a** window called to us to dismount, as they had found what was said to be the best *locanda* of the town. And a cheery little place enough it was, with all the cleanliness and comfort that one ever expects to find in an Italian inn remote from the path of ordinary travellers. We were waited upon by two bright-eyed damsels with the sharpness and politeness which naturally belongs to the Italian character. Dinner over, one of them produced from her pocket a handful of cigars and offered me one, at the same time proceeding to light and smoke one herself.

Todi was the ancient Roman Tuder. It is mentioned by Silius Italicus as being loftily situated, and famous for its temple of Mars.* It is also spoken of by Strabo and other classical writers.

It is surmounted by an old castle and partly surrounded by mediæval walls, with square towers at intervals. But more interesting than these are the extensive remains of some antique walls of Etruscan origin to be found in several parts of the town. These are composed of variously sized blocks of tufa laid together in unequal courses, without cement, offering a fine sample of the constructive workmanship of the earliest known inhabitants of Central Italy. There are also some very well preserved remains of the façade of a Roman temple, probably belonging to the time of the early empire.

The modern town, or city, as it is still called, contains between four and five thousand inhabitants. It consists of long straggling streets and a square, or piazza, with a town hall and cathedral of sturdy mediæval architecture. There are numberless picturesque nooks, lanes, and corners to be found within it, and sometimes indications of architectural taste and skill for which we may look in vain amongst modern workmanship. In common with other small Italian towns, there is a want of activity and energy within its precincts which is absolutely depressing. No shadow of ambition seems to disturb its quiet life. Remote from the great centres of

* Punic. iv. 222.

business, day by day passes without bringing any change to the still monotony of existence within its walls—scarcely reached even by a rumour of the large movements and energetic actions which stir and animate the races of men beneath.

It would be difficult to say in what manner the greater portion of the inhabitants of this town are enabled to eke out a livelihood where there seems to bé so little demand for labour, and, apparently, no commercial relationships beyond its limits. Yet here, from year to year, men and

TODI.

women live and die, some at a good old age, as appearances testify. Probably it maintains itself in a great measure on the produce of the surrounding country. Yet, in spite of its dullness and poverty, it is not without its pretensions to a certain form of social display. Every evening, in the fine weather, the principal inhabitants congregate on the terrace walks or promenade, laid out to command the whole

T

river-valley, from which the sun is seen to set like a fire, and the last glow of the fading day to vanish beyond the summits of the deep brown mountains, interweaving the sky with aerial webs of softly blended colour, and drawing the curtain of rest over still hamlet and tranquil homestead nestling peacefully beneath.

This spot was especially delightful to me at the evening hour during my stay there. It was the time of harvest; the spirit of early summer lay upon the surrounding country, not yet parched with the burning suns of the later season. An extensive valley was displayed far beneath, bounded by lofty mountains spreading their sombre slopes beyond the river, varied by vast groves, patches of cultivated land, and barren surface, all taking those subtle and delicate tints which a southern climate alone can impart. From a chasm of the hills the river emerged, and after wandering hither and thither through the valley, vanished as suddenly in a rift at the other end of it. Then the weird and melancholy songs of the reapers were wafted upwards from near and far harvest-fields, rising and falling in the stillness with their strange wild cadences, floating from bank to bank and bluff to bluff like the tender wailings of some bereaved sylvan spirit; and ere their last echoes had died on the glimmering twilight—for they seemed to linger in the air as if loth to die—the strain was taken up at some remote corner of the valley miles away, and prolonged again and again, throwing a vague spell over the scene, as the stars lit their silvery lamps one by one, and the bats and owls began to flicker through the closing shades of balm-breathing night.

The mediæval history of this town is of the usual turbulent character. A quaint incident is given by Graziani in his diary as having occurred here in the year one thousand three hundred and fourteen. "In the month of August," he says, "this year, the commune of Perugia made peace with the commune of Todi in this manner, that is, the syndic of those within and the syndic of those without kissed each other on the mouth, which peace was made at the foot of the campanile of San Lorenzo with a certain compact which appears written in our council chamber. When peace was made all the Guelphs from without entered the city. The contract was made by Sir Filippo de Gilio of Porta Santa Susanna." It is a pity so simple and satisfactory a mode of ending public difficulties has grown out of fashion in modern times.

Campano in his life of Fortebraccio narrates a stirring episode in the history of the city, which I shall here transcribe for the graphic picture which it gives of mediæval warfare and the military spirit of the time. It belongs to the year one thousand four hundred and fourteen.

"Whilst they were making great preparations for war, Braccio, having paid his soldiers a year in advance, retired into the territory of Todi before the king [Ladislaus of Naples] should arrive, who, it was reported, was approaching with twenty thousand cavalry and eight thousand infantry with as great provisions for war to assault the pope's forces as had formerly served to defeat them in Tuscany. The people of Todi, who were on the side of the pope, although they felt themselves strong by nature of their position, yet being divided into parties and factions, placed the whole army of Braccio within the city, waiting the brunt of the king's coming, imagining (as, indeed, it happened) that he would use his utmost power to make himself master of the city, seeing that it stood between Rome and Perugia. The king, accordingly, on his arrival immediately surrounded the city to besiege it, with the intention of subjugating it by famine if he should not be able to take it by force. Braccio, although he might have been able from the advantage of his more elevated position to have attacked the enemy in the plain below, nevertheless, on account of the small number of soldiers under his command, remained at first for some time within the walls. Afterwards issuing from the city almost every day he molested the enemy in such a manner that it did not appear

T 2

so much that he was besieged as that he fought in open combat, the soldiers of Braccio being so emboldened by success as several times to have approached the pavilion of the king, so that the enemy were obliged to place sentinels close to the city, fortifying themselves with bastions. Trusting in their numbers, many overran the surrounding territory, burning the houses, others reduced to ruin the edifices in the vicinity of the city, others cut down the olives and vines, which being done under the eyes of the owners, each was compelled to be a witness of the injury he suffered. When the besieged thus saw their property destroyed on every hand, they were greatly moved thereat, and finally determined to submit themselves to the king, sending the heads of the city to capitulate and conclude peace ; the ambassadors earnestly demanding that Braccio might be permitted to leave the country voluntarily with all his army and to go whither he would. The king, although many would have persuaded him to the contrary, yet at the strong instance of the ambassadors, finally consented. Five hundred infantry were then sent into the city, and Braccio, having the opportunity to leave it, went with his army to Fratticiuola. No sooner, however, had he gone away than the soldiers placed by the king within the city gave themselves to unbridled robbery, and, under cover of the night, licentiously to sack the houses of the poor citizens, commencing, as is customary with soldiers, forcibly to put everything to ruin. The inhabitants of Todi, soon repenting of the step which they had taken, once more gave themselves to the pope, and recalling Braccio to the defence of the city, threw down the royal standard, raised that of the Church, and were again besieged by Ladislaus. On the same day that this change was made in Todi certain companies sent by the king took several of Braccio's cavalry together with two hundred horses which had been put to pasture. The night following, Braccio commanded his soldiers that they should take arms, and issuing from the city at the first watch of the night, assaulted the camp

of the king with such violence **that,** having **thrown down**
their defences and cut the sentinels to pieces, they thence
passed to the trenches of the enemy, who being awakened
from sleep, whilst they **were running** to seize their arms,
were bound and **made prisoners.** There were taken and
led away **to Todi four** noble knights who had charge of
the royal standards, as they were hurrying to the pavilion
of the king. As soon as Braccio perceived that the enemy
had had time to arm themselves and that they were coming
out to fight, not wishing to be taken prisoner in the midst
of a more powerful opponent, thought it prudent to sound a
retreat. Amongst all the gallant deeds done in the war
there were none more honourable than this. The king in
person having followed them to the gates of the city, heard
the voices of the standard-bearers calling for **help ; but**
although he thought himself close upon them, they **were**
dragged up the heights with such celerity that he **suddenly**
found himself a long way from them. As **soon as they were**
within the town the soldiers commenced in **the dark** to despoil
them ; but when **a** light was brought and they saw the
distinguished aspect of their prisoners they forbore. Their
vests were richly embroidered, their spurs of gold, their
corselets and helmets gilded all over ; neither were their
horses less elaborately adorned : their trappings, bridles,
and saddles being all furnished with gold. When they
were brought before Braccio he entertained them with
much kindness ; and early on the day following he sent
them back to the king, although by the rules of **war he**
might have made them pay for their liberation. There
were taken seventy cavalry from the enemy that night. It
is said that the king after having **asked the** standard-
bearers many particulars concerning Braccio, bestowed
great praises on his humanity and high-mindedness, sending
a trumpeter to thank him in his name. The next day in
a slight skirmish **a soldier of** Braccio, much loved and
esteemed by him, was taken prisoner. The king gave him
a purple vest, **and then set** him at liberty, requesting him

to tell Braccio, that he much desired to speak with him.
Between the city and the king's camp beyond the confines
and the trench were some strong beams well secured, where
the soldiers of both sides frequently met in combat, these
to force and those to defend the obstacle ; here the soldier
addressing Braccio, told him what the king had said, at the
same time pointing out the king, who was fighting beyond
the barrier. 'Go to him,' replied Braccio, 'and tell him if
he wishes to see me I am here.'   The king, however, at the
instant approaching the barrier, Braccio immediately raised
his helmet, and with uncovered head, throwing down his
sword, dismounted his horse, and resting upon one knee
did him reverence as is customary before royalty, upon
which both retired to a long parley—the soldiers on both
sides continuing to fight with only the line of defence and
the trench between them.   The king offered Braccio three
hundred thousand ducats, if he would combine with him,
together with the command of all his army, and a city in
gift, whichever he might choose in his kingdom, except
Naples, adding that nothing should be denied to him if he
would only join him : promising all this on his faith and
royal crown.   Braccio, after thanking the king for his
graciousness in granting him an interview, who was but a
private person and of no distinction, told him that he had
always studied to maintain his faith pure and entire towards
those whom he served, and that as he was now fighting for
the pope, he should remain faithful to him, although it
might cost him his life, and that he should not abandon
him either for money, love, fear, or any manner of danger,
because he held nothing in the world so valuable as fidelity ;
but that if he could in any particular interest have served
his highness he would willingly have done so, if it were not
prejudicial to the dignity of the pope ; adding, that if he
had been in the service of the king at that time as he was
in that of the pope, he would have served him with the
same faithfulness.   Upon these words the king offered him
many compliments, and having commended his principles

departed ; the skirmishing being renewed with much **greater vehemence** than before : each party exciting **the soldiers to** a greater ardour. But with all **he could do the king was** never able to pass the line of defence which was continually surrounded by the people **of Todi,** who with their arrows kept their **enemies** at **a distance.** After having thus consumed twenty-five **days** in the siege, the king decamped ; **and** shortly afterwards, making peace with the Florentines **and taking and** imprisoning Paolo Orsini, returned first to **Rome and** then to his kingdom, where he died."

Here was **born in** the thirteenth century Jacopo de' Benedetti, called **Fra Jacopone,** the author of the Stabat Mater, and many hymns and verses. He was brought up **as** an advocate or lawyer. He married a wife of wealthy parentage who was both **beautiful and virtuous. One day during** the celebration of **a** festival, the ceiling **gave way and** Benedetti's wife suffered **a** mortal injury. On unloosing **her** dress he found that she **wore** a coarse **haircloth next** her skin. **This** and **his loss** so affected **Benedetti** that **he either** became really deranged **in his mind,** or else affected to **be so as an act** of religious penance. He attached himself as **a lay brother to a** Franciscan convent, performing **the most** menial **services, and** was made an object **of ridicule** by the whole town, receiving the nickname **of Jacopone. Many** fantastic circumstances are narrated **of him.** Once he covered himself with some resinous **matter, and** rolling himself in feathers presented himself amongst a company of merry makers, to their disgust **and** confusion. Another time **being requested to take home** some provisions **for a** feast by **a gentleman of the place,** he bore them **to the** family burial **place—"the home of all living."** Being **afterwards at Palestrina,** he wrote some verses against **the pope, Boniface the** eighth, **who had him put** into prison, **where he** languished **for a** long time. **It is said that** the pope **one** day **passing by** his prison asked him **tauntingly when he intended to come out :** "When you come in," **was the reply ;** which happened accordingly ; for shortly afterwards when the Colonna, with whom the pope was at strife, gained the upper hand, they put the pope into prison and liberated Jacopone. Such astuteness as Jacopone often showed both in his conduct and writings scarcely appears like madness. He died in thirteen hundred and six, and was buried in his native town.

The length of the Tiber from Todi to Perugia, a distance of about twenty-seven miles, offers as few points of interest and as little variety of scenery as are to be found in any similar length of its whole course. As the high road follows the river quite closely almost the whole of the distance we took the diligence of the country at an early hour of the morning to accomplish this portion of our journey. Everything wore a beautiful pastoral aspect. The river here wanders through a vast undulating plain of the most fertile territory, richly cultivated, covered with orchards, vineyards, and pleasant pastures. As we passed along the road, the horses lazily jingling their bells, we saw the swineherd tending his charge beneath the trees, here and there a flock of sheep grazing or perhaps a few cows watched by a boy or a girl with her white linen head-dress shining in the sun. Now and then a white house was seen on the upland, or perhaps a little village lifting its tall campanile from some more elevated height. The sides of the river bristled with lank poplars, vast groves of which stretch up the spreading slopes for miles. Grey willows fringed the shores, whilst the stream—a narrowing streak of azure on white beds of pebbles, sand, or baked mud— ran into cool vistas of refreshing shade, from time to time fed with little trickling rills. Hot as it was the drive was cheerful and pleasant. The driver, near whom I sat, entertained me almost the whole of the way with his views on the regeneration of Italy. Amongst other things he informed me that there was a popular superstition that if the pope should survive his twenty-fifth anniversary his delegated power would revert to St. Peter himself and be no longer availing in the hands of the pontiff. " Do you also

believe it ?" I asked. " No," he replied, " I am not speaking
of myself, but of the lower classes of uneducated people."
Presently he told me that an excellent dinner had been
ordered some days before to be ready at Diruta for the
gentlemen inside upon the arrival of the diligence, and as
there would probably be enough for all, he would ask them
to let us join them.   Accordingly, on our arrival at a little
road-side inn near that town, we were regaled on an
abundance of maccaroni, together with boiled, fried and
roast, with some very excellent wine ; not unwelcome
additions to the pleasure of a day's travelling, seasoned, as
it was, with the friendly and well-bred courtesy of our
travelling companions.

Diruta was a town of some mediæval importance, being
not infrequently concerned in the wars of Perugia and Todi.
It is in a good commanding position.   From this place a
hot length of dusty road led us by many a pretty white
villa up to Perugia.

ORVIETO

CHAPTER X.

PERUGIA, ASSISI, AND THE RIVER CLITUMNUS.

THERE is no more agreeable town in Central Italy for a summer residence than Perugia. On a spur of the Apennines commanding the prospect of the greater part of the valley of Foligno, which extends to a distance of thirty or forty miles from its foot, it enjoys a salubrious atmosphere, with a cheerful and beautiful position.* It is quiet, intensely quiet to an Anglo-Saxon fresh from the cities of England or America ; but to the lover of nature and the artist there is abundant material for the eye and the mind, whilst the student of mediæval life may feast himself in the dusty records of bygone centuries written on almost every house-front and every public building. We were happy on our arrival to find ourselves in the midst of a little colony of English and American friends from Rome, who had come here to spend the summer. I do not know of any place where the friendly and social relationships are so satisfactory as in Italy. Sojourners being led thither for the most part by a community of pursuit, the free-and-easy, half bohemian artist life allows of perfectly unconstrained intercourse. Everyone who goes to make a visit to Italy beyond the run of the mere tourist, is in a manner compelled to adopt some speciality, if he have not one already, either in art or antiquity ; so that each

* Perugia
Che com' è in monte ha il sito allegro e bello.—
FAZIO DEGLI UBERTI.

is more or less interested in the pursuit of the other, and meetings are almost always welcome and agreeable. Ours were no exception to this rule. Genial days and evenings greeted us. In fact, every day was a holiday from which a few hours were borrowed to forward a picture or to acquire material for a new one, or to work out a sketch to suggest the winter work of the sculptor. For myself the mornings of each day were almost always spent in the retirement of the town library, disinterring many a dusty tome, ancient chronicle, or local history, in order to obtain glimpses of mediæval life and manners in the city ; some extracts from which I purpose presently to lay before the reader.

Perugia is perhaps one of the oldest of Italian cities as it was once one of the most powerful of Etruria. In the fourth century before Christ it was able to withstand the Romans for a long time, though ultimately compelled to succumb to Fabius. It would not appear, however, that it was finally reduced until forty years before the Christian era, under the emperor Augustus, when it suffered the horrors of siege and famine, the city being afterwards sacked, three hundred of its chief citizens being condemned to decapita-tion. On this occasion a certain Caius Cestius Macedonius, preferring that his house should be burnt rather than delivered to the pillage of the enemy, set fire to it, where-upon the flames spread throughout the whole city, which was thus burnt to the ground. It was afterwards rebuilt by Augustus and colonized by the Romans. In the sixth century it fell into the hands of Totila, king of the Goths, after a seven years' obstinate resistance, who devastated it with fire and sword, beheading its bishop. Its mediæval history was a very troubled one, and as it includes some of the most stirring events and characteristic scenes of that hostile period it may be interesting to dwell on it a little more at length. But instead of giving a continuous his-torical account of the city, I shall present a few pictures of its state and condition in the Middle Ages.

Almost every town in Italy, little or great, has at some time or other had its local chronicler, who has written a diary or history, in a more or less fragmentary form, of the chief political and social events occurring during his life-time. The manner in which these are given is often infinitely racy and amusing. Many of them were subsequently printed, some have found later editors, whilst doubtless many still remain in the dust of centuries, awaiting the discoverer to bring them to the light.

Campano, the biographer of Fortebraccio, says that the Perugians were the most bellicose of all nations, and that even in the same house party spirit ran so high that sons were frequently opposed to their fathers, so that neither dared trust his life into the hands of the other. Treachery and suspicion prevailed; the domestic relationships even losing faith and confidence. This state of things is confirmed by the historians, although, indeed, they do not forget to tell us that there were exceptions to the rule—quiet, peaceable citizens who regarded every movement of the military spirit within the city or out of it as the worst of misfortunes, and who would willingly have pursued their way in tranquillity if they had been permitted to do so.

To furnish an idea of the state of feeling in the city, and the circumstances under which it was maintained, I shall here give a picture of its condition in the year one thousand four hundred and eighty-eight from the history of Pellini.

At that time Perugia was divided into factions by two powerful and wealthy families, the Baglioni and the Oddi, the growing jealousy between whom was fostered and finally brought to issue by the former having some offices and emoluments withdrawn from them by the pope, as was supposed, at the instigation and by the influence of the other. This was quite enough to arouse the smouldering fires of rivalry that lay between them. Immediately the whole city and territory were disorganised. But we will leave the historian to narrate the episode in his own manner.

" In those days," he says, " Guido Baglioni returned from
Spello, and seeing the differences which had arisen and the
danger of a catastrophe, reports of which were noised about
the city, summoned a good number of soldiers into Perugia
from his territories, strengthening himself with his adherents,
all the country being in arms, and the gentlemen's houses
full of friends and armed followers, and the Oddi in great
suspicion, because it was already reported that the Baglioni
wished to kill the sons of Leone degli Oddi. It happened
on the twenty-fifth of October, Giulio Cesare degli Staffa
being the head of the Signori, at one hour of the night,
whilst the minds of every one were in suspense, a little
disturbance took place in the piazza, and cries were raised
of Oddi, Oddi ! and Baglioni, Baglioni ! yet, although much
people ran thither, there was nothing more done that
evening ; but they stood in arms all night, each attentive
to his own safety. The following day, which was Sunday,
the Marchese del Monte, who had married the daughter
of Simone degli Oddi, went thither ; and with him went
Pompeo di Leone, Nicolò di Sforza and Mariotto, with
many other friends in company, although the whole country
was in an uproar, each party seeking to bring his friends
from without for the sake of his own security. On the
Monday they remained in arms in the same manner, the
shops not being opened, each guarding himself with vigi-
lance as knowing that the danger was great. The Baglioni,
for their better security, put a good number of the soldiers
from Spello in the cathedral, where they fortified themselves
by barricading the doors, only leaving aperture sufficient
for the discharge of the artillery they had placed therein,
which, although not numerous nor of great size, was by
no means inefficacious, since they were able to command
the house of the Staffa from one door and from another,
towards the Via Nuova, to bear upon the Armanni, the
Ranieri, the Arcipreti and the Sperelli ; and, in order that
no one might come into the piazza without opposition, they
had placed some at the principal entrance towards the

piazza, and on the roof of the church, opposite the tower of the Armanni, which was also provisioned and well furnished with arms and all necessaries; these also commanded the piazza and the palace of the podestà. The Corgneschi, on their part, placed many pieces of artillery and cross-bows (*balestre*) which commanded the road that leads to Sansanne; so that it was impossible for any one to enter the piazza that way without danger; and in order that the Oddi might be altogether debarred from entering the piazza, the Baglioni also had barricaded the way and guarded it with soldiers in the neighbourhood of the Cupa under the houses of the Crispolti, and in other places. They had also taken the seat of the notaries into the piazza and placed weapons and soldiers there. The Oddi, on the other side, seeing themselves almost besieged and unable to go to the piazza without great danger, set themselves to strengthen their position, with the determination to provoke the Baglioni to the contest, or, if any further tumult should arise, to defend themselves; they also being supported by many friends and adherents; amongst others by the Count Giacomo, son of Count Guido of Sterpeto, with two hundred infantry, who had fought much and was much praised for his daring. They had closed the road to the Verzaro in various places, at the Ceppo della Catena and in other places; so that all that day and the next, they did nothing else but prepare for their defence, although many neutral gentlemen and the magistrates did everything they could to make peace; to whom the Oddi made it appear that they did not know of what the Baglioni complained, nor what they would have; and as to the difference between them and the Corgneschi in the affair of Passignano, they professed that it might be easily accommodated. The intention of the Ranieri and Agamemnone della Penna to assist the Oddi being discovered, they also provided themselves with many men, and set pieces of artillery in the house of Master Filippo Capra on the hill of Porta Sole, in order to be higher than the others, so that they could shoot right into the door of the cathedral which faces the Via Nuova. They then fortified themselves in the houses, particularly Agamemnone, who strengthened his position with beams and whatever else came to hand for the safety of himself and what belonged to him, providing all that was judged useful or necessary for the occasion. On Tuesday, which was the day of St. Simon and St. Jude, the twenty-eighth of October, things remaining in this state of suspicion and fear, it happened that two young men after dining, having come to an encounter at the foot of the piazza on account of some personal quarrel, attacking each other with their swords, all the people in the piazza ran thither. It was natural that the Baglioni, being the nearest to the disturbance, should arrive there the first, ready to seize the occasion. As soon as their adherents had arrived in the piazza they began to shout the name of their party and to enter into contest with some followers of the Oddi. The Corgneschi also, hearing the tumult, rushed incontinently out of the house of Master Pietro Filippo, and without going further, placed themselves at the head of the street which goes to the Porta Sansanne, as well because the Oddi, who were already on their way to the skirmish, should not enter the piazza, as because those of their friends who were there should not be able to rejoin the others. A sharp and perilous encounter took place between the Oddi and Corgneschi under the palace of the Signori; but more by wounding each other from a distance with bolts and pikes and with small pieces of artillery which they had fixed in secure places, than with the sword and other short arms hand to hand. The Oddi, who were in much greater numbers, would have easily taken the piazza if the Baglioni had not been prompt in their help to the Corgneschi, who thus reinforced prevented the Oddi from entering it. The fight lasted several hours in the narrow streets; but when the Oddi attempted to pass by these ways—as the Baglioni attempted to do by others—to the great disadvantage of the enemies at Porta

Sansanne, and thus to enter the piazza in other directions, there were engagements in various parts. There was fighting at the same time beneath the palace of the Signori in the principal piazza, in the piazza of the Aratri, under the bridge that goes to the Via Vecchia and the Conca, where the family of the Petrini had their houses (some of which are still there) at the Ceppo della Catena, and not far from thence, at the house of the Corgneschi at San Gregorio, where barricades had been raised and strong defences made; and in all places they continued fighting valiantly until the evening with much damage of wounds and death on both sides. But besides attacking and using every effort to occupy and defend the barriers, the Baglioni, who had the advantage of the assistance of the people from without, who had been able to damage the enemy by taking them with all ardour, began to assault many houses wherein they saw the retainers and defenders of the Oddi. To some they set fire, so that presently they saw all that were within them together with the furniture burn and consume away. On that day, however, the house of the heirs of Paolo di Tancio, not far from the church of Maestà della Volta, was the only one entirely burnt down. It had been desired before the fighting commenced that in order to prevent strife or subdue it, that Guido, as the oldest and of the most authority in that family, should stand continuously with a stick in his hand and unarmed at the top of the street of the Porta Susanne, which he accordingly did, calling to his own people that they should withdraw themselves from the combat; for which reason there was much less harm done that day than there might have been. For this end also there ran thither Leandra, the wife of Sforza degli Oddi and the daughter of Braccio Baglione, and Isabetta, daughter of Guido Baglione, who with all their authority and entreaties, united with the intercessions of many reverend fathers of the Observance of St. Francis, who went in procession bearing the crucifix before them, crying 'Peace, peace!' interposing themselves with great humility, were not able to effect so much as that the fight in all the above-mentioned places should not last until the evening."

It is easy to imagine all this ; the eager and passionate countenances of the belligerents ; the women with dishevelled hair and frightened faces anxious to save husband, father, or brother ; the monks and priests rushing hither and thither with gesticulations and entreaties—all are placed graphically before us. Finally the differences became adjusted for the time being ; but fresh disturbances afterwards broke out ; houses were burnt and sacked ; the Oddi being obliged to flee the city. They established themselves at Castiglione on Lake Thrasimene ; but were thence dislodged and scattered throughout various parts of Italy.

To these factions and disturbances there was no end. Continually adventurous persons of arms, grown into power by whatever means, struggled with each other for rule ; everywhere the people suffered, and in endeavouring to free themselves from one yoke found themselves subjugated by another. Rival families sought for rule and dominion for the mere purpose of selfish aggrandisement and personal advantage. One of the most prominent of these personages was Biordo Michelotti. Nurtured amidst feudal ambitions, he early took up arms as a profession. After making himself master of Orvieto, towards the end of the fourteenth century he established himself at Diruta, and then began a warfare against Perugia ; so that more to get rid of a powerful enemy than for any friendliness the Perugians bore to him, he was finally admitted to the mastership of their city. It will be enough here to furnish two episodes from their local history at this time. One of his marriage and the other of his death, the former told by an old chronicler, as follows :—

"In the month of November, of the year one thousand three hundred and ninety-seven, Biordo ordered a great festival and triumph to be prepared in secret ; though he did not let the purpose of it be known. First of all it was

U

arranged that every family of the country and then every community, village and stronghold should bring a present. These presents were of straw, corn, wood, grain, wine, fowls, calves, sheep, eggs, and cheese ; being made spontaneously, and not by command, from the wish which the people had to show their attachment to Biordo. Biordo afterwards had it published throughout the country, that every person who was not a rebel or had not been condemned by the commune of Perugia might come with safety to the said feast. He also invited all the gentry of the neighbourhood, ordering a high festival of eight days to be proclaimed. There were invited Master Chiavello da Fabriano, together with his wife and all his family, the son of the Count Antonio da Urbino, and many other gentlemen. Moreover, he summoned a great number of the people of his territory for a body guard. The abbot of Santa Maria di Val di Ponte made him a magnificent present, so did the abbot of San Pietro and the son of Simon Guidalotti. Besides, all the districts around sent him ambassadors with very noble presents. Finally, Venice and Florence sent twelve men at arms for the tournament. . . .

"Madonna the Countess, daughter of Count Bertoldo of the house of Ursina was taken by Biordo to San Giovanni the day before. Sir Filippo di Matteuccio went for her and conducted her to Castel della Pieve, and on the thirteenth, came to Perugia. She entered by the Due Porte wearing a vestment of gold drawn over her head with many jewels ; before her were carried three pairs of coffers ; she was also preceded by six damsels in cloth vestments, for her service. She wore a wreath of asparagus round her head. She was accompanied by Master Chiavello, governor of Fabriano, and the ambassadors of Venice and Florence on horseback ; all the honourable gentlewomen going before, dancing, clothed each according to the quarter of the town to which she belonged, those who did not dance walking behind. The commune of Perugia, in order to enhance the importance of the festival gave ten florins of gold to each company. In front there were a great number of trumpeters who sounded in the manner of an invitation to come to the festival, during which no one was allowed to open his shop for the space of eight days. The banquet was laid for the Signori of San Lorenzo in the papal saloon, around which were placed a great many tables, supports being made for the torches. The table of Biordo was at the head of the saloon, raised above all the others. The masters of the feast were Baldo della Nina, Spaccalfico and Massietto Cambiatore, at whose table there were placed three hundred trenchers for each course. So that it was said in Tuscany that there was never seen before so fine a festival. The ladies were entertained altogether at the house of Biordo, which was on the hill of Porta Sole, and were a very royal company.

"The day following all the above mentioned cities, territories and other places brought presents and unique gifts ; first the ambassador of Venice, presenting one which was worth two hundred florins of gold, that of Florence being a robe of scarlet and a horse in trappings, that of Città di Castello being another robe and a horse. Orvieto presented an entire table-service all of silver ; Todi the same with two pieces of velvet. Other ambassadors did the like. Besides these there were a great number of ladies, habited with the device borne by the quarter in which Biordo dwelt, who had almost all made three vests to each person who went dancing about the piazza. On Wednesday a helmed man jousted, bearing the arms of the commune behind, that is the griffin, one of the household of Chiavello and others contending ; the joust lasting until night, when the torches had to be lighted. The prize was given to him of Chiavello's household. It was a very high festival."[*]

The account of Biordo's death is given by Graziani, one of the local historians above spoken of, in a very circumstantial way. It is as follows :—

"On the tenth of March Biordo de li Michelotti was made

[*] *Memorie di Perugia dal 1308 al 1398.* Quoted by Fabretti in his "Capitani d' Umbria." Note e documenti.

Count of Val di Chiana.   On the same day, that is the tenth of March, on Sunday morning, the said Michelotti was killed by the abbot Francesco, son of Simone di Cecolo dei Guidalotti, he was abbot of San Pietro : a man full of malice and deceit as appears by this homicide and the manner in which it occurred, as we shall proceed to narrate below.

"To recount in full all the particulars of the death of the said Biordo, it may be stated that Biordo trusted in Simone di Cecolo more than in any other man in the world, and more than if he had been a relative ; conferring with him on his most secret affairs.   One day he confided to him a plan which he had formed to raise himself very much by means of certain clever accomplices ; for he was very much beloved of them and every other person, both rich and poor, —more than any who before had held Perugia, and this was for the great benignity, suavity, and affection, which distinguished him.   After having told Simone everything, as has been said, Simone revealed it all to the other Guidalotti, who, moved with envy, at once sought to procure his death in some manner, and then to give the city into the hands of the pope ; this treachery being devised by the abbot Francesco dei Guidalotti, who did all he could to forward the design thinking thus to rise to the dignity of cardinal. And, so, as fortune would have it, on the tenth of March on Sunday morning, the above-named abbot Francesco left San Pietro and came on horseback to the end of the hill of Landone, his house being there ; he and some of his company leaving their horses there.   Then the abbot, with two of his brothers, Giovanni and Anibaldo, sons of Simone di Cecolo, went towards the house of Biordo on the hill of the Porta Sole, Armanno di Ugolino going with them, together with many other friends ; in all about twenty, all of whom had sworn an oath to the same effect.

"When they had arrived, they gave Biordo to understand that the abbot Francesco wanted to speak to him on a matter of great importance ; whereupon he quickly rose from his bed and went to the cloister, without

having any arms upon him whatever. When the abbot
entered Biordo went towards him, saying, 'I rejoice to
see you. I did not wish to trouble you to come to me,
so I have come to you.' The abbot bowed and saluted
him, and taking him by the hand presently embraced him.
Then Giovanni, Anibaldo, and the other accomplices attacking Biordo from behind, struck him in the throat with
poisoned knives, until they had killed him. Gaidone was
with Biordo, who, it is said, was also in the conspiracy;
there were also two servants with him, but they did not
help him, as was supposed, through fear. As soon as the
abbot and the company saw that Biordo was quite dead
they immediately went for their horses to their house on
the hill of Landone, and mounting them, went down to San
Pietro, staying there and sending for all their friends; but
Armanno when he was mounted did not go with the abbot,
but took the way towards the piazza, and went about the
piazza crying, 'We have killed the tyrant,' thinking by
that to lead the people with him; but not a single person
followed. By this time it had got abroad in Perugia that
Biordo was dead, although there were not twenty persons
in the piazza; almost every one being in the church at the
sermon. As soon as those who were listening to the sermon
heard of the death of Biordo, they went out and immediately
armed themselves, and then came into the piazza crying,
'Death to the traitors!' so all the people followed them
crying, 'Death to the traitors!' Andrea di Madonna Fiore
with certain companions, was amongst the first to arrive in
the piazza, who, when he saw Armanno, went towards him
crying, 'Kill, kill the traitors.' Upon which Armanno
turned his horse and galloped to San Pietro, whither the
abbot had gone with the rest of his companions. As soon
as he reached them the abbot and the others went immediately to Casalina, taking as many friends with them as
they could find. On the other side the people, being all
armed, did nothing but cry, 'Death to the traitors!' searching
for the abbot and the other Guidalotti with the intention

of killing them, all running to their houses and the houses of their followers, from which they took all the things, and then set fire to them : that is, first to the houses of Simone di Cecolo and Francesco di Nino and then to the houses of the partisans of the said Guidalotti which were all sacked and burned. At noon Francesco di Nino, uncle to the before-mentioned abbot, was found in the piazza at the shop of Leonardo, and immediately killed by one Agobio, fellow-cousin of Biordo. Shortly afterwards Sigisnolfo, going through the town on horseback seeking for the Guidalotti and their followers to kill them, was informed that Simone di Cecolo, father of the abbot, was hid in the district of Sansanne in the house of Antonio de la Mona, apothecary ; so they went thither and killed him, afterwards throwing him out of the window. After vespers Giacopo di Bartolommeo and another were found near the fountain of Buzago, going to rejoin the abbot at Casalina, who were both slain. On the same day Gaidone was hanged near Capo Cavallo : he had fled ; and as it was believed that he belonged to the band of traitors they hanged him. It is said that the conspiracy was arranged at San Pietro, where the abbot had intended to give a feast to which Biordo was to have been asked with many other citizens, and there they were all to have been killed ; thus it was arranged, all of which was revealed by Luca Torsciano, whose head was cut off, because he belonged to the faction. The same day the news was sent to Madonna Baldina, the mother of Biordo, and to Madonna the Countess, his wife, and to Cecolino : the commune sending them word to Todi, where they were staying. Cecolino was recommended to remain in Todi until they sent for him ; and this the commune did, because Cecolino was a man very hasty and terrible, and they feared he might do some great mischief : so that Cecolino after having accompanied the ladies as far as the confines of Perugia returned to Todi. In the meanwhile the blood of Biordo was gathered up and put into a basin, and was buried the following night in the church of San Francesco together with the body in a coffin.

When the before-mentioned women arrived, there was a great weeping and an honourable funeral was ordained, the commune of Perugia causing a helmet of silver to be made for his tomb and a standard with the device of a white griffin upon it. Afterwards there were made many banners with his arms upon them. On the Sunday and Monday the people were occupied continually in carrying away grain, wine and corn from the abbey of San Pietro, and on Tuesday it was set on fire, in order that there might be an abbey no longer, since it was said that it had been found on record, that many times treachery against the state of Perugia had been plotted within its walls ; and therefore all was burnt save the church. On the Tuesday, that was the twelfth of March, it was determined to raze the fortress of Sant Apollinare, which belonged to the abbey. On the ninth day after the death of Biordo, that was the eighteenth of the month, there was published a proclamation throughout the city, that the shops should not be opened. The ceremonial of the funeral was prepared in the palace of the captains, in which there was raised an elevated platform, upon which was placed the coffin covered with black, so that every one might see it ; and about it was erected a square frame-work upon which were placed burning torches, many mourning men and women standing around, and many retainers on horseback covered with black even to the ground, with banners in their hands ; and they went through all the city crying aloud and making great lamentation and weeping, saying, ' Our lord and master !' And almost all the people wept and said that the father of the people was dead ; and much people remained in the piazza covered with black cloaks ; although every one was armed, for fear lest some disturbance should arise. And so the coffin was borne about the piazza amidst such grievous mourning as would have made a heart of stone weep. Then it was carried back to the palace, Biordo's mother tearing her hair with so great violence as to leave none on her head. This was in the *pergola* of the palace in which the mother and wife of Biordo stood dressed in mourning ; and then the widow had all her hair cut off, upon which the lamentations were once more renewed in such a manner that it may not be told or recounted.   Around the coffin a great number of torches were placed and all the priests and friars, as many as could be found, and much people, both men and women, went as far as the palace of the Signori accompanying the coffin ; many persons remaining in the piazza out of suspicion.   Also the country persons made great lamentation ; for to them Biordo had been very favourable and a great benefactor."

But by far the most illustrious and distinguished of these local captains or governors, who were little kings in their territories, was Braccio da Montone surnamed Fortebraccio. He was born in Perugia in one thousand three hundred and sixty eight ; his family at that time owning the feudal territory of Montone, a fortress lying some distance to the north of Perugia towards Città di Castello.   He distinguished himself in arms when still a youth by repressing a plot against his brothers at that place, and reinstating them in their possession.   He began life as a military adventurer, but all his ambition was finally concentrated in the desire to possess himself of the rulership of his native town.   More than once he had attempted to seize it by force of arms, but in vain ; every hand was raised against him.   Even the women, once when he had won his way into the city, inciting their sons and husbands to resistance, poured on the devoted foe boiling water and live ashes, hurling upon them all the missiles within their reach.   As to the men, the historian says, they fought not as army against army, but as man against man ; as if their enmity were not a matter of public difference, but one of private hatred and personal vengeance, crying for the blood of each individual opponent.   Against such obstinate bravery, Braccio could do nothing.   He rallied his troops in vain.   At last he was driven out of the city, to the great joy of the Perugians, and their sorrow also, for he left them the sore task of opening and filling many new graves.

It was only after the assassination of Biordo Michelotti

that a better opportunity favoured him with success. Whilst
various powers were contending for their rights over Perugia
Braccio mustered all the forces that he could, meeting the
Perugians and their allies under Malatesta di Rimini,
near San Giovanni on the banks of the Tiber below the
city. It was on this occasion that Braccio introduced a
new method of fighting which Campano says was always
afterwards adopted. Instead of marshalling all his army
together, he divided it into squadrons, appointing a re-
liable commander over each. The two armies met on a
plain near the bridge between the hills and the river. Before the battle commenced Braccio took care to provide
ample means of refreshment for his soldiers, organizing
attendants to carry through his army supplies of water to
reinvigorate the men under the heat of a midsummer sun:
the battle being fought upon a dry and arid plain thickly
covered with dust. This arrangement probably decided
the fortunes of the day, for whilst the soldiers of Braccio
were thus able to refresh themselves from time to time, the
opposing troops under Malatesta, overcome with the blaze
of a July sun, their eyes and mouths filled with hot dust,
bathed in perspiration, and having no opportunity of removing their helmets for a moment, were at last so borne
down by the continued strokes of the enemy as to be
unable to use their swords, and after considerable slaughter
were finally led away unresisting prisoners. When the
Perugians within the city heard of their sad defeat at the
hand of the foe whom they had formerly so successfully
resisted, they were filled with consternation. A profound
silence reigned throughout the town, more terrible, as the
historian says, than any spoken complaints could be. No one
dared to look another in the face in the heaviness of his
own grief: whilst the women shut themselves up in their
houses mourning both their living and their dead.

In the meantime the Council of Ten deliberated as to what
was the best thing to do. There could be only one conclusion. If the city must be saved from outrage, fire and

slaughter, it must be given up to Braccio. It was a bitter decision, but it was done.

No sooner was this conclusion arrived at than the whole city began to prepare for the entrance of their conqueror as for a public festival. The streets along which he and his army would be supposed to pass were lined with carpets and tapestries covering the walls of the houses, the ground being strewn with flowers. Not only were valuable stuffs hung from the windows, but also gold chains and costly jewellery—even to the ornaments worn by the women— suspended in wreaths reaching almost to the ground, dazzied the eyes with their splendour on every side. The whole piazza was covered with an awning to ward off the rays of the sun. Every one opened his treasures, whether for private use or for commerce, to the public gaze. The Palazzo Publico, or Town Hall, surpassed all the rest. Carpets from French looms, of exquisite workmanship decorated the windows ; vases of silver and gold were ranged in its front, exposed to the eyes of all. All this was done to let the conqueror know they trusted him with everything. Braccio however did not make his triumphal entry in the manner that was expected. He crept in suspiciously through another gate where no sort of preparation had been made for him, and only on arriving at the piazza amidst the fes- tive sounds of trumpet and pipe was he assured that no treachery lay behind all this display. Here the magistrates, nobles, and chief citizens were called upon to swear alle- giance to his jurisdiction ; and the oath was taken, bitterly enough, doubtless, by many who put on a cordial front and a smiling face, to force a seeming welcome.

The Perugians, however, had, after all, perhaps little reason to regret the necessity that thrust the adventurous man-at-arms upon them, since he did everything to make his rule a light and equitable one, and, perhaps, kept out the dominion of more lawless and ruthless despots.

It is hard now to recall the fierce vindictive spirit of these troubled times. How bitter was the cherished hatred for a wrong, real or imaginary; how relentless the revenge that followed it. A single event extracted from the diary of Graziani will illustrate this better than a volume written upon it.

"On the tenth of February," he says, "one thousand four hundred and thirty-seven, in the country of Acquapendente there were three shepherd boys taking care of their charge, and chatting together, when one said to another, ' Let us see what it is to hang a man.' So being agreed, one attached a rope to one of the others, the third raising him from the ground by the neck; then he who had placed the rope about his neck tied the other end of it to the branch of an oak. At this instant a wolf was seen to approach them, upon which the two fled, leaving the other hanging. When the wolf went away the two returned, finding their companion dead. So they took him down and buried him. On the Sunday the father of him who was dead, went, as was the custom, to pay his son a visit, and to take him bread. Not finding him in the pasture, he asked his companions about him, and so, by much questioning, one of them told him what had occurred. Then the father, as soon as he understood that his son was dead, seized the shepherd who had told him, and finding where they had buried him, took out a knife, and killed him on the spot; and then, cutting him open, drew forth his liver and took it home, and invited the father of him whom he had slain to come and eat with him. When he came, he gave him the liver of his son, telling him after he had eaten, that it was a part of his son. Then the father of the one who was hanged took the slayer of his son and killed him. Then the mother went shrieking to the mother of him who was hanged, and killed her likewise. And so from one to another, and from another to somebody else, it was said that by the end of February, that is in less than a month, for this cause, between men women and heirs, about thirty-six persons had been slain."

If the people were impulsive in their revenge, they were

scarcely less so in their religion. The same historian has left us a very characteristic picture in the following account of the preaching of a friar in Perugia.

"On the nineteenth of September (one thousand four hundred and ninety-two), on Wednesday, Berardino di Quillo of Siena, a friar of the Order of the Observance of St. Francis, from Assisi, commenced to say mass, and to preach at the top of the piazza at Perugia. It was said that in Assisi he had accomplished a great work, more especially in making the peace between those who had been long enemies, one for the death of a father, another for that of his brothers, another of his sons. On the first day no shop was opened until the sermon was over ; and there was much people. On the Thursday there was a proclamation that no person should open his shop, neither should any servant or workman be permitted to work during the sermon. Nevertheless, it was allowed that if any person, either from engagements of public business, or any special service, could not come to the sermon at the sounding of the bell of San Lorenzo, he should not be taken or imprisoned afterwards. And always there was much people, gentlemen and ladies. On the twenty-third of September, on Sunday, as well as could be judged and reckoned, there were more than three thousand persons at the sermon. He preached on the sacred Scriptures, reproving persons of every vice and wickedness, and expounding the Christian life. Then he denounced head-dresses, false hair, and every vain decoration of the women ; and the gaming-table, cards, dice, counterfeits, and amulets of the men : so that within fifteen days the women sent all their false hair, head-dresses and ornaments, and the men their dice, cards, tables, and such like in great quantity to the convent of St. Francis : and on the twenty-ninth of October, the friar Berardino caused all these diabolical things (*cose diaboliche*) to be gathered in the piazza, and there had laid a pile of wood, between the fountain and the bishop's palace, on which all the aforesaid were placed things and on Sunday they were set on fire, after the sermon. The fire was so large that it would be impossible to describe it : things of the highest value being burned in it. So great was the rush of men and women to avoid the flames, that many would have stood in danger of their lives, if it had not been for the assistance of the citizens. At this sermon there was an infinite number of persons."

A still more singular picture is presented to us in the account of a religious impersonification, or species of miracle-play, which forms an interesting comparison with its modern survivor in Bavaria.

"On the fifth January (fourteen hundred and forty-eight) there came to Perugia a certain Friar Robert of Leccie, of the Order of the Observance of Saint Francis. He was twenty-two years of age, and came to preach the lent sermons. On the twenty-ninth of March, which was Good Friday, he commenced to preach in the piazza every day. On Holy Thursday he preached on the Communion, and invited all the people for Good Friday ; and at the end of his sermon on the Passion, he caused this representation to be made : that is, he preached at the head of the piazza, outside of the gate of San Lorenzo, where there was a terrace arranged, reaching from the gate to the corner, towards the house of Cherubino degli Armanni ; and there, when they should have displayed the crucifix, there came from San Lorenzo, Eliseo de Cristofano, a barber of the gate of St. Agnolo, in the likeness of Christ, naked, with the cross on his shoulder, the crown of thorns on his head, and his body appearing all beaten and scourged, as Christ was beaten. And there appeared armed men, who led him to be crucified ; and they went round the people, down towards the fountain, until they came to the entrance of the Scudellare ; and they then went up to the Audience Chamber of the Exchange, and thence to the above-mentioned terrace, and there, in the middle of the terrace, they were met by one in the character of the Virgin Mary, dressed all in black, weeping piteously, in the manner of the mystery of the passion of Jesus Christ : and when they had reached the place where Friar Robert stood, they remained there some time, the cross being still carried : and all the people wept and cried for mercy. Then the cross was laid down, and an image of Christ which had been prepared beforehand, was placed upon the cross, and it was raised, and then the cries of the people were much greater than before, and Our Lady began to lament at the foot of the cross, together with St. John and Mary Magdalene and Mary Salome, who pronounced some verses of the Lament of the Passion. And then came Nicodemus, and Joseph of Arimathea, and took away the body of Christ and placed it in the lap of Our Lady ; and then they placed it in the tomb, every one continually weeping with a loud voice. And many said that there was never in Perugia so great and pious devotion as this. And that morning there were six persons made friars : one was the above-mentioned Eliseo, a foolish youth, Tomaso di Marchegino, Bino, who was with the priors,[*] the son of Bocco del Borgho di Sant Antonio, and Ricciere di Francescone di Tanolo.   Many others had also previously taken upon them the monkish garb by reason of the preaching of the said Friar Robert."

If the historian had ended his narrative here one might have had the more faith in the powerful mode of appeal made by the earnest friar : but he carries it on a little further :—

"At the end of three or four months," he says, "the said Eliseo di Cristofano of the Porta St. Agnolo came out of the monastery and returned to his business of barber, and was afterwards called by the name of Domenedio (Lord-God), and then he took a wife and became a greater ribald than he was before."

I shall only make one more extract from these curious old records.   It is the description of a singular custom of the city, which was called a "game," which no doubt helped to keep up the belligerent spirit of the times.   It went by the name of the Battle of Stones (La Battaglia di Sassi),

* The priors were the chief persons or magistrates of the city.

and is thus described by Campano in his Life of Braccio Fortebraccio.

" The whole city was divided into two parts, the one at the top, and the other at the bottom of the piazza, furnished with new and unaccustomed arms ; although there were some, in order to be more light and nimble, who only carried a shield, wearing a helmet and boots of raw and indurated hide ; or instead of a shield, a hood was worn, these being called lancers, for the facility they had in throwing and sheltering themselves. These, on account of their dexterity, led the first battle, and then, when it was fairly commenced, retired behind another class of combatants, called armed troops. The armour of these was much heavier than that borne in battle. They wore on their feet certain light shoes, made of linen cloth folded three times, stuffed with stags' hair ; on the legs, up to the knee, they wore the same material covered with very hard double leather, the knee being protected with iron greaves covered over with scarlet cloth. The body was defended by a cuirass, under which were placed waddings of tow and cotton sewn in linen, which lay close to the person, covering the shoulders and back, and falling to the elbows like sleeves. They also wore collars of cloth and cotton, covered with very hard raw hide about the throat and neck. The head was covered with a helmet, which was pointed in front like the beak of a falcon ; and in order that they might the better be able to see the stones in the air and use their own with more advantage against the adversary, there were two large holes cut in the front, leaving the sight exposed. At the top of this helmet there was a roll woven of hard felt three times doubled, spread out in the form of a cap surmounted by a plume of purple or silver, according to the calling of him who wore it : this was tipped with a crest of various colours. The shoulders were covered half way down to the waist with a red mantle, all the rest of the back being ornamented with beautiful vestments. These were they who were called armed troops, whose function was not so much to contend

with the adversary, as to act as reserves to sustain the
battle, although they often enough fought themselves, and
for this purpose carried a cudgel, tied to their right arm,
and a shield on the left.   When all the people armed in
various ways were congregated in the piazza, each retired
to the one side or the other, and thus divided into parties,
one occupied the top, and the other the bottom of the
piazza, the fighting taking place in the midst.   The first to
enter upon the battle were the most spirited and robust of
the young men, fighting until the hour of tierce ; then the
boys alone, armed also for defence, throwing stones, the
one against the other, for two hours continuously.   The
rest of the day was occupied in fighting promiscuously
both young and old.   Those with the protective head-gear
were placed in front, whose office it was to throw at the
adversary from a distance, and as neither of these would
retire, they at last closed upon each other, whereupon the
armed troops came forward.   It was considered a disgrace
for the latter to throw stones, but rushing into the midst, they
used their cudgels and their shields, not desisting because
others were throwing stones at them in the meantime.   It
was a fine sight (*bellissimo spettacolo*) to see first one fall
down wounded, and then another rolled over on the ground,
some protected by their shields flinging themselves with
their full weight on the adversary, or throwing themselves
into the thick of the fight, and giving it their opponents on
the face and eyes with shield and cudgel.   The victory
consisted in occupying the middle of the piazza, the enemy
having been driven from it.   But the finest sight of all was
to see the old men, who, standing at the windows, as soon
as they saw the party they were attached to give way or
flee, without having respect to their years or infirmities (so
great was the enthusiasm of the parties), rush out of the
houses, and taking off their mantles and vests, run to give
them help and rally them.   Two thousand citizens frequently
fought in this manner in the piazza.   Nor did the strife
ever pass without bloodshed, every year ten or twenty men

remaining either **dead or** disabled.   **This diversion was not,** however, prolonged throughout the **year.   It only com-** menced in the month **of** March, continuing for **the two** months following, **and** was only practised **on** holidays.   **The** parents **of those who were** killed never recognising any injury **or enmity whatever,** considered **the** deaths the result **of** accident **or** misfortune.   **The combat was never** ter- **minated** until **one** of the parties was driven from **its posi- tion.**   Finally, whoever called for peace, whether **boy or man, the** combatants separated.   **Every** one said that **there was no game in Italy** so desperate **as** this ; **and it** was **believed that on** this account the people had **become so** vigorous in body and undaunted in mind.   The soldiers **of** Braccio frequently took **part with** the youths, **and entered** into the battle, but they were **easily** worsted by the **Peru-** gians.   **It** is said that **Braccio, once** standing **at a window** which overlooked the piazza, was asked **to command a truce,** the encounter being **so** obstinate that neither party **would** give way, so that many were falling.   'Do **you wish,'** he replied 'that I should be like the mayor of **Sinigaglia ?'**   Which is a **proverb** used **when a** command, however **often** given, is not **obeyed ;** perhaps even **he** who commands being disposed to follow an opposite course."

Perugia is dignified by many very noble works of art. Here Pietro Vanucci, **called** Perugino, lived and worked with a **mind** always calm, enriched by some of the sweetest and **tenderest** imagery that ever blossomed from the **human soul.**   The Cambio, or Exchange, still bears upon **its walls** some of the **glories of** his pencil : prophet, warrior, **and** philosopher, **all refined to a** delicate **spiritualism which** causes them **to** appeal **to the soul rather than the eye.**   He seems to have lived **in** a world **quite remote from the** clash **and** din of the middle **ages, tenanted by calm** and happy beings, **to** whom **all storms were lulled in the** peace of a **tranquil mind, accordant with itself** and with **that by** which **it was** surrounded.

The principal piazza has remained unchanged.   Its old

X

fountain with its half obliterated sculptures gave us many hours delightful occupation in the attempt to spell out its quaint fancies. Sometimes in the afternoons, when the shadows began to stretch along the sward, we would recline before the glorious façade of Agostino Ducci at the church of the confraternity of Saints Andrea and Bernardino, studying with delighted eyes the moving assemblage of angelic forms that float and wave over its surface, drawing the soul with them in mazy ecstasies of delight. Sometimes we would follow the courses of the hills, and, seated amongst the olives, strive to carry away upon paper some memorial of the prospect by which we were surrounded. Thus passed the artist's holiday, whose life has so much to make it always a holiday when it is ordinarily prosperous and happy.

About ten miles from Perugia, connected with the Tiber by a small tributary, is Assisi, an old-fashioned mediæval town built on a rise at the foot of the Apennines. Once it was a busy and important little place : now its vitality is absorbed in the neighbourhood of the more active and wealthy Perugia. It is but the shadow of what it was. Its long dreary streets only echo emptily to the feet of a few passers ; its ancient mansions falling to decay. Here and there at picturesque corners are seen shrines of the Madonna painted centuries ago, before which the tiny lamp still burns and the votive wreath is laid ; their fine old frescoes gradually crumbling from the walls. Above its terraced ways, overlooking the whole town and the broad Umbrian plain, a broken old castle keeps grim watch and ward with sturdy walls resisting the wintry blast, which here sometimes rushes from the gorges of the hills with terrible fury. At one side of the town and somewhat lower in elevation rises the church of St. Francis and the convent with its cloistered galleries and spiring cypresses, venerable in religious history.

Assisi is of very ancient origin. It was probably a town in the earliest days of Rome. A fine portico of an ancient temple of Minerva still remains, which is now built into a church in the piazza. It is supposed to have been the

birthplace of the Latin poet Propertius, alluded to in his
epistle to Tullus : " Umbria, rich in fertile land joining close
to the champaign country beneath, gave me birth." *

Metastasio the famous dramatic poet was also born here.
But it derives far more of its celebrity from having been the
home and birthplace of St. Francis, whose influence had so
wide and large a power throughout Europe in the Middle
Ages. He was born in one thousand one hundred and
eighty-two ; the son of a well-to-do cloth merchant. In
early life he appears to have been one of the gayest and
most spirited young gallants of his time, singing troubadour
songs in the streets—always ready to join in the con-
vivialities of his companions, without any traces of the
asceticism for which he was afterwards distinguished. He
must have taken part in the embroilments which were
constantly occurring between his native town and Perugia,
since he once lay a prisoner for a whole year at the latter
place. As he grew into manhood more serious sentiments
were gradually impressed upon his mind. Like every newly
awakened soul he at first sought blindly after his real
destiny and function through endless doubts and perplexi-
ties. It resolved itself to him afterwards in a literal accep-
tation of the doctrines of Christianity, which he received
rather from the side of dogma than interpreted as reasonable laws. His final step was to adopt the condition of entire
and absolute poverty. From a few followers his doctrines
—or rather his example ; for he was a man of few words, and
taught no more orally than might be easily set down upon
a sheet of foolscap—influenced the whole of Christendom,
reaching from the highest grade of society to the lowest.
In England the order which he instituted was called that of
the Grey Friars. Perhaps no one ever lived a more con-
sistent life. His rule of poverty was never broken. When
he gave up his last mantle, all but the garment which he wore

* Proxima supposito contingens Umbria campo
  Me genuit, terris fertilis uberibus.
                                    El. i. 22.

nearest his skin, to a destitute beggar, he said, " This man's misery covers us with confusion ; for we have chosen poverty as a great treasure, and lo ! he is poorer than any one of us."   He carried neither scrip nor purse ; never accumulating anything ; but always having his needs supplied, either by the labour of his hands or the charity of others.   That which he professed and followed was the very chivalry of religion.   " Truly this is the camp and army of the knights of God," exclaimed Cardinal Ugolino as he came upon the straw huts which the new order had erected near Assisi. Nothing is more striking in the character of this noble-hearted enthusiast than his love for the whole creation— his recognition of the purposes of God throughout the universe.   He called the sun his brother and death his sister ; the fire that burnt him and the pains that tore him in his last illness were addressed in similar terms.   The birds were his brothers and sisters : every creature was dear to him. The poet could not have had a better illustration that,

> He prayeth well who loveth well
> Both man and bird and beast.

His mission was a great one.   He impressed upon all Christendom by a fine example, when absolute power and riches, ill-gotten though they might be, were considered the highest earthly good and worthiest object of life, that their attainment far from being indispensable to happiness was frequently a hinderance to it.   When his country, and indeed the whole of Europe, were torn with factions he came to reinforce the blessings of peace and good will.   To the implacable and remorseless cruelty of his time he taught tenderness and gentleness.   He placed reason and right before the intoxications of ambition ; and though his own life was an exaggerated one, perhaps nothing less would have served to oppose and curb the redundant extravagancies of the age in which he lived.   Whatever may appear to have been the mistakes of such a life, looking at it with the social views of to-day, it was undoubtedly based on a truly heroic sentiment which had its warrantable mission then.

It was to commemorate him that the fine church here which bears his name was built—or rather it may be called three churches, one standing above the other. Never had man a nobler monument raised to his memory. Commanding some of the sweetest and most picturesque scenery of Italy, it stands midway between the summits of the Apennines rising behind it and the low-lying plain of Foligno that sweeps from the foot of the hill to Perugia on the one side and Spoleto on the other, a distance of forty miles. A river winds beneath it, issuing from the recesses of the mountains, following a northward course to the Tiber through a considerable part of this fertile plain. The situation is thus described by Dante in his 'Paradise.'

> Betwixt Tupino and the stream descending
> Down from the hill the blest Ubaldo chose,
> A fertile tract is from the mount depending;
> Whence to Perugia heat and cold do come
> Through Porta Sole; and behind it those
> Of Nocera and Gualdo mourn their doom.
> On that side where the mountain falls away
> Most gently, to the world a sun was born,
> As from the Ganges springs the solar ray.
> Whoso would therefore call the place aright—
> Let it no longer of its fame be shorn,
> And orient, not Ascesi be it hight.*

---

* Wright's translation. These are the words of Dante :

> Intra Tupino e l'acqua che discende
>   Del colle eletto dal beato Ubaldo,
>   Fertile costa d'alto monte pende,
> Onde Perugia sente freddo e caldo
>   Da Porta Sole ; e diretro le piange
>   Per greve giogo Nocera con Gualdo.
> Di quella costa, là dov'ella frange
>   Più sua rattezza, nacque al mondo un Sole
>   Come fa questo talvolta di Gange.
> Però chi d'esso loco fa parole
>   Non dica Ascesi, chè direbbe corto,
>   Ma Oriente, se proprio dir vuole.
>
>   Par. xi. 43.

The lowest of the three churches of St. Francis is the most
modern.   It is the sepulchral crypt formed from a hollow in
the rock where the remains of the saint were found within the
present century ; the two upper churches were commenced
early in the thirteenth century ; a hundred years elapsing
before their completion.   The lower of these two is the ideal
of a Christian temple as a place of pensive retirement.   It
consists of a nave and transept composed of low, wide-span-
ning arches; every inch of the walls being covered either
with pictures or ornamental decoration.   It is pervaded by
a solemn gloom, even on bright days; the light being
only sparingly admitted through painted windows.

Of the many precious works of art enshrined in these
religious shades I shall only mention one, probably the
masterpiece of Giotto, painted at the close of the thirteenth
century, which decorates the ceiling above the high altar.
It is a large fresco in four compartments, three of them representing the characteristic virtues of St. Francis, Poverty,
Chastity and Obedience, and the fourth his glorification,
surrounded by the hosts of heaven.   They are epic in treatment and abstrusely allegorical in their mode of expression.   In one of them St. Francis is being married to Poverty
by our Lord.   She is represented as a tattered female, with
her feet amongst thorns, her head being surrounded with
roses.   Angels witness the ceremony.   Two little boys in
the foreground throw mud at the espoused couple, a dog
barking viciously at a little distance.*

* Towards the end of the thirteenth century the doctrines of St.
Francis had obtained so wide an influence and became so largely abused,
that vast numbers of persons of all ages and both sexes left their houses
and homes for the profession of poverty—even to destitution.   This was
productive of many evils and very great disorders; so much so that
Giotto himself, who had lent his pencil to illustrate the nobility of poverty
of spirit, and to protest against the inordinate desire of acquisition, thought
it necessary to use his pen as a corrective to the prevailing frenzy, in a
poem found by Trucchi in the Laurentian Library, and reprinted in his
' Poesie Inedite.'   " No 'l commendo," he says, " chè rade volte stremo è
senza vizio" (I do not advocate it, for rarely are extremes without
sin): adding that if any should say it was commended by our Lord,

The third church built above this is in direct contrast to it. It has a lofty ceiling ornamented with golden stars upon an ultramarine ground. It is full of light and air, and though some of its brilliant colours have suffered during the lapse of almost six hundred years, there are still abundant signs left of its former splendour. The fine puristic frescoes that decorate the walls have been attributed to Giotto ; but the discriminating art-student will probably come to the conclusion that but few of them can be from his own immediate hand.

It was a noble idea to set forth the blossoming of the virtues hardest to follow in this elaborate structure—the mortal sowing and the immortal reaping—the growth from darkness into light—the groping amongst shadowy forms of dimly discerned glories, till elevated into the regions of a loftier radiance, they glow with a new lustre imparting light to the day and fire to the sun.

Adjoining the church is the convent of St. Francis, founded during the lifetime of the saint, early in the thirteenth century. It consists of cloisters, cells and galleries, constructed upon vast mural archways built against the hill side. Strange to say this convent was singularly privileged to be the holder of property : so that instead of being a community of poor friars living by labour or alms

---

> Che però 'l suo aver poco
> Si fu per noi scampare dall'avarizia,
> E non per darci via d'usar malizia.

(That his doctrine of possessing little was given forth that we might avoid avarice, and not to open the way to evil.) In the same way Guido Cavalcanti calls poverty,

> Sposa d'ogni cosa persa
> Per la quale è sommersa
> D'onor al mondo ogni viva radice.

(The spouse of each polluted thing, by which is subverted every living root of honour in the world.)

Guido Cavalcanti's poem is translated at length in Mr. D. G. Rossetti's 'Dante and his Circle:' a valuable selection of conscientiously reproduced examples of the *primi secoli* too little known.

as their founder did, it was the seat of a wealthy religious body, and became a sort of aristocratic retreat for men of culture and refinement, who inhabited roomy and wholesome apartments ; very different from those of other convents of the same order. It is now suppressed with other similar institutions, and altogether gives an impression of intense melancholy—an impression that is deepened if one enters the church at eventide as the setting sun throws his last struggling beams through the painted pane, and instead of the full choir of former days, one hears the forlorn voices of a few religious brothers mournfully repeating the evening offices of the church which are echoed from empty walls and deserted benches.

The mediæval condition of Assisi was, of course, an unsettled one. The jealousy of its rulers and those of Perugia constantly bred ill-feeling between them, which at last diffusing itself amongst the people, was turned to the bitterest enmity ; so much so that even traces of it are left to this day in the occasional disparagement with which the inhabitants of the one place speak of those of the other without any apparent cause. One picture from Campano of the taking of the town by Piccinino of Perugia in the year one thousand four hundred and forty-two will sufficiently illustrate this.

" Piccinino, after having deferred the attack of Assisi until the twenty-eighth of November, finally determined to advance upon it at all hazards, and receiving opportune help from Perugia, he distributed the people in this manner : Pazzaglia, Pierbrunoro, and Riccio, from Città di Castello, with all their companies, were sent towards the upper fortress : Piergiovampaolo with the Perugians towards San Francesco ; whilst he and his troops spread themselves about the other parts of the city, giving orders to all that when the sign of onset was given, they should approach the walls, and placing ladders against them, should make every effort to enter the city. By particular information he had also the secret knowledge of an ancient aqueduct which commencing outside the city above the fortress, being smaller towards the place called the Carceri, and opening into the city at the market-place, appeared to offer a convenient passage for as many soldiers as he could wish, if it were cleared of the stakes and rubbish which had been formerly placed there to bar the entrance.   He accordingly sent thither Pazzaglia and Riccio, with three hundred foot, who, sawing asunder the upright beams which closed it, opened a way which easily admitted the soldiers one by one.   Thus making use of the aqueduct, he sent a thousand of the best men of the army into the city, which occupied the whole night.   The Perugian writers, however, do not give so large a number. In the morning a little before dawn, it is said, they were discovered in the city by one carrying a lighted torch, who was passing a place where there were no houses, and hearing persons near, called out several times, 'Who is there?' At last they replied, 'Friends.'   Whereupon, perceiving they were enemies, he went away and commenced shouting, 'To arms, to arms: the enemy is amongst us!'   This caused those who were on guard to give notice to the other citizens and soldiers, who took their arms and ran to the place whence they heard the cries.   In the meanwhile Pazzaglia and his company, perceiving they were discovered, although the full number of soldiers ordered by Piccinino had not yet entered the aqueduct, emerged, and mounting the walls, cried, 'Ladders, ladders ; come up, come up!' which being heard by Piccinino, who happened to be near, he was quickly at the foot of the walls, and flinging himself from his horse, made the attack at a small aperture, which the Assisans had opened for the purpose of skirmishing, large enough to admit one man at a time ; the gates being kept closed. Through this Piccinino entered, and, afterwards, his horse, upon which being mounted, he commanded that the breach should be widened, so that a man on horseback might pass through, which was immediately done, so that his troops were able to enter with ease.   In the meanwhile the soldiers on guard and the people within the city had attacked those who had entered by the aqueduct, and were in close engage-

ment with them when the cavalry of Piccinino came up
shouting 'Braccio, Braccio! Piccinino, Piccinino!' throwing
themselves with such energy upon the others that they were
forced to retire to the fortress. Immediately Count Carlo
Fortebraccio went thither with a good number of cavalry,
whereupon the foreign troops in the service of the Assisans to
the number of eight hundred, surrendered themselves ; all
of whom, at the desire of Piccinino, were spared uninjured.
Whilst this was going on at the fortress, Piergiovampaolo,
who as already stated was with the Perugians at the part
near San Francesco, when he heard the cries of his party,
also mounted the walls and entered the city, driving away
the guard from the gates, setting fire to them, and throwing down the defences which the Assisans had raised, thus
opening a way for his troops, who entered the city, repulsing
the few that resisted, and setting themselves to pillage the
houses. Piergiovampaolo went to San Francesco making
many prisoners, who had ran thither expecting to find security in that sacred place : he also took many things thence.
Alessandro Sforza, brother of Count Francesco, who had
come to Assisi, as has been said, on the twenty-first of the
month, to animate the courage of the citizens, promising
them succour, when he found the enemy within the city,
knowing his impotency to oppose them, retired to the larger
fortress with a good number of the principal citizens who
had followed him thither. By the magnanimity of Piccinino
these were liberated on the following day. Alessandro having
signified to Piccinino that he wished to speak with him, the
latter sent his secretary to him, to whom Alessandro said,
that for himself he asked neither grace nor favour, but that
he desired extremely that those citizens of Assisi who had
taken shelter with him in the fortress might be liberated.
To this Piccinino agreed ; allowing them to issue from their
retreat on his word of honour ; so that they went about the
city without fear of violence, unmolested by any one. But
the soldiers of Piccinino having in divers places overcome
the enemy, and having the victory in their hands, leaving off

fighting began to sack the houses, making prisoners of the citizens they met, and, without any regard, scattering misery and ruin at their pleasure.   An anonymous writer of Perugia narrating the occurrence, says, that such was the consternation, the uproar, the cries of the women, the children, and the old men, one bewailing a son, another a father, another a brother, that the very soldiers who had stripped the houses and dragged out the women, compassionating their distress, offered them the safety of their lives and the opportunity of escape ; but they, all disordered, bewailing themselves and their ill-fortune, refused everything, only asking their death.   Of these many were led out of the city, but more by those soldiers who had been placed on guard than by others, because they had more confidence in them, and went voluntarily.   It is also narrated that many Perugians joining this undertaking, not from any desire which they had for it, but by order of their superiors, pitying the misery and wretchedness of these women, did their utmost to procure the safety of their persons and their goods, but that they drew upon themselves and their property the greater injury, by not trusting themselves to the Perugians ; for, instead of seeking safety from them, they would rather place themselves in the hands of the foreigners ; so great was the hatred they had conceived towards them.   There is also a very notable fact told of this occurrence.   During this revolution in affairs, a great number of women and children with their effects had sought refuge in the convent of Santa Chiara of the order of St. Francis, which was very large and celebrated, thinking to find security there, as well for the sake of religion as for the excellence of the convent. Whilst everything was being submitted to the sack of the soldiers, Niccolò Piccinino came up, and seeing there so many women and children, said to the women, and specially to the nuns, that everywhere being overrun by the soldiery, this was no longer a fitting place for them to remain, and that they might choose where they would go, promising them escort and safety ; and at the same time naming various places in the vicinity, and amongst others his own city, Perugia. Upon which, first the nuns and then the other women with one voice indignantly cried, 'We go to Perugia! May consuming fires enter into it; but not we!' Piccinino growing angry at this, as something too insolent, immediately turned to his men crying, 'To the pillage!' and so presently everything went to ruin without regard to the sisterhood or religion : the example being followed in every other temple and sacred place, nowhere being secure from the lawlessness of the soldiers, all being equally submitted to sack and destruction. Only San Francesco was saved from the first onset which Piergiovampaolo had made from the outside, because Piccinino had sent a guard thither in observance of a promise which he had made to the reverend fathers of that community, who in that fearful night were of no little service to the people ; passing through the town, by permission obtained from the captain, and wherever they found women, either in the houses or in the streets, taking them to San Francesco, where, by their means, many were placed in safety. The loss and damage to the city was immense ; for there was no place, public or private, sacred or profane, which was not made the prey of the soldiers, who with their customary liberty and licence, without any restraint from their general, used the greatest cruelty in carrying off women and girls to obtain money for them, and to give them to the service of others, of whom many were redeemed by the Perugians, not for their own interest, but to get them out of the hands of the soldiers and send them back to their homes."

On this occasion all the public archives as well as vast quantities of private documents were burnt, which were sufficient to maintain a large bonfire for three days.

Whilst at Assisi the pilgrim of the Tiber must not omit to visit one of its famous tributaries, the Clitumnus, which under another name falls into it near Diruta. Its source is to be found a few miles beyond Trevi. One delightful afternoon, in company with a friend, I explored its upper

course. It has many classical associations. The younger
Pliny gives so circumstantial a description of it in a letter
to his friend Romanus, as it existed in the first century of
the Christian era, that I cannot do better than transcribe it
here in full.

" Have you ever seen," he says, " the source of the river
Clitumnus ? As I never heard you mention it, I imagine
not. Let me therefore advise you to visit it immediately.
It is but lately, indeed, that I had that pleasure, and I
condemn myself for not having viewed it sooner. At the
foot of a little hill covered with venerable and shady cypress-
trees, a spring issues, which gushing out in different and
unequal streams, forms itself, after several windings, into a
spacious basin, so extremely clear, that you may see the
pebbles and the little pieces of money which are thrown
into it as they lie at the bottom. From thence it is carried
off, not so much by the declivity of the ground, as by its
own weight and exuberance. It is navigable almost as soon
as it has quitted its source, and wide enough to admit a free
passage for vessels to pass each other as they sail with or
against the stream. The current runs so strong, though the
ground is level, that the large barges which go down the
river have no occasion to make use of their oars, while those
which ascend find it difficult to advance with the assistance
of oars and poles ; and this vicissitude of labour and ease is
exceedingly amusing when one sails up and down merely
for pleasure. The banks on each side are shaded with
great numbers of verdant ash and poplar-trees, as distinctly
reflected in the stream as if they were actually existing in
it. The water is as cold as snow, and as lucid too. Near
it stands an ancient and venerable temple, wherein is placed
a statue representing the river-god Clitumnus in his proper
vestment; and, indeed, the prophetic oracles here delivered
sufficiently testify the immediate presence of that divinity.
Several little chapels are scattered round, dedicated to
particular gods, distinguished by different names, and some
of them, too, presiding over different fountains. For, besides

the principal spring, which is, as it were, the parent of all
the rest, there are several smaller streams, which, taking
their rise from various sources, lose themselves in the river,
over which a bridge is thrown that separates the sacred part
from that which lies open to common use.   Vessels are
allowed to come above this, but no person is permitted to
swim except below it.   The Hispellates [inhabitants of
Spello] to whom Augustus gave this place, furnish a public
bath, and likewise entertain all strangers at their own expense.   Several villas, attracted by the beauty of this river,
are situated upon its borders.   In short, every surrounding
object will afford you entertainment.   You may also amuse
yourself with numberless inscriptions fixed upon the pillars
and walls by different persons, celebrating the virtues of the
fountain and the divinity who presides over it.   There are
many of them you will greatly admire, as there are some
that will make you laugh ; but I must correct myself when
I say so ; you are too humane, I know, to laugh upon such
an occasion.   Farewell."*

The cypresses have vanished from its source, and the
channel of the stream must have been since contracted, or
else the barges at that time must have been very narrow ;
as it would be difficult now to navigate it with more than
one barge at a time : there would certainly be no room for
the use of oars in any case.

Suetonius, in his 'Life of Caligula,' says that, "Only
once did he take an active part in military affairs, and
then not from any set purpose, but during his journey to
Mevania [Bevagna], to see the river Clitumnus and its
grove.'

It was not only held sacred in itself, but the animals
pastured on its banks were supposed to have gained their
whiteness from drinking its waters.   In allusion to this
belief, Virgil, in singing the praises of Italy, thus apostro-
phises it : "Hence the white flocks, Clitumnus, and the
bull, principal victim, which often bathed in thy sacred

* Ep. viii. 8.   (Melmoth's translation.)

stream, leads the Roman Triumph to the temples of the gods."*

It still retains its ancient character. Crystalline in its purity—"limpid and clear as the mind of the just," it rushes swiftly forwards through vineyards and orchards, each turn revealing some new and delightful piece of

TEMPLE OF THE CLITUMNUS.

rusticity. Sometimes we came upon an aged tree covered with ivy ; sometimes a patch of newly-reaped stubble ; sometimes we found little nooks and corners filled with luxuriant blossoms. Long green trailers were clearly seen in its

* Hinc albi, Clitumne, greges et maxima taurus
  Victima, sæpe tuo perfusi flumine sacro
  Romanos ad templa Deûm duxere triumphos.
                                        Geor. ii. 146.

bed, waving to and fro as the stream went over them. On a hot day it was inevitable that one should be tempted to the luxury of a bath. I quickly undressed, and plunging into the water was immediately seized with a most benumbing coldness. A few strokes, in the vain attempt to head the current, and I was on the bank again, shivering in the hot sunshine. Near a little village called Pissignano, which thrusts up the fragment of an old mediæval tower from the olive slopes, a short distance before reaching the source of the stream, we found the famous temple that still ornaments its banks. It consists of a façade with pediment and tympanum supported by four columns ; two carved in imbricated foliage and two in spiral flutings. There are several inscriptions upon it ; the passage for conveying away the blood of the sacrifices is also still to be seen. At the back of the temple there is the raised carving of a cross surrounded by ornamental work, which has given rise to the supposition that it might have been a temple dedicated to Christian worship ; but it is far more probable that the Christian symbol was of later insertion. It is built of the calcareous stone of the district, and still remains in excellent preservation, though somewhat injured by an earthquake that occurred in this part of Umbria in eighteen hundred and thirty-one. The upper part of the temple has within it a modern altar set with nosegays and hung about with pictures ; worthless excepting for the purpose for which they were placed there. Readers of ' Childe Harold ' will hardly require to be reminded of Lord Byron's description of this interesting old relic and its situation.

> But thou, Clitumnus, in thy sweetest wave
> Of the most living crystal that was e'er
> The haunt of river nymph, to gaze and lave
> Her limbs where nothing hid them, thou dost rear
> Thy grassy banks whereon the milk-white steer
> Grazes ; the purest god of gentle waters,
> And most serene of aspect and most clear ;
> Surely that stream was unprofaned by slaughters—
> A mirror and a bath for Beauty's youngest daughters !

And on thy happy shore a temple still
Of small and delicate proportion, keeps
Upon a mild declivity of hill
Its memory of thee; beneath it sweeps
Thy current's calmness; oft from out it leaps
The finny darter with the glittering scales
Who dwells and revels in thy glassy deeps,
While chance some scattered water-lily sails
Down where the shallower wave still tells its bubbling tales.

Hard by the temple a mill, turned by the river, greets the
ear with its homely sound, near which a weeping-willow
dips its pendant branches into the water.

A little farther its source is reached at a place called
Le Vene. It gushes out from the foot of a mountain in
several copious springs which, after flowing hither and
thither amongst the water-flags and rushes, unite into one
stream. The spot is a very beautiful one. On the one
side rises a range of lofty hills connected with the Apennines : on the other the wide Umbrian valley stretches,
laughing with corn, wine, and oil. Far across, another
mountain-range bounds the plain, white clouds gathered
about its peaks and the sunshine resting there as it did
when the milk-white steer was led to the stream to receive
its ablutions in preparation for the sacrifice.

CHURCH AND CONVENT OF ST. FRANCIS AT ASSISI.

Y

CHAPTER XI.

FROM PERUGIA TO THE SOURCE.

A NOTHER locality connected with the Tiber by a small
stream or torrent, is the famous lake and plains of
Thrasimene, where the celebrated battle was fought, two
hundred and fifty years before the Christian era, in which
the Carthaginian general, Hannibal, defeated the Romans
so signally : one of the very few occasions upon which the
Romans suffered an absolutely disastrous defeat at the
hands of their enemies.   The lake is now called the Lake of
Perugia, from which town it is about sixteen miles distant.
The battle occurred during the second Punic war ; after
Hannibal had made his memorable and hazardous passage of
the Alps, and ravaging the heart of Italy, was marching
straight for Rome, when he was met here by the Roman
army under the Consul Flaminius. Flaminius had been
stationed at Arretium (Arezzo), of which the Carthaginians
being aware, they avoided coming in contact with him at
that place by taking a more easterly line of march through
Fæsula (Fiesole), possibly with the object of securing a
more advantageous position for an engagement.   The
Roman consul was at this time awaiting reinforcements
under his colleague, Cneius Servilius ; but when he saw
the Carthaginians pass him along the plain of Arezzo on
their way to Rome and the ravages they were committing
with fire and sword—which they took care to render as
apparent to him as possible—without regard to the wiser
counsel of his officers, he prepared to follow them.

Trending southwards from the plain lying beneath the town of Cortona, a range of considerable hills, called the Gualandro, bends downwards to the Lake of Thrasimene, only allowing a narrow pass between the shores on the one side and the rising ground on the other, thence opening into a wider plain, very much narrowed again at the southern extremity at the little town of Passignano, where the hills once more approach the lake, thus inclosing an irregularly extended semicircular space with the lake on the one side and the hills on the other. The battle has been circumstantially described by the old historians Livy and Polybius. It was fought early in the morning. The heights were occupied by the Carthaginian general with the pick of his Spanish and African troops, the lighter infantry occupying a lower position, whilst the cavalry were disposed about the immediate entrance of the defile. The whole plain was covered with a dense mist which had risen from the lake, effectually veiling the Roman army from a sight of the enemy. It is strange that the Romans should not have taken the precaution to reconnoitre their course previously to entering so dangerous a locality. As it was, they marched straight into the trap. No sooner had the whole army entered the defile than the foe poured upon them with all the advantages of surprise ; the Romans being still more confused from the mist that enveloped them, concealing the position of the enemy and their number. In vain the consul rode hither and thither in the attempt to rally his panic-stricken troops. They were scarcely able to see or hear him. At last the soldiers being hemmed in on every side found their only chance lay in the use of their swords, so that the battle came to be, in a great measure, a personal combat. Some of the companies, indeed, fought so bravely that they perished to a man on the spot where they first stood. What was most re-markable was that an earthquake occurred in the thick of the engagement, which toppled down mountains, overthrew cities and changed the course of rivers, without being so much as perceived on either side ; so great was their ardour in fighting. In the midst of the fight Flaminius was seen urging on his troops, when there rode forth a horseman of the enemy covered with blood and dust, crying, " So this is he who is the slayer of our comrades and the devastator of our fields : he also shall be sacrificed to the manes of the dead!" and riding irresistibly through the ranks which surrounded him, he pierced him mortally through the body with his lance. Upon this the whole army laid down their arms and fled wildly, precipitately, without knowing the direction in which they were going. Some fell on the bodies of the slain and were smothered by others falling on the top of them, some ran indiscriminately on the arms of the enemy, as if seeking their own death, others driven to the edge of the lake were fain to take the water as far as they could walk in it, but were thence pursued by the cavalry and cut to pieces, whilst others swam far from land only to be drowned or to return and meet the fate of their companions. Nearly six thousand of the van of the army had cut their way gallantly through the enemy at an early stage of the engagement, escaping to the southern end of the plain, where they awaited the dispersion of the mist only to see the total defeat of their comrades. Seizing their standards, hastily, they retreated, but being pursued, overcome by famine and fatigue, they were induced to relinquish their arms under promise of safety. " A promise," says Livy, sarcastically, " kept with Punic fidelity, for they were immediately loaded with chains." Thus ended this great battle. For three fearful hours the work of slaughter proceeded without intermission. The little stream that courses the plain ran blood instead of water, and is known by the name of Sanguinetto, or the Runlet of Blood, to this day.

In this battle fifteen thousand Romans were slain, and one thousand five hundred of the enemy their conquerors ; many afterwards, on both sides, dying of their wounds. The loss has even been computed as much greater. Hannibal had his own soldiers buried upon the field. The body of Flaminius could not be found.

LAKE THRASIMENE. SITE OF BATTLE.

The spot and its associations have inspired some of the happiest lines of 'Childe Harold.'

> I roam
> By Thrasimene's lake, in the defiles
> Fatal to Roman rashness, more at home;
> For there the Carthaginian's warlike wiles
> Come back before me, as his skill beguiles
> The host between the mountains and the shore,
> Where Courage falls in her despairing files,
> And torrents, swoll'n to rivers with their gore,
> Reek through the sultry plain, with legions scattered o'er.
>
> Like to a forest fell'd by mountain winds;
> And such the storm of battle on this day,
> And such the frenzy, whose convulsion blinds
> To all save carnage, that, beneath the fray,
> An earthquake reel'd unheededly away!

None felt stern Nature rocking at his feet,
And yawning forth a grave for those who lay
Upon their bucklers for a winding-sheet;
Such is the absorbing hate when warring nations meet!

Far other scene is Thrasimene now;
Her lake a sheet of silver, and her plain
Rent by no ravage save the gentle plough;
Her aged trees rise thick as once the slain
Lay where their roots are; but a brook hath ta'en—
A little rill of scanty stream and bed—
A name of blood from that day's sanguine rain;
And Sanguinetto tells ye where the dead
Made the earth wet and turn'd the unwilling waters red.

For the purpose of enjoying the sweet scenery of this charming spot and exploring the old battle-field, I took up my abode at a little inn at Passignano, on the borders of the lake. One afternoon I walked to the small town of Tuoro, which rises from the plain situated on an elevated mound covered with olives, the site of many a fierce struggle on that dreadful day. It was a wretched little town, without drainage, the streets being unpaved and strewn with rubbish, whilst the houses wore the air of falling completely to decay. In vain I went from alley to alley: the hot hours of a midsummer day had not yet passed: all the inhabitants had betaken themselves to rest; only a few hungry dogs prowled about the street. At last I found a cobbler at his stall, who took me to a little *bettola*, or wine-shop, a dingy little cellar, where a few persons sat gossiping in the cool, whilst enjoying the refreshing draught of some thin wine. I entered into conversation with an intelligent-looking man of the group. Hearing my errand, he proffered to take me to the top of the bell-tower of the church, which commanded the whole plain and to point out to me the various supposed sites of the battle and probable manœuvrings; as he had learned them from a military man whom he had accompanied on a special survey of the ground. Indeed, the whole position was clearly to be seen—what infinite advantages would be gained by the first occupier of the spot, and how any attempt to take it would be fraught

with the greatest difficulty.   As we returned, he complained
bitterly of the **poverty** of the district, **and spoke of a project**
for draining the **lake from which** the **miserable population**
hoped to **reap much advantage.**

Although **the scenery about** the **Lake of Thrasimene**
is by **no means the finest in Italy, yet there is something
in the broad sheet of water, spotted** with **its lovely islands
and the** low-flowing mountain **lines,** by which **it is surrounded, which fills the mind with** soothing **impressions ;
sometimes the prospect from the heights expanding before
the eye in pictures of exquisite loveliness.   The poverty of
the district** gives **it a still more** pathetic interest.   **The lake**
has very little fish in it, **and the** hilly district being **none of
the richest, the fruits of the earth are dearly won by the**
hardest toil.   One evening, as **I roamed the uplands, I met a**
bronze-faced lad of fourteen.   **There was a look of intelligence**
through his rusticity which caused me **to enter into conversa-**
tion with him.   **He told me he was a farm-labourer ;** and in
answer to **my** questions as to his **earnings, said that** he
was paid in kind, and never received **money as** wages.   I
said, I supposed then that he was **paid pretty** generously.
" On the contrary," he said, " we receive barely enough for
a subsistence, **and as we have to** take our produce to market
we sometimes obtain very little for it—scarcely enough to
give us the necessaries of life."   **All** this was conveyed to
me with a quiet self-possession of manner and that innate
air of breeding which distinguishes even the peasant classes
in many parts of Italy.   With all his **poverty he seemed**
cheerful and happy ; and when **I gave him a trifle at part-**
ing he looked pleased and surprised, **and went on his way**
with the contentment **of a prince.**

Once more prosecuting **our onward journey from Perugia**
we had thence a **welcome addition to** our little party in a
congenial artist friend, Mr. E. Vedder. We started at an
early hour of a brilliant morning, by the public diligence—a
mode of travelling, which in Italy always offers quaint points
of interest and specialities of character met with in no other

way.   Commencing the **descent of the hill upon** which the
town is built, **our** road at first **lay between** groves of olives
and well-cultivated slopes; but **presently a most glorious
panorama opened itself** before us.   **In the midst of a very
lovely valley, in which** the soft lines of the hills **were
gradually lost, the river** was seen embowered in **luxuriant foliage, patches of** the clear blue of the sky mirrored between the sharply-defined reflections of its banks.
Across the stream a delicately-curved bridge was thrown,
looking almost too frail to support itself.   The effect was
quite magical: the thin veil of the morning giving an appearance of intangibility **to the prospect, as if it** would
vanish with a breath.   **The scene was infinitely** varied;
verdure **of all shades and tints,** nodding groves, towered
heights, swelling hills spotted **with villas and farms;** then,
nearest **the river, low-lying groups of houses were clustered**
as if out of love for the meandering **stream that wandered
hither and** thither until it **was** lost **to** the sight.   After a
while the hills subsided in **gentler slopes.**   **The** banks of the
river were diversified with straggling poplars surrounded
with pastoral groves of grey old oaks, whose large boles
rose from a carpet of emerald grass upon which the shadows
stretched as if in shelter from the heat of the sun, which
now began to burn down fiercely from the sky.   On the
other side of the stream well-wooded hills arose; here and
there **a white homestead peeping** from the foliage, or
a lófty **castle in grey blank ruin,** the centre of many a
mediæval **struggle and feudal quarrel.**

    Long before the **sun had reached the zenith we** arrived
at the little town of Fratta, where **we** stopped **both** to
explore the district and to exercise **our pencils in recording**
a very characteristic passage of the river.   **Fratta is now**
generally called Umbertidi; **as** there are no fewer than
three **other towns in Umbria bearing the former** name.
Just outside of **the town we found a** cheerful and pleasant
little inn that promised well for **a** cleanly and comfortable
domicile.   On signifying our desire for some refreshment

To face page 316.

THE TIBER, NEAR PERUGIA

the table was presently spread in an **abundant, if not** sumptuous manner ; **our** repast numbering **amongst its** dainties the **luxury of caviare** in addition **to the several** other appetizers **which usually** form **a part of an** Italian meal.

Unlike most **of the towns in this part of** Italy, Fratta, instead **of** being placed on a **height, stands upon the** level bank of the river, which is here **crossed** by **a wide** stone **bridge.** It contains an old moated castle, **now** shorn **of** its terrors and gradually falling **to decay.**   There is **something** exceedingly charming about the neighbourhood **of this** old-fashioned **town.**   Shady **lanes and** pleasant **field** paths accompany the course of the **river, bordered** with black-branched willows **and scented** poplar **shrubs.** Without being absolutely romantic, the banks of the **stream** offer exquisite passages **of soft** characteristic beauty—just the thing to satisfy **and** delight **the artist's quieter and tenderer** moods.

Fratta was **founded** by the miserable **remnants of the Roman** army **defeated** at Thrasimene.   **It had the usual** mediæval vicissitudes of pillage **and burning.**   Fortebraccio once made **a raid upon its** territory, as Campano relates in his biography.   He says, "That after having sacked many places of the **country,** he moved **his** camp alongside of the **Tiber, not far** from Fratta, **to the** district held by Perugia, **and commenced to** make it his prey.   As the country **people** had no suspicion whatever of his intention—having **driven** their cattle to pasture and set themselves **to work** in the fields—he took a great number of the **peasantry,** together **with** their **flocks and herds.   The** Perugian soldiers who **were in** the district, **under the command of** Ceccholino forced **him to the combat ; but being repulsed at the first encounter, he lost** some of his cavalry, and flying **at** full speed, sheltered himself on a neighbouring hill.   Braccio, **having** ravaged **the banks of the river, went with his** army **to the** bridge of Pattolo.   In the meanwhile, Ceccholino, having **drawn** some soldiers from a village **near, galloped** off to Perugia." This was in order to prevent the further progress of the enemy : but Braccio, after having devastated the country about Fratta, retired to Todi, rewarding his soldiers with the spoil they had taken.

In all these raids and warfares the country people appear to have been the first and worst sufferers. At any moment liable to have their crops destroyed, their cattle stolen, their homes ruined and burned, their families outraged or slain, nothing could have been more insecure than the peasant life of that time. Their feudal lords might defend their castles or escape from them ; there was no defence or escape for their retainers. Compelled at any hour to take arms on behalf of their territorial governor, or to prosecute his quarrels, their domestic peace was destroyed, their honest gains lost, their occupations suspended in these brawls and feuds, out of which they were sure to come sufferers. So that in looking back, we must confess that the poorest rustic toiler of to-day is in a position of ease and comfort compared with the insecurity of the peasants' condition in these turbulent ages.

From Fratta the river traverses a plain between low-lying hills—a pleasant and cheerful country. As we passed along the road, peaceful rustic labours were being followed everywhere. The housewife sang at the door of her cottage, the ploughman called to his oxen, the thresher swung his slow flail, women stood up to their knees in the river washing clothes and chatting merrily. Bathers came down to the deeper pools and plunged into its waters, little children dabbled on its banks, and hissing geese stalked about in straggling rows. The river here becomes narrowed to a small stream, the additions made by its tributaries being in a great measure lost in the course of a few miles along its hot pebbly bed. A little before reaching Città di Castello, the sloping banks were covered with groves of oak, amongst which the blue morning mist still lingered ; the hills being broken into conical summits, surmounted here and there with a white church or glittering homestead.

It was high noon as we entered Città di Castello. Every blind and door was closed to the sun. As we rattled along the dazzling white pavement not a soul was visible, not even a dog. It was like a city of the dead. By the deserted loggias long green vine-sprays dangled in the sun. Grass grew in the streets. In the heart of a large town we were in perfect solitude.

We took up our abode at the Cannoniera, once a palace of the Vitelli, an historic family, governing the place in the fifteenth century, noticeable also as amongst the first patrons of the painter Raphael. Curiously enough, in many of these towns removed from the beat of ordinary travellers we found ourselves better off in regard to accommodation than in most of those situated nearer to Rome.

No sooner was our arrival noised about the town than all the vendors of curiosities and refuse lumber of any time since the Middle Ages poured upon us like birds of prey on their victim. Every one who had a piece of canvas that had once been a picture immediately brought it out. I am afraid I was very disrespectful to these antique treasures ; but V., who hoped to find something good amongst them, was deluged with demands upon his attention. Many a time I was stopped in the street with the inducement of a great name to inspect some undiscovered gem of art. Unfortunately, I had had too much experience in these researches to be led aside by them. I knew the cracked and chipped remains of the almond-eyed Madonna, with the plethoric infant in her lap, before I had seen her ; the tattered and soiled fragments of tapestry, and broken bits of earthenware were not unfamiliar to me ; the bag of obliterated coins was an easy acquaintance ; the rusty nails, buckles, lamps, arrow-heads, snuff-boxes, surviving dislocations of worn-out tables and chairs, I was perfectly well acquainted with : so I referred them all to V. as a *compratore* (or buyer), who did not seem to succeed very well in convincing the people that *everything* which was decayed, worm-eaten, and unsightly, was not necessarily valuable.

Città di Castello was the ancient Tifernum. The younger Pliny had a villa near, which he describes very circumstantially in a letter to his friend Apollinaris. It had a fitness of situation here, as he held the office of conservator of the river and surveyor of its banks. No appliance of art appears to have been wanting to have made it one of the most delightful and elegant of retreats. It had numerous rooms and extensive pleasure-grounds, with box and other trees clipped into fantastic forms. Here he used to spend the summer season in retired and learned leisure. Sometimes he engaged in field sports ; but when he did so he used to take his tablets for writing with him, so that, as he says, in case the game was not plentiful, he might at least come home with something. He tells his friend that he sometimes supped by the side of a fine polished marble basin so artfully contrived that it was always full without overflowing, the surface of the water serving as a table, the larger dishes being placed round the margin, and the smaller ones floating about in the form of little vessels and waterfowl. He thus describes the situation of the villa. "Though the country abounds with great plenty of water, there are no marshes ; for, as it lies upon a rising ground, whatever water it receives without absorbing, runs off into the Tiber. This river, which winds through the middle of the meadows, is navigable only in the winter and spring, at which season it transports the produce of the lands to Rome ; but its channel is so extremely low in the summer, that it scarcely deserves the name of a river ; towards the autumn, however, it begins again to renew its claim to that title. You could not be more agreeably entertained, than by taking a view of the face of this country from the top of one of our neighbouring mountains. You would suppose that not a real but some imaginary landscape, painted by the most exquisite pencil, lay before you : such a harmonious variety of objects meets the eye, which way soever it turns."

The political position of Città di Castello in the Middle

Ages was similar to that of most of the other Italian cities at that time; that is to say, it was under the feudal rule introduced by the Goths and other European nations at the destruction of the Roman empire—a military system in which the soldier who distinguished himself received a territory as the reward of his bravery or success, over which he was the recognised ruler, having the power to call out the people at any time on military service. These feuds or lordships were all subject to the higher authority of the sovereign, whose *cattanei*, or captains, were scattered throughout their several dominions for military and political ends. Of course this state of things gave rise to endless abuses and constantly recurring warfare, producing frequent subversions of one rule to another, in which the mere adventurer sometimes came in for the best share. In the twelfth century, a better system of things partially prevailed in the revival, to some extent, of civil rule, in the advocacy and furtherance of which the noble-minded Arnold of Brescia perished a martyr. The various cities attempted to put down the power of their military rulers or tyrants, and reduce them to the condition of civilians. Hereupon the divisions of interest and ambition were set the one against the other; leagues being frequently entered into and almost as frequently broken. Not only were there wars between neighbouring cities and territories, but within the walls of the same city discord reigned, through the domineering of the great and powerful wishing to reduce the people to their rule; sometimes two or three factions contending for supremacy with each other and against the citizens; though the latter, often enough, took part with one or the other side. Neither were the head governments better off. Embroiled amongst themselves, they had little time to give to individual rights and wrongs. Bitterness and animosity prevailed everywhere, so that, as Borghini said, "Blind Italy divided against itself, consuming itself with its own strength, would destroy the beautiful garden of the world." It was this state of things that makes the Italian history of this period the most intricate and perplexing of that of all Europe; its endless vicissitudes and revolutions being almost impossible to follow.

In the latter half of the fifteenth century Nicolò Vitelli contested possession of the city with the pope, who was represented by the warlike cardinal, Giuliano della Rovere. Niccolò, though at first defeated, afterwards entered the city, and was permitted to remain there as ruler on swearing fidelity to the pope. The Vitelli thenceforward became principals of the city, retaining their position for long afterwards.

The old chronicles of the city afford some curious pictures of mediæval life. One of these gives a singular instance of an antique custom transmitted to more modern times. It happened in the year sixteen hundred and thirty-two, that a woman of Anastasia, in Valle Urbana, had a carbuncle on her chin, which increased so rapidly as to cause suspicion that it might be a plague-spot. Without having recourse to any other aid, she vowed to St. Florido, the patron saint of the city, that she would go to his sepulchre and miraculous image, and suspend there the clothing she wore; and so she was healed: thus precisely following the ancient custom of suspending the garments in the temple of a god after extreme danger, as of ship-wreck. As Horace mockingly says after his emancipation from the charms of the wily Pyrrha—

> Me in my vow'd
> Picture, the sacred wall declares to have hung
> My dank and dropping weeds
> To the stern god of sea.*

Possibly, also, in the case just mentioned, a pictured or

---

* Me tabulâ sacer
Votivâ paries indicat uvida
Suspendisse potenti
Vestimenta maris deo.
        Carm. I. v.

written tablet would commemorate the fact; thus making the resemblance to the ancient custom still more complete.

A curious entry in the town chronicles under the eleventh of March, fifteen hundred and nine, states that the bishop confirmed the regulations in regard to women's clothing and funerals, disregard of which was to be punished by excommunication. The regulation was prescribed by the council. Every woman was compelled to be dressed according to the amount of dowry she possessed. Those having a hundred and ten florins, or anything less, only being allowed to have one gala dress, which was to consist of brocade velvet, with a plain skirt of crimson joined on to purple. To the peasants cloth of grain was only allowed for trimming, not for dress; to these also was forbidden the use of either gold or silver money. For funerals, six florins were allowed for wax candles to doctors and officials of the pope; to all others not more than three florins. By a special brief of Julius the second, the Vitelli and some others in office were exempted from this regulation. Still more curious are the sumptuary laws of fifteen hundred and sixty-one; the council prescribing not only the dress of the people, but what should be eaten and drunk. Jewels were prohibited, as well as gold and silver in clothing or adornment, a little being conceded to wives of forty, and brides of the first three years. On occasions of baptisms, weddings, or initiation into the monastic life, the viands were to consist of no more than three courses. These regulations were confirmed by a bull of Pius the' Fourth.

The description of the taking of the city as given by Campano, the biographer of Braccio Fortebraccio, is a very stirring incident. He says that Braccio came to Città di Castello "and encamping not far from the walls gave the inhabitants to understand by a trumpeter, that if they did not surrender themselves to him he proclaimed war against them. The minds of the Castellani were filled with fear at the arrival of Braccio, as in the case of sudden war happens to every man, however brave he may be. The banished from the city, of whom there were many in the camp of Braccio, greatly augmented the fear; for the Castellani had not a sufficient force to defend the city, and they saw it was of no use to ask succour of the pope, seeing that he had ceded authority to Braccio; but if they should surrender themselves, the banished persons, who for a long time had followed the field, would make themselves masters of the city. On the other hand should they oppose themselves to those who pretended to have a right over them, they saw clearly that they would have to suffer all the greatest evils that can come of siege, famine, and the arms of the enemy."

In this difficulty the Castellani, who had already begun to be disturbed by civil discords, sent ambassadors to Braccio to sue for terms of peace; but the sole conditions upon which he would treat with them were that they should give up their city entirely to his rule, upon which he promised, that he would not only forbear to interfere with their property and claims as citizens, but that he would identify their own rights and interests with his own. Whilst the Castellani were deliberating upon these proposals with much difference of opinion, the season of harvest was fast passing, all labour being quite suspended, thus threatening them with famine in case of siege. At last they attempted to purchase an immunity from their enemy by offering him the tribute or subsidy of five thousand ducats the year, on condition that he would leave them their freedom. To this offer they joined the most earnest entreaties, submitting that their friendship would be of more value than their servitude, and that though this payment would be made with the greatest difficulty they would rather suffer it than lose the name of liberty which they had so long held dear. Braccio, knowing that the besieged must soon begin to feel the pangs of famine and that they had little hope of foreign help, refused their money, designating their former submission to the papal rule as neither more nor less than a servitude already suffered, adding much more which was rather in accordance with his wishes than to their satisfaction.

When the Castellani found that their embassy had succeeded so unsatisfactorily they came to the conclusion to hold on the siege whatever might be the result; Braccio in the meanwhile fortifying his position and giving out that whoever issued from the gates should be taken prisoner. At this juncture the soldiers of Braccio began to cut down the olives and destroy the vineyards in the neighbourhood of the city; burning the villages, sacking the houses, and devastating the whole country. But the Castellani gave themselves every hour with more diligence to maintain the garrison, storing the walls, towers, and other places with stones and arms for their defence, and though not without grave fears as to the result, they appeared to make light of it before the enemy. When Braccio saw this he sent to Perugia for more soldiers and five pieces of artillery. Between citizens and peasants the Castellani numbered five thousand infantry, some of them bowmen, but the greater portion, clad in breastplates and bearing shields, were formidable from the various weapons they bore, of which their many civil strifes had taught them the skilful use. The arrival of the troops from Perugia added more to the fears of the besieged than to the hopes of Braccio, who was unwilling to risk the flower of his army on the doubtful issue of a dangerous siege: these Perugians being accustomed, as the historian says, to running, jumping, and the use and management of horses, almost as soon as they were born; they were also in the habit of fighting frequent duels, and even in times of peace were well practised in the use of arms and the government of war. Their very bravery or temerity, even, was an embarrassment to Braccio, who had to restrain them from the almost certain sacrifice of their lives to their daring. The desire, however, not to lose the opportunity of gaining possession of the city at last overbore other considerations, so that he was finally induced to make an attack upon it. For this purpose he

caused an immense machine of wood in the form of a
testudo to be raised to as great a height as possible, and
having filled it with veteran soldiers caused it to be drawn
to the walls in the vicinity of the tower which stood above
the gate of the city.   He also drew up two pieces of
artillery in front of the tower, placing wings of crossbowmen
on either side for the assault ; Perugian infantry being
distributed about the fortifications with ladders, having
orders to be prepared to scale the walls and enter the city
whilst the Castellani were occupied in defending the tower.
No sooner had the attack commenced than the Castellani
on the walls, dismayed at the number of the enemy and
their formidable appearance, began to deplore their ill-
fortune, as if the city had been already taken.   The panic
quickly spread itself, so that presently, instead of defending
the city, every one was seeking safety in flight and concealment.   The gates were opened, some of the principal
persons being delivered up as hostages to the conqueror.

Leaving Città di Castello, the river traverses a vast plain
with sloping hills on the left, crowned with several picturesque
towns and mediæval fortresses.   This plain is very fertile
and well-cultivated.   Long rows of young maple or elm
("amicta vitibus ulmo") support festoons of enwreathing
vines.   Here and there shady lanes run underneath the
boughs of umbrageous oaks which throw down deep black
shadows in the glaring sunshine.   At the foot of the hills
to the left the river runs, a small stream in its white dusty
bed.   Presently we came to a little village called San
Giustino, where the driver, wishing to regale his horses,
advised us to stop an hour, which, he told us, might be
pleasantly occupied in looking over an old mediæval castle
which had been adapted as a modern residence.   We had
no reason to regret this arrangement, as the old place was
exceedingly interesting.   The castle consisted of sturdy
walls surmounted by towered battlements, surrounded by
a dried-up moat.   Along one side a very gracefully constructed open gallery passed with arches supported on

elegantly-shaped columns. A lofty clock-tower commanded splendid views of the whole valley, with its varied culture and sparkling villages half embosomed in trees or perched on the mountain heights. The castle was surrounded with quaint gardens, containing an abundance of lemon trees with their golden fruit glowing amongst the rich green leaves. Laurel avenues impervious to the sun, and long alleys of fantastically-clipped box carried the mind back to the times of hoop and patch and further still. A maze of thick close hedges, in which the gardener in vain tried to cause us to lose ourselves, thanks to V.'s talent for geography, whom I took care to follow closely, completed the old-world fashion of the place. The interior of this enchanted abode did not contain much more than some very fine mural decorations and a few good family portraits, as the owner, it appeared, seldom or never resided there. For the rest, a great proportion of the rooms was entirely occupied by silkworms. Ample sheets were hung up, upon which were deposited myriads of variously-tinted eggs. Large frames were also placed about containing trays or shelves, upon which were numberless moths just emerged from the cocoon or worms spinning themselves into it. The whole place, indeed, was peopled with these little creatures, doubtless a source of considerable revenue to their owner.

Following the road from this place we were struck with the number of wayside shrines and black crosses to which were nailed the symbols of the passion of our Lord, as the nails, spear, sponge, etc., doubtless the relics of the time when the road was traversed by pilgrims to the holy sepulchre. Presently we entered the arched gateway of Borgo San Sepolcro.

Borgo San Sepolcro is a quaint little town surrounded by walls with bastions at the angles. It had a very curious origin. There was once a rocky mound here which stood in the midst of a vast forest, upon which the snow lay so thick and long that it was named Nevia. Here some

pilgrims from the holy sepulchre at Jerusalem in the tenth
century, wearied with much journeying stopped to repose ;
and as they slept by a fountain they received a divine
command in a dream to build a church on the spot.   Accordingly gathering together what they could, they formed
a little chapel, in which they deposited the relics they had
brought with them from the Holy Land.   To this place
the people of the surrounding country resorted for purposes
of devotion, and from time to time built houses there, which
at last formed a town, taking its name from the circumstances that had given it birth.   The Calmaldolese monks
afterwards founded an abbey there, owning a great part of
the territory ; but the inhabitants shook off their dependence
in the thirteenth century, and torn by factions, joined the
Aretini.   Their town passed subsequently under the rule of
the bishops of Arezzo, the Visconti, and Fortebraccio, by
whom it was given to the pope, and finally became subject
to that of Florence.

One of the chief attractions of Borgo is its numerous
and beautiful works of art.   It was the birthplace of Pietro
della Francesca, and contains some of his finest paintings.
Pietro was a remarkable man in more respects than one.
Vasari says he was the first geometrician of his time.   He
wrote many books.   At the age of sixty, twenty-six years
before he died, he became blind.   We may imagine what a
loss his sight must have been to him.   His works are of
the very noblest order.   There is an unaffected tenderness
and sweetness in his angels and female figures not even
reached by Pietro Perugino ; their loveliness is that of
innocence and youth ; they can be scarcely called abstrac-
tions, and yet one hardly knows where to match their
flower-like grace and sweet spiritual bearing in the world
of fact.   His finest work is in the Monte di Pietà.   It is a
fresco of the Resurrection.   The Saviour leaves the tomb
bearing a banner of victory.   It is impressive from its
vigour of treatment and intense originality both in conception and execution.   It is also painted in a fine key of

colour peculiarly its own.   Altogether it gives a perfectly new impression of an over-familiar subject in art.

As we strolled about in the evening we came upon the *pallone* ground, just outside and against the walls of the city.   As this is the national game of Italy, it may be worth while to describe it for those who have not seen it.

It is played upon a ground measuring about two hundred and fifty feet in length, and about sixty wide ; always with a high wall on one side.   The players are three at a side. They generally wear a thin close-fitting garment.   On their right hand a large oval covering of wood is fixed endwise, which is grooved into raised squares diminishing upwards.   The balls are of hide, well oiled.   They are hollow, being filled by an air-pump, when in use, and closed by a valve.   The player about to strike the ball in the first instance stands at the top of an inclined plank, opposite to the deliverer of the ball, who faces him at some yards distance.   The striker then runs down the plank, at the same time the bowler makes a few steps forward, delivering the ball at the right moment, which, being struck, gains great impetus, flying the whole length of the ground. It is then to be kept up within assigned limits from one side to the other as long as possible.   It is a game of very considerable excitement ; the animation being sometimes increased by the ball flying amongst the spectators, whose ducking and running do not always prevent them from receiving an ugly blow.

As we followed our evening walk by the border of the fields, V. and I were much amused by the roundabout way a man bestowed maledictions upon a refractory pig which of course would go every way but the one desired.   After vainly attempting to drive it in the direction he wished, the man sat down wiping his forehead, exclaiming with great vehemence, *Accidente a chi ti voglia bene !* (May an apoplexy seize him who wishes you well !)   A form of adjuration in-tended to convey unutterable things to the swine, whose mere friend and well-wisher was to suffer so terrible a misfortune.

From Borgo San Sepolcro the river flows through scenery of the same character as before : grey villages on the cliffs, old castles occupying the heights.   As we passed along the road the landscape was enlivened by bands of happy girls reaping in the fields, protected from the sun by broad-brimmed straw hats.   Presently the prospect opened into a level plain in which the bed of the river was expanded into the form of the lake, but not a drop of water was visible. When we reached this spot I heard a suppressed chuckling in the interior of the carriage (I was sitting with the driver) which presently exploded into peals of derisive laughter. It appeared B. and the others had been watching their opportunity for a joke until the little feeble stream which had hitherto occupied the bed of the river should vanish altogether; at last it came.   "Where is the venerable old man seated amongst the sedges," they asked, tauntingly, "with the water-pot discharging copious streams, which you promised to show us ?   Where are the nymphs, naiades, and other inhabitants of the sacred flood ?"   On my explaining the cause of their merriment to the driver, however, he reassured me.   "*Non abbia paura, signore,*" said he, "*fra poco la ritroveremo*"—Never fear, sir, we shall find it again presently—adding that the scanty stream had been diverted temporarily from its proper course for the purpose of turning some mills, and sure enough we shortly came on it again, though in no great quantity.

A few miles beyond, the river passes through a deep artificial cutting, made with much labour in eighteen hundred and fifty-five, when an enormous landslip choked up the bed of the stream, which immediately rose in consequence to so great a height that the inhabitants had to flee the neighbouring little town of Pieve San Stefano, which remained a long time under water with all the adjacent country.   Now the signs of the misfortune are no longer seen, but a bit of white marble let into the wall of the church near the roof shows how severe and disastrous it must have been.

Pieve San Stefano is a homely little town running along
the river, in a fertile country, deriving its chief support from
corn and grain. The day of our arrival was a market day,
so that the little place was full of business and animation.
The country people had assembled from all the surrounding districts, the women wearing broad-brimmed Tuscan
hats and the young rustic gallants tricked out in their best.
Many a little romantic gossip did we observe going on
between the young girls and their sweethearts, or would be
sweethearts, whilst their mothers and fathers were occupied
in cheapening purchases or vending their wares—not as
Englishmen buy and sell, but with infinite gesticulation
and a storm of talk. Perhaps the only opportunity for
lovers to meet each other who live widely apart may be on
such occasions as these, when acquaintances are formed,
and for the most part prosecuted. This is the last town
situated on the Tiber, or the first from its source. Thenceforward for leagues all is mountainous desolation or hardly-
won culture ; the scattered groups of houses found here and
there on its course scarcely deserving the name of villages.

Numerous ravines run from the river here amongst the
mountains, each with its half hidden rillet at the bottom,
clear and unstained as a naiad's mirror. In the evening
V. and I explored one of these little streams, sketch-book
in hand, through all its crinkly bays and miniature falls, a
tiny tributary to the waters of Old Father Tiber.

We had here reached the last stage but one of our
journey. Pieve San Stefano is but about twenty miles
from the source of the Tiber. We engaged the services of
the son of the landlord of the little inn at which we were
stopping—which, by the way, was an excellent one in a
simple rural fashion—as organiser of the expedition ; and
we had reason to congratulate ourselves in having done so ;
for Tomaso, besides being a cheerful, well-looking, fine-
spirited fellow, knew all the country round to the extent of
at least a day's journey. As the whole way lay entirely
amongst the Apennines, and was of the most rugged

description, without roads, and, in some places, scarcely
the semblance of a path, the only mode of accomplishing
the journey was either on foot or on the backs of asses.
Engaging a number of these, we started before daylight.
As we did so my own mind was filled with the anticipations
of an object accomplished which had long been present
with me. I realised the feelings of a pilgrim when all the
interests, hopes, and sentiments that have accompanied his
journey crowd upon his soul in the nearness of the goal of
his wishes. The mountains seemed to gain a large restful
calm in the glimmering of the dawn, and the heavens to
smile down in more serious peacefulness, at a purpose well-
nigh fulfilled ; for thus we clothe the appearances of nature
with our own moods, and claim her aspects as significant of
our own feelings ; perhaps they are so.

Instead of following the upward course of the stream
Tomaso proposed that we should go a more circuitous route
amongst the mountains, and then trace it downwards to
the place we had left in the morning, as the road by the
immediate banks of the river was so abrupt and broken
that it would be much more difficult to traverse in this
direction. To this there could be no reasonable objection.
The ride (or walk ; for it was as much the one as the other)
was a most enchanting one. The vast mountains were
everywhere around us. Sometimes opening into wide
valleys, sometimes closing into narrow gorges ; sometimes
our road lay along the craggy back of a desolate hill-top,
then it would dive into the shadowy recesses of a sombre
wood. When the sun had well risen, hot and bright, we arrived
at a little mountain farmhouse, with goats browsing about,
at the door of which was suspended a leavy branch, the old-
fashioned " bush " that indicates the sale of wine. I proposed that we should stop a few moments and refresh
ourselves, which we did ; a most extravagant charge being
demanded for the same. As we again pursued our way,
Tomaso came to me mysteriously, saying that he had been
told, at the place we had just left, that two *malviventi*

(brigands) had been there the previous day, and that
there was a band of thirteen lurking in the forest into
which we had to penetrate to find the source of the
river.   This was not very cheering ; for although we
were not without arms, even if we should be able to use
them, they might not avail against such odds.   Presently
we gained a lofty ridge overlooking a vast valley or basin
surrounded with rocks tumbled about in the wildest
confusion.   It was bounded on the one side by a vast
range of mountain called Le Balze, the greater part of it
covered with a dense forest in which was to be found the
object of our journey.   At the foot of this mountain was a
church and a group of a few rude houses, dignified with the
name borne by the mountain.   Hither Tomaso escorted us.
It was about the hour of noon.   We were soon surrounded by
every man, woman, and child in the place.   Hot, wearied,
and dusty, as we all were, my friends, not unreasonably,
resigned themselves to the prospect of a good rest and a
refreshing meal ; their astonishment being great when I
proposed to set off immediately in search of the object of
our pilgrimage.   In vain I argued and enforced, until at
last I was obliged to confess that as Tomaso had been told
that there was a band of brigands in the woods, I did not
consider it prudent to remain long enough for it to be
noised abroad that four Englishmen were about to enter
their precincts, but that if we went immediately there was
less danger of being molested, as we heard that they were
at some distance from the spot where we were wishing to go,
lying in wait for a landowner of the district.   This being
confirmed by the people of the place, my friends all agreed
that, tired and heated as we were, it would be better to go
at once.

Accordingly an old man undertook to be our guide.   By
the side of the little stream which here constitutes the first
vein of the Tiber, we penetrated the wood.   It was an
immense beech-forest, perhaps some part of it virgin to the
tread of man.   The trees were almost all great gnarled

veterans, which had borne the snows of many winters : now they stood basking above their blackened shadows in the blazing sunshine. The little stream tumbled from ledge to ledge of splintered rock (here a limestone in which small nummulites and other organic remains are visible) some- times creeping into a hazel thicket green with long ferns and soft moss, and then leaping once more merrily into the sunlight. Presently it split into numerous little rills. We followed the longest of these. It led us to a carpet of smooth green turf amidst an opening of the trees ; and there, bubbling out of the green sod, embroidered with white strawberry blossoms, the delicate blue of the cranes- bill and dwarf willow herb, a copious little stream arose. Here the old man paused, and resting upon his staff, raised his age-dimmed eyes, and pointing to the gushing water, said, " *E questo si chiama il Tevere a Roma !*" (And this is called the Tiber at Rome.) My mind was filled with emotion. The baby river ! It was like being present at the birth of one who should alter and control the destiny of the world. It was as if all the incidents of the long journey were focussed at this point. The whole history and asso- ciations of the stream arose within me with a crushing sensation of overpowering vastness, from the first settle- ment founded on its banks, through the grandeur of the lordly Rome of Augustus, to the modern ecclesiastical city. I thought of the many lives that had been lived out on its banks, and the many battles that had been fought there. I thought of the lands it passed through : the low-lying marshes of Ostia, the solemn undulating Campagna, the sunny mountains and valleys of Umbria, the spreading fields of corn, vine, and olive, the towering cities, the quiet homesteads, the rocky nooks and fastnesses in its course, and the mighty influence the denizens of its shores had had in the history of mankind and civilisation. All were brought before me, as drowning men are said to see the whole course of their lives at an instant. We stooped and drank of the cool clear water where it first saw the light. We reverently

gathered some of the flowers that bent above its little basin;
and then we went away. I with the words still ringing
in my ears, "And this is called the Tiber at Rome!"

As we followed the stream in its downward course I
half regretted not having sat down to make some record
with my pencil of a spot almost sacred to me. But, indeed,
I could not have settled my mind to such a task at that
moment. Besides, the immediate source offered nothing
for the pencil to seize. It was but a carpet of soft green

NEAR THE SOURCE OF THE TIBER.

grass in an opening of the wood out of which the clear
stream welled. Some such regrets must have been felt by
my artist friends; for when we had reached the point where
the little streams flow together, V. and B. looked about
wistfully, and then sitting under the shade of one of the
oldest of the beeches that twisted its contorted trunk as if in
pain, they made me two precious drawings, though we were
not without some kind of nervousness at the delay so near
the haunts of the lawless troop of *malviventi*. We were not

molested, however, and we soon had the satisfaction of sitting down to a good hearty meal with an hour's quiet rest after it.

The mountain upon which the Tiber takes its rise is but a part of a larger and more elevated chain, the highest point of which is called Monte Fumajolo, which bounds one side of a vast irregular basin of limestone rocks, whose romantic peaks lift themselves in sublime majesty around It is here that the Apennine range, after gradually trending eastwards from the junction of the Nar, makes its nearest approach to the Adriatic. Indeed the Marecchia, which falls into the Adriatic at Rimini, has its source very near to that of the Tiber ; so that the spot must be about the apex of the watershed. The miniature republic of San Marino and, I believe, the town of Rimini itself are to be seen from the more elevated summits in clear weather.

As we left the place, the afternoon shadows were beginning to lengthen on the broken slopes ; but long before the evening red had transformed the splintered pinnacles into pillars of living gold, we lost sight of the miserable *osteria* with its friendly loiterers, the quiet church nestled amongst the hills, and the smiling patches of green field in our downward journey.

Our return road lay on the banks and sometimes in the bed of the river. We followed the stream from the spot where it issued out of the beech forest, over barren spurs of the mountains crested with fringes of dark pine, down to a lonely and desolate valley, shut in by dun and misty blue peaks. Then we entered the portals of a solemn wood with grey trunks of trees everywhere around us and impenetrable foliage above our heads, the deep silence only broken by fitful songs of birds. To this succeeded a blank district of barren shale, cleft into great gullies by many a wintry torrent. Presently we found ourselves at an enormous height above the river upon the ledge of a precipice which shot down almost perpendicularly on one side to the bed of the stream. This spot, we were told, was called La Balza della Donna (The Woman's Rock) from a woman

having once thrown herself down from it ; but whether it
was through

"Amor ch' a null' amato amar perdona,"

("Love which brooks not disregard"), or from some less
romantic cause, our guides were unable to inform us. A
little past this place we came upon a very singular and
picturesque spot. It was an elevated rock shut within
a deep dim gorge, about which the river twisted, almost
running round it. Upon this rock were built a few
gloomy-looking houses and a quaint old-world mill. It
was reached from the hither side by a widely-spanning one-
arched bridge. It was called Val Savignone. The imagination of a Doré could suggest nothing more wildly
desolate than this romantic little fastness with the stream
murmuring round it, the vast peaks rising above it, shut out
from all excepting the sun for a few hours at midday and
the stars at night. What it must be in the winter, when
the shallow waters of the summer season are changed to
raging torrents which fill the bed of the stream and roar at
the base of the rock as if to tear it down, and the heavens
pour their surcharged floods upon it from above, may be
partly imagined. We were sorry to have to pass by this
place without the opportunity of even a hasty drawing ; but
as the day was fast going and we had still many miles
before us, we were obliged to leave its solitudes unrecorded.
Henceforwards we chiefly followed the bed of the river.
At Balsciano, a small village perched upon the cliffs, the
hills began to subside. As we passed the steep acclivity upon which the village stands, we were greatly
amazed and amused to see some goats running and
skipping down what appeared to be almost like the surface
of a perpendicular wall of rock. They seemed to be supported on nothing, and though the shale followed them
in loose fragments at every turn, not one of them made a
false step. Presently these heights declined, and we found
ourselves between easy slopes, which led us through paths
of willow and dwarf poplar, once more to our temporary

domicile at Pieve San Stefano, but not before the crescent
moon showed a pale disk, and the stars were sparkling like
diamonds in the sky.

A few miles distant from Pieve San Stefano, towards
Borgo San Sepolcro, the Singerna empties itself into the
Tiber. It was in a hamlet upon its banks that Michael
Angelo was born—a place which appears to be but vaguely
known to his biographers. This we determined to visit;
but instead of following the course of the river, Tomaso
proposed to take us across country to Caprese (the name of

CAPRESE.

the memorable spot). The next day we arranged to do
this; H., who was somewhat fatigued with our long journey
of the previous day, agreeing to go with the carriage on the
high road 'to Borgo, and await us at a certain spot, where
we proposed to rejoin him in the evening. We accordingly
set out with a relay of asses, under the charge of Tomaso

and their owner, a bluff country fellow who minded his
business, but had no words to throw away.   After a few
hours' journey we reached the Singerna as it wound its
willow-fringed way through an open recess of the hills, the
conical elevation upon which Caprese is situated rising on
the farther side of it.   As we sat down to sketch, the sun
began to slope downwards, throwing soft grey shadows in
the mellowing sunshine.   We then climbed the hills, scram-
bling over volcanic cinders and amongst the disordered
fragments of the torrent-ploughed road.   At last we gained
the summit, and we were amply repaid for our labours, if
there had been nothing more than the fine view which there
met us.   Beneath us lay an unlevel plain bounded by the
broken summits of the Apennine range.   At the foot of the
elevation upon which we stood the river wound through its
bed of white boulders, bordered with poplars at intervals,
a faint murmur of which just reached our ears.   There were
no more than a few miserable houses on its summit, the
highest portion of which contained nothing but the remains
of a ruined castle, the old municipal building in which
Michel Angelo was born, and a little modern chapel.   As
the person who had the key of the communal chambers
was down below at his agricultural labours in the valley, we
despatched a messenger to him, and besides that, commenced
to ring the chapel bell, the sound of which went booming
across the valley until it died in the echoes of the hills.
Presently the holder of the keys came and opened the door
of the building for us.   The outside was partly covered
with stone tablets, upon which were sculptured initials,
coats of arms, or other devices of the various syndics or
governors of the district, some of them quite obliterated by
time and weather.   In vain I sought one bearing any device
of the Buonarroti.   Besides these there was a modern white
marble slab let into the wall commemorating the formation
of the kingdom of Italy under Victor Emmanuel.   The house
is built of good solid stone masonry, consisting of three
rooms and a garret on the second floor, which generally
constitutes the habitable portion of an Italian house.   On

the ground floor there are some cells giving out of a central chamber which look as if they might have been formed for prisons.   The chamber in which Michel Angelo was born is about twenty-six feet long by seventeen broad.   It is entered by a simple arched doorway and is lighted by a little oblong window.   Over the doorway of this chamber is a rude modern inscription in distemper, which, translated, runs as follows : " Here was born the immortal Michel Angelo Buonarotti in the year one thousand four hundred and seventy-four.   He lived eighty-nine years and died in Rome in the year one thousand five hundred and sixty-four."   In the year of Michel Angelo's birth, his father, who was a man of name and note in Florence, was appointed *podestà* or governor of Caprese and Chiusi, and accordingly removed hither with his wife, who here gave birth to her second child, the illustrious artist.   They only remained here a year, after which, the term of office being expired, they returned to Florence.

The sun was fast sinking to his fall as we descended the hill of Caprese, and we had still a dozen miles of journey before we could reach the place where H. would be already awaiting us.   As we had to follow the bed of the river the whole distance, we were obliged to keep on our donkeys if we wished to retain dry feet, as the stream had to be continually forded in its crossings from one side to the other ; the bed being much wider than the space occupied by the stream.   It was a most uneasy journey for the poor brutes that bore us, the boulders and pebbles being of all sizes, so that every step was an uncertain one.   It offered many charmingly picturesque turns.   Sometimes bordered with soft pastoral slopes, and sometimes hung with great plumes of sombre foliage.   Once or twice, on the spreading shoals, herds of white oxen came down to drink, grouping themselves in the most picturesque manner under the trees. Presently the daylight died quite away and the bright stars came out above us, as we pursued our way in silence, our rustic guide dimly seen stalking in front of us, answering every question in monosyllables, or not at all, never once

turning to look behind him.   One little episode impressed
itself strongly on my mind.   We had left the bed of the
stream for a little distance, and were threading our way
along one of its banks.   Tall trees were arched above us,
through which the bright stars twinkled by fits.   Bats flew
hither and thither ; whilst the night-moth dashed by through
the night which was his day : the owl at intervals giving
forth his solemn whoop.   The seclusion, the stillness, the uncertain glimmer of light, the soft sense of luxury and beauty
diffused around, filled the mind with the most soothing reflections, recalling all the romance and tenderness of "youth
and buried time."

At last, as the river bed opened into a broader estuary,
we descried the lights of the Madonnina, or Lesser Madonna
—for such was the name given to a few houses on the road
where the Singerna flows into the Tiber, from a small
shrine of the Madonna existing there.   Here we found H.
awaiting us with some anxiety.   Dismissing our rustic
guide and Tomaso, with whom we parted with a hearty
shaking of hands, we were presently on our way to Borgo
San Sepolcro, where we arrived to a welcome supper before
midnight.

The next day on our way to Arezzo, the nearest point
of the railway, we crossed the river near Anghiara, at the
site of a celebrated battle, some account of which will close
our historical records of the classic stream.   The engagement took place on the twenty-ninth of June, one thousand
four hundred and forty, between Piccinino, commander of the
Milanese army, and the Florentines under Giovanni Paolo
Orsini.   The circumstances are thus given in Baldeschi's
life of Piccinino.*

---

* There is also a rhymed account of this battle in the Magliabecchian
Library at Florence, which has some spirited passages.   This for example:

> E si vedean gli elmetti sfavillare
> Pe' colpi delle accette e mazze forti ;
> Ognun fa prova di quel che sa fare,
> Come poltron non voglion esser morti :   [Carone

"When Piccinino with his Lombardese soldiers stood in front of Città di Castello, hearing that Francesco Sforza was ravaging Lombardy with fire and sword and had approached the very gates of Milan, the latter were very anxious to return thither in defence of their homes and countries. With great difficulty Piccinino quieted them under the promise of a speedy return, but in the meantime determined to attack the enemy, who were near to Anghiara; and "with this design," the historian says, "issuing secretly from his position with several horsemen (a good part of the night still remaining) went to reconnoitre their camp. The day following, having commanded his soldiers to be prepared to march at an early hour, he came to Borgo, leaving his baggage, and making known his design to the officers of his regiment, afterwards despatching his son Francesco in advance with two companies of horse who were on guard that day. No sooner had this been done than he prepared to follow, calculating that as it was the festival of St. Peter and the day already far advanced, the discipline of the camp would be relaxed, and that, taking them by surprise, he would have little difficulty in routing them. In this he would not have been disappointed if Micheletto, the captain of the cavalry, had not anticipated the danger, for whilst a part of the soldiers, half unarmed, sheltered themselves in their tents from the heat of the noonday sun, and whilst others, oppressed with food and sleep, lay stretched in the shade, he alone, fully armed, had set himself the task of going round the camp, which was near the walls of Anghiara, and seeing from an elevation an unusual cloud of dust in the distance, raised the alarm, informing the other captains of the coming of the enemy, upon which the whole camp immediately began to arm, each having time to rouse himself and exchange a few

---

Carone in questo dì debbe sudare:
Ciascun della salute cerca i porti;
E dov' è men la battaglia divisa
Quivi si mette Niccolò di Pisa.

words with his comrades.   When all was ready, Micheletto
went with a company of cavalry and occupied the bridge,
which was little more than three hundred paces from the
foot of the hills.   Here a stream, running between steep
banks into the Tiber, divides the plain.   At this place
Micheletto awaited the enemy.   When they came up, those
in advance, seeing the enemy above them, although previously bent on the attack, were somewhat cooled, this
happening out of all their expectations, yet, nevertheless,
they rushed upon them, and commencing the battle, they at
first drove them from the bridge to the place they had
come from, but afterwards, being overcome by the numbers
that poured upon them from the camp, they retired by
degrees towards the bridge.   Piccinino, in the meanwhile,
sending other companies in aid of the first, caused the
battle to be renewed, the same thing being done on the
other side.   Thus as the one side and the other gave itself
to reinforce its own party, presently the whole of the troops
were engaged, a sharp and cruel battle taking place between
them, neither captains nor soldiers pausing to take breath
for a moment.   So ardently did they fight, that when the
quarters became too close for the use of lances and
pikes they fought with their knives.   When the battle had
thus continued with the utmost fury for more than three
hours the soldiers of Piccinino, both because they were not
fighting on their own ground and were tired with the
journey of twelve miles which they had made, and because
evening now approaching, a wind arose from the hills
where the enemy was stationed, blowing so much dust into
their faces and into their eyes as to take away from them
both sight and breathing, were obliged to turn their backs
on their opponents."

In spite of the poet-chronicler's assertion, that everybody
wielded a bloody sword (" *Ciascuno ha la sua spada in-
sanguinata* "), the historian informs us that " not many were
killed on either side, but prisoners were made of eighteen
hundred cavalry and thirteen hundred soldiers of Borgo,

whom Piccinino had enrolled as if for a manifest prey. About sixty women whom Niccolò had placed along the road with vessels of water to refresh his troops were trampled to death with the horses. He saved himself and the remnant of his troops by regaining Borgo, laying it altogether upon adverse fortune that he had been conquered that day."

L'ADDIO.

AND now my task is done. As I write this the day
has once more sloped downwards ; the mountains
are purple and dark against the sky ; the landscape is
subdued to a sombre grey ; the oxen are loosed from the
yoke ; the flocks of sheep go home ; the peasant lays aside
his labour for repose ; the mechanic leaves his toil ; the
birds retire to rest. Again comes the solemn hour of
twilight, the magic time of the south, "when the desire of
the travelled pilgrim turns towards home, and the softened
heart is filled with pensive memories of past partings, whilst
the vesper bell from afar seems to mourn the dying of the
day." And still the old river flows on to the sea through
sunlight and starlight, and will continue to flow when the
footsteps that now tread its banks shall be stayed upon its
shores for ever, and new generations rise with new thoughts
and feelings, as its crumbling monuments and perishing
memorials slowly sink into oblivion and mingle their many
memories with the silent dust. Farewell !

INDEX.

THE END.

LONDON : PRINTED BY WILLIAM CLOWES AND SONS, STAMFORD STREET
AND CHARING CROSS.

Just Published, *Crown 8vo., price 6s., cloth,*

THE SHEPHERD'S GARDEN.

By WILLIAM DAVIES.

OPINIONS OF THE PRESS.

" Mr. Davies's songs are such as Isaak Walton's milkmaid might have sung to Piscator and Venator when they were returning through meadows, after their day's fishing. They run the gamut of all simple feelings—from the prattle of mere gladness to the gravity of tempered meditations, or the gush of childlike sorrows. The melodies are as charming as they are varied, and the descriptions are full of the sweetness, vitality, and movement of country sights and sounds. . . . The volume is delightful."—*Daily News.*

" He has written pieces which might have been produced by Herrick or Suckling, by Wither or Carew."—*Pall Mall Gazette.*

" This very delightful book."—*Evening Standard.*

" Many of the shorter pieces would have a charming effect set to music by Mr. Sullivan or Signor Pinsuti, and sung by Mr. Leslie's choir."—*Athenæum.*

" Brightness, colour, purity, and freshness, with something of the innocent mirth of children on a May morning, are eminently the characteristics of this dainty volume. . . . They are full of high feeling, of purity, and of refinement."—*Manchester Courier.*

" The spirit of pastoral poetry which gives such freshness and simplicity to the poems of Spenser, the Fletchers, Browne, and Marvel—which sparkles like dew on the page of Keats, conveys pleasant anodyne in the meditative verses of Wordsworth, and shines in full lustre in the masterful lines of Burns and Ramsay,— gives grace and elegance to 'The Shepherd's Garden.' . . . . . Happy conceits and truthful imagery abound in· this elegant volume."—*Morning Post.*

" We can discover in every line of his own writing that he knows well and loves deeply the kind of art he seeks to reproduce, and understands the sources of its peculiar grace."—*Globe.*

" A more genuine, poetic region than ' The Shepherd's Garden ' we have seldom entered ; its flowers are precious gems ; its bowers are calm and classic shades."—*Literary World.*

" The songs and madrigals are so fresh, so musical; they breathe the very spirit of pastoral life, and are so thoroughly spontaneous that there is never the least suspicion of affectation." —*Graphic.*

" Full of taste and tenderness."—*Warrington Guardian.*

" Very charming and sweet."—*Figaro.*

SAMPSON LOW & CO., FLEET STERET, LONDON.